Strawberry Jam on Tuesdays

ANTONY COOK

Strawberry Jam on Tuesdays
Copyright © 2021 by Antony Cook

All illustrations by Antony Cook.

Tellwell Talent
www.tellwell.ca

ISBN
978-0-2288-6191-1 (Hardcover)
978-0-2288-6190-4 (Paperback)
978-0-2288-6192-8 (eBook)

To my daughters: Jessie, Autumn, and Alison.
May you forever know how much you are loved.

Everything in this book is completely true except the parts that aren't. Time, some alcohol and a bit of ego are probably the biggest culprits between fiction and truth, and I leave it to the reader to sort out which is which.

All characters and places are also true, except for legal reasons, in which case:

This is a work of fiction. Names, places, characters and incidentals are either the product of the author's imagination or used fictitiously. Any resemblance to any actual person, or their image, living or dead, organization, event or location, are entirely coincidental.

That said, you know who you are. xoxo

Preface

I will always have my father's left arm, my mother's right foot, and my daughter's out-stretched hands. They are my history, my story, my burden to carry through time.

Their silence taunts me in this cold empty room. My father's arm points in accusation, my mother's foot shrivels in shame, and my daughter's hands plead with me to catch her as she sinks into a murky abyss.

In my dreams, I have tried to save them a thousand times, but failed on all counts. I know better than to hold onto something already severed, yet I still cling to these lifeless appendages as if life itself depended on it.

Time breaks everything in the end. It has to. There is no other way to let go of the illusion. An illusion where everything stays the same and change is a choice, not a constant.

So, I drift in the wake of my past, unattached and unresistant. I search for truth among the discarded wreckage and try to recognize the difference between what was real and what never was.

Only then will I be able to find the Time Keeper.

PART 1

Chapter 1

(Rayleigh, Essex, 1910)

The train always came at night. It pulled the same two empty flats and a passenger carriage that had seen better days. Shortly before midnight, the protesting heaves of the Great Eastern ground to a halt as two dozen uniformed men exited the train and immediately set to work. It took the best part of the night to daisy-chain the cargo onto the straw-laden beds. It was heavy, dirty work but when the locomotive finally retreated, William Clover gave a sigh of relief.

It's over, he thought, holding the remainder of the balance he was owed in cash. As the owner of the Hambro Hill brick fields, he had done what was necessary but was in no mood to celebrate. He told himself it wasn't blood money. He told himself he was aiding in the safety of the British Commonwealth, but deep down, he knew it was all lies. Simply put, he could never speak of this arrangement again.

William trod carefully as he left the railway siding. He followed the path around the steep edges of the clay pits and headed toward a large, roofed shelter. It was a utilitarian structure, nothing more. It served its purpose, and he knew the boy would be there, waiting as always.

By all accounts, William Clover was a devoted religious man. Lately, however, he had serious doubts about his God. He was never a man to question his lot in life, but he could not ignore the fact that his business was in serious trouble.

In theory, the Salvation Army was a good thing, thought William. They promoted many of the same qualities he demanded from himself. He even understood the benefits of sobriety until, as he liked to call them, "The Christian Bastards" had opened a competing brick business in the neighbouring town of Hadleigh. Ever since, he had watched his profits dwindle to piss and it hadn't taken long to realized there was just no way Clover Bricks could compete with London's re-located homeless. All they were willing to work for was food, shelter, and a few bullshit kitchen scraps of human dignity.

If there was any vindication for William Clover, it was from the growing radical movement—the Skeleton Army. Its members were mainly fucked-off pub owners angry with declining alcohol sales, but many of William's labourers had also joined just to fuel their own cause. He tried not to smile as he reached the drying shed door. He had read of the troubles in West Sussex, and he couldn't resist the thought of his lads pelting dead rats and feces at the parading Sally Anners.

"Make it clean," instructed William to his second eldest son. "And no lines," he added as they walked down the tables of wet clay.

It was a ritual they had performed for many weeks and Don did not need reminding. They moved swiftly among the rows and before long, the two fell into unison, matching each other's pace and skill. There was little sound as they worked. The drying shed creaked occasionally, and Don's faint, inaudible mumble barely registered above the sound of baby swallows chirping hungrily from their nests.

"That'll do boy," said William when they had reached the end. "Better go back home and sleep."

His son looked up and nodded. He finished washing his hands in a bucket of cold water and started to leave.

"Hey," said William. "You did good."

His son smiled and William kissed the top of his head.

"Now go, before your mother finds out."

William straightened his aching back and pulled a wooden pipe from his pocket. He drew the smoke deeply and watched as his son hopped awkwardly among the clay ditches. He knew the boy was different—that had been obvious for years. His eldest William, then Rob, Johnny, and daughter Ivy had all managed to avoid the scarlet plague, but Don had not been so lucky. He had always blamed the merciless fever for Don's lack of brains, but he was still unsure why the boy chose to be such a loner.

He stood in the silence and revelled in his favourite time of the day. It was a time where the night and the morning sunrise met in what he always imagined as communal forgiveness. It was the moment when William Clover felt almost invisible, a moment where he felt weightless, like the wisps of his smoking pipe. To further validate his point, a fox, no more than ten feet away, casually trotted by unbothered. It had something in its mouth, a chicken, a kitten maybe. William couldn't tell, but it was dead whatever it was.

He finally turned and headed for his ram shackled office. There were big plans once for a permanent building, but like many things in life, they had fallen to the wayside. As he walked, he could feel the man's stare. William had seen him hiding in the shadows of the drying sheds and there was no doubt why he was there.

"I knew it," cursed William, his mind suddenly racing with fear. "They've come to tie-up the last remaining loose end -me."

He shook his head in disbelief, then slowed his pace not to look panicked. For William, there was only one hope, and though it lay in a drawer not five hundred feet away, the chances of using it were as slim as finding a rat turd in a rice barrel.

It was while sitting on the toilet, several days after his meeting with the army, that William understood the severity of his secret deal. As he waited for his bowels to stir, he picked up a discarded encyclopedia that reluctantly he had bought for his children.

"Typical," he said, realizing several pages had been ripped out and used as toilet paper. "Bloody hooligans the lot of 'em."

He was just about to close the book when a picture of the Egyptian Pyramids caught his eye.

"The killing of servants, architects, and labourers," read William, "was common practice at the time of a Pharaoh's death. Not only was this to aid the King in the Underworld, but also it kept any knowledge of the burial chamber from being looted by thieves." William stopped in midloaf. "Jesus," he said, wondering if the same fate awaited him. *What have I got myself into?* He suddenly felt incredibly stupid, having so readily trusted perfect strangers. "God forgive me," he said, ripping his own page from the encyclopedia. "Or the devil," he added, "whoever gets me first."

Chapter 2

The gun calmed his nerves as William closed the drawer to his desk. The piece was a Webley MK 1 pistol used by his uncle Charlie in the recent Boer War. It was fired last by Charlie himself. He had come back from the war with something called "shell shock" and his head never quite sorted itself out.

When Tuberculosis had swept through Rayleigh and Charlie showed all the signs, he wrote a letter to his mother explaining how he couldn't face the hospital again, then blew his brains out on the cliffs of Westcliff-on-sea.

William opened the cylinder chamber and inserted six .455 calibre bullets. He had kept it in meticulous condition, and there was no hesitation the gun would do what was necessary. All he could do was wait.

There was no warning to the man's arrival. William heard no footsteps or preamble. The door simply opened and the stranger walked in without hesitation. William remained seated with the Webley pistol pointed in the direction of the man. He had expected to look up into the face of a stone-cold mercenary, but the man staring back was anything but.

He was a portly fellow, about thirty-ish, wearing a tattered regimental jacket and ripped trousers. It was an odd contrast to the spit and polish of the military, and it looked to William that the stranger had been sleeping in his clothes for some time. The man stopped a few feet from the desk. He reached into his inner blazer pocket, and without breaking gaze, tried unsuccessfully to remove an object.

"You're from the army then?" said William more like a statement than a question.

The man looked surprised. "Yes," he replied still distracted with his pocket.

William was confused. Something wasn't right. If the army had sent someone to clean-up loose ends, then either the assassin was a master of disguise, or the army had drastically lowered their Special Forces requirements.

Finally, after a frustrating struggle, the man stepped forward and unceremoniously placed a heavy weighted object onto the wooden desk. It made a thud that vibrated through William's chair, and looking down, he instantly recognized the familiar shape.

"Alright," said William, "it's a clay brick, one of mine." He could see the W. CLOVER stamped clearly on the brick's frog. "So what?"

The man answered slowly. "I want . . . to find the person . . . who threw . . . this . . . brick."

"What army are you from again?" said William, completely baffled by the whole situation.

"God's army," the man replied.

With relief, William's entire body relaxed. He almost laughed out loud as he eased his grip on the gun. *Of course,* thought William, recognizing the uniform. *The misguided wanker is from the Salvation Army. How could I have been so paranoid?*

With a new surge of energy, William felt in control again. He was still unsure what the man was wanting, so he decided to push back, knowing there was no bounty on his head.

"Why the fuck would you want to do that?" William said somewhat aggressively.

"Because," answered the man, "that brick . . . killed my wife."

A cold silence took over the room, and for a long moment William could do nothing but stare at the brick. It was probably his imagination, but he thought he saw something dark red at one end of the clay slab.

"I'm from Shoreham," the man continued with tears in his eyes. "Last week, my wife and I were parading with our fellow Salvationists when the Skeletons attacked. They're a nasty bunch of non-believers, I'm sure you know a few. When they attacked, we tried to run, but there was no place to go. I think fighting back just made it worse."

William said nothing. He understood the man wanted to say his peace, and somewhere deep down he could respect that.

"They came at us with everything. Bricks, bats, dead animals, chains, whatever they thought might inflict the most damage. I saw the brick too late. I tried, I tried to stop it, but there were just too many bodies. It hit my poor Mary in the side of her head, and she was dead before she hit the ground. All I know is your brick killed my wife and I'm here for my pound of flesh."

William waited a moment to collect his thoughts, then deliberately got to his feet. He firmed his grip on the Welby and let it fall to his side in plain sight.

"I'm terribly sorry for your loss, I really am, but I'm afraid I can't help you. I make a lot of bricks, and I'm not responsible for them once they leave the yard. That brick could have come from anywhere. Christ, most of London's Liverpool Street station is made from my bricks. My advice to you is to go home. You'll find no revenge here."

"Well, someone's got to pay," replied the man, standing his ground. "My wife is dead, and your name is on the murder weapon. Oh, and just so you know," the man added as an afterthought, "I saw what you did last night with the money."

William unconsciously took a step closer in outrage. No one was supposed to know about his business. He had struggled for weeks to come up with the perfect hiding place and there was no chance in hell he was going to be blackmailed by a conniving little shit.

"You saw nothing," William snarled. "Now get the fuck out."

He waved the gun at the man to emphasize the point, but without warning, the man suddenly bolted forwards. It was a vicious, powerful lunge, and William, having no time to react, felt the full weight of the man's body as they both toppled to the floor. *Jesus,* thought William, cringing from the impact. *Whatever happened to turning the other cheek?*

From above, William noticed the brick. Somehow the man had reclaimed it from his desk and was in the process of re-directing it toward his head.

"See!" the man yelled in rage. "See how you like it!"

At the last possibly moment, William turned. He took advantage of the man's downward momentum, and as the brick passed by, barely missing his skull, William plowed the man's head ruthlessly into the ground.

It stunned him long enough for William to climb to his feet, and in one fell swoop, William Clover's boot connected squarely with the man's face. The man's nose broke instantly. A small spray of blood confirmed it was a direct hit, and William breathed hard, trying to catch his breath. He was annoyed now, and touching his throbbing head, wanted nothing more than to finish this and get on with his day.

His attacker looked rough. It seemed he had wasted whatever energy he had and now stood swaying with his arms up in an unsteady boxer's stance. As the man attempted a lethargic right jab, William ducked effortlessly and aimed a lead hook punch with his left. It was called the one punch knockout for a reason and William's fist connected hard, sending his assailant's brain ricocheting around his head.

It was over. The man dropped like a sack of wet cement and William didn't bother looking back. He walked toward the office door and out into the cool morning air.

There was movement across the fields down into Pitsea valley. The village and surrounding farms had begun to stir and William could see the first few tendrils of chimney smoke start to rise in the distance.

He reached into his trouser pocket and felt for his pipe. It was broken and he dismissively threw the pieces to the ground. *Of all the Bible-thumpers in the world,* thought William, *and I got the poor sod who wanted to play Humpty Dumpty.*

He decided not to get the police constable involved. The stranger, he felt, had been through enough. Instead, he would tell his work lads that one of the barn horses had kicked the man at morning chores, and his son John could dog cart him to the train station at the bottom of Crown Hill Road.

"I thought I sent you home to bed?" said William, suddenly noticing his son by the woodpile.

Don just shrugged, smiled, and said nothing. William wasn't surprised. Nothing really surprised him about Don anymore.

"There's a man in my office," William said. "He's not feeling too well. I need you to go find your brother Johnny and tell him to hook-up Laddie to the cart."

He looked over, expecting his son to comply, but the boy didn't move. Instead, Don just stared at the open office door. William turned just as the now conscious man appeared in the opening. He leaned against the door frame to steady himself and spoke.

"I told you someone had to pay," he said and raised William's pistol, pointing it at Don.

"Leave the boy out of this," said William, stepping into the line of fire.

"Come here boy, or I'll shoot your father dead."

"Don't you dare!" ordered William as Don started to walk.

"Well, suit yourself," retorted the man and shifted the pistol's aim to the centre of William Clover's chest.

Don started to cry. He was scared and didn't understand what was happening. He clung to his father in terror, and William tried to calm him by softly humming one of Don's made-up tunes.

If I could just buy a bit more time, thought William, *just a little more time.* He looked around desperately for any kind of weapon, but nothing was in reach. *So this is it,* he thought, swallowing hard. *This is what my life has come down to.*

In a last-ditch effort, William got ready to charge. *At least,* he thought, *there is enough time for Don to get away.* He watched the man closely for his chance. Any slight distraction would do, but when the moment finally came, it was William that turned his head away first.

From across the clay pits, the distinct sound of work boots echoed from the drying shed walls. *Of course,* thought William, realizing the time. It was his work crew coming for their back pay and William couldn't have been more relieved. The man looked up, then swung his head back to William and Don. He looked confused and desperate. He put down the gun, then lifted it again, unsure of what to do.

All the man had wanted was some kind of restitution, someone to listen and understand what he felt. But no one could. His Mary was gone and he had no idea how to go on. He felt as if his God had abandoned him, and his soul had been stomped on and fed to the dogs. His pain was all he had left and he just wanted it to end.

"Put the gun down, friend," said William. "We can fix this."

But the man was looking through William now, distant, and unreachable. "There is no fixing this," he replied in defeat. "Everything is broken."

He closed his eyes and grimaced in anticipation. He lifted Charlie's pistol to his temple, and as the gang of unsuspecting workers stumbled into view, the man pulled the trigger and followed the previous gun owner into oblivion.

Chapter 3

(Rayleigh, Essex, 1993)

The Jam's "Town Called Malice" brought me back from the edge. It blared through the darkness from a cassette deck inside a carelessly parked car. Its engine still idled as I tried to open my eyes, but all I could see were fleeting images of legs silhouetted against the car's blinding front headlights. The boot to the head hadn't knocked me out. I hadn't seen stars like I was supposed to. Just a momentary pause in my brain as my naked body crushed hard into the wet grass.

My wrists and ankles had been tied and I was pissed. Drunk yes, but also mad as fuck that I had been caught off guard. The marmalade that had been unceremoniously spread on my chest felt uncomfortably sticky and as hard as I tried not to think of insects crawling into my orifices, my paranoia thought otherwise.

By the time I managed to stand, the car was gone. With my hands and feet bound, all I could do were short, naked bunny hops forwards. It wasn't pretty, but considering everything I had been through, I was past caring about what oncoming traffic was thinking. I took one more unsteady hop and lost my balance. I careened through some rather unfriendly undergrowth and found myself lying on my back, my chest now covered in a variety of roadside kibble.

"You fucking bastards. Did you know about this?" demanded a voice somewhere in the darkness.

"I knew you were done for," I replied laughing, "but no idea I was supposed to join you."

Thinking back through the day's events, I had to stop and wonder exactly where my mate Dave's stag had gone wrong. There was a flood of possibilities, but as I laid in the dark, I really had to blame the stripper. It was clear we had all been shafted the moment the door of the Mexican restaurant opened. All seven of us, as drunk as we were, recognized the absence of tits on the man wearing a powder blue negligee and a curly blue wig.

"Wheth's my boy Dave then?" he asked in the awkward silence.

"Fuck me," said Dave as his enchiladas drooped. "What the hell was that?"

It took a second for both parties to understand the situation. This was not the gig our stripper had expected, and it certainly wasn't what we had paid for. In hindsight, it was a true "Mexican stand-off," and it appeared no one's dignity was going to get away unscathed.

To his credit, our stripper's dance routine to Madonna's "Like a Virgin" was technically impressive, but unfortunately not well received. Even Dave's attempt at pulling a scroll from the man's buttocks did little to raise our deflated expectations.

"Christ," I heard Dave's friend Olly say after the stripper had left. "How am I going to forget that one?" It was a fair question and so was the answer.

"Drink, you fuckers!" yelled Dave. "Drink until you get the 'willies' all out."

"How long does that take?" I asked.

"Last time it took three days and half a carrot cake."

I didn't ask.

It was less than an hour later, at Rayleigh's notorious Pink Toothbrush night club, that I found myself holding on to the venue's toilet. I had slam danced my stomach into full convulsions and was enjoying a visual recap, in reverse, of the last twelve hours of consumption. From what I could see, there was no 'willy' in my puke, and I sat immobilized on the piss-soaked floor and waited for the noon kebab to reappear.

Outside the cubical I had heard a few patrons come and go, but I had been somewhat preoccupied to respond to their cheers of encouragement. Inside, things were as expected. The pink ceiling and wall paint flaked in large chunks, and basically anything that wasn't essential for shitting was broken or destroyed.

I sat with my back against the door and wiped my mouth.

"Don't force it," I mumbled, reading the graffiti scratched into the paint. "Wise words," I had to agree.

I followed an arrow that started at the words "Pull here for art degree" and almost laughed when I realized it was pointing at the broken toilet paper dispenser.

I would have missed it if I hadn't pulled a piece of wet toilet paper from the bottom of my shoe. The portrait was small, maybe a couple of inches tall, but definitely an image I knew well. The design was simple enough. It was a sideways oval with a shaft that widened in thickness. I had tried to research its meaning, but all I knew was it belonged to the Time Keeper and the bastard was close.

Like many times before, I felt the feeling of déjà vu take over. It always happened when the Time Keeper was near. Somewhere in my present, another memory was demanding to be remembered, and I closed my eyes and waited for the feeling to pass.

"You alright, treacle!?" I suddenly heard Dave yell.

He had the men's door half-open, and from behind him, I could hear the security staff yelling to "drink up and fuck off!"

"Shit," I said looking down at my watch. "It's after one."

"Yeah, I know," replied Dave. "We were all wondering where you were."

I had lost track of time, or more accurately, time had lost track of me.

"Come on," said Dave, pulling me to my feet. "Apparently there's another surprise waiting for me."

The plan was simple. Billy, the club's bouncer, was going to drive us all out to a remote roundabout in the country. There, we would wrestle the groom to the ground, take off his kit, and leave the poor guy tied naked to the wooden traffic barricade. It seemed reasonable enough for a stag night finale, and Dave, after rolling around in the car boot, was for the most part accommodating.

I was picking up the remainder of his clothes when someone tackled me from behind. I hit the ground hard, and it took a few seconds of struggling to realize I wasn't being let off so easily. I guessed I should have known better. The best man's rule book clearly stated, "No groom is to be left behind naked unless accompanied by his best man."

The blue glow of a television gave us hope there might be someone still awake. It was well past three o'clock when we hopped up a farmer's driveway, Dave still dragging half a wooden fence. We weren't sure what else to do. As far as we could see, there were no other lights in the surrounding darkness. With our hands and feet still tied, we knocked on the front door with our heads. Surprisingly, we heard movement from inside. Something clonked on the floor and then after a brief moment, the door opened.

"Errr . . . excuse me mate, you got any wire cutters?" Dave asked as casually as any naked stranger could.

A man in his forties stood in front of us, his face instantly breaking out into a grin.

"You've got to be kidding," he said. "I did this to a mate of mine last month. Hey, Sandy!" he yelled. "Come look at these prize-winning geezers."

We heard a window open from above and then a woman's laugh echo into the night.

"Where's your key?" I whispered, starting to shiver.

A taxi had dropped us off at Dave's parents, and I was still amazed that the driver hadn't been in the slightest bit bothered that his passengers were both completely naked.

"In my jeans," said Dave.

"Well, that doesn't help. Is there a spare?" I asked.

"That was the spare," he replied. "Tell you what," remembered Dave, "Mum always leaves the second storey window open a crack. See if you can reach up and get in."

I'm not sure how it looked as Dave bunked me up. My ass cheeks and bits hovered dangerously over his head but after a couple of tries, I grabbed the brick window ledge and heaved my body up.

"It's locked," I hissed, struggling to hold my weight.

"Yeah, I know," said Dave.

"What do you mean you know?" I gasped, but it was too late.

From below, Dave rang the doorbell and pounded on the brass door knocker.

"Pay back, bitch!" he shouted as the exterior house lights turned on.

Dave's mum and dad stood on their doorstep looking up curiously. Then seconds later, Dave's twenty-something twin sisters appeared and did the same.

"You wanna take a family picture!?" I yelled, feeling rather exposed.

"No, it's ok," replied Dave. "We'll wait for my Nan first."

Chapter 4

Two bodies lay outside William Clover's office, a man with no name and a twelve-year-old boy. The man was dead. There was no question. The left side of his head had blown wide open and brain fragments glistened in the morning sun. The boy, Don, was unconscious but still very much alive. He rested peacefully in the shade of the woodpile having fainted a few seconds after the initial carnage.

"Who killed this man's wife?" demanded William. "I know some of you bastards were at the Shoreham rally."

The men looked down to avoid their boss' stare. William could see several Skeleton Army tattoos on his men's arms, and he knew he would never get to the truth.

"Well, this poor Sally Anner and his wife were there," said William, pointing at the crumpled body. "Apparently one of our bricks knocked his wife's head off. It's fresh, came out of our kiln last firing. Anyone feel like fessing up? . . . Anyone?"

There was no answer.

"I didn't bleed'n think so. As far as I'm concerned, you're all as guilty as each other."

He let his words sink in and watched as the eldest of the five workers wiped small flecks of blood from his face.

"Look," reasoned William, changing tact. "If the police come snooping, who knows what they'll do. My guess is that they'll try one of you for murder, and that will be the end of Clover bricks. Somehow, I don't think having a reputation for our bricks killing people is good publicity. So, if you want to keep your job and not get hung, I'm thinking our friend here needs to disappear."

William looked around. There were no objections. Two of the larger men each picked up a leg of the corpse and dragged the dead weight into the office. They left a wake of streaky blood, neither noticing the sickly thud of the dead man's head clunking over the threshold.

"You," said William, pointing to the fittest of his crew. "Go find my son Rob at Shirley House. Help him drag over the large oilskin, and for God's sake, keep your mouth shut. Ok boys," said William, turning back to the dead man. "Time to light the kilns."

The easiest way to get rid of a body, thought William Clover, *is to burn the thing to a crisp.* He had a kiln and a good cover story, but there was one small problem—the dead man wasn't going to fit.

He handed the bow saw to his nearest worker and nodded encouragingly. "Go on then," said William, "start cutting."

The man reluctantly took it and stared down at the stiffening body.

"Where should I start?" he asked nervously.

"Try his leg," someone suggested.

"Ok," he said, lining up the cut, "but for Christ's sake, someone stop the body from rolling."

It took only one stroke of the serrated blade to sink deep into the man's upper thigh. The flesh gave way with little resistance and the man felt it wasn't unlike carving the Sunday roast. He continued for a few more strokes then, hitting the dead man's leg bone, wedged the saw blade tight. He cursed as he wrenched it free and tried again. Once more the blade stuck and after several more attempts, the worker yanked out the saw and sat down breathing hard.

"Someone else have a go," he gasped. "I'm flipp'n knackered."

Another worker stepped forwards and took the saw.

"You got the wrong tool," he said, shaking his head. "You need an axe to do the job right."

The man looked like he had some experience at dismembering, and moments later, the woodpile's axe was brought to him from outside. Confidently, the worker raised the axe above his head. He let out a guttural scream, then drove the axe blade into the open incision. There was a loud and unmistakable crack and instantly the dead man's femur was pulverized into a thousand pieces.

The unexpected meat carnage hit everything in a twenty-foot radius. Flesh and bone sprayed from the impact as if a small bomb had exploded, and instantly the men, the walls, and furniture were all covered in a fleshy wet shrapnel. The hardest hit was the man still holding the corpse. There had been no time to turn and with his mouth still wide open, he received a direct hit to the face. He held on for a moment and then vomited his breakfast onto the dead man's leg. The sight of semi-digested tomatoes and bacon was enough to curdle the strongest man's stomach and William Clover looked away in disgust.

Jesus Christ, he thought, barely holding down his own breakfast. *I'm never eating blood sausage again.*

Chapter 5

The dog attempted a half-hearted tail wag as I stepped over its basket and slipped out the door. It was still dark and only a few hours had passed since Dave's impromptu family reunion on his parent's front step.

A car waited for me in the rain and I got in still half-drunk. At the wheel was my cousin Bloggs. He had always been a bit of a crazy bastard and even now, in his late twenties, nothing had really changed. His claim to fame, apart from shooting down a grocery store advertising blimp, was working at the local Matchbox factory. Over the years, he had worked his way up to the position of chief engineer where he had mastered the essential skill of inserting steering wheels into toy cars.

"It'll be piss easy, cousin," said Bloggs. "All ya gotta do is pour pints for a couple hours and then when the coast is clear, bunk off and enjoy the rest of the show."

"Sounds great," I replied. "But who's going to be at this London Irish Day thing?"

"What's that guy's name that did the Live Aid thing?" asked Bloggs.

"Geldof," I said. "Bob's going to be there?"

"Sure," replied my cousin, "and some Van Morrison guy, I can't remember."

By the time we arrived, the six official steps to pouring a Guinness were completely out the window. I sat in a plastic chair and poured brown soapy foam to angry Irishmen until I ran out of cups.

"This is fucking mental!" I yelled to my cousin.

"I know! Wish we were serving an Irish funeral!" he yelled back.

"Why?" I asked.

"There's one less drunk at a funeral."

Bob was still playing his set when I finally got relieved. He was dressed in a yellow suit covered with sunflowers, and I just had time to barge my way to the front before I heard the harp-like piano introduction to "I Don't Like Mondays" by the Boomtown Rats. The crowd around me erupted in cheers and Geldof started to sing.

"The silicon chip inside her head . . ." and then fuck, I felt it happen again.

Damn it, Time Keeper, I thought. *Why are you doing this?* It was the same old feeling. A sense I had already done this moment before, and I looked around angrily, trying to see where he was.

An on-looker jostled past me, and then I caught a glimpse of a man's upper arm. *There you are,* I thought, recognizing a tattoo with the Time Keeper's insignia.

"Hey, fucker!" I yelled, but it was no use, the man had disappeared. In an instant, he had been swallowed by a surge of drunken partygoers, and I was left standing in a mud trodden field, and sadly out of beer.

For dramatic effect, the band stopped dead at the lyrics "TELL ME WHY?" Everything went quiet as Bob raised his fist high into the air and stared out into the crowd. It felt like he was demanding an answer, but I had none. I wanted to yell out he should talk to the Time Keeper, but the music suddenly continued and I really didn't think he cared.

I still had a Pogues' song in my head as my cousin and I drove through London. I had found him by chance as I rolled around in some kind of dance scrum, and we finished the night listening to Shane Macgowan belt out a toothless Irish ballad that everyone seemed to know except myself.

I looked down again at the scrap of soaked paper. I was fairly sure I had read the address correctly though Hackney didn't seem like the most inviting place. We had passed several smashed cars as I searched for the correct road, and I found out later that I had just missed a violent riot in the local bagel shop the night before.

I said my goodbyes to Bloggs and watched as his car taillights disappeared around the corner. It was quiet on the street, and I stood for a moment just listening to the sounds of a place I knew nothing about. *This better be it,* I thought, walking up the path to number twelve. I was just about to knock when I smelt a distinct odour of rotten eggs.

"Jesus," I said out loud, realizing the stench was coming from the other side of the door. "What the hell is that?"

I hesitated for a second then knocked anyway.

I was relieved to see Petie Pie Bottom open the door. He welcomed me like the old friend I was, and after dropping my pack, I followed him down the hall to the kitchen.

By the stove, I found the source of the smell. It came from a large pot filled with charcoal grey sand, and I watched as Peter's roommate, Russell, frantically stirred it with a wooden spoon.

"What's cooking?" I asked.

"Gunpowder, old chap," he replied, and I realized he wasn't kidding. "Gotta get it right or I'll flunk my Uni course."

I really hoped he did get it right. As far as I understood, you couldn't make gunpowder only half-right.

The next morning, I awoke on a worn-out Victorian couch in the upstairs lounge. It was raining again, and I stared up at a gaudy crystal chandelier that had been gathering dust for decades. I watched as a slow stream of water ran down the light fixture and landed next me on the floor. The water made a rhythmic slap as it hit the wet carpet and I made a mental note not to step in the puddle when I got out of my sleeping bag.

Eventually, I got up and stepped in the puddle.

"Oh for fuck's sake," I said, looking for my backpack.

It leaned against a small end table, and I sat down next to it and pulled off my wet socks. On the table, I noticed a small pile of grainy black and white photographs. Several of them had fallen onto the floor, and I picked them up to take a closer look.

It was hard to tell what I was seeing. Some of the pictures were out of focus, a few over or underexposed. There was one of Peter that looked interesting. He was holding a bicycle lamp standing by some type of stone staircase. He didn't look particularly happy. I got the feeling there was more to the story, but, with things to do, I let it go for another time.

Ten minutes later, I had climbed the back garden wall and stood at the entrance to a local market. Most of the merchants had dried off from the rain, and I started to meander through the rows, picking at a few odds and sods as I went.

I was looking for a wedding present, preferably a cheap one, but as far as I could see, everything on offer was shit. I was about to give up when I came across a table stacked high with books. If there had been some sort of order, I couldn't figure it out, so I began searching the piles, pulling books out at random. Buried between *the Wonder Book of Animals* and a 1970's *Blue Peter Annual*, I found a thick burgundy book.

"Hey, how much?" I asked, holding up the book.

The vendor looked up from his newspaper and did some math.

"A tenner," he replied, looking hopeful.

"I'll give you three."

"I'll do you for a fiver, but that's the lot. Take it or leave it."

I took it and left as the new proud owner of *The Motherhood Book* circa 1930. It was a bit out-of-date, but I figured there had to be some good advice on how to keep a baby alive. The clincher, however, had to be the recipes at the back of the book. It was even worth the extra two pounds to find out how to cook sheep's brains in milk.

Jumping back into Peter's garden, I realized someone was home. The lights in the kitchen were on and the door to the cement patio was open. A moment later, Russell appeared in the doorway. He stepped out of the kitchen, and if it wasn't for a five-foot cardboard tube on his arm, everything would have looked perfectly normal.

"What are you doing?" I asked, pointing at his new appendage.

"Potatoes," he replied as if it was the most obvious thing in the world.

I watched as he walked over to a row of potatoes lined-up on the garden table. Using a small tree branch in his other hand, he carefully nudged one of the potatoes into the open end of the cardboard tube.

This isn't looking good, I thought as Russell started to count down. On "one" he made a grand sweeping gesture with his bionic arm and launched the vegetable projectile up and out of sight in the direction of the market.

"What the hell are you doing!?" I yelled.

"Fulcrum, my boy, it's all about the bloody fulcrum."

It isn't my place to argue, I thought, so I went to the kitchen fridge and opened a can of lager. I sat and watched Russell load a second potato.

"Put your back into it this time," I said encouragingly.

"Yes, yes," he agreed. "That one was just a test."

For the next half hour, Russell practised his technique. By the last potato, I had given him a 10 out of 10 and he flopped down on the lawn in triumph.

"Hey, what's with all those black and white pics upstairs?" I asked once Russell had caught his breath.

"Ah, the church," he said. "Do you wanna go?"

"What, to mass, you mean?" I asked.

But before he could answer, Peter came into the garden.

"Hey, do you know anything about what's going on at the market?"

"No," Russell and I both said innocently.

"It looked like the police were trying to break-up a fight. Apparently, someone lobbed a potato at the bagel shop again. I think they're on the verge of another bloody riot."

It turned out that Russell and Pie Bottom had stumbled onto "the church" by accident. It had sat abandoned directly across from a pub off Liverpool Street, and a loose plywood panel blowing in the wind was just too much of an invitation to pass up.

Inside, they had discovered an abandoned crypt buried in the bowels of the building, and I found myself deep below the road, after midnight, standing in the same stone passage.

I could hear Russell and Peter through the darkness. They had already gone ahead, and I followed slowly, not wanting to step on anything I shouldn't. I tapped my flashlight, realizing its batteries were already dying, and brushed away a cobweb.

"Fuck," I said, getting annoyed. "This is not fun."

Again, I brushed another web from my face and it tickled slightly as I felt my frustration build. *What is this shit?* I thought, swatting my face with both hands. I shinned my light above me and screamed.

"Fucking Christ shit fuck!" I yelled, staring into the empty eye sockets of a human skull.

It dangled precariously above me from a stone shelf, and I could plainly see I had been walking through the remnants of its hair. I had just enough time to curse again before the skull fell and hit me on the head.

"For fuck's sake," I said, suddenly feeling the ground shake.

"Get down!" I heard Peter yell.

I dropped to the floor in confusion just in time to hear a deafening blow. An instant later, I felt a warm blast of air and my back and legs were sprinkled by tiny bits of debris.

"What's happening!?" I screamed as loose bones and dust crashed around me.

"It's Russell!" cried Peter, jumping over me. "He's blowing up bodies!"

I held the back of Peter's shirt and followed the beam of his bicycle lamp as we heard two more explosions. Thankfully, they were only distant rumbles, and we climbed the stone staircase and dove for cover. I cleared the last strands of the dead man's hair from my sweater and waited.

"He probably blew himself up," said Peter, not sounding in the slightest bit surprised.

"Does he do this often?" I asked.

"Well, not with homemade gunpowder," replied Peter. "I'm still a bit annoyed at him for putting the cat in the microwave."

Five minutes later, Russell emerged waving a femur leg bone triumphantly in the air.

"Are you a complete moron?" I asked Russell when he finally walked over to us.

"Ah sorry, chaps!" he replied shouting. "I just thought it all would be a bit of fun!"

"Fun!?" yelled Peter. "I think I just soiled my best trousers."

"What, your good ones?" asked Russell.

"Yeah, my bloody Dahl's."

It was common knowledge that Pie Bottom's favourite trousers were once worn by the late great author of *Charlie and the Chocolate Factory*, Roald Dahl. Peter had acquired them from Mr. Dahl's widow in a bizarre garden accident and he wore them with pride, honouring the man's legacy.

"This is no good at all," continued Peter.

"Oh, don't be like that," said Russell, still holding the leg bone. "Chances are they weren't Dahl's best pair of trousers anyway. More than likely he crapped in them himself."

"You really think so?" said Peter hopefully.

"Of course," said Russell, putting his arm around Peter. "And that, my friend, is a connection no one else in the world will ever have."

Late the next morning, I woke again in the Great room on the second floor. It wasn't the rain's rhythmic tapping this time that gently woke me, but a pounding on the front door from downstairs. I reluctantly got up and once again stepped on the wet carpet.

"Fuck," I said as my first word of the day and headed down the stairs already in a foul mood.

Without thinking, I picked up Russell's prize femur that was sticking out of an old umbrella stand. It felt deceivingly light in my hand, and I decided it probably would make a better potato stuffer than any kind of weapon.

The door banged again and I opened it to find a police officer standing on the front step.

"Ah yes, good morning," stated the officer. "I'm wanting to speak to . . ." he looked down at a small notebook, "a Russell Williamson and one Peter Dixon. We've had some complaints about flying projectiles and our investigation has been focusing on this area. Just wanted to ask a few questions to some of our repeat offenders."

If I had learned anything watching detective shows on television, it was not to talk to the police while holding part of a dead body. Fortunately, my hand was still behind the door and as I mumbled a confusing excuse as to why Peter and Russell weren't home, I gradually bent my right arm down and dropped the bone casually on the hall carpet.

"We've had complaints about you lot before," the officer continued. "We'll be back later this afternoon." And with a stern look, he turned and left.

I closed the door and sighed. *Shit, that was close,* I thought, and decided it was time for me to go. Granted, I reasoned, blowing up dead people was certainly memorable, but under interrogation, I knew I would crack about the potatoes. The best I could do was to leave a note warning the boys. I mentioned that I didn't think you could dust potatoes for fingerprints, but I suggested the leg and the gunpowder were probably better moved out of the house.

I did the dishes, then changed my wet socks one last time. Grabbing my backpack, I took a final look around. I smiled and thought maybe Russell was right. Maybe this was all a good laugh, then realizing the time, I hoofed it over the back wall and hurried to catch the Fenchurch Street train.

Chapter 6

William had hoped cutting the body would have been a much easier job. *Obviously,* he thought, *dissection isn't a job requirement for making bricks,* but he had to admit he was a little disappointed in his crew's squeamish disposition. Taking matters into his own hands, he went outside and found his uncle's pistol still lying on the ground. It rested next to a half-dried pool of the dead man's blood and William picked it up.

"Goddamn it," he said as he walked toward the pig pens. "Who thought it would end like this?"

Reaching the enclosure, he climbed into the pen of the oldest sow, Betsy. He stood for a second, then patted the old girl on her head one last time. William sighed and lifted the pistol.

"I'm sorry, old girl," he said, and without hesitation, fired a bullet into her skull, dropping the pig instantly.

He turned, leaving the carcass still twitching in the mud. He hated many things at that moment but knew emotion was the least of his worries.

He stood at the edge of the brick field's pond. Cautiously, William looked around but saw only a poorly constructed raft lying on the far side of the bank. He knew the children had built it. *And despite my warnings, it is typical,* he thought, *that Don is the one who fell in.*

He looked around one last time to be sure, then tossed the gun as far out into the water as possible. The impact hardly made a splash and he hoped the cursed weapon would sink deep into the silt, never to be found again.

William had the morning fox to thank for his plan. He'd had to think fast to cover the dead man's tracks and just to make sure, he went through his alibi one more time.

He would claim he had seen a rabid fox that morning. It certainly wasn't unheard of and his attempt to shoot the damn thing would logically explain the pistol shot. He would then say he had discovered the crazed animal had burrowed into Betsy's pen and attacked her. William knew any farmer would agree. There was no other way to stop rabid contamination other than butcher and burn, and William intended to do both before the day was out.

He checked on the boy around noon. His bedroom was hardly bigger than a cupboard and William stepped over the boy's comics and sat next to his sleeping son. He could tell he had been crying and he watched Don until finally he opened his eyes.

It took him a moment to recognize his father, but then Don reached for him and sobbed uncontrollably.

He held on tight to his father's shirt, and through the muffled tears, William heard his son repeat the same question, "Why?"

"You know, some people are just so unhappy they don't want to be in this world anymore," William said calmly. "That man missed his wife so much that he just wanted to be happy with her in heaven."

"Yes, sir," replied his son.

"You know, I think it would be best if we could keep what we saw to ourselves. I think it would upset your mother and the rest of the lads are going to do the same. Do you think you can be a big boy and do that?" asked William.

"I think so," said Don, trying to hold back his tears. "It's just every time I close my eyes, all I see is that man's head exploding."

Don leaned forwards and started to cry again, this time muffling his sobs into the mattress. William waited. He knew it would be hard for the boy. Even with all the death and suffering of farm life, William knew a man blowing his brains out was not the same as cutting a chicken's head off. After a few minutes, Don lifted his head and dried his stinging red eyes.

"I wish I could wake up like Daniel and know it was all a dream," he said.

"Who's Daniel?" asked William.

"Dreamy Daniel," his son answered. "From the 'Lot-O-Fun' comic. He goes on adventures and then just wakes up at the end of the story. I wish I could do that."

"Well, maybe in time you won't think about it as much," William responded.

"Maybe," the boy answered, sounding unconvinced.

William sighed. *What am I going to do?* he thought. Looking at the boy, he saw the same distant stare he had seen in his Uncle Charlie, and William had to admit that his son seemed more traumatized than he had hoped.

He had promised himself he would never take another dirty job from the army. He had been even more adamant not to survey a job offer in Scotland needing Clover bricks. But, as William held his boy, it occurred to him that Scotland could be the perfect excuse.

Time and distance, thought William, making up his mind.

"Ok then. Pack your duffle, son," he said to Don. "We're going on an adventure, just like your friend Daniel."

Chapter 7

The new curate appeared on Tuesday morning, staring through the kitchen window at 66 Daws Heath Road. His pale face and rimless glasses caught Ida Clover off guard. In her surprise, she dropped the plate she was washing and the crash instantly triggered an onslaught of barks from the dogs and the cats running for cover.

The curate had several matters to discuss. First and foremost was the incident the previous Sunday during the vicar's sermon. It seemed that several boys, including the Clovers, had taken it upon themselves to release an array of caterpillars and large slugs under the pews.

Also, there was the issue of Mr. Clover. He had been absent for several Sundays and the curate was poised with a speech about leading by example which he felt obligated to recite.

He had just been able to open the scullery door a few inches when Ida wedged the door with her foot.

"I think it's best if you see the children first, young curate," she said, deliberately stalling. "Get them to show you their pets," she encouraged. "They're supposed to be down by the brick fields stacking bricks."

She took off her apron and scanned the room quickly. *The place is a bloody wreck,* she thought, feeling a little unprepared. She watched as the curate strolled off down the path, and cursing her absent husband, piled what was left of the dirty plates and cutlery into the oven.

He smiled as he headed through the barnyard toward a field of chickens. Secretly, he had always wanted to be a farmer and he inhaled deeply, finding romance in smelling several kinds of animal shit.

Passing the ferret cages, he stopped and tried to pet the head of one of the sleeping animals. For his troubles, he almost had his finger bitten off and he made a mental note not to stick his fingers through any more cages.

He wiped his brow as the path turned and the curate found himself suddenly standing in front of an open area penned with pigs. He counted twelve sties in all, and peering over a wooden fence, he saw eleven were occupied. A couple of the animals looked up, snorting disapprovingly, but since he wasn't offering any food, they turned and went back to more important pig matters.

He found the children setting up for a game of cricket. He recognized a few other boys from the neighbouring farms and was about to mention the Sunday caterpillar incident when he was told to play wicket keeper.

"Wicket keeper?" he said to one of the Clover boys. "But I'm not dressed for it."

"What do you mean?" he replied. "Those look like trousers to me."

By the end of the first innings, Rob Clover had decided the curate was a complete dick. It wasn't the curate's ability to catch that annoyed him, but simply the man's demand for honesty. It seemed that no minor infraction got past the judging eyes of the keeper, and Rob had just about enough of being yelled at for standing out of position.

It was only when Sarah the pig crashed through the yard that Rob had a glimmer of hope the game was going to end. Instinctively, the panicked animal made straight for the backside of the unsuspecting curate and with all the power of a steam locomotive, the pig sent him flying several feet into the air.

To add to the curate's misfortune, he landed on the charging sow and rode the bucking swine down the entire length of the makeshift cricket pitch. By the time Sarah had crashed through the bails and wickets, the curate had hit the ground with little grace and even less dignity.

"How's zat!" yelled Rob Clover, throwing his arms into the air. "Game over."

He heard a few cheers as his friends instantly bolted, and without waiting to see if the curate was still breathing, Rob ran to join the new game of "catch the pig."

The curate lay on the ground for some time. He was afraid to move, but eventually he climbed to his feet and surveyed the damage. There was a large tear in his left trouser knee but apart from a scraped elbow and a ferret bitten finger, he was relieved to find he was relatively unscathed.

He walked back to the broken wickets and spotted his glasses in the mud. He picked them up and was happy to discover the lenses were still intact. He adjusted a slight bend in one of the wires and then reached into his front pocket for a small, starched handkerchief.

The curate was still polishing the lenses when he looked up into the face of a rather unhappy looking horse. By the sounds of it, the horse had been worked hard and the animal snorted heavily, just in time to smear his glasses once again. As the dust settled, the curate could see it was the local milkman, Domper Horner, holding the reins. *Oh great,* thought the curate, *just what I need.*

As far as the curate was concerned, Domper was a cantankerous, bitter old bugger. Recently, he had argued with him over a delivery of some curdled milk, and after getting nowhere, was reprimanded for not having put the milk into the ice box fast enough. *If at all possible,* thought the curate, *Milko Dom is looking worse than usual.* Not only was the man unshaven and his white jacket smeared with dirt, but just above Domper's left eye patch there was a large purple lump.

It was well known, even in the short time the curate had been in the Rayleigh parish, that Domper Horner had only one good eye. His other eye was made of glass and the curate couldn't help but think he had lost the argument over the sour milk by the distraction of not knowing which of Domper's eyes to follow.

"What happened to your eye?" asked the curate, trying to keep things pleasant.

"I bloody lost it!" exclaimed the milkman.

"What again?" replied the curate without thinking.

Domper was about to reply when he was suddenly interrupted by a squealing pig running past the wagon. It was followed moments later by several screaming children and Domper cursed at the passing hooligans not to spook his horse. A few of the slower children stopped at the wagon and caught their breath. They were breathing hard as they looked up at the milkman.

"Hey, Mr. Horner, what happened to you eye?" asked Johnny half bent over.

"Well, if you have to know," he answered reluctantly, "old Daisy hoofed me one in the old coconut this morning. Knocked me eye clean out. Bloody thing rolled away, couldn't find it anywhere."

"We'll find it," said Rob excitedly. "We'll all go over to your barn and have a look," he offered.

"Well, it can't hurt I suppose," said Domper, touching the lump on his head, "but you mind your business, and for Christ's sake, don't touch anything important."

He watched as the children ran to catch up with the pack, then motioned the curate to get out of his way as he flicked the horse's reins.

"Let's hope Mrs. Clover knows where her ice box is," Domper said as the cart began to move. "Hate to see perfectly good milk go to waste."

So much for the youth of today, thought the curate, picking up the children's worn-out cricket bat. *Maybe,* he thought, *I can work the subject into my sermon, though, after talking with Milko Dom, the theme of an eye for an eye seems to be a tad more relevant.*

He smiled and almost laughed as he walked past the Clover brick kiln. Its two large steel doors hung half-open and having never actually seen inside, the curate pulled on one of the heavy doors and took a quick look.

To his dismay, the kiln was only half-filled with bricks. *Obviously,* he thought, *the children haven't finished their job.* It occurred to the curate that helping put the last bricks in place would show just what a good sport God really was. He looked around and found what he thought were the remainder of the un-fired bricks still sitting on the drying shed tables. *Easy enough,* thought the curate, rolling up his sleeves. And with a silent prayer to Saint Joseph, he began transferring the remaining bricks to the kiln.

After an hour, the curate was drenched in sweat. He had cleared several tables and was feeling rather pleased. His only wish was to see the expression on the children's faces when they realized they wouldn't be in trouble. *Maybe after that,* he thought, *they may even consider Sunday school.*

At the back of the shed he found one last pile. They were covered by an old canvas sheet, and picking up the closest brick, the curate was surprised to find it felt slightly heavier than the rest. *Must be getting tired,* he thought, dismissing any other explanation. He stacked the first load onto a wooden wheelbarrow and grunted as he lifted the handles.

"Dear God," he said out loud, feeling the strain on his lower back, "give me strength."

By the time the last brick was in place, there was hardly any room left. The curate latched both kiln doors, massaged his aching back, then decided he was done for the day.

Mrs. Clover would simply have to wait for another day, thought the curate, picking up his jacket. If he was just quiet enough, he could grab his bicycle and be gone before anyone was the wiser.

He was nearly clear of the front gate when a voice from the scully window beckoned.

"Damn, damn, damn," muttered the curate under his breath.

"Yoo-hoo" called Mrs. Clover, running up the path. "Tea's getting cold, young curate," she announced, and begrudgingly the curate was led back into the house.

"Oh yes," said Mrs. Clover, or Ida as she had insisted on being called. "My family comes from a very long line of respectable gentry. There's of course my father, a Thorington. He had the largest landholdings in Thundersley at one time. Did you see the children down there?" she asked, finally pausing for a bite of scone.

"Yes, yes, indeed," replied the curate, a little surprised at the chance to speak. "They were very diligent at finishing their brick stacking," he lied.

Ida Clover nodded with polite suspicion, then leaned forwards as she poured the curate's tea. From the curate's vantage point, all he saw was Mrs. Clover's fleshy cleavage.

Good God, he thought, trying to look away, then changed the subject to poor Domper Horner.

"Yes," she said, "he told me the whole story when he filled my jugs. I do hope the children can find his eye. Sugar?" asked Ida.

"No, thank you, Mrs. Clover," said the curate, "but I would like a drop of milk."

With relief, he reached the small jug before Ida, and with a polite *no trouble* sort of smile, he quickly tipped the milk container in the direction of his teacup. *That's odd,* thought the curate, feeling something shift inside the jug.

It made an odd clanking sound and then without warning, something plopped into his cup. The splash soaked the freshly starched tablecloth, but neither the curate nor Ida Clover reacted. Instead, they both stared, frozen, at the fragile bone China cup and watched as some type of spherical object bobbed just below the surface of the brown, tepid liquid.

At first glance, the curate thought the object resembled a small chicken egg, but as it rolled over in his cup, there was no mistaking the stare of a fake glass eye.

"Well, it seems like we found Domper's missing eyeball," the curate announced with calm disgust. He set down his cup and got up to leave. "I'm sure the children will take it back," he said, glancing down at the table one more time.

He was never sure if Domper's eye had actually winked at him. The late afternoon sun had a tendency to cast odd, peculiar shadows, but it was enough for the curate to decide the Clovers were a family to steer well clear of in the future. As far as he was concerned, they were all as mad as each other, and he left, praying not to trip over any more lost body parts on the way out.

Chapter 8

Essex, as far as I remembered, was a violent place back in the seventies. It was a time when red cast iron phone boxes reeked of piss, and anything that couldn't be stolen was either smashed or burned.

Looking back, it was no wonder I ran away from school on my second day. Even at five years old, I suspected anarchy was a better social condition than conformity.

It only took a moment to break my mother's grip. I didn't have a plan but bricking it down the school hill road looked like the path of least resistance. Several mothers took up the chase, but a few hippies wearing clogs and bell-bottoms were no match for my last attempt at freedom.

I hid, I remember, for a long time near the bottom of the road. I had jumped a garden wall and had curled myself tightly under some type of bush. I heard voices and footsteps for a while but eventually things became quiet.

I was found later that afternoon, fast asleep in my bed. My parents had left the front door open, and it hadn't taken a great deal of detective work to follow parts of my discarded school uniform up the stairs to my room.

Once the police left, I found my mother crying at the dining room table. I was surprised to see her so upset. Even when she had thrown my brother's shoes out the window because the laces weren't the same length, she had never lost it quite the same way.

"I thought I had lost you," she said, blowing her nose.

"But I knew exactly where I was," I replied in my defence.

On the third day, I walked to school by myself. Maybe my mother understood I needed my freedom or, at least, the illusion of it. Regardless, it worked. I never ran away from school again. It wasn't that I didn't want to, I just think I learned better ways of annoying the "Establishment" by sticking around.

The walk from the bus stop to my old house was easy. I passed the overgrown garden of the crazy bird lady, Mrs. Tree's house with the blind poodle, and the Thipthorpe's cottage whose daughter only ate banana sandwiches.

When I reached the house, I stopped and stared from across the street. It had changed, but somehow remained as familiar as the day I left. My old family home was basically a two storey A-frame with the house next door mirroring the design. *It's odd,* I thought, *how these twin peaks still dominate the rest of the road.* To my father, it had always been an impressive display of personal success, though I preferred to remind him the house was only paid for because he cut his arm off at work.

The accident, for better or worse, happened before I was born. In fact, my father's three years off work was probably the reason for my appearance.

It was not a clean chop but more of a messy mangle. A large spinning drill called a milling machine caught my father's sleeve and with very little ceremony, ripped and twisted his arm till it hung by only a thin strip of dying flesh.

What remained I have as a plaster cast that rests on top of my underwear drawer. I see it everyday, the only left arm I ever knew of my father's. Each morning and every night it is there. A constant reminder that sometimes "struggle" is far better than complacency, and that safety guards, like clean underwear, are necessary regardless of what you might think.

For the briefest moment, a figure passed by my parent's old bedroom window. There were no cars in the driveway, and I had presumed nobody was home. I watched to see if they would return and hoped, whoever it was, hadn't called the police. But I hadn't have worried, I knew who was there, the feeling was unavoidable.

When they appeared again, the Time Keeper did not move. He stood in the middle of the three second storey windows and bowed his hooded head like the first time we met. I'm not sure why I wasn't surprised. In some way I half expected his presence, and I felt a sadness come over me, something I had never felt for him before. I thought about waving, but that just seemed wrong, so I stared back and wondered if maybe he was trapped or tied to the house like myself.

I was not sure what haunted me about my childhood home. I had often come back and made my pilgrimage up the hill for reasons I couldn't explain. Possibly, it was the feeling that my time there was incomplete. That I was taken away, at an early age, to a new life in Canada before my spirit was ready. *Maybe it is that simple,* I thought. *Just the inability to accept change. Maybe my ghost of childhood past refuses to let go.*

Whatever the reason, I knew it wasn't bringing anything back. Maybe gaining peace from the past had more to do with realizing that not all things wanted to be held.

"So, what's with you, Time Keeper?" I asked out loud. "Do you need my help? Or do I need yours?"

The question hung in the air as I turned and walked further up the road. I had no doubt I would see him again, that was a given, but one day, I hoped, I would find my answer.

I was seven when the Time Keeper first appeared. He came while I slept, and it was only when I woke from my dream through a fishpond in the ceiling, that I realized I wasn't alone. He stood at the bottom of my bed, dressed like a monk, silently reading from an open book. I was ready to believe I was still sleeping until he moved towards me, and I heard the unmistakable sound of feet crunching on my bedroom carpet.

What made it worse was the fact I couldn't see the apparition's face. His robed hood covered most of his upper body, and whether it was for dramatic effect or not, he had lowered his head so that all his features were hidden.

By the time he reached me, I was about ready to yell. He turned to face me and had started to lean over my bed when I broke free of my paralysis and slammed on my wall light switch. It took a second, but as my eyes adjusted, I discovered the room was empty. Whoever or whatever had visited me was gone, and my only proof was simply a memory too real to be imagined.

My last recollection of the Time Keeper that night was a talisman that hung from his neck. It was a strange sort of design with a sideways oval and a protruding stem. I hadn't thought much of it at the time but as the years went on, I understood his odd-looking necklace had more to say.

I was eating strawberry jam on toast when my budgie Sammy died. It was a Tuesday, October 2nd, 1977, to be precise. He was quite dead when I checked on him that morning. He lay at the bottom of the cage, his legs straight up and as solid as a clay brick.

It was my first experience with the finality of death. I tried to grasp some kind of meaning, but the motionless plume of green feathers gave little answers. I tried to eat my toast through the tears, but it was no use. Eventually, I made my way to school, by myself, late, my eyes red and sore from crying.

I buried Sammy that evening. A small wooden cross with two tail feathers marking the spot. It was there, with my hands muddied from grave digging, that I vowed to honour my friend's two and a half years of life. It seemed obvious enough. I would only eat strawberry jam on Tuesdays for the rest of my life.

"Ay, you want one of these doughnuts?" a friend would ask.

"Does it have jam in it?" I would reply.

"Yeah."

"What day is it?" I'd ask.

"Wednesday."

"Oh," would be my reply. "Can't eat jam on Wednesdays."

I was fifteen when I finally decided I had served my budgie justice and deprived myself of enough missed jam opportunities. There was only so much culinary peer pressure I could take, and I released myself into a strange new world of jam freedom.

Notable Deaths on October 2nd

Rock Hudson, 1985 (actor, *Written on the Wind*)

George Savalas, 1985 (actor, *Kojak*)

Peter Medawar, 1987 (zoologist and Nobel Prize winner)

Alec Issigonis, 1988 (designer of the Mini car)

Hazen Argue, 1991 (Canadian politician)

William Berger, 1993 (actor, *The Adventures of Hercules*)

Henry Ringling North, 1993 (circus owner)

Chapter 9

I had stayed the night at Petie Pie Bottom's father's house, Naughty Norman. His wife had left years ago, and it wasn't uncommon, growing up, to find Peter and his brothers all eating dinner in their canoes around the living room television.

Naughty had left for a swim by the time I made it downstairs. I sat at the kitchen table and warmed myself with a tea and the midmorning sun.

Most pressing was the best man speech I had to write. I had never written one before, and I felt some mounting pressure to pull off some type of intelligent, heartfelt observations about a friend I had known forever.

The plan was to take the bus back into Southend and head for the library. *If anything,* I thought, *at least it will be a quite place to reflect on the past few weeks.*

I grabbed my backpack and followed Norman's written instructions on how to lock up and where to hide the key. With that done, I had just enough time to get down to the main arterial road and catch the 23A into town. I closed the front gate, turned, and then abruptly stopped.

"The fuck?" I said, staring at a man in monk's clothes, sitting on the front garden wall.

"Been waiting for you," he said, turning his head toward me. "Thanks for coming back."

I grasped for some reasonable explanation, then finally blurted out the only thing I could think of. "You're the Time Keeper."

"The Time Keeper—is that what you think I am?" he said smiling. "Far from it, my friend, but I gotta say, I like it. You mind if I take off this robe?" he asked.

I was about to respond when he threw down his cigarette and wrenched the balky wool material over his head.

"Cor, that's better," he gasped, "been itching in that thing for ages."

I looked at him and felt somehow let down. The man that had followed me for years, popping up randomly and technically haunting me, was now casually standing in front of me as if it was the most natural thing in the world. To add to my disappointment, he really didn't look very impressive. Apart from a receding hairline, he wore a pair of old worn boots, a pair of patched up bell-bottom jeans, and a tie-dye t-shirt that had the caption "Save The Humans" printed on it.

"I really didn't come back for you," I said apologetically. "I just wanted to see the old house, ya know?"

"Oh," replied the Time Keeper, a little disappointed.

"Well anyway," he said, "I thought it was time we met. You know, I really think we can help each other."

"With what?" I asked.

"Let me put it this way," he began, then paused to get his words right. "It's all about the memories. They'll mess you right up if you don't know how to ride them."

"Ride a memory?" I replied confused.

"Yeah man, they're like waves. All ya gotta do is jump on, do a cut back now and then, and ride that puppy all the way to the original moment it was created."

"So you're a surfer?" I said, trying hard to follow.

"In a sense," he replied. "I've been riding your memories for a while. All you have to do is think of one, and I'll take the drop. That's where you get your déjà vu, it's just me hang'n ten."

"Well, thanks for nothing," I said. "Can't help feeling a little used right about now."

"Ah, don't be like that. You have some gnarly waves, mate."

"Thanks, I guess," I replied, still a little suspicious. "So, why me?" I asked, trying to get to the point.

"To be honest, I'm hoping one of your waves will get me out of this place. I seem to be in limbo here, just like the rest of them."

"The rest of them? There's more of you? And everyone smokes?" I asked.

"Yeah, it's all a bit confusing. The rules seem to change all the time. For some reason I can smoke, but I can't drink, so that really bites. Not sure about the others, we all tend to keep to ourselves."

I thought about it for a moment before answering. "So, am I the only one that can see you?"

"Pretty much, but there are a few that can. Children seem to see me more. Do you see that lady walking her dog over there? Well, she thinks you're talking to the lamp post."

I looked across the road just as an old purple rinse granny looked away to avoid my stare.

"So how exactly are you supposed to help me?" I asked, completely lost.

I turned, expecting an answer but realized I was alone. The Time Keeper had vanished or caught a wave I guessed. *That was a bit rude,* I thought, feeling somewhat dismissed. Certainly no marks for hippy surfer etiquette I concluded, then looked at my watch, and ran for the bus.

The Southend Central Library looked sadly out-of-date after its modern face-lift thirty years earlier. In contrast, it couldn't have been further removed from the Victorian train station next door, but I was glad to see that mindless vandalism did not discriminate between architecture.

I climbed the stairs to the second floor of the library and used the card catalogue to find book titles on how to write speeches. I found two on the subject of weddings, but as I flicked through the pages, I decided that jokes about wife beating and female domestic chores were not topics I thought would go down well. After a quick think, I tried my luck on books about farm animals. It was a promising direction, but as hard as I tried, I couldn't work bestiality into my speech.

Finally, after a few hours of random doodles, I came up with something I thought was pretty good. It bordered on arrogance and self-defecation, and I had to admit, I was rather pleased with myself having worked in two naked references.

Folding the papers, I headed down to the first floor lobby. To the left of the main entrance was an art exhibit I hadn't noticed. As far as I could tell, large photographs of intense looking people hung suspended from the ceiling. None of which, it seemed, were having a very good time and I decided to take a few minutes and walk through the small gallery.

One picture in particular caught my attention. The photograph was of a man being held back by police. A caption explained he had just found out that his son was being held hostage at gun point just outside the frame of the camera. His expression was real. It was unconscious, primal, and heart-wrenching. Next to it was a second picture of a man bursting out in anguish having found that his entire family had just died in a plane crash.

"Terrible," I heard a voice say from behind me.

I turned and to my surprise, I saw the Time Keeper sitting on a bench.

"It's funny," he said as I sat down next to him, "how the living try to avoid pain."

"How so?" I whispered, not wanting to be accused of talking to an empty chair.

"Well, from the other side here, it all seems a bit pathetic. We turn off the news because it reminds us of how vulnerable we are. We numb ourselves with drugs and meds to avoid even the potential of pain. I think even the tooth fairy was invented to explain pain to a child. "

The Time Keeper was silent as we both stared across the walkway.

"You know, there's a little girl I see sometimes," he continued. "She died of a heart defect when she was very young. Sweet thing, always smiling. But you know what she wants more than anything?"

I shook my head.

"She just wants to feel. Feel the wind, feel pain, feel anything to make her believe she's really alive. "

"But she's not," I replied.

I looked again at the photographs in front of me. It was all there. Despair, pain, fear, anguish, all examples of what I thought made me uniquely real.

"So how do we save the humans?" I asked, referring to the Time Keeper's t-shirt.

"That's debatable," he said smiling, "but I think it starts by surrendering."

"To what?" I asked.

"To everything," he replied. "The good, the bad, and every emotion in-between. You don't know how lucky you are."

Considering the Time Keeper's etiquette, I was surprised he followed me out of the library and stood next to me at the bus stop.

"Can you give me a ride?" he asked.

"Can't you just get on the bus?" I muttered under my breath.

"No, no, surf me back. Just think of the old house and I'll catch the wave," he explained.

"So I'm your own personal taxi now?" I said a little too loud.

"Ah, don't hassle me, man, we're friends, right?"

I looked up in disbelief. "Me hassle you?"

Reluctantly, I closed my eyes. I thought of the old house on Fairfield Road and by the time I opened them again, he was gone. *Hang ten,* I thought as the bus pulled to a stop, and I stepped on board feeling I had already lived this moment somewhere else.

I walked up the path to Flossy's rose-covered cottage and closed the iron gate behind me. I had made the trek many times through the years, and I had no doubt where I would find her. I followed the side path along the pebble-dash wall, then turned into the back garden and saw that the faded blue kitchen door, as always, was propped wide open.

"Hello, Floss," I said, stepping into the kitchen.

She squinted for a moment, then recognized me.

"Oh, hello dear," she said, reaching for a glass. "Just hang on a minute while I put my teeth in."

For as long as I had known, my Great Auntie Flossy had always sat in the same chair. It faced into her garden, and though she could turn on her television by an extension on her walking stick, I suspected the outdoors gave her more pleasure than the BBC.

She was the wife of my grandmother's brother, Rob Clover, and as married couples went, they had always seemed a little odd. For starters, neither of them could walk. Flossy had a set of antique polio leg braces, but Great Uncle Robert was quite immobile. How she dragged the old boy to the bedroom every night, I will never know, but she did, and I had to respect the poor girl, regardless of how much she despised him.

Rob Clover was a milkman until he crashed his float. The accident made sure he never worked or walked again, and looking back, it was a shame I didn't know either of them any other way. As a kid, Great Uncle Rob used to scare the fuck out of me. It was his eyes that did it. All of a sudden, they would start to roll back into his head until only the fleshy whites of his eyeballs showed. I never did find out what that was all about, though it seems obvious, there must have been some kind of brain damage going on.

It was just Flossy now. Rob's eyeballs had rolled back permanently a few years ago, and I sat down in his empty chair and thought about what his world had looked like.

"Tea then?" she asked as if I popped in on a daily schedule.

In reality, it had been getting on six years, but it didn't seem to bother Flossy. I watched as she boiled the kettle from her chair, then fiddled with her postwar gas stove and browned toast on one side. We talked while I ate. I mainly listened as she berated a neighbour and the window cleaner. None of it really mattered, I was just glad to hear the old girl was still dishing out the shit.

It was dark when I got up to leave. I placed the washed dishes on the draining board and was about to kiss her goodbye when she gave me one last job.

"Now before you go, dear, I want you to go get something for me."

She directed me to a shelf in her bedroom wardrobe and I brought out the box she had asked me to retrieve.

"They're for you," Floss said as I opened the dusty lid.

Inside were several small oil paintings. I had seen them before and knew they were my Great Uncle Rob's. Honestly, I thought they were kind of shit, but I lifted a few off the pile and faked my interest in the painted rural scenes of Victorian Essex.

"What's on the back?" I asked, flipping the last painting over.

"Well, I wasn't going to spend money on canvases, so I got Rob to cut up one of his old atlases. Anyway, he would have liked you to have them. Go on, take them. They're no use to me."

I faked a grateful smile and secured the lid with a rubber band. *Great,* I thought, *more crap to lug around,* but I slid the thin box into my pack and kissed her cheek, unknowingly for the last time.

Chapter 10

"Erected by his parents in memory of Michael S. Brown, their beloved son that was done to death" read William Clover, standing in front of Michael Brown's grave.

He had remembered the tragic story from the previous year, and arriving early for his meeting with the artillery Major, Don and William had ventured into the East Wemyss Cemetery and paid their respects.

As he continued reading, it did not go unnoticed that he shared the same first name as the slain boy's father. William rested a hand on the shoulder of his son and unconsciously drew him closer. *Death, it seems, is following us everywhere,* thought William, and try as he might, he could not shake the images from the past few days.

Before leaving for Scotland, William Clover had left strict instructions with his workers. He had already managed to drag the man's body into the kiln, but since the dismembering hadn't gone so well, he positioned the corpse, with the help of a sledgehammer, into a haphazard fetal position. He had covered the body with bricks and after checking that there were no limbs sticking out, he had prepared the five fire boxes with wood and the butchered remains of his dead sow.

All that is left, thought William, *is for my workers to put the correct bricks into the kiln. Couldn't be too hard?* he thought, *certainly easier than dismembering a body.* The only thing he hadn't counted on was an ambitious curate and his men leaving for their tea.

The journey to Scotland had been laborious and slow. It involved several steam trains and transfers, but eventually they had made their way north, grateful to be away from the carnage of Essex.

When they had arrived at Buckhaven station, the wind was blowing at almost gale force. Having no choice, the father and son trudged along the Fife Coastal Path and leaned into the wind, both feeling the sting of the salty sea air. Around them, the wheels and riggings of mining elevators stood as reminders of where they were. Literally below their feet, coal miners had worked the tunnels for generations, digging the rock that for many became their permanent graves.

Finally, as the two crested a gentle hill, both William and Don slowed to admire the remains of Macduff's Castle.

"Would you look at that!" yelled William over the sound of the wind. "Would have been pretty impressive in its day!"

Only two towers remained and a partial wall, but it was enough to ignite the imagination of his son.

"Can I climb it?" asked Don enthusiastically.

"We'll see," replied his father. "Let's get this meeting over with first."

They found the major beside the western tower. The man was staring out to sea, his hands purposely placed on his hips.

"Bloody good view," he said, turning to greet William. "You must be the structural engineer. About time, I say. Look, we've got a wee bit of bother here. We've been letting off the cannons up here, you know, for a bit of practice, and we've managed not only to knock down bits of the castle but caused a few cave-ins in the passages underneath the cliffs."

William thought he should correct the man. By no means was he an engineer, but he decided to hold his tongue. He didn't really care.

"Have you thought of moving the artillery?" William asked.

"Aye, but there's no where else to go. If we shift the whole operation north, we're going to collapse all the coal shafts."

To William, it seemed the problem wasn't engineering, but stupidity.

"Well," William said with false enthusiasm, "let's go look at those caves."

To the right of the men, a foot path meandered down the steep, grassy cliff. William hadn't bothered to wait for the major, and by the time the man had reached the pebbled beach, William was happily puffing on his new acquired pipe.

They stepped together through the entrance of what the army major called Court Cave. It was cool and dank and though the light had been reduced to only a sliver, there was still enough for William to make out a recent mud slide that rose to meet the roof of the cave's back passage.

"They say this was the passage Macduff himself escaped through when Macbeth besieged his castle at Kennoway," spoke the major.

"I doubt anyone will be escaping through it these days," replied William. *Even an idiot,* he thought, *could see the cave is highly unstable.* "You're going to need a bunch of support pillars in here. One there, one there, and three right across the middle," pointed William. "Better get out while the going's good," he added and left without waiting for a response.

The second cave, the Doo Cave, gave William just as much concern. Within a few steps of entering the east cave, William had to stop.

"Jesus!" he exclaimed. "This thing's just about to go."

Around him there were several recent mini avalanches and he turned with the same uneasy panic as before.

"What the hell are those for?" asked William, looking at a series of carved squares near the cave's entrance.

"Pigeon boxes," replied William's guide. "Back in the Middle Ages, they were kept in here to provide fresh meat in winter. You see, the cattle got so scrawny they weren't worth killing. But that all changed when they invented the turnip."

"Oh," said William, "I bloody hate turnips."

The last cave William entered was more reassuring. Jonathan's cave, north of the castle, seemed relatively sound with only the beginnings of some natural coastal erosion. There was a steep drop to the floor, but the entrance was large and the chamber was well lit from the wide opening.

"You see those drawings," the major pointed out. "They're the oldest Pictish markings in Scotland. There are more markings in this cave than in the whole of England."

William felt somehow that the man wanted him to be impressed, but he wasn't. In fact, he was getting a little tired of the local history lesson.

"Look at this one," pointed the man. "See the human figure, and look, it's right next to a fish."

"Yeah, I see it," said William, stepping closer. "Looks like he's fucking it."

Outside, William Clover squinted in the daylight.

"I'll tell you what," said William. "I'll write some recommendations to your head of command. Bricks, lots of bricks, and the sooner the better."

William shook the man's hand and looked back along the shore. *Now, where's my son?* he thought, looking up and finding the answer.

"Jesus Christ," said William, spotting the boy on top of one of the castle's towers.

His legs were buckling and from William's vantage point far below, Don looked like he was about to fall. William tried to shout but it was no use. The wind snatched his voice and carried it out to sea. All William could do was watch as his son flailed helplessly, his mind already imagining Don's broken body on the jagged rocks below.

Chapter 11

So, the big wedding day came. Everyone had their clothes on, clean shirts, ties, and polished leather shoes. At Dave's parents', there was the usual wedding mayhem. Even the dog had contributed to the chaos. It had crapped on the kitchen floor, and I decided beer and the back garden was the best choice to avoid fecal or emotional mine fields.

I was particularly proud of the necktie I was wearing. It was silk with an Art Deco design in yellow, red, and dark blue. My mother had shoplifted it several Boxing Days ago and ever since, it became a tradition to shoplift with mum on the day after Christmas.

My tie flapped in the breeze as we arrived at the church. Dave had organized a procession of motor scooters to accompany him to the century old chapel and about ten custom Vespas and Lambrettas pulled into the church parking lot decked out in bows and streamers.

To my surprise, the vicar had joined the entourage and had taken a few puffs of a joint. I wasn't sure if that was spiritually ethical, but then Adam and Eve had been chatting with a talking snake, so who knew what the hell they were on?

"Don't leave the roach ends on the ground," was the vicar's last words as we entered the church. "They don't help with the parish goat's digestion."

I was close to passing out by the time the bride and groom had exchanged vows and exited the church. I only owned one suit and hadn't planned on buying another. The problem was my suit jacket was tailored for winter in Canada, and the thick jacket material felt more like a wool blanket than a slick fashion statement.

To make matters worse, I had decided I wasn't going to loosen my tie or take off my jacket until I had read the best man speech. It was an honourable sentiment but naively impractical. Even the goat looked hot in the baking sun, and I wondered if its balls were as sweaty as mine. Sadly, the removal of my jacket wouldn't have made any difference to the outcome of my speech.

It tanked, even with the snare drum and cymbal I had set up for added effect. I was in trouble from the start. A joke about two antennas getting married and having a "brilliant reception" got little response and the harder I banged the drum for punctuation, the less enthusiasm I seemed to generate. Somewhere near the middle of the speech, I desperately ad-libbed a reference to goat sex, but it was simply too late. I limped to the finish with a spirited, half-defeated toast to fertility, loosened my tie, and made a beeline straight for the bar.

It didn't take long to feel better. A few pints later and wearing my tie as a headband, I had almost forgotten my toast master inadequacy. The disco part of the night had kicked into full swing and on hearing the opening few bars of "Town Called Malice," I cheered along with some of the bachelor party lads and hit the dance floor running.

They say to dance like no one is watching, but I know better. I dance like everyone is watching and I air drummed around the floor, confident that my drum technique was massively impressive. I suspect it wasn't. I'm sure I looked like a complete twat thrashing my arms like I was having a seizure, but I really didn't give a shit. I closed my eyes, and like the Time Keeper suggested, I surrendered to everything.

"Hey!" I shouted to the vicar a few songs later.

He had been twisting away on the dance floor holding a large glass of wine.

"Is that water or wine?" I asked.

"Ah, well," he responded, "that all depends on what you believe."

"Well, there's a Scottish guy at the bar that claims he can make vodka from potatoes, so I'm keeping my options open."

I sat down with him at the end of the song and casually brought up the subject of the Time Keeper.

"So tell me," I asked, "do you ever get visited by ghosts?"

"All the time," he replied.

He reached for the table wine and poured the remainder of the bottle into his glass.

"You do?" I asked a little surprised.

"Oh yes," he continued, "mainly poor souls that have lost their way or the ones that don't want to let go."

"Wow," I said, "who knew. Ok, well it seems I'm talking to the right person because there's this guy that's been popping up in my life since I was seven."

The vicar sipped from his glass.

"What does he want?" he finally asked.

"All he said was that he was stuck and he needed my help to get out."

"Well, there you have it," replied the vicar.

"Have what?"

"Your answer. For some reason this spirit needs your specific help. My best advice is just to listen and understand what he really wants . . . Ah," said the vicar, interrupting himself. "The power of love," he half sang. "A force from above . . . make love your goal."

I knew the song the DJ was playing. It was by the band Frankie Goes to Hollywood.

"Gosh, that's such a great song. You know, love is the one emotion that can transcend everything."

"Do you think it really can?" I asked.

"Well," he said smiling "I've bet my life on it."

Chapter 12

William reached the top of the spiral staircase and screamed at the top of his voice.

"Christ all mighty, boy, what the hell were you thinking!? You could have gotten yourself killed!"

"I'm fine," replied Don, not wanting to face his father. "That man helped me anyway."

"What man?" replied William still out of breath.

"The man that was here," replied Don. "Didn't you see him on the way up?"

"No, I didn't."

"Well, he sort of just appeared when I got to the top. He told me not to get too close to the edge, then grabbed me just as I lost my balance."

"It's a bloody good job he did," said William. "Jesus, I thought you were a goner. Any idea who he was? I'd like to thank him."

"No," said Don, shaking his head. "I just sat down and he left."

"Well, maybe we'll see him below."

"I don't think so," replied Don "He looked like he was in a bit of a hurry."

They climbed down the ancient tower and walked the pebbled beach to the shore. They saw no one as they made their way to the water's edge, and despite William's search along the horizon, nothing moved except a few seagulls high above the cliffs.

He watched as his son searched the rock pools and knew it had been the right decision to come. Despite the boy's habit of attracting trouble, William had seen a change in his son. If he was being completely honest, he had also felt one in himself.

He was ready for a change, William admitted. He was physically and mentally drained, and deep down he knew it was time to let the brick company go. He was tired of the struggle, tired of the backbreaking work, *and just for once,* he thought, *I want to start living my life for real.*

Maybe all men go through this, he pondered. *You reach an age and wonder, what's the fucking point? What's the point of slaving away day after day, year after year?* He was finding it difficult to see the difference between blowing his brains out and simply working to death. *At least the poor bastard in my office,* thought William, *had the guts to end things on his terms.*

Above, William noticed a small black dot in the sky. He heard a faint buzz and shielded his eyes to get a better look.

"Aeroplane!" he cried out to Don. Without waiting, he pointed and yelled again.

This time the boy turned and looked up to where his father was gesturing. As the object got larger, the two of them stood and watched with fascination. They had seen other aeroplanes, but the novelty never seemed to wear off.

"Do you hear the sound of its engine?" asked William. "I reckon it's in trouble."

"Do you think it's going to crash?" replied Don.

"I don't know, son, let's see what happens."

The Time Keeper watched from the opening of Jonathan's Cave. He knew Gustov Hamel, the man flying the plane, had earlier landed the fourth stage of the Daily Mail Air Race in Edinburgh. He knew the 20-year-old was going to crash later that day. He knew it would be north of Dumfries and he also knew Hamel would walk away unscathed. Why he knew that, the Time Keeper couldn't say, he just did. It didn't bother him anymore. There was nothing he could really do. Time, he had concluded, really didn't give a shit.

He still couldn't understand why he had bothered grabbing for the boy. Intuitively, he understood Don Clover was meant to die, but hopelessly, possibly instinctively, he reached out anyway and touched the boy's arm. It wasn't clear how their energies intertwined. That was definitely not meant to happen. What was clear was that the boy had not fallen. Somehow the Time Keeper's arm had pulled him back, and Don Clover was safe from a fate that would have sent him plummeting to the rocks below.

As he sat among the cave etchings, he tried to make sense of what had just happened. His arm still tingled as his head spun thinking of the ramifications. For the briefest moment, he had been able to touch a world that he thought was lost. He had altered a destiny and literally shifted time.

"How was that possible?" he said, still rubbing his arm. "I thought time was untouchable?"

Clearly something isn't right, thought the Time Keeper. He wasn't sure if it was just him or some kind of weird anomaly he had stumbled on. *But either way,* he thought, *if somehow that was a way out, then what is there to lose?*

He sighed as he watched the monoplane disappear into the distance. In four years, he knew the pilot would be dead, lost in the English Channel. He understood he couldn't save everybody, but looking at the boy leaping over the rocks, he was happy to have made one tiny difference in the universe.

The snow fell around me in silent, heavy chunks. It felt like I had walked for hours, but finally, through the thicket of white drifting tendrils, I arrived.

I stood with my breath drifting away in small insignificant clouds and I strained to look up, taking in the immensity of the structure in front of me. The wall seemed to have no end. High above, it was lost in a haze of heavy cloud, and as far as I could see, the wall stretched east and west, vanishing into points of oblivion.

Beyond the wall, I thought I heard the muffled sounds of footsteps and a car engine accelerating. It was hard to tell exactly, but whatever it was, I felt abandoned like a traveller on the wrong side of a walled city. From somewhere in the distance, I could hear the sound of bells. It was a piercing repetitive tone, and before I could resist, an invisible force held me and pulled me back from where I had come.

I struggled as the wall disappeared. Nothing made sense and I flailed helplessly, suddenly opening my eyes to find myself once again laying on Dave's parents' living room couch. The doorbell rang again, and for the second Sunday in a row, I got up with a heavy head, stepped over the sleeping dog, and cracked open the front door.

"Are you ready?" asked the man standing in silhouette against the morning sun.

"What?" was my best response as the man repeated his question.

I must have looked as confused as I felt because he added, "We're all packed and there's just a wee bit of room for you. You did say eight o'clock, did you not?"

It took me another moment, but eventually I recognized the man as my vodka-making Scottish friend from the reception bar. Somewhere in the distant rooms of my recollection, I realized I had talked my way into a ride to Scotland.

There was a few more seconds of awkward silence and then flipping my inner voice with my outer, I thought *yeah, yeah, brilliant, just give me a minute*, and then out loud I said, "Fuck it, why not?"

Twenty minutes later, I was sitting in the back seat of a Ford Fiesta motoring north along the A130. I had hoped I would be able to sleep off my throbbing headache, but sadly it was not to be.

Mrs. Vodka had taken the opportunity to interrogate me on everything and anything Canadian. She started by naming a friend who had moved to Canada as someone that I might know, and after several more miles, she was naming all of the provincial capitals of Canada. Mercifully, as she was halfway through naming Canadian animals alphabetically, we pulled into a Little Chef restaurant on the side of the road.

To be perfectly honest, I wasn't interested in food. Most of the morning I had been wrestling with a sketchy stomach, and once inside, I bypassed several families shovelling down peas and chips and made straight for the toilets.

As a rule, I can shit anywhere. In a box, with a fox, drinking tea, by the sea. I've crapped in holes with French campers, in paper bags, in the woods, and in the ninth hole of a local golf club. There was even a time where I defined multitasking by eating my dinner on the toilet.

Probably my worst ever shit was at a seedy night club in Toronto. I guess patrons had been breaking toilet seats or using them as weapons because the bar had the bright idea of removing them all together. You could get a toilet seat, you just had to ask the bartender. Not the most discreet way to attend to your business, and when it was handed over, the seat was unceremoniously plonked on the counter between whatever food and drink was being served.

As if that wasn't disturbing enough, attached to the plastic seat was a long metal chain bolted to a large hunk of wood. Initially, I was rather offended to think the owner presumed I would try and steal the thing, but then watching a drunken idiot whip the toilet seat around the dance floor, I realized next to midget tossing, the toilet seat hammer toss was not a bad alternative.

My best shit ever to date was at a Burger King restaurant on Princes Street in Edinburgh. Not only was the cubical completely enclosed, but it was tiled floor to ceiling with the best grouting job I have ever seen. It was so clean you could have eaten off the toilet seat. I didn't, but truly a magnificent place to spend some quality time.

My shit at the Little Chef's restaurant was wet, loud, and explosive. I hadn't sat completely down when it launched, and sounding like I had just stepped on a kitten, I wasn't sure it had even touched the sides on the way out. *Christ,* I thought, feeling the burn, *someone should really invent a way to freeze toilet paper.*

I knew I was taking longer than I should, but I didn't have much of a choice. I was sure my new Scottish friends were likely getting a wee bit impatient, so I did the only reasonable thing possible and pretended I was done. I pulled out a wad of waxy toilet paper and was half done cleaning when another load came down the pipeline with impressive gusto.

"Goddamn it!" I yelled, losing my patience. "Hurry the fuck up!"

I had never actually yelled at my poo before, but I imagine even human excrement needed a good talking to once in a while. Finally, after several minutes, I was done, and I once again ran through the restaurant, still in the process of buckling my belt.

With relief, I spotted the Scottish couple's car idling in the parking lot. I was grateful they hadn't left without me. Nothing was said as I got in and closed the door. I wasn't sure if it was because I trailed an after stink or Mrs. Vodka was too embarrassed by my vocal performance. Either way, it didn't matter. I learned long ago never to apologize for my poo.

Annan was a pleasant town as far as I could make out. The Vodka's house was on a hill directly overlooking the boiler factory where Mr. Vodka had worked his entire life. It seemed a simple life to me, a safe, predictable existence, and I felt bad that my bowels had possibly caused permanent trauma in their lives.

It was still early evening when I finished my toast. The Vodka's had settled in for the night watching television and I thought it best to leave them in peace and go for a walk.

I crossed the road and found a path that led through a farmer's field. It meandered for some time until it came to a large grassy clearing. Beyond, the land gently sloped to the water's edge, and without knowing it, I found myself on the Solway Firth that fed into the Atlantic. Before me lay a swirl of coloured mud and sand that had been formed by the retreating tide. It reminded me of a five-year-old mixing paint with their hands, and as I watched the gold and blazing purples set in the sky, I was stilled by the feeling that I was a part of something larger than I could ever comprehend.

"Lovely, isn't it?" came a voice from behind.

I half jumped, completely caught off guard, and turned to find the Time Keeper leaning against a large rock.

"Fuck, stop doing that," I snapped. "You're beginning to creep me out."

"Sorry, mate," said the Time Keeper with a smug smile. "I've been over the hill visiting Lockerbie."

I knew Lockerbie. Everyone knew Lockerbie. It had only been a few years since the Pan Am airliner was blown up, killing everyone on board and taking out a large chunk of the town.

"What's going on there?" I asked.

"There's still a few lost souls out walking around. Can't blame 'em. I'd be pretty pissed too. It's like they just can't seem to make the leap from being alive to realizing their dead."

"Can you help them?" I asked.

"I've tried," replied the Time Keeper, "but you're up against a wall of anger with most of them. It's like when a baby's born; it ain't very happy being wrenched out of its nice warm little world. And as I said, most of us prefer to keep to ourselves, so I'm not looking to inflict any more aggro."

The Time Keeper looked into the distance, then spoke solemnly without turning.

"I've been around long enough to know everyone has their time."

I let his words hang in the air before I asked, "Including you?"

"Yeah, even me," he replied.

"You know . . ." I started to ask, thinking about the vicar's advice, "I wish I could figure out how to help you?"

There was no response, and before I even looked up, I knew he was gone.

"What a fucker," I said. He really was a bit of an asshole.

I took one last gaze out across the estuary. *It truly is beautiful*, I thought, then turned and climbed back up to the trail.

By midmorning of the following day, I was on a bus heading east to Edinburgh. The Vodkas had unceremoniously dumped me in Dumfries at first light, but to their credit, they kept up a brave face as gracious hosts right until their final goodbye waves.

About an hour into the trip, the bus had to stop for a herd of sheep crossing the road. As we waited, I started up a conversation with a girl sitting across the aisle. She was in her mid-twenties, a cute hippy tree hugger, wearing Doc Martins and an exotic-looking sun dress. Margoat, as it turned out, was from Liverpool. In some ways, she was a lot like me. We were both a little lost, travelling the country with hardly any money, and I spent the rest of the ride taking notes ranging from hitchhiking tips to the legalities of claiming squatters' rights.

We said goodbye at the bus station, and I pulled out my map of the city. It was rather vague, but after several wrong turns, I finally found a room at a backpacker's hostel for a tenner a night. There wasn't much use hanging around the place. For my money, I was assigned a bunk in a room with fifteen other people, access to a kitchen I had no use for, and all the cold showers I could handle.

In my pocket, I had been given an address. It was for a pub called the Water Shed and I was told, by a co-worker back in Canada, I could score a few free pints if I went on a night when his friend was working. To my luck, he was. It was a bit of a shit hole, but after introducing myself and lying about how good a friend I was to my co-worker, a complimentary pint of cider miraculously appeared.

If there's anything I hate more than macaroni and cheese, it has to be cider. I hate cider. It's an acid thing I guess, but I have learned that when you're given a free pint of anything—well, maybe not piss—you shut up and drink it. Unfortunately, the trouble started when a second pint appeared. I was only half done my first, and immediately my stomach told me this wasn't going to end well. *Alright,* I thought, *I can do two pints.* All it took was a bit of mind over matter, and after chugging the second glass down, I felt I had managed to pull it off.

I tried hard to conceal my empty glass. The last thing I needed was another pint. I picked a moment when my Canadian bartender was distracted, then left for a quick piss before leaving. I gave one final wave on my way out, then realized my new Canadian friend was pointing down to another lonely pint. *Oh for fuck's sake,* I thought, handing it to the Canadians. They really did take care of their own, even if they killed you with kindness along the way.

"Well, what are you going to do?" I said, repeating my Cousin Drunk's famous words.

Then, taking a deep breath, I accepted the fact I would be seeing my haggis and chips once more before the night was through.

As predicted, my dinner made its reappearance after midnight on the floor of a red telephone box. The haggis and chips came up surprisingly easy, though there still was no sign of any "willy." Standing in the large puddle of regurgitated cider and floating sheep stomach, my only thought was that my father was right. There always were diced carrots in your vomit. He had sworn there was a tiny leprechaun chopping them up as you chucked a load, but I was in no shape to start looking.

Instead, I decided to call a girl I was sort of dating back in Canada. Her number was written on a folded piece of paper and in my stupor, I dropped it in the stinking mess at my feet.

"Oh crap," I said, feeling for it through the puke. "The things you do for love."

I was a little surprised to find she wasn't that thrilled to be accepting a collect call from me. I thought I held it together pretty well, but when she realized she was paying to hear me sing some drunken rendition of an ABBA song, our conversation, and relationship, abruptly ended.

Chapter 13

It was hay season at Shirley House when William and Don returned. They had taken their time getting back and besides scything the hay, there were fences to fix, and an over-due apology to the greengrocer for an escaped cow that had eaten half his produce.

One of the best days of their trip was spent watching aeroplanes at an air strip outside of Edinburgh. Two had landed but only one managed to continue. Engine trouble had grounded a French pilot, and with smoke billowing from the plane's engine, it was a thrilling day for the hundreds of spectators.

They had also spent time in London. The boy had never seen the great city and William, truth be told, had wanted to do a bit of snooping on the Salvation Army. After a walk around the Embankment and Westminster Cathedral, they made a small detour to find a workhouse on Great Peter Street. It wasn't hard to spot. A large number of homeless men were milling about outside, and William approached one of the least threatening looking men and bummed a light for his pipe.

It hadn't gone unnoticed that the matches he was offered were the Salvation Army workhouse brand "The Lights in Darkest England." He had casually pressed the man for details, and when he mentioned Hadleigh and the farm colony he hoped to be sent to, William forced himself not to betray his emotions.

"Oh yeah," said the homeless man, "there's a kitchen, dining room, dormitories, even a bloody hospital down there."

"I thought it was just a farm?" said William.

"Well, I heard there's been a bit of an expansion lately." The man leaned in and lowered his voice. "Just on the q.t. mind you, I heard the brickmaking is funding a plan to ship a bunch of men out to Canada."

How am I supposed to compete with that? thought William, feeling the reality of the situation crashing down. As far as he was concerned, the Clover Brick company was screwed, and the sooner he could close up shop, he realized, the better.

Rob, Johnny, Will, and Don had nearly finished stacking the winter hay when William decided to move his hidden money. He pulled open the door to the drying shed and stood in the large open space. The bricks were still there, just as he had left them, and William walked over to the nearest row and picked up the closest clay block. It felt wet. *It's not supposed to be wet,* William thought. *My bricks had plenty of time to dry.*

"What the hell is this?" he said with a twinge of uneasiness. "These aren't my bricks."

Puzzled and with a rising panic, William turned toward the open door. Instead of walking, he started to run, and kicking a stray chicken out of the way, he didn't stop until he had reached the farm's only well.

He strained to raise the well's metal bucket, but finally it pulled free. William placed it on the ground and quickly dropped the clay into the water. He knew the water would help break down the brick, and rolling up his shirt sleeves, he groped and squeezed in the freezing water until nothing but small reddish-brown lumps remained.

"Nothing!" he yelled in despair. "No coin, no gold, nothing."

Something is very wrong, he thought, tipping the contents of the bucket onto the grass.

"What the hell is going on?" he said, turning back in the direction of the drying shed once again. "As God as my witness, if someone's touched my money, I'll have their bleed'n head."

It was clear to William that his bricks and money were gone. A large pile of broken and twisted clay lay scattered by his feet, and despite all of William's frantic searching, there were no gold coins anywhere to be found.

"Where's Rob!?" screamed William, demanding an explanation. "Where's the bugger I left in charge?"

In a fit of rage, he grabbed the large tabletop and wrenched it up and over into the air. More semi-dried bricks crashed to the floor, and William stomped out of the shed, not caring about the mess he had left behind.

William found his son resting against the wheel of the pony trap. Rob got to his feet sensing trouble and braced himself against his father's wrath. He knew he had messed up but couldn't understand why his father was in such a rage.

"Where are the bricks I told you not to touch!?" screamed William.

"I don't know," replied Robert, going pale with fear.

"What do you mean, you don't know? They didn't just walk off by themselves."

Rob wasn't sure how to answer. He had followed his father's instructions, but a day into the kiln firing, he had noticed the drying tables had been cleared.

"Someone must have put them in the kiln," blurted out Rob. "I didn't touch them."

William had the boy by the scruff of his neck. He didn't know whether to lash out at the boy or blame himself. He tried hard to comprehend the enormity of the situation, then after a moment, released the boy and told him to ready the cart.

"Where are you going?" asked Rob, thankful to be spared.

"To Tom Shelly's. If he has my bricks, I'm damn well going to get them back," replied William.

Rob stepped back as his father cracked the horse's reigns and charged past him in a cloud of dust. The trap bounced and skidded as it gained speed, and Rob knew his father would not spare the horse until he had reached the other side of Rayleigh.

The Shelly's were having their tea when Will Clover pulled to a halt in front of the house. Tom had noticed the cart through the scullery window and got up, a little annoyed at the unwelcome intrusion.

I've been meaning to have a talk with the brick maker, he thought, and opening the front door, he walked down the garden path, guessing it was as good a time as any.

Desperately, William spoke. "Those bricks you bought for your last job," said William. "Have you used them yet?"

"I have," replied Tom in an annoyed tone. "And I have to say, they were shit. Not your usual quality at all."

"What was wrong with them?" he asked.

"Cracks, and lots of them. A few even broke in half as soon as my lads picked them up."

"Then I'll make you new ones," offered Will, "just give me the old ones back."

"Too late," replied Tom. "The thatcher's have already done the roof. Besides, by the time there will be any real structural issue, I'll be long past this world. Look, I hate to do this to you," continued Tom hesitating, "but I'm going to have to use another company for my next job. I just can't risk another crappy batch. I'm sorry, Will."

William didn't care. He had already lost several clients to the Sally Anners and the ones that remained, he presumed weren't far behind. He turned, and with sunken shoulders, walked back to his trap like a man that had just aged twenty years.

"Do you want to come in for some tea?" asked Tom Shelly feeling guilty, but William Clover waved him off, thinking he was in need of something a lot stronger.

He eased his horse into a slow trot and then cursed himself for the fool he had been. He was deep in self-pity when, at the last second, he pulled hard on the reigns, and narrowly missed a man riding his bicycle. It was a close call and William halted the cart to make sure the man was alright. To his surprise, the man on the bike was the new curate from Rayleigh Church.

"Oh," said William, "it's you."

"Hello, Mr. Clover," replied the curate. "Fancy meeting you here."

"What are the chances? Must be a miracle?" retorted William.

"Well, God does work in mysterious ways."

William was just about to move on when the curate blurted out, "I just wanted to say how lovely your children are."

"Oh yeah?" replied William.

"Yes, we had a grand game of cricket several weeks ago while you were gone. I hope you didn't mind. I'm afraid it took them away from their chores for a couple of hours."

"Wouldn't be the first time," said William sarcastically.

"Yes, it was quite a day with Mr. Horner losing his eye and everything."

"What again?" said William.

"To be honest, Mr. Clover, I actually helped pitch in while the children looked for his eye."

"And how did you do that?" inquired William with a little more interest.

"Well, I didn't want to get the children in trouble, so I finished stacking the kiln with the rest of the bricks from the shed."

"You did what!?" screamed William.

Without thinking, William leapt down from his cart and landed directly in front of the unsuspecting man.

"You stupid, stupid man!" shouted William inches from the curate's face.

"Well, I just assumed . . ." babbled the curate.

"That just makes an 'ass' out of 'u' and 'me', doesn't it?" replied William. "Jesus fucking Christ."

He closed his eyes and tried to hold back his fury. William imagined how good it would feel to ring the curate's neck but thought better of it. He was about to climb back on to the trap when the curate spoke one more time.

"I hope that language sees fit for a donation in our penance box this Sunday?"

"Here's my donation," said William Clover, turning around and hitting the curate squarely on the man's jaw.

He dropped instantly, pulling the bicycle down with him. Surprisingly, the curate was still conscious, and he looked up groggily with blood trickling from his lower lip.

"If I ever, ever see you on my property again," shouted William, "I will make sure you meet your maker a damn site quicker than you expect!"

He let his pointed finger linger for greater emphasis, then climbed back on to his trap, and left the bewildered curate entangled in a pile of limbs and bicycle parts.

Three shots of single malt scotch and six pints of ale found William Clover deep in self disgust. He was, for the most part, a silent, no nonsense drunk, and the crowded pub took little notice as he hunched over the back-room table. He was about to go piss or order another jar, William hadn't quite decided, when he was approached by two half-drunken men, both recent ex-Clover Brick employees. He looked up despairingly as the two boys came closer.

"Buy us a round, would ya, boss?" slurred one of the lads.

"Sorry, boys," replied William in a barely audible voice. "Got nothing left."

"Cor, pull the other one," joked the other worker. "Bet you made a pretty penny off that last fucking job, you tight miser."

"Well, it's all gone now," William replied with a stone-cold stare.

"What do you mean?"

"I mean it's gone. The whole lot got buried in the clay."

"In the brick fields, you mean?" asked the first boy.

"Yeah, something like that," replied William. "But don't you worry, I'll get you your back pay."

He left the two men barley standing and headed for the exit. *The drink has made me say too much and the sooner I get home,* thought William, *the better.* His hand was on the iron pull of the pub door when he heard his name being called above the rumble of the other patrons. Turning, he saw one of the lads he had just talked to standing on a chair. He was banging his goblet on an adjacent post, and after a few moments, the pub fell silent. All eyes, including William's, focused on the boy. *Oh shit,* thought William as he waited for the boy to speak. *What have I done?*

"Your attention please!" shouted the boy, barely able to keep his balance. "It has just come to my attention that I don't have any money."

There was a roar of laughter.

"No, no, it's true," the boy continued, waving his arms to hush a couple of hecklers. "I have no money because the one man who owes me, and some of you too . . ." he said, pointing around the room, ". . . seems to have forgotten where he put it. So who's with me in having a good old treasure hunt and digging up Hambro Hill?"

"There will be none of that," interrupted William before anyone else could respond. "Any man I find digging a hole in my brick fields can consider it their own grave. I told you boys, and anyone else I have unfinished business with—I'll get you your money. The Clovers always pays their debts."

He walked outside and found his old complacent horse. He lit a lamp on the side of the trap and then used the same match to light his pipe. *What a fool am I,* thought William, *to think things were finally going to get easier.* He had let slip the one chance he had been given to make something of himself, and now he could only wait and face the backlash of rumours that were bound to follow.

William wondered who would show up first in the morning. Would it be men with shovels wanting their money? The local police inquiring about an altercation with a clergy member? Or a detective looking for a missing person? It really didn't matter anymore, he decided. He was done trying to find meaning to his life. Life, he concluded, was nothing but a series of random acts that pushed and pulled till someone won and someone lost. There was nothing more. It all just came down to simple chance, and in a strange way, William felt better for finally understanding his place.

There was only the faintest lustre of gold in the setting sky as William navigated the streets of Rayleigh. His horse, Laddie, instinctively knew the way back to Shirley House and William did little to steer the animal other than hold the reins. On the silent night air, he could hear the train whistle coming from Wheatly Crossing, and if he was not mistaken, a horn blast from a boat on the River Crouch a few miles to the north.

He had passed through the main part of town before he heard another unmistakable sound. It was a sombre, harmonic voice, and William cursed again at the Salvation Army at Hadleigh and its brass band rehearsals. Surprisingly, he recognized the song, and recalling the words to William Blake's "Jerusalem," he began to sing along.

"Bring me my bow of burning gold," he bellowed, "bring me my arrows of desire."

When he reached the line "bring me my chariot of fire," William started to laugh. The irony was not lost on him as he thought about his own burnt gold. Even his poor horse and cart had little fire left in them.

"Probably closer to the knackers' yard than anything else," retorted William.

He closed his eyes. The drink was doing its job and William felt his shoulders drop as his body relaxed. He thought about flying and the planes he had seen with his son. He imagined how it would feel to navigate the skies somewhere between earth and the heavens, and he ached for a place where he could breathe and be untouched.

"What the hell am I going to do?" he asked in defeat. "What am I going to do?"

He had lost everything, or at least that's how it felt, and William realized he was standing at the same crossroads as his Uncle Charlie and the man from his office. *Is this how they felt,* thought William, *just before pulling the trigger?* He didn't believe he was far off. *The only difference,* thought William, *is that I'm not ready to give up.*

"I will not cease from mental fight," he recited from the last verse of "Jerusalem."

"Nor shall my sword sleep in my hand." Which, if he had to think about it, was the best way not to cut his dick off while sleeping.

` "No," he said to himself, "I've survived worst. The rumours of buried treasure will pass, the curate knows better than to press charges, and whatever is left of the dead man's ashes are entombed in a thousand bricks and being shipped across the county."

Secretly, he had to thank the Salvation Army. By losing the brick company, he had been freed. He could start again and gain everything he wanted, with or without the gold. *Maybe one day, I could even fly my own plane,* he thought. The possibilities were endless, and in a moment of pure clarity, he understood that until "things" finally broke, he wouldn't be able to appreciate anything more the universe had to offer.

PART 2

Chapter 14

(Buckhaven, Fife, Scotland, 1993)

Bill Cook looked at me for a moment then silently made up his mind.

"Aye, you look like a Cook," he said. "You'd better come in."

I had never met my relative before. In truth, I hadn't known he had existed till only a few weeks earlier.

He stood on his front step and sized me up. I can't think I gave a great first impression. I had been roughing it for several weeks, and I'm sure he wasn't impressed with my long hair. But something must have sparked inside the eighty-year-old. Maybe a memory of a time long ago when he himself lived another life. Whatever the case, he nodded his approval and my third cousin twice removed invited me in.

Bill wasn't far off from what I imagined. An old man with liver spots and a few grey hairs that still clung to his worn-out body. He shuffled slowly into the kitchen and reached for the kettle.

"Hey, I can do that," I offered, but he waved me off.

"I might be old, but I'm not useless," he said with a smile. "But don't worry, I'll put you to work."

It was coming up to ten o'clock when I finished washing the dirty plates from the evening tea. It was still light out, and staring out of the kitchen window, I could see an oil rig being pulled out to sea.

"Hey, Bill, I thought Buckhaven was a mining town?" I asked.

"Aye," he replied from the living room. "But not now. I blame Thatcher, though to be fair, we had a few bad cave-ins that didn't help." Bill turned off the t.v. "What a load of shite."

I had watched the first half of the football game but from the sounds of it, it hadn't ended well.

"Well, I'm off to bed," he said. "You're all set then?"

"Yep, no problem," I replied, grateful to have a room of my own. "And thanks again," I added.

I shut the bedroom door and since there were no chairs, I sat in a wheelchair by the side of the bed. It belonged to Bill's daughter, Janice. She had suffered from MS for years, and lucky for me, was away at a care facility for the week.

An oxygen tank stood next to the bed, and leaning over, I cranked the tank valve open. A clear plastic mask had fallen to the floor and I reached over and held it to my face. *This is more like it,* I thought, inhaling several deep breaths. *A bit of a cheap buzz, but what the hell.* I closed my eyes and let the gas seep deep into my lungs. After a few minutes, I turned off the tank and felt wide awake.

What do to? What to do? I thought, looking around the room. In the corner, my pack leaned against the wall and having no urge to even consider sleep, I decided to organize what little possessions I owned. I pulled out the entire contents and laid them on the bed. Only then did I notice the squashed box of paintings I had forgotten all about.

In all, there were twenty-three paintings, a lot more than I first thought. Carefully I laid the works out on the floor and inspected each one. The paintings weren't very big, maybe six by ten inches. They were all outdoor scenes, some with farm animals, some of town shops, and one of a house with the name "Shirley" painted at the bottom right hand corner.

It was obvious my Great Uncle had not had any formal training as an artist. But, to give him his due, he had tried to blend the colours and somehow grasp an elementary idea of perspective. Strangely, it seemed, he had also latched onto the idea of combining both a foreground and background. *Maybe Great Uncle Googly Eyes had read a how-to book,* I thought, but in every painted scene each main subject was countered by tiny subtle images from behind.

I once saw the paintings at the local library in Eastwood. I was just a boy, and it was my grandmother, Googly Eyes' sister, that had dragged me by bus to go see the exhibit. The paintings had been displayed on large white boards, and I guess the collection would have been of some mild interest to history buffs and the local old timers. Regardless, even at six years old, I thought the paintings were crap. A year earlier, I had painted a picture of my budgie and won first prize in a competition at school, so I hadn't really understood what all the fuss was about.

They looked different now, the paintings. Maybe I just saw them in a different way. I was sure each of them had a story to tell, and whatever memory they held for Great Uncle Rob, it was important enough for him to preserve it.

I packed the paintings back in their box and yawned. I was starting to come down from my oxygen hit, and sluggishly I made my way to the shower. I made a mental note to visit Flossy once more, then sat on a plastic handicapped seat and let the lukewarm water soak my lanky pale skin.

The next morning, I found my way down to the beach. The wind blew me along as I trudged north along the coast and among the sea-ground beach pebbles—bits of worn smooth glass twinkling in the sun. I found myself looking down as I walked. I scanned the rocks below my feet, feeling a need to look for something. A shell maybe? a piece of driftwood? I really didn't know.

I kept searching until eventually I stopped at a small smooth rock that was just as ordinary as the ten thousand others. It was hard to explain why one particular pebble spoke to me, but it did. It was small enough to fit into the palm of my hand and I picked it up, squeezing it with satisfaction. It felt solid and timeless and I realized it was something I was meant to have. A simple reminder that would always bring me back to where I now stood.

I slipped it into my pocket, still feeling the weight of the stone in my palm. *Funny,* I thought, *how that happens.* How the body can remember weight without having to hold it. It was as if memory could truly transcend the senses.

I was given a collection of rocks once. They sat in a large glass jar and were suppose to represent how life should be balanced. Inside, there were three sizes. The largest rocks were to go in first. According to the theory, the largest rocks symbolized the grounding aspects of your life such as your health, family, and children. Then you were to add smaller pebbles. They were to embody the less important stuff like your job, money, and house. And lastly, sand was to be added, representing the "really, really small stuff"—the stuff we shouldn't have to sweat.

On top of that, one additional ingredient was supposed to be added—chocolate milk. It was poured into the sand and explained how fun and personal goals were suppose to be achieved. And there you had it. One self-contained balanced diet of life, neatly arranged in a geological diorama with the lid screwed on tight.

And life would be great if chocolate milk didn't go sour or the glass jar didn't break. But it does, and it stinks, and it is messy, and the shards of glass will cut you if you are not careful. I never did like that jar. Possibly because of its naivety, but mainly because of the restriction. Who knows, maybe Augustus Gloop would agree?

The cave was there, just as Bill had described. Earlier, he had handed me a guidebook about the Wemyss Caves, but there was no mistaking the charred blackened entrance of Jonathan's cave.

From the guidebook I learned the burnt walls were from a fire a few years back. Apparently, a couple of local teenagers had decided to steal a Volkswagen Beetle, drive it into the cave, and then set fire to it.

Iron grills now stood at the mouth of the cave. I thought they would be permanently sealed but on closer inspection, I found the gate unlocked. It swung open easily, and I lowered myself a few feet and dropped to the floor below. It was cold in the semi-darkness and untying my jacket from around my waist, I slipped it back on.

The guide gave a brief summary of the cave. I wasn't too bothered about a hermit named "Jonathan the nail maker," so I flipped the page over and took a look at the map of the cave walls. I followed its instructions to the first etching, and standing in front of it, compared the design with the drawing on the map.

Ok, I thought, *that's fair. It does look like a horse,* but moving to the second carving, I had to disagree. It clearly was a man fucking a fish. My guidebook had described it as "a man with tool" and I guessed, for all intents and purposes, it was correct. The final carving was described as a kind of merchant's mark, but it wasn't. Without question, it was the mark of the Time Keeper. The symbol of the side oval and elongated post was undeniable.

"So, you have been here, you bastard," I said out loud. "I wonder if it was you that carved 'man bonking fish'?"

To be sure, I couldn't rule him out. It seemed he was everywhere these days. I touched the mark with my finger, and instantly a boy skipping rocks flashed in my mind. *I've been here before,* I thought, shaking my head to refocus.

"That's impossible," I said, trying not to buy into the feeling. "This has to be the Time Keeper's doing."

I climbed out of the cave and breathed the sharp, cleansing air of the ocean. *That's better,* I thought, feeling the déjà vu leave.

"So, where the hell is he?"

I scanned the beach and then down toward the town. There was nothing but waves and empty coastline.

"Where are you hiding, Time Keeper?" I asked again, and then looking up, I knew.

The castle, according to my guidebook, was called Macduff's Castle. I had heard once that a distant relative of mine named Mary Black had lived there, but its main bragging rites had more to do with it being mentioned in Shakespeare's *Macbeth.*

As far as I could make out from my reading, the castle had been standing in one form or another since 1057 A.D. It seemed also that someone had forgot to pay the maintenance fees around 1666, as things went downhill rather quickly from that point on. What remained was somewhat confusing. I could tell a lot had been knocked down through the years, but one turret still remained, patched up by modern brick and cement.

It was an impressive tower. It stood four floors high and I could see a lookout at the very top of its spiral staircase.

"Crap, not another bloody iron gate," I said, reaching the base of the tower.

I rattled the bars, but they held fast. I thought it was the only entrance to the staircase, until I noticed several bricks knocked out just above the original stone arch.

"Ah ha!" I yelled in triumph.

Just enough space to squeeze through, I figured, and thanking the local youth for their contribution to natural selection, I started to climb.

I only had a few more steps to reach the top when I saw the Time Keeper. He was sitting, talking to himself, and I stopped just below his feet.

Without saying hello, I asked, "Was that you who carved the man fucking the fish?" and pointed downward in the general direction of the caves.

I had hoped for a cheeky sly comeback, but instead the Time Keeper completely ignored my question. He looked like he was in the middle of calculating some complex mathematical equation, so instead of waiting, I climbed past him and out onto the top of the tower.

I was not ready for the force of the wind. It pummelled me into an involuntarily crouch and I held on to the last piece of staircase as I took in the panoramic view. Around me, the sea roared as loud as the wind. Far below, gulls screamed bloody murder, and everywhere I dared to turn, the great expanse of the ocean blurred with the sky as one.

I felt something as well. Something sad and terrible, as if somebody had just died. It washed over me suddenly, as strong as a pounding wave, and my stomach clenched as I forced myself back down into the safety of the turret.

"What the fuck was that?" I demanded over the whistle of the wind.

The Time Keeper hadn't moved, but with reluctance, he eventually turned toward me.

"Something happened to me today," he replied. "Something I can't explain. I think I moved time."

"What? You can't do that. You're just a hippy memory surfer."

"I agree. But didn't you feel it?" asked the Time Keeper.

"Yes" I admitted.

"It's because I stopped it from happening."

"Stopped what?"

"The boy," said the Time Keeper. "I grabbed the falling kid from the edge and yanked him back."

"Shit," I said, not having a better response. "That's not supposed to happen."

"Nope," agreed the Time Keeper again, "but it did."

We sat in silence while the Time Keeper slipped back into his meditative state. I wasn't sure what to do, so after a while, I got up to leave.

"Wait," said the Time Keeper, standing up. "I want to show you something."

Reluctantly, I followed him back up the stairs and into the daylight. With unsteady legs, I stood next to the Time Keeper and tried not to look down.

"Hold it," he asked, shaking his hand impatiently.

I hesitated, not sure any of this was a good idea.

"Are you jumping?" I asked.

"No, no," reassured the Time Keeper. "I can't actually physically touch you. You'll just feel a slight tingling. Or at least, that's what I think should happen."

He shook his whole arm, and closing my eyes, I reached out and braced myself for whatever was about to happen. I was still waiting when I heard his voice.

"Open your eyes," said the Time Keeper.

At first, nothing appeared to have changed. I looked down at my hand and saw that we were actually holding hands as far as one could with a non-physical entity.

"See anything different?" asked the Time Keeper.

I looked out to sea and then down to the beach.

"There," I said, "down by the shore. They weren't there a minute ago."

From my vantage point, I could make out five small children. There was something unnatural about the scene, and after a moment, I figured out what was wrong.

"That's odd," I said. "It's like they're all in their own private little world."

"Yes," agreed the Time Keeper. "That's how they are around here. It's like everyone's looking for something they lost."

"Where's here?" I had to ask.

"Where do ya think? This is the In-Between, or as I like to call it, the Narrows."

"Do you mean everyone here is dead?" I asked.

"Dead to you, yes, but more 'lost in time' to me." The Time Keeper sighed and looked straight at me. "I want you to turn around now but keep a hold of my hand. Very important," he said. "Got it?"

I knew what was behind me. To tell the truth, I was a little afraid to look.

"Ok," I replied and slowly began to shuffle my feet.

It took some time to reposition myself, but once my back faced the water, I was able to look up and see the entire expanse of East Wemyss Cemetery.

"Fuuuuckkk," is all that came out of my mouth.

Before me, strewn among the pathways and tombstones, were dozens of hopeless looking people. Many wandered aimlessly as if lost with no direction, while others looked angry, waving their arms at seemingly nothing. I watched as I followed an Edwardian dressed woman shuffle past a vicious-looking, fur-clad Viking. Neither gave the other the slightest attention and it occurred to me that neither time nor fashion meant anything in a wasteland of hopelessness.

"Those are the ones that never get out," said the Time Keeper. "They would rather run in a hamster wheel of eternity than choose to let go. You see, some of them weren't ready to die, others just didn't expect it, and then there are the ones that still think they're alive. It's all really messed up, like they got their wires crossed or something. Maybe it's the fear of the unknown, I don't know, but whatever it is, it only makes them hold on even tighter. See that one there," continued the Time Keeper, pointing at a boy in a brown Victorian suit.

"Yes," I replied.

"Well, that's Michael Brown. He was murdered for carrying his employer's wages back from the bank. Got his head smashed in, and then he choked to death after having his hat shoved down his throat."

"God, that's horrible," I said.

"Yeah, no kidding," he replied. "But here's what I'm thinking. What if I can save him? I saved one boy today, maybe I can save another?"

"How are you going to do that? Don't you need to ride a wave back to the exact moment?" I asked.

The Time Keeper grinned slightly. "Oh, there are ways," he said, "but I'll need to find a Snatch to do it."

"A Snatch?" I asked, feeling lost.

"Yeah, a Snatch," replied the Time Keeper. "They're the lowest form of scum around here, pretty much the mafia of the Narrows. You want a specific memory wave, you go to them. They have them all—the Titanic sinking, the battle of Hastings, walking on the moon, whatever you want."

"And where do they get them?" I asked.

"Mainly old age homes and hospitals. You ever get a memory blank? You know like waking up the next day from a night out and having a tattoo on your ass and two sheep in your bed?"

"Ok, yes, it's happened," I admitted.

"Well, more than likely your memories were ripped off. Seniors and coma patients are the easiest pray. The Snatches find a way in through the unconscious and literally go through your memory files, trashing the place as they go. By the time they're gone, all you got left for Christmas is Dementia or Alzheimer's. It's fucking barbaric, if you ask me."

"So what do they want?" I replied. "For a memory? What's the going rate these days?"

"Your life energy," answered the Time Keeper. "They literally suck what's left of the life out of you. If they get enough, then they can do life over, you know like reincarnation? Only problem is if they completely drain you. Then you're really screwed, erased like you never existed at all. Eventually, everyone here will fade and cease to exist. Unless they can find what they need to move on. Easier said than done in a place that turns a meaningful life into a meaningless exit."

"What about you then?" I asked. "What makes you so different?"

The Time Keeper avoided my gaze. "Nothing, I guess. I'm not really sure I am. Anyway, I'm off to find one of those scum sucking wankers. In the meantime, go take a look at Michael Brown's grave. It's the white marble plinth over there with an angel on top. Who knows, maybe it will have disappeared by the time you get there."

Without warning, the Time Keeper vanished. I felt a painful snap on my left hand, and I cursed, still gazing out across the cemetery. It took me a second, but then I noticed it was empty. There wasn't a soul as far as I could see, and I realized my glimpse into the Narrows was over. I stared a little longer, almost in disbelief, then turned and started down the spiral stairs to the hole I had climbed through.

I had only made it to the third level when I was forced to sit down. Nausea had suddenly taken hold and I could only guess that hopping between realms of existence wasn't so good on the system. As the pain increased, I felt my eyes begin to roll, and I leaned back as an inky blackness oozed through my brain.

My last conscious thought was wondering if a Snatch was going to find me. I really didn't care, there were enough bad memories I could do without. The only memory I didn't want to lose was being naked, at nineteen, with three women in a bathtub. As long as the bastards left that, I would still be a happy man.

Chapter 15

Nevel Fink, by all accounts, was not a happy man. By nature, he was a recluse, choosing a solitary existence with little interest in friends. There were, however, a few scattered acquaintances, but it was clear their relationship was based on his brick expertise rather than his stale, dismissive personality.

This day, however, was different. Even the very dead ninety-two-year-old Mrs. Pitts had done little to dampen Nevel Fink's spirits. He sat in the dead woman's kitchen and smiled as he thumbed the small black notebook. *It's a shame about the old girl,* he thought. *She has been more than accommodating.* Unfortunately, there was no choice. There could be no connection to his newfound information, and he took comfort in the fact her head was silenced by only three hits against the living room coffee table.

He looked down at the notebook one more time and ran his fingers over the embossed cover of the Essex Police shield.

"After all this time," said Nevel, shaking his head. "And to think of all the brick companies in Essex, it had to be the bloody Clovers."

For possibly the tenth time that afternoon, Nevel opened the yellow paged book. He read aloud the words of the Rayleigh police officer that had long preceded his newly dead wife.

"Tuesday May 3rd, 1910—Responded to the complaint of Mrs. Tyrell, 44 Woodlands Close. She claimed her lodger did not return to settle his account and insisted on an inquiry into his last known whereabouts. The man in question, a Mr. Albert Fink, of no fixed address, had left in the early evening, having mentioned an appointment at Hambro Hill brick fields later that night. On questioning several employees of the brick works, including the owner, William Clover, I conducted a brief search of the property. No new information was discovered regarding the aforementioned meeting. Mr. Fink, in all likelihood, skipped town to pursue other interests. Note made to check train station on patrol route."

All that Nevel had ever wanted was to prove his father had not abandoned him. *It might seem trivial to some,* thought Nevel, but ever since the day he had lost both his parents, he had made it his mission to find the truth.

Through the years, he had read and reread every article and police report he could find. He had even gone as far as tracking down two original eyewitnesses, but nothing ever explained or justified the facts that had haunted him for the past eighty-three years.

According to the records, his parents had never stood a chance. As parading members of the Salvation Army, the rally in Shoreham was already destined for disaster. The Skeleton anti-movement, it was revealed, had been planning an attack for weeks and the Salvationists, like lambs to the slaughter, walked smack into the middle of the awaiting arsenal.

It was never proven who had actually thrown the brick. It had sailed through the air on a steep trajectory, and according to the Shoreham Herald, "it had landed with such force on the skull of Mary Fink that her head was reduced to nothing more than a bloody pulp of flesh, bone, and scattered brains."

It was the dead woman's husband, his father, that had reportedly removed the brick from his wife's head. A soft, plopping sound echoed above the street as brains and muscle released their suction, and as Albert Fink stood, holding the unlikely murder weapon, onlookers recalled Albert's last words before fading into the surrounding chaos—"I have nothing left but to meet the maker."

Eleven years since the day he lost both his parents, Nevel stood in front of the hundred-foot chalk cross. It had been carved into the surrounding Shoreham hillside and as the dedication ceremony commenced, he watched as volunteer workers were invited up onto the rickety stage.

He listened as the Salvation Army band finished their rendition of "Lest We Forget" and when the crowd fell silent, the town's mayor stood up to speak.

"Lest we forget," began the mayor. "Lest we forget those that went before us and gave us what we have today. Hard working honest men and women just like the ones before us now. Please," urged the mayor, "a round of applause." With his arm, the mayor made a wide sweeping gesture, then added for good measure, "Meet the makers!"

Cheers and claps erupted throughout the crowd, but Nevel did not move. He had been struck dumb by the mayor's last words, and as he stared at the odd-looking bunch of volunteers, Nevel understood everything.

"My father," he said, drowned by the noise of the crowd. "He said he was going to meet THE maker, not meet MY maker. Of course," said Nevel. "He wasn't about to off himself and meet his God, he was going to find the makers of the brick that killed my mother."

It all makes perfect sense, he thought, desperately trying to recall police reports and facts. *Yes, that's right,* he remembered, snapping his fingers. The only Skeleton radicals arrested in the Shoreham riots were from Essex. *That's where my father went, across the Thames to Tilbury.*

There was only one unanswered question left for Nevel. What was the name of the maker printed on the blood-soaked brick?

"Do you have any idea how long I've been looking for this?" asked Nevel to the body of Mrs. Pitts.

He had moved to the living room and had sat down to finish his third cup of tea. A small pool of blood had soaked into the faded shag carpet, and Nevel had been careful not to step into the offensive mess.

"I mean, it has literally taken me decades," he stated. "Do you think I even like bricks?" he asked. "Sure, I'm known as the leading authority on Essex bricks, great, big deal, but like everything in this life, dear, I did it because the end always justifies the means. You know what the funny thing was?" asked Nevel, hearing no reply. "What, cat got your tongue? The funny thing was," continued Nevel, "it had very little to do with bricks to find you."

Nevel laughed at the irony and took another sip of his tea.

"Well, since you're so interested, I'll tell you. I was in the Rayleigh Police Station last week and as a highly respected member of the British Brick Society, I was asked to access the condition of the original brick structure. Boring stuff really, so I'll spare you the details. What was interesting though, was that I had to take a piss. I know," agreed Nevel with himself, "at my age, things don't get any easier. But on the way, do you know what I found? Come on, take a guess? No? Well, it was a plaque dedicated to your husband and every other constable that had worked for over fifty years in the force. So, I said to myself, Nev, I bet a few of those people would have been around at the same time as my father went missing. Maybe I could go through their notebooks and see what I could find. So yes, confession time, I wasn't a museum curator interested in displaying police memorabilia. Fine, you got me, big deal. But you didn't have to threaten to call the police. That was just plain rude."

Nevel felt his anger once again rise. He had been surprised how quickly it had spiralled out of control lately, and he made a mental note to try and not kill anyone so quickly next time.

"Anyway, this won't do," said Nevel impatiently. "I'll let myself out and thank you once again for all your hospitality."

He washed his teacup and placed it back in the cupboard. He then re-boxed the dead constable's things and placed them back under a spare bed in the front room.

As he closed Mrs Pitt's front door, Nevel felt lighter. He tapped his pocket just to make sure the notebook was still there and tried to figure out what had changed. *Everything* was his answer. Everything had changed. He now had direction, he now knew exactly where he was going. *At long last,* he thought, *I can finish what my father could not, and after too many miserable years of futile searching, I will finally have my answers.*

Chapter 16

I was worried about the Time Keeper. Nothing had changed at the Michael Brown grave site. Even the dried seagull shit on top of the statue had stayed the same. I waited a few extra days, then decided to head back to Edinburgh before I completely emptied the oxygen tank in my room.

I said my goodbyes and figured the Time Keeper would make his appearance when he needed to. It wasn't like I had any control over his visits, and after a few hours of travel, I stepped off the bus in St. Andrew's square and thought about my next move.

Ten minutes after phoning, Margoat appeared skidding to a stop on a brand-new bicycle. I figured the bike was stolen, but I really didn't care. She wore the obligatory hippy nose ring and was still wearing the same sundress from the bus. As we walked to the pub, I snuck a few casual glances at her ass and boobs and wasn't surprised that accompanying her leather necklace and bracelets, she had a few well-placed tats.

"How's the squatting going?" I asked, sipping my beer.

"Great," she replied "You should come over and stay if you'd like. Just don't piss off the Argentinean street jugglers."

She turned, and after bumming a cigarette and a pen from the table behind us, "Goat" as she liked to be called, wrote down directions on a paper napkin.

Outside, an impromptu drum circle was setting up. I could hear the hand drums starting to clunk and though it was tempting to join, I needed some air. A little buzzed, I got up to leave and I left Goat with a skinny dude with dreads handing out drums. I navigated my way clear of several double-decker buses and was about to enter Princes Street Gardens when I heard the shot. It thundered across the sky with such force that I inadvertently ducked.

"Damn," I said. "The one o'clock cannon got me again."

The howitzer had been fired for years, originally aimed out to sea to help ships reset their chronometers. Nowadays, "firing the one o'clock gun" was better known as a lunch time wank, and though tradition had out-weighed necessity, the cannon still provided the simple pleasure of making American tourists crap their new tartan trousers.

I passed through the iron gate and let my shoulders relax. I stepped aside to let a mum and her push chair pass and I walked casually along, people watching as I went. A man on his bicycle with trouser clips and saddle bag navigated between pedestrians, and I stopped for a moment to watch a hack game of soccer in full swing. Several couples had brought picnic blankets, and as I passed an array of food stuff in various stages of consumption, I couldn't help notice an obvious bonking session happening under a brown and orange throw.

For me, my own public horn doggery happened at the Canadian Opera Company in a dark director's booth. It doesn't matter how I got there, but since there was no director in sight, and *The Barber of Seville* really held little interest, a girlfriend and I wasted little time at making a performance of our own. I will always remember slamming the poor girl against half inch glass while watching well-to-do opera goers yawn and occasionally nod off.

It wasn't a bad neighbourhood. I might have walked past the house if it wasn't for the boarded-up windows and a toilet on the front lawn. I wiped kebab sauce from my chin and walked up the front garden path.

"Hello!" I called out, opening the broken door to the house.

There was no response, and smelling a waft of weed, I cautiously looked down the hallway to find the source. The hallway had been left behind in the 1970s. I couldn't help but note the black and orange shag carpet and the green-pea coloured wallpaper that desperately tried to hang to the walls.

There was a kitchen at the end of the hall and an open door about halfway down to the right. I could hear a rhythmic slapping coming from what I presumed was once the family room and, as I entered, an object suddenly careened past, barley missing my head.

"Jesus," I said, stepping back. "What the fuck?"

"It's ok, you come in now," replied a voice with a heavy accent.

Ducking slightly, I realized I had already pissed off the Argentinean jugglers. They were standing at either end of the room lobbing clubs at each other. To their credit, however, they didn't seem to miss a beat as I stepped between them.

Taking in the scene, I recognized Goat sprawled out on the couch. She was with the dread dude from the afternoon drum circle and by the way his arm draped around her, it was clear they were a new temporary item. Both had spliffs on the go and Goat looked half in the bag as I tried to get her attention.

"Hey, Goat, it's me, your bus buddy," I announced.

"Oh . . . hey," she said in a semi-conscious state.

I waited, but she didn't offer anything more. I was hoping there would have been some kind of introduction or grand tour, but she was well and truly fucked.

Learning my lesson, I slowly eased into the kitchen. Fortunately, the coast was clear and I found two people sitting at an old wooden table. I put down my pack and tried introducing myself. The guy had a beer on the go and a mouth full of curry. The girl, I guessed in her early twenties, must have been tripping on something, as she was concentrating hard on an imaginary dimension on the other side of the wall.

I still had a few bites of my kebab, so I sat down at the table and fiddled with the wrapper. The man, maybe ten years older than the girl, finally finished chewing, swallowed and pointed at the Canadian flag on my backpack.

"Canadian . . . yes? . . . You?" he asked in broken English.

"Yes . . . yes," I replied a bit too enthusiastically.

"I like Canadian yes . . . very good hockey. Montreal the Habs, yes?"

"Sure," I replied, having never played hockey in my life.

He smiled, stood up, and finding a semi-clean glass in the sink, poured me some of his beer. Somehow, I fluffed my way through Richard and Lafleur trivia simply by nodding at everything he said. Occasionally, I would add an "ah" or "hum" just for added effect, though to be honest, I was a little distracted by the girl that still stared motionless at the wall.

"That is my cousin, Loretta. She'll be ok. A bit loco," said my new hockey friend, "but very talented."

He winked with the expectation I knew what the hell he was implying, then poured another beer, and in broken English told me he had opened up for the Spice Girls the week before.

"Wow, that's amazing," I said, not believing a word.

But as it turned out, he was telling the truth.

"You know, they give me fifty pounds to stand at record store and juggle in front of angry people. How do you say . . . a press conference, yes?"

"Yes," I agreed "Oh, okay, you juggled because the Spice Girls were late?"

"Yes, that is right."

"Cool," I said. "Maybe you could juggle at a hockey game next?"

Suddenly, Loretta pushed her chair back and stood up. She looked at me and touched a gold crucifix around her neck. She grabbed my hand and announced she wanted to take me to her bedroom. Not sure what to do, I looked at her cousin.

"Yes, go, go, my friend," he said smiling, "very talented."

That's what I am afraid of, I thought, but it was too late. Loretta had already started to pull me away and I did the only honorable thing and follow her with my beer.

I sat on the edge of Loretta's bed and felt a cold draught. I could see the broken window high on the far wall and as she lit candles, the flames made shadows that danced around the room.

Without saying a word, she gently leaned me backwards, parted my legs, and bent down onto her knees. *Jesus,* I thought, guessing this was the talent portion of the evening.

Closing my eyes, I waited, and then waited some more. Even in my limited sexual experience, I knew something was taking too long. I was about to ask if everything was ok when, from under the bed, I heard a scraping sound as if something heavy was being moved. It was followed by the sound of two latches opening, and I instantly bolted upright, just a little concerned.

On the floor, in front of me, was an open suitcase. The lid was obstructing my view and I watched as Loretta reached into the case and took out two wide leather straps. I swallowed hard and with a rising panic realized we were going Medieval. *This isn't good,* I thought as she harnessed the leather over her shoulders and with a smile of anticipation, she started to play.

I have heard it said that life is stranger than fiction, and at that moment, the erupting sound of an accordion truly made me a believer. It cut through the air with such deep genuine emotion that I felt a little stupid and ashamed.

"That was beautiful," I said after she finished the first song. "You really are talented."

"This was my grandmother's favourite," she said, starting into a sad melancholy ballad. "You like?"

I nodded, not wanting to ruin the moment, and I sat motionless, hardly breathing at the fragile perfection. It was hard not to close my eyes, but at some point I must have fallen asleep. Loretta played on into my dreams, and it wasn't until I was nudged awake that I realized she had stopped and her accordion had been packed away.

"Thank you," I said half-asleep.

I thought about lying down again, but I got the sense she wasn't interested in sharing her bed. As painful as it was, I staggered to my feet, hugged her briefly, and headed back down the hallway.

Except for a dozen or so drained beer bottles, the kitchen was empty. I grabbed my pack and after trying several locked doors, I found myself alone in what could only be described as "the room where everyone throws their shit."

Among the jumble of crap, I found a chunk of foam. It was just long enough to curl up onto and dropping it next to a stack of wooden planks,

I lay down among the sawdust and decided that "squatting" was a bit overrated.

I tried to sleep, but it wasn't happening. I lay listening to the rumble of late-night traffic, and just when I thought I might drift-off, an electronic beeping screamed at me from behind my head. Groggily, I rolled over and discovered a small digital display plugged into a wall socket.

From what I could tell, it was demanding power credits, and it must have been extremely angry as I was pretty sure it told me to "fuck off."

"Right back at cha," I mumbled in response.

I had no idea what time it was, but the sun had started to rise, and I figured it was as good a time as any to take my morning dump.

The problem, I discovered after finding the bathroom, was the fact there was no toilet. Just a large hole where the toilet should have been. It was then I remembered the toilet on the front lawn.

"Fuck," I said, feeling my morning turd start to prairie dog. "What am I going to do now?"

As far as I figured, there were three options. I could either shit in the hole in front of me like the French, shit on the relocated toilet in the front garden or do my damnedest to delay operations and hit Burger King on Princes Street.

"You know what?" I said to myself. "My ass deserves better." And grabbing my pack, I brushed the sawdust from my hair and prayed I could hang on.

The Time Keeper, dejected and exhausted, sat outside the East Wemyss public toilets. It was now quarter past twelve on Friday February 19th, 1909 and he was still trying to figure out what had just happened.

He wasn't alone. A fierce, axe-wielding Nordic Viking stood over him, yelling at the top of his lungs.

"What in the name of the God Balder were you doing!?"

The Time Keeper tried to answer but couldn't find the words. He was still reeling from having been dragged out of the inner lavatory and deposited on the ground like a sack of coal.

"What do you think?" finally retorted the Time Keeper weakly. "I was trying to save the boy."

"You can't!" boomed the warrior. "Who told you that you could? Trying will just destroy you."

He was right, admitted the Time Keeper. He had never felt so weak and tired. He felt drained not only in energy but also from being witness to the last fifteen minutes of shameless brutality.

He had seen many gruesome scenes surfing through time, but this had been different. He was invested, driven even, and yet he had failed to stop the murder. He watched as Constable Stewart ran past him and into the public toilets. The Time Keeper knew there was no chance for the boy now. Not only had Mickey Brown been knocked unconsciousness, but his attacker, Alexander Edmonstone, had strangled the boy, and just for good measure, shoved the boy's cap down his throat.

The Time Keeper couldn't understand it. He had arrived early enough, having surfed a memory wave he had haggled from a local Snatch. He had picked his moment perfectly, and reaching out like before, had tried to push the assailant away. But nothing had happened. There was no connection, no resistance, the Time Keeper's hands simply passed straight through the attacker and the poor boy's beating had continued. He had tried and then tried again, each time with the same result. Nothing seemed to work, and by the time the fifteen-year-old clerk gargled at his final attempt of life, the Time Keeper knew he was in trouble.

He had started to suddenly feel weak as if he was slowly sinking into quicksand. All he could do was thrash his arms about like a drowning man.

"What would have happened to me if you hadn't pulled me out?" asked the Time Keeper.

The Axe warrior looked at him with confusion. "You didn't buy a memory wave, did you?" he asked.

The Time Keeper didn't answer; he didn't have to.

"You stupid moron," he continued. "Look, if you want to stay here, then my advice to you is to keep a low profile. Don't do stupid shit like try and change the past."

"But I've done it," protested the Time Keeper. "I've touched the living and saved a falling boy."

The Axe Man looked at him with mild disgust. "I'm sorry, but dead is dead. You just can't start changing people's clocks. Yes, I've seen it done, but it always ends badly. I'm surprised you're still here. "

"What do you mean?" asked the Time Keeper.

"I mean, a gentle tap or an extension into the living you can get away with, but a full submersion usually ends in total obliteration. There's rules about all this.

"For example, what a cluster fuck the sinking of the Titanic was. There were hundreds of idiots like you trying to hang on to their drowning relatives. They all were just trying to keep their loved ones alive any way they could. I never saw so many In-Betweeners vanish in front of me, just fizzed into fine white powder. If you ask me, the only thing you're doing by saving someone who should be dead is prolonging their suffering.

"Do you know what happened to some the Titanic survivors? They died anyway. Some poisoned themselves, others jumped out of buildings, and quite a few were hit by cars. Fred Fleet hung himself, Jack Thayer cut his own throat, and poor old Washington Dodge shot himself in the head. It just goes to prove you can't change something you're not a part of anymore."

"So why did you help me?" asked the Time Keeper. "You had nothing to gain."

The Axe Man looked up and gave a half-hearted snort.

"Well, that's where you're wrong. I had a lot to gain," he said smiling. "I've been in this godforsaken place way too long. Five minutes, five hundred years, I couldn't tell you anymore. The one thing I can tell you is that the only true way to save yourself is to give away what you need."

That seems a little counterintuitive, thought the Time Keeper. *Yet, truth be told, it was the Axe Man's "mission statement" that just saved my ass.* After a short while, he spoke the only words he thought would do it justice.

"Thank you," he said, bowing his head in gratitude.

"Yeah, well don't count on it again," replied the Axe Man, starting to walk off. "I saved you this time, but let's not make a habit of it."

"I'll see you around then!?" the Time Keeper shouted back, but there was no reply.

The Axe Man had disappeared into a laneway, and once again the Time Keeper was alone. He sat a little longer and watched as the School

Wynd alley started to fill with onlookers. Many tried to pull themselves up and over the lavatory wall to catch a glimpse of the unidentified body. The constable, obviously shaken, was helped through the crowd, and a little later, he heard the doctor pronounce Michael Brown dead.

Finally, he got up and walked down toward the cliffs. He took in the big open sky of the North and tried to cry. He already knew he couldn't but felt it was the right thing to do. He missed the release, he missed so much of a world he wasn't apart of anymore.

"Give away what you need?" mouthed the Time Keeper silently.

Easier said than done, he thought. There were just so many things he missed and needed. Beer, sex, a good shit, a nice bloody steak, all reasonable pleasures of being human. *But what do I really need the most?* thought the Time Keeper, trying to be completely honest. *Well, for one thing, I need to get the fuck out of this place.* Surfing was just that—skimming the surface. There was no depth in the Narrows.

"And what else?" he asked. "To be heard," he said, surprising himself. "Yes, to be heard." And then added, "To be understood, loved, and forgiven. I guess the basics never change, regardless of dimension."

How he was going to give away what he needed he had no idea, but for the first time since entering the Narrows, the Time Keeper embraced the idea of hope.

He turned as the murderer Edmonstone emerged from the Court cave with an empty brown leather bag. Presumably, it was the bank bag that had contained the wage money, and the Time Keeper watched as the killer tried to bury it under several rocks by the shore.

He knew Alexander Edmonstone wouldn't last long on the run. He knew he would be caught in Manchester and eventually hung the following year. But it was the evil in the man that disturbed him the most. It was the same evil he had felt from the Snatch and it saddened him to think how much devastation one person could inflict on another.

Christ, thought the Time Keeper, *evil is disguised in so many things. How will I ever be able to tell the difference?*

Chapter 17

I had a plan. Not a very good plan, but a plan none the less. I was going to hitchhike my way to Cambridge University. I was inspired not only by my lack of money but also from a friend that recently travelled to the western coast of Canada.

She had carried a large cardboard cut-out of a thumb and claimed she had never waited more than five minutes for a ride. Unfortunately, I didn't have any cardboard or oversized breasts, which I suspected had more to do with her success, and after two long hours without a ride, I slumped down outside a petrol station somewhere along the A1 motorway.

I sat for some time thinking what was worse, sleeping in a ditch or on a piece of shitty foam? Neither I decided sounded appealing, so getting up, I bought a cheap bacon and tomato sandwich and headed back to the on ramp for a second go. I was just thinking the sandwich wasn't so bad when an eighteen-wheeler slowed and pulled up alongside of me. It hissed to a stop and I jumped, almost dropping my crusts.

"You Canadian, mate!?" the driver shouted down at me.

I figured he had spotted my Canadian flag, and looking up, I craned my neck to the open window above.

"Need a ride then?" he asked.

I still had a mouthful of food but nodded with relief, gave a thumbs-up, and climbed into the cab and into my first official ride as a "hitcher."

The driver seemed pretty relaxed about our arrangement. It was obvious he had picked up people before. I, on the other hand, not knowing what to do, felt obligated to convince the trucker that I wasn't some kind of threat.

"So where you headed?" asked the driver.

"Cambridge," I answered.

"Oh yeah, what's in Cambridge?"

"A girl," I replied.

The trucker laughed and nodded.

"I'm actually from Southend in Essex," I explained. "Went to Canada when I was ten but still keep in touch with a few friends from primary school."

"Southend," he said. "Fucking hell. Used to go down there for the weekend and get well pissed."

It was my turn to laugh. "I guess some things never change."

In truth, all I had was an address and phone number. Not much to really go on, but after a chance meeting with Sarah's mother back in my old neighbourhood, I wasn't going to be asked twice for an open invitation to visit her daughter.

The trucker let me out just north of Newcastle, and after eleven hours, several bags of crisps, and five rides, I found myself crawling up a motorway embankment somewhere, I hoped, on the outskirts of Cambridge.

I reached Sarah's rental house a little drunk. I had stopped at a pub to find my bearings and while I waited for a taxi, I had drank a couple of pints, eaten a Scottish pie, and pissed against a red telephone box outside.

I hugged her politely as she welcomed me in. I'm not sure what either of us were expecting, but it was clear within the first five minutes that Sarah's mother had been hoping for some kind of love connection. Sadly, it was not meant to be. I'm sure what was presented to Sarah was not what a proper Cambridge girl was dreaming of, and in all fairness, Sarah had hit a few branches of the chunky tree on her way down.

I think we were both relieved when a roommate broke the awkwardness and came in through the back door. She introduced herself as Lisa and seemed lovely despite her facial hair. In terms of volume, it was very impressive, and I really tried to have a normal conversation while avoiding words such as hairy, groom, and shag. Eventually though, I had to ask.

"What's with the beard?" I said as casually as possible.

"If you have to know, I struggle from bulimia. It's a hormonal thing."

"Well that blows chunks, "I said without thinking.

She looked at me, but I ignored her stare.

"So," I said moving on, "what's there to do around here?"

"Big day tomorrow," replied Sarah. "We all get our exam results."

"Sounds like a party to me," I said, lightening the mood.

"Should be something," she agreed.

I looked over at Lisa.

"You up for a bit of hair . . . hell-raising tomorrow?" I asked.

"Been waiting for this day for four bloody years," she replied. Lisa walked to the fridge and pulled out a bottle of wine and a bottle of champagne. "Ready to get started?" she asked, holding up both bottles.

"Yes please," answered Sarah. "Let's start with the wine. What about my long-lost school chum?"

"Sure, that sounds great," I replied. "We can shave the bubbly for later."

By morning, several graduating students had gathered at the house. I opened the door to a cute and thankfully beardless student named Tams. She hadn't very high hopes about passing the year, so I worked the sympathetic angle and promised I'd be there in case she needed a shoulder to cry on.

Jock showed up not long after. He wasn't a student but his sister Janet was. Unfortunately, he had come down from Newcastle only to discover she had already moved out, but the more the merrier I always say, and with his large bottle of whisky, he joined the growing entourage.

I liked Jock. You could just tell he was a crazy bastard. Even as I watched him roll a loose tobacco cigarette, it didn't surprise me when he told me how he had stuck his fingers down his throat and spewed in his best friend's tobacco tin.

When we finally got going, our first stop was not the local pub but surprisingly the vicar's rectory. Apparently, the vicar was always up for a glass of sherry, and I began to wonder if all the clergy of England had some purvey dark side I wasn't aware of.

"You've never been to the Chapel at King's College?" the vicar asked.

"No," I replied, starting to feel the whisky. "What is it?"

"Well, it's the closest place you'll ever get to God," he replied, slurring slightly.

"Sounds great. Do they charge by the hour?" I asked.

"No, by the soul," the clergyman said.

"Well, not so sure how much I have of that left," I replied. "I'll bring some pound coins just in case."

I had to admit I was impressed. Not only by the Chapel's architecture but also at the massive walls of painted stained glass. There was a story to each of the cartoonish windows. In fact, an entire sequence of events spanned the church from Christ's Crucifixion to the Last Judgment.

In some ways, I realized old Googly Eyes' paintings told a story too. I had never thought about my great uncle's paintings being anything other than crappy historical renderings, but as I stared at the intensely coloured panels, it was obvious that paint was Rob Clover's form of communication.

"Who knew," I said out loud, catching up to the rest of the group.

"Who knew what?" asked Jock.

"Who knew bulimic chicks with beards got sexier the more you drank?"

"Well," replied Jock, "wouldn't be the first girl I made puke."

By midafternoon, I found myself standing on a pub table in Bene't Street. I felt pretty damn good. Jock must have felt the same because he was at the other end of the table crouched in a mock sumo wrestler's stance.

His shirt was off, revealing a really bad tattooed lion on the front of his fat Newcastle gut. Around us, we were being yelled at to get down, and I noticed the bar owner crossing the room toward us.

Poor Tams wasn't looking so hot. She had been gearing up to brace herself for scholarly failure, and she had pretty much checked out of the festivities.

"Hey, Tams!" I yelled. "Get up here, we need a referee!" I reached down and yanked her half-comatose body on top of the table. "Ok, we need you to count it down," I said but looking up, I realized Jock had already started to charge.

I had been winding him up, mocking his shitty tattoo, and there was no mercy in his intent. He first took out Tams on the way over, then plowed directly into my chest with a meaty thud. I gave a grunt as we careened through the air, and I felt very little in my drunken state as we folded into an empty table and chairs. With Jock on top, I couldn't tell where Tams had ended up. I heard screaming from somewhere and before we had untangled ourselves, a heavy hand lifted me from the neck of my sweater and half pulled, half walked Jock and I to the bar's exit.

On the way out, I noticed a shelf of books. As a parting gift, I reached out and grabbed one, but it didn't seem to want to budge. *That's odd,* I thought, giving it one more really hard yank. The owner tried to wrestle my arm free, but it was too late. The bookcase and all of its contents came crashing down.

"Well, that's stupid!" I yelled. "Who drills holes in books and threads string through them?"

My drunken brain was still trying to figure out the logic when I felt something metallic knock into the back of my legs. I spun around, lost my balance, and fell into the driver of a motorized wheelchair.

"Arrh, for fuck's sake!" I yelled, not usually in the habit of fighting the handicapped. "Get off me."

I reached out and pushed myself clear, crashing to the pavement in a drunken heap.

"You know," started a computer-generated voice, "I could say many things right now. I could tell you about my theory of unification and how it determines everything in the universe . . . but I won't. Instead," the voice continued, "I will express a common colloquialism that you will directly understand. Go fuck yourself, dick head." And with that, the man in the wheelchair drove off.

"That was kind of nervy," I said, feeling a little indignant.

"Do you know who that was?" Sarah asked, trying to pick me up.

"No," I said.

"Stephen Hawking."

"Stephen who?"

"Stephen Hawking, you know, international acclaimed physicist and author of *A Brief History of Time*."

"Oh, that Stephen Hawking," I said. "Well, he should have learned how to drive first."

Tams had finally reached emotional rock bottom. It was official, she had failed her courses and was slumped on a bench on the other side of Sarah's kitchen.

Now's my chance, I thought, cutting across the kitchen floor that had turned into an impromptu rave. All that had been needed was a tape deck and a strobe light and as I air drummed between the other dancers, I was caught frozen in a series of unflattering tableaus.

By the time I reached Tams, she was unresponsive. I lifted her head and I felt her body shift then fold into my lap. The music had got louder and as I looked down at her, she opened her eyes and smiled. I leaned down and kissed her lightly. It felt nice and possibly meaningful.

If only I could just keep her conscious, I thought, but there appeared to be little hope. She was fading fast, and I sat there stroking her hair, at peace in the raving chaos.

I wasn't sure how long I had been sitting, but my stomach had decided it was time for pay back. I needed a toilet fast and doing my best to wriggle out from under Tams' body, I accidentally let her head clonk on the wooden bench. She moaned slightly as I stumbled out of the kitchen, and I thought I still might have a chance with her if I made my number twos relatively quick. I aimed for the hallway toilet and felt reasonably confident that I would make it. I turned the doorknob and pulled.

"Shit," I cursed.

It was locked and from inside I caught a few muffled moans and a girl's squealing voice demanding to be fucked harder. It sounded like Jock was getting his leg over, and though I would usually yell some type of encouragement, I was more concerned about my exploding bottom.

Behind me, in the middle of the living room, a vacuum cleaner caught my eye. It stood next to a coffee table, and to my luck, I saw an empty juice bottle and a family-sized bag of crisps. I think they were salt and vinegar flavoured, but there was no time to check. I couldn't tell if I was about to vomit or crap myself, so I grabbed the vacuum, the bottle, and the crisp packet, and squatted down behind the ripped love seat.

It came hard and violent. I could do nothing but hold onto the nozzle of the vacuum and let the steady stream of sick spew into the pipe. Immediately following, I knew I had to shit and with one hand still holding the hose upright, I frantically unbuttoned my jeans and pulled down my underwear. *Damn impressive,* I thought, flicking off the juice bottle cap with my thumb. I lined up the crisp bag under my ass and without a second thought, shoved my pecker into the open end of the glass bottle.

It was a triple bill. Puke, pee, and ass spray evacuated my body in complete unison. It was a beautiful thing. A drummer's dream of pure ambidexterity. I finished by waddling over to a box of tissues on the mantle and cleaned the best I could. I placed the used-up tissues into the crisp bag and rolled the vacuum back into the middle of the room.

"Just as I found it," I said, positioning the bottle of piss on the table.

Then, with the job done, I left the room without a shred of dignity.

The music was still blaring when I got back to the kitchen. Someone had unplugged the strobe and I looked over to where I had left Tams. She wasn't there, but in her place, sat bearded Lisa.

"Hey ya," I said, sliding in next to her, "where's Tams?"

"We put her to bed!" replied Lisa, shouting in my ear. "She was so wasted she was making out with all the losers!"

"Probably a good job then!" I shouted back.

Upstairs, I knocked tentatively at Tams' door. There was no answer, so I cracked it open and found her out cold. On the floor, next to her, was a bowl half-full of vomit. I couldn't help feeling it was all a bit of a turnoff, so I left her, with her diced carrots, to sleep the night away.

Down the hall, I found Jock in his sister's empty room. He sat on the floor and I joined him, grabbing the whisky bottle from his hand.

"You know, I really do like your tattoo," I said, taking a swig of Jack.

Jock managed a snort, then lowered his head once again. Downstairs, I heard the music stop. It seemed the party had finally shut down and in place of the rhythmic drone, I heard the sound of rain dripping from a leaky gutter.

"Show me the way to go home," Jock suddenly mumbled. "I'm tired and I wanna go to bed."

I knew the song. "I had a little drink about an hour ago," I joined in, "and it's gone straight to my head."

I lost track how many times we sang the stupid verses. Each time became more intense, and it was probably a good half hour before Sarah told us to shut up and our wall thumping finally stopped.

I curled into a spare bed with lace pillows and listened to the sound of the rain. I closed my eyes and instantly I was lulled into a dreamless sleep by the ticking of an imaginary clock and a faint uneasiness that time was beginning to run out.

Chapter 18

Nevel had started his interrogation by picking up the Clover brick. He closed her back door and as he turned the key to lock it, he heard Flossy Clover's voice call from across the room.

"What the hell do you think you're doing? If you're after my gold, you're wasting your time. Now bugger off before I poke your eyes out with my knitting needles."

It was a futile threat, but Nevel smiled all the same. He knew she could hardly stand, let alone run, but he gently placed the brick on the table and sat just out of striking range.

"Do you remember me?" Nevel asked.

Flossy stared for a moment, then seemed to recognize him.

"You're the man from the British Brick Society. Nathen or something?"

"That's right," Nevel conceded. "But I'm here on a very different matter today. Today you are going to tell me what happened to my father?"

Flossy looked confused.

"How would I know something like that? Do I know him?"

"Well," said Nevel Fink, "let's find out."

He reached for the old woman's arm and took hold of her bony wrist. Her resistance was more than he had expected but without the slightest hesitation, he raised his free hand, and punched her directly in the face.

Five minutes later, Flossy woke in a haze of pain. Her right arm and upper body had been tied by an electrical cord, and through her swollen eye she saw that the wooden kitchen table had been moved closer.

Nevel held her left arm flat against the table and seethed with anger.

"This is how it's going to work," he explained. "I ask a question, and if I think you're not telling me the truth, I smash a finger. Quite simple, yes? Good, now here we go. In May of 1910, my father visited the Hambro Hill brick fields and never returned. What happened to him?"

"I don't know nothing," streaked Flossy on the verge of hysteria.

Slam went the brick on her first finger. Without a doubt, every bone in her little finger was pulverized instantly. Blood dripped from the brick as Nevel raised it for a second time.

"Maybe this will jog your memory?" And without asking another question, Nevel slammed the Clover brick down a second time, making the table tremble under the impact.

"I heard there was a man!" cried Flossy. "In the barn at Shirley. He was a hobo, a drunk. Use to sleep in there in the winter. Rob told me he found him dead one day in the manger. No one knew who he was, so Rob's father dragged him into the brick fields and buried him."

"My father was no drunk!" screamed Nevel, slamming down the blood-stained brick once more. "Lies, lies, lies."

When he let her arm go, nothing but a soup of bone and skin remained. Flossy was pale from shock, but despite her pain, she managed to stare at Nevel with unnerving defiance. He swallowed hard but then shrugged it off. *Defiance doesn't matter,* thought Nevel, *that is just part of the game. All it means is that things are just going to take a little longer than I expected.*

The black and white television sat in reaching distance of Flossy. The soap opera *EastEnders* blared from the set, and Nevel leaned over and turned the volume up to an uncomfortable ear-grating level.

To Flossy's right, an electric heater glowed bright orange. It was very old, early post-war, guessed Nevel, and it was obvious the two rusty safety bars did little to protect the exposed glowing element coils. In one aggressive swoop, Nevel grabbed a fist full of Flossy's grey hair and held her face up to the electric heater. He enjoyed her screams, even her pitiful begging gave Nevel a certain sick pleasure. He breathed in the smell of singed hair and burning flesh and leaned in, almost touching the side of Flossy's head.

"How do you like your steak!?" he yelled over the noise of the television. "Mine? I like mine medium rare," he confessed. "Should be about right," Nevel announced and yanked Flossy's head once again back into her chair.

This time, there was no defiance staring back. In its place was a hideous, almost unrecognizable portrait of a destroyed human being. One side of her face smouldered as her brazened flesh oozed and wept from multiple blisters. Even Nevel felt a little sick as he looked at Flossy's charred mouth. What skin hadn't burned was now a raw brilliant red, and much of her face had swollen, forcing shut one of her eyes.

Nevel leaned over and turned down the television volume. He listened to her deep gasping breaths and waited patiently as Flossy gained some type of composure.

"You must understand, my dear Flossy," said Nevel in an almost apologetic tone, "but this pains me greatly to do this. All I wanted was the truth. Was that too much to ask?"

He waited again, but there was no response. All he heard was the sound of sucking as saliva uncontrollably dripped from the side of Flossy's useless mouth.

"In some ways, you brought this on yourself. If you had just answered my questions honestly, I would not have needed to go to such extremes." Nevel sighed. "I think I have changed my mind. I really do prefer my meat cooked well done."

He reached for her hair but was stopped by a half-raised stump.

"Please," Flossy gurgled, almost in a whisper. "I'll tell you what I know. Just stop . . . please."

"Well?" waited Nevel, trying hard to hold back his anger.

"Rob and his brother Johnny told me once their father shot one of his sows. Said it had been attacked by a rabid fox. Said their father had butchered it and put it in the brick kiln to burn."

"What's that got to do with my father?" asked Nevel, even more agitated.

"You remember Don," she said. "He liked you. Don't know why, but he did. One night, years ago, we were just peeling potatoes, when out of the blue, he just suddenly said, 'It wasn't a pig.' I asked him what the dickens he was talking about, and he said it wasn't a pig his father had put in the kiln. It was a sad man that had shot himself." She coughed and more blood trickled from her mouth. "You'll have to figure out the rest by yourself," she said. "That's all I know."

Her head slumped forwards and Nevel realized she had passed out.

"No, no, no," he said in frustration. "I'm not done with you yet."

He slapped her hard on the side of the head and Flossy gave a low moan.

"Come on, girl," said Nevel. "Stay with us."

It took a full minute before Flossy showed signs of consciousness. She opened her one good eye slowly and groaned as Nevel pulled her head back.

"There you are," said Nevel smiling. "Nearly done. Just a few more questions and I'll leave you to it."

Nevel picked up the Clover brick and stood over the disfigured woman. He wasn't sure what he was going to do, but he knew he couldn't keep her alive.

"Be careful of that brick," Flossy said suddenly. "That could be a bit of your father in there."

She coughed and gave a weak laugh. In a final renewed act of defiance, Flossy Clover raised her remaining index and middle fingers into a letter V.

She took one last deep rasping breath and silently mouthed her last living words, "Up yours, fuck hole."

Chapter 19

The nondescript countryside flashed past like a dream I couldn't remember. I still felt pretty much wankered from the night before, and not feeling like reading my new book, I slumped back into my chair and closed my eyes.

I had been the first up earlier that morning. My plan was to get rid of the crisp packet and juice bottle, but they were no where to be found. All I could guess was that someone had wanted a midnight snack and I laughed out loud at the thought of some poor bastard crunching shit flavoured crisps and then trying to wash out the taste with a bottle of piss.

There was still tea in the pot when Sarah shuffled into the kitchen. She wore a pair of pink bunny rabbit slippers and we chatted for a few minutes before I wrestled on my pack.

"Gotta love that Jock," I said, trying to smooth things over.

I sensed a few lines had been crossed the night before and though she hid it well, I think Sarah was relived I was leaving.

"He's definitely something," she replied, shaking her head.

"Hang on a minute," she said, getting up. "I've got something for you."

She returned a few moments later and handed me a small, wrapped package.

"What's that?" I asked.

"Oh, just a small reminder of your stay."

I ripped open the brown paper and smiled.

"Perfect," I said, holding up a worn copy of a Wilbur Smith novel.

"It's been signed too," she added.

I opened the cover and laughed. Not only was there a hole drilled through the middle of the book, but across the slightly crumpled title page there was a distinct tire track from a motorized wheelchair.

I woke somewhere on the East Midland line between Cambridge and London's King's Cross. More people had got on the train, but the seats opposite me were still unoccupied. On the floor, I noticed my book. As I reached down to pick it up, a voice startled me from across the aisle.

"Whatcha reading?" they asked.

I was about to answer, when looking up, I saw the Time Keeper casually sitting with his legs crossed.

"What happened to you?" I said with a mixture of relief and surprise. "I thought you were saving that dead kid?"

The Time Keeper waved his hand dismissively. "Yeah well . . . that didn't go so well."

"Oh," I replied, deciding to leave the topic alone. "So what have you been up to? I haven't seen you for a while."

"I met a friend," the Time Keeper replied. "Some kind of fourth century Nordic Viking. A bit rough around the edges but a stand-up bloke all the same."

"Cool," I said encouragingly.

For the first time in our conversation, I realized something was different. I couldn't quite put my finger on it, but the Time Keeper had softened somehow, and I wasn't sure why.

"Where you headed?" he asked as he stood up and surveyed the rest of the train carriage.

"Down to Flossy's in Eastwood," I replied. "I've got some paintings I want her to explain. What about you?"

"Not sure, just keeping a low profile at the moment."

Suddenly he turned, dismissing whatever had caught his attention.

"I tell ya what," he said. "If you're going that way, why don't I go down to Southend and hang out on the pier? It's been years since I've done that. Can you set me up a memory wave?"

I thought about it. "Sure, I don't care."

There were many memories I could have chosen. All warm and coated with the sticky fondness of youth. I was about to choose my childhood classic that included the standard mix of Rossi's ice cream and marmaite sandwiches, when I stopped. I smiled to myself and asked the Time Keeper if he was ready.

"Ok, here it comes," I announced, and with my eyes tightly shut, I conjured a memory as descriptive and vivid as I could recall.

I wasn't trying to be mean. Just a bit of pay back for leaving me to wrench my guts out in the tower of Macduff's castle. Moments later, I knew I had hit the mark. The faint yelling of "you bastard" rang in my head, and I smiled, thinking about the Time Keeper spinning at some nauseating speed.

I had sent him back alright, to a memory when I was seven. I could still feel the sick churning in my stomach as a carnie spun the Big Wheel bucket mercilessly. I remember yelling for him to stop, a blur of the old pier's amusement park, and then an uncontrollable release of diced carrot shrapnel that sprayed everybody on the ride. For a moment, I swore I caught a whiff of vomit, but then, it was gone.

I had to say I felt rather pleased with myself. It wasn't often I could use a memory to my advantage. In fact, I didn't realize they were usable at all. But there it was, the Time Keeper covered in puke.

To give him his due, the Time Keeper had taught me a thing or two lately. Most importantly, that *time* was really quite flexible. Memories weren't just for the *past*. They actually existed in the present as well as the future. It was all just a matter of perspective.

At the next station, I watched a man run for the train. *Come on, run you fat wanker!* I yelled in my head, but it was too late. The train accelerated and the out-of-breath commuter had no choice but to watch the expectation of his present slip into the past.

I always looked for my uncle and aunt's house. It's not hard to spot by train. If you paid close attention riding the Southend Victoria line, you would see it just past the airport on the other side of the tracks. Most passengers wouldn't give the house a second glance. To me however, there was one architectural feature that screamed every time I passed by.

It was nothing more than a black terra-cotta drainpipe. It ran up the back side of their house, and if I had known the trouble it would cause, I would never have bothered climbing it.

I made two tactical errors the morning I forgot my wallet. The first was not to put back the rubbish bin that I used as a step-up on to the pipe, and secondly, I shouldn't have pushed off the side of the house using the down spout as leverage.

Everything would have been fine if my aunt hadn't unexpectedly pulled up in her car. But, I panicked, and jumped down to avoid the embarrassment of breaking into my relative's second storey window. I will admit I heard something crack, but I swear the drainpipe was perfectly intact when I walked around to the front of the house.

By the time I arrived back to the house that evening, things were in full swing. The police had been called, the bin lid had been fingerprinted, and neighbours' statements had been taken. It all seemed a little excessive for an abused drainpipe, but doing the only logical thing, I denied everything.

I guess that was my third tactical error, but there was no turning back. My uncle didn't believe me—I didn't believe me—but that was my story and I held onto it like a drowning man clinging to a piece of string. Seven years later, I saw the same uncle. Without even saying hello, he looked straight at me and pointed his finger.

"You broke my bloody drainpipe, didn't you?"

And again, I denied everything. Except that night I left an old piece of drainpipe in his bed, in the guest room of my parents' house. It was not uncommon, from that day on, for me to randomly receive pieces of drainpipe in the mail. Sometimes they were disguised as Christmas presents, but mainly they were wrapped in brown paper and stamped "Inspected" by customs for "National Security reasons." I received what was to be my last drainpipe package shortly before I was to leave on a major trip. It would take me to several continents ending after three months in England for Christmas.

What better way to shove it to my uncle, I thought, *than to drop the chunk of pipe between his Paxo balls.* I had fantasized for weeks what his expression would be. I pictured a mixture of shock and amazement and possibly a formal written apology, but it was not meant to be. Instead, I received a face full of disgust. He stared at me briefly, then without saying a word, stood up, left the room, and refused to talk to me again.

I don't think we ever really settled the issue. Well, not until years later when I finally figured it out. Both my uncle and I had been played. Played by the biggest one-armed shit disturber of them all—my father.

Through it all, the old man had watched from the sidelines, enjoying every minute. I even suspect some of the drainpipe pieces were from him. I guess it really goes to show that the ones you least expect, sometimes are the guiltiest.

Chapter 20

I walked the steps again, up to Flossy's house. I wanted to find a way to fire the old girl up, and I was armed with something even better than yelling "bingo" at a seniors' home on game night. In a white pastry box, I carried four fresh cream buns. They were the most expensive I could find and kicking Flossy's side gate back into place, I walked down the side of the house and into her back garden.

As usual, I turned, expecting to see the blue door propped open, but instead, the door was locked tight. *That's odd,* I thought, putting the cake box down next to a couple of untouched milk bottles.

"Hey, you in there, Floss!?" I yelled, knocking and rattling the handle.

Unless Floss had gotten a ride somewhere, she certainly should have been home. I sat down on the step and leaned back on the locked door.

"Now what?" I said, looking at the box of cakes. "Seems a bit of a shame just to leave them here. Well, just one then," I convinced myself, and flipping open the lid, I grabbed the bun that oozed the most strawberry jam.

I was just about to take a bite when I wondered what day of the week it was. *Old habits die hard,* I thought, and smiled as I crammed as much cake into my mouth as I could. I washed it down with a half pint of Flossy's unclaimed milk, then got up and made my way to a telephone box in front of Eastwood Park.

I had just enough change to make the call and after a few rings, I connected with Southend Hospital.

"Err yes, hi, right, I'm looking for my great aunt. Just wondering if possibly she's in for a stay?"

I gave her name and waited.

"No, no record of a Flossy Clover anywhere in your system? Humm I see, ok well thanks very much."

I hung up feeling somewhat relieved. It was suggested I try the larger hospitals in the area but with no more change, I gave up and headed back to the house. *So where the hell are you?* I thought. Something wasn't adding up, and I had decided I wasn't leaving till I found out. I had my book and time to kill, so settling in for an afternoon stakeout, I lay back under one of Flossy's apple trees and promptly fell asleep.

It was the rusty squeal of Flossy's gate opening that pulled me back into the afternoon. It took me a second to remember where I was, but then, looking up, I saw a man carrying a cheap plastic bag.

"Hello?" I called out, making him jump in surprise.

He was an elderly gentleman, somewhere in his late seventies I guessed, and if I hadn't made him shit his pants, I certainly nearly gave him a heart attack.

"Do you know if Mrs. Clover is home?" he asked, recovering his composure. "I'm from Meals on Wheels. I came earlier, but no one answered. Just thought I'd give it one more go. Are you a friend?"

"A relative," I said, getting up and brushing myself off.

We both agreed that something wasn't right. I had just started to tell him about my phone call to the hospital when I heard more footsteps come from around the corner of the house.

This time, a window cleaner appeared. He was carrying an A-frame ladder and a not-so clean bucket of suds. Apparently, Thursdays were a busy day for Flossy and the cleaner explained he had come around to collect his money for the month.

I finished telling my phone call story, and it was decided that Squeegee Luigi would put his ladder up and take a look through an unobstructed side window.

"Can you see anything!?" I yelled as the cleaner got into position.

"I see something," he replied. "I can't tell just what, but there's definitely something glowing orange in there."

That was enough, I decided. I walked over to the back door and hoofed the latch hard with my foot. It made a dramatic crack as the wood frame split and the door slammed inwards, violently crashing against the wall.

Inside, I saw Flossy sitting in her worn-out chair. Her head was tilted to one side and there was no question she was dead.

One eye stared blankly out into the back garden, but her other wasn't doing so well. It hung from its socket like a ping-pong ball on a piece of string and for a second my brain couldn't comprehend why half of her skull was missing. The window cleaner came up behind me and almost vomited.

"Oh dear God," I heard him say, and then without adding anything more, he retreated to check on his diced carrots.

The orange glow was from an electric heater that was still radiating at full capacity. It was obvious this was no accident. Great Auntie Flossy had been viciously attacked and left to burn to a crisp. *BBQ*, I thought, *that's what I smelled*. It sat heavy in the room, and I shuddered at the realization that I was enjoying the aroma. I stepped closer and awkwardly manoeuvred between Flossy's body and the heater. I stared for a moment, transfixed on the blistered charred flesh.

"Jesus fucking Christ," I said, "what a way to go."

Then, without another thought, I flicked off the power switch and backed out of the room.

Several hours later, I was still in Flossy's back garden. The police had arrived along with a doctor, the forensic unit, a coroner, two detectives, an ambulance, a fire truck, and a few nosy neighbours for good measure. I had been questioned along with Reggie, the Meals on Wheels' pensioner, and the window cleaner, whose name I found out was actually Stan.

At some point late into the afternoon, the three of us helped ourselves to the lukewarm lunch in Reggie's bag. I offered up the last three cream buns and with the remaining milk bottles, our impromptu picnic strangely felt like a schoolboy's nosh-up straight out of a Beano comic.

Finally, as darkness descended, Flossy's body was stretchered out of the house. I was escorted by a police officer back into the murder scene and with the portable lights of the mobile forensic team, I saw just how extensive the blood splatter had reached.

I found what I was asked to find in a drawer by Flossy's telephone. A simple address book, a little blood soaked, but still easily legible. Sadly, there weren't too many people to call. William, Rob, Don, John, and my Grandmother Ivy, had all been dead for years. Floss and Uncle Googly Eyes had never had kids, and flicking through the pages, there were only a couple of distant nieces and nephews I hardly knew.

The only real number of significance was Flossy's sister-in-law, Maury Clover. She had been married to John Clover until his death and since she still lived close by, I decided I would make the trek over the following day and break the news.

It felt odd not seeing Flossy in her chair. The room suddenly felt unfamiliar and cold. I looked around one last time, then realized something was missing. Flossy's Clover brick was gone. Quickly, I scanned around the door and under some nearby furniture. *Shit,* I thought, *I wonder if that's what finished her off?*

I was about to mention it to a detective when I overheard Stan the window cleaner ask if he was still going to get paid. Presumably, that was the moment the detectives decided the three stooges were now in the way, and before I could say anything more, we were ushered through the front gate and thanked for our trouble.

Stan biked off in a huff with his ladder and bucket, and I caught a ride with Reggie to Naughty Norman's. Through the afternoon, I had pieced bits of Reggie's life together. He was eighty-seven and still going strong. He attributed a lot of that to never being married and the discipline of the army having served in the Second World War. He had wanted to be a pilot but ended up as a cook working the mess hall in Croyden. After the war, he had continued cooking. He worked in several nursing homes and hospitals, deciding to retire when he undercooked thirty roast chickens and gave half the senior home dysentery for dessert.

I thanked him for the ride, shook his hand, and wished him all the best. I doubted I would ever see him again, and getting out of the car, I went to find Norman's hidden spare house key. It was a complicated affair, especially in the dark.. I had to blindly count a number of bricks down and across at the side of the house. It took me a couple of tries, but finally I got it right and let myself in.

A note was waiting by the kettle. It was from Norman saying he would be back late, but if I wanted a job, I should call Peter in London as soon as possible.

I made some tea and thought about the last ten hours. Who would do such a thing? I asked. It made no sense brutalizing an old defenceless woman. I had overheard the detectives speculating about probable cause, but I believed it was more than just a simple robbery gone wrong. Her murder was as twisted and fucked up as it got. What if I had come across the attacker? All I had in my defence were four cream buns, and I didn't think they would have been much help, even against a diabetic.

I finished my tea and turned out the lights. In the dark, I made my way down the hall and fumbled my way upstairs to the spare room. *Tomorrow, I thought, is another day. How much more fucked up can life get?* And getting into bed, I answered my own question.

Plenty.

Chapter 21

The Time Keeper felt as alive as he was going to get for a dead guy. He breathed in the cool sea air and tried to remember how it once felt.

He had washed the sick from his body and stood looking out across the Thames estuary. The tide had started to go out, and he watched as a boy, far in the distance, stumbled and slid to shore through the expanding mud. It took a while, but eventually, he came close enough for the Time Keeper to realize the boy was an In-Betweener. Usually, he simply ignored them. There was just no point, but this time was different.

"Give away what you need," the Time Keeper started repeating to himself, and with the boy no more than ten feet away, he called out. "You alright, son?" he asked.

There was no response, so the Time Keeper repeated the question. In a daze of uncertainty, the boy raised his head. He looked around, confused at who the man on the beach was talking to.

"Yeah you," continued the Time Keeper. "I said, are you alright?"

"What, you some kind of faggot?" replied the boy.

"No no, you got it all wrong. I just wanted to know if I can help. That's all," said the Time Keeper.

"Well, you could have thrown me a life jacket before I fuck'n drowned," the boy replied. "Look, just stay away from me, homo, I got enough shit to deal with."

Bloody typical, thought the Time Keeper. *Try and do a good thing and all you get are insults.* His natural instinct was to say screw it, but then remembering his newfound mantra, he pulled himself together and tried again to offer up some help.

"Hey!" yelled the Time Keeper, catching up to the boy. "I don't wanna be here any more than you do. Trust me. I just thought you could use a friend."

"A friend isn't going to help me, I'm dead. I messed up. I didn't wanna die."

"Yeah, well none of us wanted to," replied the Time Keeper, "but that's where we're at."

"You ever been to your own funeral?" asked the boy. "If knowing you're dead isn't bad enough, then listening to your friends and family say your death was a tragic waste doesn't really help. It was my fault. Do you get it? I was the one who said life jackets were gay and took it off when no one was looking. It's my own stupid fucking dumbass goddamn fault."

They stood facing each other on the beach. Between them, a man with rolled up trousers snored lightly in a rented deckchair.

"Well . . . I forgive you," said the Time Keeper.

"Why the fuck would you say that?" asked the boy.

"Because it's a start. I think without forgiveness, we can't really be free."

The Time Keeper wasn't sure where his words had just come from. He spoke what he felt, and he realized his honesty had reached the boy.

"That's retarded," he said in response. "You're retarded."

"Maybe," agreed the Time Keeper, "but tell me now if you've got any better suggestions."

The boy folded his legs and sat down on the sand. He stared for a long time out toward the thin sliver of ocean, then spoke with tears in his eyes.

"I don't know how long I've been walking the mud, but you are the only person to have ever talked to me."

More silence followed before the boy quietly whispered two last words.

"Thank you."

The Time Keeper reached down and touched the boy's shoulder. It was a simple gesture, and for the slightest unexpected moment, he felt he had passed along what the axe man had given him. *Maybe there is something to all this?* he thought. *Maybe there is a way out after all.*

Chapter 22

There wasn't much left of the dead pigeon. Just a few scraps of bone and half a feathered wing. It lay on the ground at my feet and stepping over it, I entered into what was once the site of the original Hambro Hill brick fields. I closed the farmer's gate and stood looking across three empty fields. I saw nothing remotely suggesting a once thriving brick business, and even if there was, I figured it would have been picked over and levelled years ago. In the distance, I could see an endless sea of houses and lamp posts. They weaved through a landscape of concrete, and I knew somewhere in the middle I would find my Great Auntie Maury.

"So this is where it all started," I said to myself, feeling somewhat nostalgic.

It was hard to imagine what it would have been like. I had heard a few stories through the years, but looking at the rows of plowed earth, there was nothing to give me any great new insights.

My mission was to find my own Clover brick. It would be slim pickings I knew, but somewhere in the three remaining fields, there had to be something worth finding. I started my search at the ditch closest to the motorway. At one time, there were houses built there for workers, and since they were knocked down to make way for a wider arterial road, it seemed like a logical place to start.

Sadly the stinging nettles got me first, followed closely by some type of thorny branch. It scraped across my face just in time for me to trip over a discarded car bumper and topple headfirst into an old blown out tire.

"Fuuuuccccckkkk!" I yelled in frustration. "Jesus fucking fuck!"

To add insult to my injuries, ditch water from inside the tire had soaked my leg.

"Great, looks like I just pissed myself."

Moving slower, I stepped further down the ditch. Two more dead things and a broken traffic cone later, I found a drainage pipe that looked like it was built before the new road. On either side of the pipe, old, cemented bricks held the structure in place. Several looked loose enough to wiggle and with a few good kicks, I pried a couple away from their original position. I had to admit I felt a bit of Clover Fever as I frantically brushed dirt from the inside frog. *Could it be this easy?* I thought, reading the maker's name.

"J. Price," I said out loud. "That isn't right."

In frustration, I threw the brick further down the ditch and cursed again as it crashed into something metallic. *What a complete waste of time,* I thought, pulling myself out of the ditch. Enough was enough, and abandoning my search, I headed toward the north trail that led to the Clover housing estate.

Between the second and third field, I noticed something definitely circular on the ground. I guessed it to be thirty feet across and having watched enough *Time Team* archaeology television, I realized the anomaly suggested some kind of previous structure. I knelt and dug my hands into the earth. The ground was soft and after only a couple of scoops, I found what I was looking for.

"Charcoal," I said, staring at my black hands. "Definitely something burnt."

There was nothing else it could be. It had to be the original Clover brick kiln. I had heard stories about the kiln. How it took three whole days to fire the bricks and how William Clover always sat watch, telling ghost stories to scare his workers awake.

I looked at the ring of grass and smiled. I could almost see my great grandfather sitting there. I imagined he would have been smoking his pipe, puffing slowly to add to the suspense. The sound of the fires would no doubt have been spitting and cracking around him, and it wasn't hard to think that the flickering shadows would make even the holiest of men look evil.

Shrieking Boy's Grove

"Now I expect you have heard of that terrible wood at the end of Kingsley Lane. Or the awful crime committed there, so earning its terrible name.

Many hundred of years ago, tis said, a woodman was given the task, of clearing the undergrowth away, so the trees could grow taller and fast.

He had a boy to help him clear, the growth as he cut it away. But the poor little lad was small and weak, he was tired before the end of the day.

The woodman was riled, and grumbled and raged, but the boy was too tired to do much. So the man swung his axe and smote the boy from his shoulders, his head was struck.

A hollow tree he hid him in, and said he had run away. But the headless boy sits on a gate, and shrieks by night and by day.

The woodman was haunted by the boy's ghost, and used to get drunk in the Hart. But he couldn't escape the bloodcurdling yells, so from the parish did depart.

Now across the big common, at the end of the lane, the wood is still standing there. Guarded by the ghost of the headless boy, to go there alone, I you dare." —William Clover

Considering Maury didn't know she was pregnant until she gave birth, the simple country girl did remarkably well for herself.

Married to John Clover, William's youngest son, Maury had little business interest until her husband died from an unexpected blood clot. Even then, if it wasn't for Don, her dead husband's brother, Hambro Hill brick field would have never entertained its second lease on life.

Don was not good with change. For him, Shirley House and the brick fields were all he cared to know. He had tried to adapt. He had tried to find work, but after his last employer attempted to drown him in the village pond, Don retreated to his bedroom at John and Maury's and had little to do with the outside world ever again.

It was not long after her husband's funeral that Maury discovered a line of freshly made bricks in her back garden. They were methodically lined-up down the centre of the lawn, and without warning, the sight brought tears to her eyes.

"What are you making bricks for you soppy old fool?" she asked Don as she wiped her eyes.

"I don't know," he replied, "just kinda missed it."

In time, a sort of ritual developed. Don would make bricks in the day, and after he went to bed, Maury would throw the wet clay back into the mud hole at the bottom of the garden. She enjoyed the ritual. There was something about it that made her feel closer to her dead husband. Possibly it was the stories Johnny had told her, but whatever the reason, she knew it helped with the emptiness.

Maury couldn't remember how long they had followed their brick ritual. Maybe six months, over a year possibly, but when a rather overly enthusiastic member of the British Brick Society knocked at her door, she wasn't sure how much she wanted to share.

The man from the B.B.S. introduced himself as Nevel Fink. He was tall and well-mannered, and after insisting Maury check the authenticity of his membership card, Mr. Fink launched into a lengthy explanation regarding the study of historical Essex bricks.

Maury had listened with little enthusiasm. When he finally paused to take a breath, she told the man he needn't have bothered. All of the Clover property, she explained, had already been sold, and what wasn't built on were just simple farmer's fields.

To get rid of the man, she drew a crude map of the area and circled where she thought the old kiln was located. *It seems harmless enough,* she thought, then shut the door and thought nothing more of it.

Only later did she realize the man had returned. She had looked through the kitchen window and to her amazement, saw Don talking to the same man from the B.B.S. In front of her brother-in-law was a half-finished row of bricks, and she watched as the brick enthusiast frantically wrote down notes on a small pad of paper.

"Oie!" shouted Maury out of the open window. "What the bloody hell do you think you're doing?"

"Isn't this fascinating?" replied Mr. Fink. "True history in the making."

"Well maybe," she replied, "but I've got washing to hang."

She picked up her basket and walked outside. The man was just putting away his camera when Maury reached him. She was about to ask him to leave when Don spoke excitedly.

"I'm going to get my picture in a magazine," he said.

"What magazine?" demanded Maury, turning to Nevel.

"*Historical Brick Monthly,*" he replied.

"Never heard of it," she said.

"Well, yes it's small," admitted Nevel, "but Don is such a treasure trove of information, it would be a shame not to share all that knowledge."

Maury thought for a moment and then asked how much the article would pay.

"Oh, I'm afraid this is all on a volunteer basis, Mrs. Clover," answered Fink. "I'm sorry, but there's just no money in bricks."

Several weeks later, Flossy had come for a visit. She was rather annoyed by the number of cars parked on the road, and as Maury politely sipped her tea and listened to Flossy's rant, the doorbell rang with an annoying shrill.

"Not again," said Maury. "That's the eighth time today. I'm going to bloody murder that brick fellow if I ever see him again."

As with the previous seven interruptions, a man asking for a map of the brick fields stood on Maury's doorstep. He had read the latest *Historical Brick Monthly,* and like many of his fellow enthusiasts, had travelled half the country to see for himself the original site of Hambro Hill.

It was unfortunate how quickly things got out of hand. Don had asked about building a kiln next to the shed, and there were already several small holes dug in her back garden, apparently taken for soil analysis.

Flossy could see it was all too much for her sister-in-law. *In fact, it's typical,* she thought.

"Not a clue in the world," she said, shaking her head.

"About what?" asked Maury.

"Do you know you have a genuine business opportunity here?"

"No," said Maury.

"My God, woman, just think about it. You get yourself some glossy brochures, get Don to demonstrate his brickmaking skills, sell a whack load of t-shirts, and we'll be in the money. I bet if we bring up the old story of William Clover hiding his gold, we could even get a story in the local paper."

"Really?" doubted Maury.

"Of course," said Floss. "Now give me that pen over there and a piece of paper."

Five minutes later, a bucket sat outside with a sign that read "Donations" taped to it.

"And that's just the beginning," Flossy said, looking up. "How do you feel about converting your living room into a bit of a gift shop?"

Without question, The Clover Brick Company at Hambro Hill had always been regarded as one of the finest bricks of its time. Today, after decades of brick manufacturing, the Clover name was still recognized as a sign of impeccable quality. It is where the phrase "Clovered it" originated, meaning by definition: to execute a job to the highest degree.

Very few pristine examples remain of the "original" Clover brick. If not for Don gathering up the last few bricks and giving them as Christmas presents, none would have survived today.

"Who would have thought?" said Flossy in 1976 while reading an article from *the Southend Standard*. "Original Clover bricks are so high in demand that some poor chap woke up this morning to find bricks missing from the side of his house."

In the early stages, it was decided that Maury and Don would be in charge of the shop and garden tour. Flossy nominated herself as chief publicist, and her cover story of two innocent widows and a retarded brother-in-law trying to preserve the family history caught on quicker than expected. Almost overnight their pictures appeared in newspapers, and even Mr. Fink was allowed to write a follow-up article with the condition he heavily emphasize the family's need for donations.

Flossy's big break, however, came when she was asked to be on BBC's program *Lost Treasures of England*. It was, in all fairness, an Academy Award-winning performance, and the week after the program aired, the gift shop completely sold out of rubber Clover bricks. The program had looked into the claim that the owner of Hambro Hill brick fields, William Clover, had buried his company's fortune somewhere on the property. Whether he forgot where he put it or never had the opportunity to retrieve it, that was never discovered. But to Flossy Clover, daughter-in-law to the late William Clover, there was no doubt in her mind, or in her acting ability, that the treasure was there. All anyone had to do was come and find it.

Unfortunately, to date, no Clover treasure has ever been found. Apart from one Roman coin and a few bits of crappy Anglo-Saxon pottery, nothing came close to the fantasy of a metal detector's dreams. But in compensation, one small souvenir and tea shop offered a multitude of parting gifts. From key chains to hats, from soaps to t-shirts, all of the shop's merchandise reminded the purchaser that "X Marked the Spot" and to "Keep Calm and Throw a Brick."

It was only when the gracious hosts had waved goodbye and the visitors were all gone that the real truth was revealed. The only Clover treasure that existed was in the tills of the "Brick Souvenir and Tea Shop." All that was left to do was count and watch as the Clover family profits exceeded the entire fiscal earnings of the Clover Brick Company.

As if the proposed brick parade, the bronze brick statue, or the well-known poem entitled "Will's Gold" wasn't enough, my brother and I were both unknowingly enlisted into Flossy's empire in 1974.

Pulled from school just after lunch, we were driven to our grandparents' house and told to change into our pyjamas. It was an odd request in the middle of the day, but we did as we were told, then sat on either side of our grandmother as she read ghost stories and tales of buried treasure.

I wish someone had told me what was going on as it all felt rather confusing. I doubt the phrase "propaganda campaign" would have meant much to me at the time, but in reality, that was exactly what was happening.

I still remember old Flossy standing behind the photograph's lights, yelling instructions.

"Tilt your head," she would suggest—or the best catch phrase that my brother and I would repeat for years to come—"You're not looking scared enough."

By the time the newspaper article and accompanying photo was published, I was happy to have forgotten the whole experience. I doubt we were ever paid for our cameo, and maybe, in retrospect, that was why Flossy tried to slip me a fiver every time I used to visit.

All I know is that I did my part for the "family." Inadvertently, I gave my best performance to a cause I knew nothing about, and whatever skeletons and side deals came of it, I have decided to leave them buried in the same illusive hole as the Clover treasure.

"Did you hear?" I asked Maury, stepping into the gift shop.

"Yeah, I heard," she replied. "Your Uncle Colin called me this morning. As far as I'm concerned, the old cow got what she deserved. Been skimming off the top for years."

"Fair enough," I said, "but I would hold off saying that to the police. They might think you did it or something."

She stopped unloading a box of brick shaped lollipops and looked at me with concern.

"Do you think I've got anything to worry about?" she asked, "I mean, in terms of my safety?"

"Well, the police think it was a robbery gone bad, but I'm not so sure. If they had come just for the brick, they could have been halfway to London before she was out of her chair. It just feels like something else was going on, especially finding Floss' kitchen door locked from the inside."

"Bloody hell!" exclaimed Maury.

I waited for a moment, then asked if she had any thoughts about what she wanted to do with the shop.

"I've been thinking it might be time to shut things down," she replied. "Burt from next door thinks if we put our savings together, we could bugger off to Tenerife and buy a retirement villa."

Maury was probably right. Things had been spiralling down for some time. Even Don's brickmaking show had been stopped years before his death. Maury had fought a good fight against the town council, but when Don burned down her garden shed, there was no arguing the cease and desist order.

"Here," she said, handing me a plate of leftover sandwiches. "Go sit in the tearoom while I clean up."

I took the plate and found a table.

"Wow," I said out loud. "This is really quite posh."

I had never actually sat in the tearoom before and looking around at the decor, I tried not to spill crumbs on the fancy lace tablecloth.

"Hey, what's that church over there?" I asked, looking out the window.

"That?" said Maury from the other room. "Oh, that's Holy Trinity in Rayleigh. Suppose that's where we'll have Flossy's send-off. It's the same view you used to see from old Shirely House. In fact, when Johnny and I sold the last of the land, the builders gave us this house pretty much on the exact same spot."

I was on my third soggy cucumber and cheese sandwich when my brain suddenly made the connection. *Hang on a minute,* I thought, sliding back my chair. I walked back into the gift shop and found my pack.

"Here," I said, placing a rather beaten-up box of paintings on the counter. "They were Great Uncle Rob's. Flossy gave them to me. Funny now I think about it, but she was kind of insistent I take them."

Maury opened the box and gaped. "I bloody know what these are alright," she said. "The old cow wouldn't let me touch them. We could have made a mint flogging the prints on drink coasters and postcards."

She was still shaking her head when I found the painting I was looking for.

"See," I said, flipping the cardboard over and reading Rob's handwriting. "Looking east from the parlour window."

"Well look at that," she said, "been a long time since it looked like that."

"What do you mean?" I said, holding up the picture to compare the view. "Pretty much the same thing. Just now there's five hundred houses in the way."

I was surprised to find Maury more interested in the back of Rob's paintings. I hadn't taken much notice, but Maury pointed out the cardboard canvases were nothing but cut up pages from an old-world atlas. Some of the backings had stories and poems handwritten by Rob, and Maury figured they must have had some relevance to the corresponding scene.

"Did you ever hear the story of the 'Shrieking Boy's Grove'?" I asked.

"Long before you were rusting your nappy pins, my dear. Do you mind if I keep these?" asked Maury. "I think there's enough ghost stories here for a small book."

"Sure," I said, handing her the loose pile, "and don't worry, my finder's fee is quite reasonable."

Chapter 23

Nevel blew out a sigh of relief as his passenger door slammed shut. He still couldn't believe he had pulled it off. All afternoon, he had nervously told lie after lie to the police, and as he drove out of Eastwood, he realized how completely exhausted he was. He certainly hadn't planned on staying at Flossy's the entire afternoon. *God,* he thought, *how was I to know some punk-ass relative from Canada was going to be snoozing in her back garden?* He smiled and thought how quickly he had made up the Meals on Wheels story.

"You're a saucy one, Mr. Fink," Nevel said smiling.

He had returned to Flossy's house for one thing only—to look for Rob Clover's paintings. The previous night had made him too angry to even think straight, and it was only later as he scrubbed blood splatter from his body that he realized his missed opportunity.

It seems such a long time ago, thought Nevel, *when I first realized the significance of Rob's paintings. Things were so different then,* he mused, remembering the afternoon he had found Don kneeling over several rows of freshly made bricks.

He had only popped in at the house to drop off a stack of the latest *Historical Brick Monthly.* No one had been in the shop, and walking into the back garden, he had found Don humming away, methodically pushing small flat stones into the wet formed clay.

"Hey," said Nevel, interrupting Don. "Looks like you've been hard at work."

Don looked up and smiled. He liked Mr. Fink and got to his feet, wiping his hands on the front of his trousers.

"What's with the stones in the bricks?" asked Nevel. "Something to do with the firing process?" he suggested.

"Don't know," replied Don. "Just something my father and I used to do. It was just a game we played. You know, like putting six pence in the Christmas pudding."

"That's a pretty fun game," said Nevel, trying to conceal his interest. "It must have been hard trying to collect all those stones."

"Well," said Don, looking around a little uncertain. "My father and I didn't use stones."

"Really?" replied Nevel "Then what on earth did you use?"

Don looked around again and then whispered, "Coins, but only when the trains came, mind you. On those nights, father seemed to have lots of money."

"Fascinating," replied Nevel. "So, what did you do with all those bricks?"

"They got dried and stacked in the drying sheds. No one was supposed to touch them, except one day they all got put in the kiln by mistake. By the time father found out, all the bricks had gone."

"Gone where?"

"Don't know. Probably got carted away with all the other bricks and used to build houses."

"I bet your father wasn't too happy?" suggested Nevel.

"I'd say," agreed Don. "My brother Rob was supposed to be in charge. I don't think father ever forgave him. All I remember is for weeks afterwards, Rob would go off on his bike to try and find them."

"Do you think he had any luck?" asked Nevel.

"No, I don't think so. If he did, he never told me. All he used to do was come home and paint pictures of where he'd been. Don't know what good that did?"

Nevel parked his car in front of his house and got out. All he wanted to do was make some toast, then crawl into bed. He needed time to think, and a good night's sleep had always served him well.

As far as he was concerned, every single Clover needed to die. Maury was definitely next, but after dealing with the police all afternoon, he knew he had to tread lightly. He smiled, thinking of the possibilities. He pulled up the bed covers and placed Flossy's brick next to him on a pillow.

"Good night, father," whispered Nevel, kissing the crimson clay. "I hope I can make you proud."

He closed his eyes and rolled onto his side. After several minutes, Nevel was still awake. His head spun with images of his father being chopped and burned like scrap butcher meat. *How could they?* he thought with a sick disgust. *What kind of animals were they?*

Finally, only after he had decided how Maury would die, did Nevel fall sleep. It was a deep stone-cold slumber, and even the sound of Flossy's brick hitting the bedroom floor did little to pull Nevel from the depths of his revenge.

Chapter 24

I hadn't taken ten steps out of London Bridge train station before a woman approached and asked for money. She wanted twenty pounds for baby nappies, and I politely told her to "fuck off."

I crossed the street and made my way down London Bridge Road. Around me, a noisy barrage of traffic and exhaust fumes swirled past, and though I knew I was on the south side of the Thames, it was still hard to distinguish London's betting shops and cafes from any other rundown city I had visited.

Fortunately, it didn't take long to find the glossy black door. I pressed the buzzer as instructed, and after manoeuvring through a sea of unopened junk mail and bicycles chained to radiators, I climbed five sets of stairs to find Peter waiting.

"Fuck, I'm knackered," I said, letting Petie take my pack. "Couldn't you find anything on the ground floor?"

"Yeah, well we were in a bit of a rush to find something," he replied.

I followed him up one more set of stairs, and then unceremoniously collapsed onto the closet couch in his living room.

"What do you think of the new place?" Peter asked as I scanned the room from my horizontal position.

"Nice," I said without moving, "but tell me, what the hell happened to Russell's potatoes?"

"Well, the police said they were considering bringing in a projectile analyst, so we decided it was probably time to do a runner."

Peter handed me a cup of tea from the open kitchen, and I sat up, noticing the view from the living room's two large windows. London Bridge was in my direct line of sight, and I watched fascinated as a black-suited mass of bodies surged toward another world on the other side of the Thames.

London Bridge, as it turned out, wasn't in London, well at least not the original. Back in the early 1960s, someone at the city administration had the bright idea to sell the thing. Everybody knew the bridge had been "Falling Down" for years, and a buyer from the States had put up the money and shipped it, brick by brick, back to Lake Havasu in Arizona. The only problem was the American bridge enthusiast was under the assumption he was receiving London's famous Tower Bridge instead. I guessed after three years of reassembly, it was kind of hard to send it back.

"What's with the traffic light?" I asked, looking down to the end of the main hallway.

"That was Russell's contribution," Peter replied. "It was the one thing he insisted I hold onto. It's hooked up to the bathroom light, so you know when someone is stinking up the place."

"Where is Russell?" I asked. "Didn't he come with you?"

"Er . . . No," said Peter. "We decided it was best to go our separate ways. Harder for the police to track," he added.

Peter had three roommates. Eileen who was Irish and only wore black, an Austrian named Rebecca who led a secret drunken double life away from her Jehovah's Witness family, and a New Zealander named Johanna who desperately tried to have sex with anything that moved and failed miserably.

"Around here, if someone's away, their room is yours. Unfortunately, we're all here this week, so you'll have to make do with the couch."

I looked down at a deflated blow-up doll crumpled in the corner.

"What happened to her?" I asked.

"Urshula?" replied Pete. "I think she's partied out."

Later, I tried out the bathroom for myself. From a sitting position, I could see Southwark Cathedral's clock tower, and I made a mental note if ever I needed to time my poo. The view from a standing position, however, looked out across the vast array of train tracks that merged into London Bridge station. I'm not sure what it was but peeing while locking eyes with train passengers just felt wrong.

By the time I turned off the traffic light and walked back into the living room, Peter's flatmate Rebecca had appeared. She was a well-built, stocky woman in her early thirties. She had a pretty farm girl face, and she offered me a beer as I sat down again on the couch.

She was looking at a pile of photographs, and I picked up a few that lay on the coffee table. Rebecca explained she worked for a landscape company, and after each location job, her boss made the employees take pictures with cheap throwaway cameras. I was looking at an uninteresting photo of George Michael's lawn when Rebecca started to laugh.

"What's so funny?" I asked.

"Here, take a look," she said, handing me a small pile of prints.

"Holy crap," I blurted out, leafing through more of the images.

It was apparent that this pile of pics was not of landscapes or potted plants. They were holiday snaps of a couple in Greece, several showing a naked woman in rather compromising positions.

"That's the girlfriend of one of my co-workers," said Rebecca, laughing again. "He must have thrown his camera into the developing pile so he wouldn't have to pay."

We sorted through the holiday snaps and chose the top three. Rebecca taped them to the fridge, and then grabbed two more cans of lager.

"Are you up for another?" she asked.

"Hell yeah," I replied and realized all I had to do to go to bed was keel over on my side.

The night was loud outside on the streets of London. It was hard to get used to the constant shouts and hum of the city. I watched from the window as a couple of homeless men struck up a drunken exchange. Eventually, one of the men stumbled off, and the other started to wank in his sleeping bag.

I must have slept without realizing, but I awoke unable to breathe. Something was definitely wrong, and I felt a heavy pressure on my chest. In the dark, I tried to move and was about to call out in panic when to my groggy surprise, I realized someone was on top of me.

"Rebecca?" I asked, thinking Urshula was out of commission.

She didn't answer, but instead, leaned closer and tried to kiss me. I squirmed the best I could, but apparently I wasn't going anywhere.

"Hold on, hold on," I whispered, trying to buy some time."I gotta pee."

She released her hold, and instantly I took a deep breath. I made my way down to the bathroom and sat on the toilet not knowing what to do. Rain had started to tap on the cracked window as I waited out the situation. *I can't stay in the toilet all night,* I thought, so after twenty minutes, according to the cathedral clock, I cracked open the door and tiptoed down the hall.

This is going to be a bit awkward, I thought, opening the door to the living room, but to my relief, the room was empty. I gathered my blankets and pillow, and to play it safe, I found a spot in the hallway next to the washer and dryer. It would have been a good location if no one had used the toilet. Unfortunately, both Peter and Joanna had felt the urge, and after tripping them both, my sleep was further interpreted by the intense glare of a red, amber, and green traffic light.

Hearing the first trains squeal out of London Bridge station, I knew I was done sleeping. It was early, maybe six o'clock, and down the hall I heard someone knocking about in the kitchen. I felt like an old man, having only slept a few hours, so wrapping my blanket around me, I slowly shuffled back down the hall to the living room.

"What were you doing sleeping in the hallway?" Peter asked with concern.

"Oh, I don't know," I replied "I was feeling a little sick and felt I needed to be next to a major appliance."

Peter looked confused, but he handed me a mug of tea, and I decided my vacuum cleaner story could wait for another day.

"There's probably work tomorrow," he said, changing the subject "Just let me know later if you're interested."

Peter said goodbye and I heard him wrestle his bicycle down several flights of stairs. I yawned and was about to head down the hall to his empty room when the phone rang.

"Ay, cousin," I said. "What's going on?"

It was my cousin Anita, better known as Cousin Drunk. By her panicked tone, something was definitely up.

"You coming to Flossy's funeral?" she said.

"When is it?" I asked.

"Today at 11 a.m.?"

"Oh fuck," I said and looked at the living room clock.

It said 7:23 a.m. in glowing red digital numbers, and I made a quick calculation and realized I could still make it if I hurried. *So much for working,* I thought, as I frantically started packing. I loved my cousin, but wished she wasn't such a scatterbrain. Our last trip together had her accidentally setting her hair on fire, flashing her tits, and nearly getting arrested for pissing on the wall of a cathedral. *Yeah,* I smiled, *she was alright.*

Chapter 25

Not far off the coast of Southend-on-Sea and left of the sunken ship Montgomery, a strange and almost apocalyptic scene can be found in the Red Sands of the Thames estuary. Seven giant towers rise from the ocean floor, each with a set of rusted legs that look like something from a science fiction novel. They are called the Maunsell Forts, and they stand as relics from the Second World War in various stages of decay.

Originally built as early defence forts against Hitler's bombing campaigns, all seven buildings were fitted with anti-aircraft guns at the height of the war. In all, twenty-two planes and thirty V1 flying bombs were shot down before the enemy had a chance to drop their payloads on London.

What a perfect place, thought the Time Keeper, *to have the first meeting of the Narrows.* He had managed to gather a few unlikely candidates willing to listen to his newfound ideas. He was beginning to feel he had a real talent for connection, and ever since the boy on the beach, he had approached In-Betweeners everywhere, trying to enlist their help.

Not including himself, there were four others. They sat watching their tea slosh with the motion of the fort, and the Time Keeper tried desperately to steer back the conversation.

"Well, what's wrong talking about my cat?" said an elderly woman, holding her knitting. "I mean, you said we could talk about anything we wanted, and for me, that's my pussy."

"I had a cat once," added a man in a business suit.

There was a bullet hole in the side of his head, and by the way he had tried to style his hair over the gaping wound, it was obvious he felt a little self-conscious.

"Yeah, I knew some heavy cats," joined in another man that claimed to be the bandleader Glen Miller. "Boy, they were the cat's meow."

"Yes, yes," interrupted the Time Keeper. "Very good sharing, but we're here today to talk about how to move on from this place."

"I'm not leaving until I know my Ginger-puff is well taken care of. The neglect my poor Gingie has suffered is just heartbreaking," said the old woman, putting down her needles.

The last man at the table had yet to speak. He wore an Iron Cross military medal around his neck, and by his heavy boots and sheep skin jacket, there was no doubt he was a German war pilot.

"I don't think the Kraut speaks English," said Glen Miller. "What's the word for cat in German?"

"Katze or Katzchen, I believe," replied the man having the bad hair day.

"Ah," nodded the pilot smiling. "Ich mag katzchen!"

"Okay, okay," said the Time Keeper, raising his voice. "I get it, we all like cats, very good."

He was thinking he finally had their attention when the woman mentioned she once owned a budgie that could talk.

"Look, people!" yelled the Time Keeper, slamming his tin mug on the table. "I invited you here today because I want to show you something."

From around his neck, he produced the amulet he had worn for as long as he could remember.

"You see this," he said, holding it up for everyone to see. "This is how we get out of here."

"Well, let's get a move on, old boy," said Glen Miller. "I've got sound check in an hour."

The Time Keeper looked around and then walked over to a dusty window pane. With his finger, he drew a circle on the dirty glass.

"See this circle, it's like the one on my medallion," said the Time Keeper.

"No, it isn't," said bad hair guy. "That's a circle, your necklace is more like an oval."

"Well, you get the idea," replied the Time Keeper.

"If you're going to explain something to us, then you better draw it properly," added the old lady.

The Time Keeper sighed. "Fine," he said and drew something more or less like an oval on the next pane over. "There," he finally said. "Happy?"

"It's the wrong way round," said Mr. Miller. "You drew an egg. Your thingie goes the other way like a musical whole note."

The Time Keeper stared at the dead band leader. He counted to ten to calm his rising frustration, then asked Glen Miller where he thought he was.

"Can't quite say for sure. I remember getting that bomb dropped on my head flying over the English Channel, but I haven't quite figured out what happened," he answered.

"Oh," said the Time Keeper, "that's a real bummer. Well, I can clear that up for you and everyone else here. You're dead. You're all bloody dead. Dead . . . dead . . . dead."

"That's a little harsh, don't you think?" retorted the old woman.

"Well, what else do you think you are?" asked the Time Keeper.

There was silence as he stared back. He could see, for the first time, a dark deep pain behind them and he realized that the Narrows was nothing more than a hiding place for the dead to deny and avoid the truth.

The man with the head wound spoke next. "I see what I want to see," he said, looking toward the oval on the window. "I don't need to listen to you."

It sounded to the Time Keeper that no one wanted to acknowledge they were dead. Whatever pain or circumstance had brought them to this place, it still held them back from moving forward.

"So tell me this, what's better?" asked the Time Keeper, now having their full attention. "Looping around and around in circles, or ovals, until we fade into oblivion? Or getting off the merry-go-round and walking a straight line out of here?"

He walked back over to the window and added a straight line from the oval to the dried putty at the edge of the window frame.

"The way out," whispered the Time Keeper. "It really is the meaning of everything."

He held his finger to the pane and stood motionless.

"But where would we go?" said the man with the bad hair.

"Out, of course, like out out," replied the Time Keeper, "to what lies beyond the wall."

The group looked at each other confused. Even the German pilot shrugged his shoulders, joining in.

"I'm sorry, dear," said the old woman, "but I think you're the only one that wants to leave."

Chapter 26

Just past the Pink Toothbrush night club, I slowed my pace. I could see the bell tower of Holy Trinity Church and knew I was going to make it. *All I need,* I thought, *is a place to change.* I looked around, and seeing an open charity shop, I crossed the road and stepped inside.

"Hey, where are your ties?" I asked, not trying to sound too impatient.

"Down on the left by the bras and underwear," the volunteer pensioner replied.

I found the display and chose the least offensive tie out of the five.

"I'm going to have to try it on," I said. "Where's your changing rooms?"

"What, for a tie?" she said.

"Yeah, I need to see the full presentation."

She looked at me a little suspiciously, but I didn't have time to care. I gave her a quick wink, then pulled my backpack into an open cubical.

Pulling the curtain closed, I did a bit of creative manoeuvring. I changed into my crumpled best man suit and tried to ignore the fermented smell of stale beer and cigarettes. I had to admit, the tie didn't look half bad, and whipping back the curtain, I stepped out, posing like a catalogue model with one hand in my pocket.

"Oh my! Don't you look lovely," said the sale's clerk.

"Right back atcha, baby," I said, pretending to shoot her with my finger. "How much for the tie?"

"Ah, don't worry about it," said the volunteer. "You just made my day."

From a distance, I saw a banner tied to the coach gate entrance of the church. For a moment, I was horrified to think it was advertising the funeral, but getting closer, I could see it actually read "Free Breakfast on Saturdays." I stepped past a couple of hearse drivers having a smoke and entered the ancient stone church through a large Gothic door. Inside was a lobby with a donation box and a small stack of postcards for sale. There were stairs to my right, presumably leading to the choir balcony, and seeing no one around, I found a large alcove and stashed my pack.

To be honest, I was expecting a much larger turn out. It was a little disappointing as I scanned the pews, and it was sad to think the free Saturday breakfast probably pulled a bigger crowd. Flossy's casket rested near the altar in the centre of the isle. There were a few wreaths draped over it, and I was relieved that the decision had been made to keep the lid closed.

My uncle and his partner were seated in the front row. Behind, Maury and Burt sat with expressions of grief that almost looked convincing. Cousin Bloggs had shown, an aunt from Southend, a few people I didn't know, and my Cousin Drunk. I slipped into the pew next to her.

"You made it, cuz, well done," whispered Anita.

"Yeah, all good," I replied, surprised at how cheerful I was sounding.

"I heard Floss was a bit of a dog's breakfast when you found her?"

"You could say that again," I agreed.

I looked up just as the organ exploded into life, and a solemn victor entered the altar from a side chamber door. He stood patiently waiting for the music to stop, and as I took a final look around, I recognized Squeegee Luigi and gave him a slight appreciative nod.

We listened as the victor rambled off a few passages and quotes appropriate for someone he had never met, and when he offered the chance for anyone to say a few words, it was my cousin that whispered in my ear.

"Hey, do you think I should say something?"

"Like what?" I replied.

"I don't know, maybe about running free and reuniting with her husband?"

"Christ," I whispered back, "if that was the case, I have a feeling Rob would be running in the opposite direction. Probably to hell, if that's what it took."

We both tried to suppress a laugh and I snorted as we bowed our heads.

Sadly, there were no takers to speak and fifteen minutes later the funeral service was over. *Maybe that's how she wanted it,* I thought. Outlive your enemies and piss off the rest. Could have been worse I guessed, and I watched as the funeral home representatives carried out Flossy's body for her last and final ride.

Outside, I made the rounds. I shook a few hands and feigned interest by asking a few mundane questions. I was itching to get over to the pub reception, but I saw Stan the window cleaner and went over to thank him for coming.

"No problem," he said, "just felt I had to." He gave a nervous grin, then mentioned he had been talking to the detective on the case before the service. "Says they think the murder weapon was a blunt instrument like a brick. He said the forensics found clay fragments embedded in your auntie's head." He looked away, then scratched the back of his head. "Hate to bring it up, but any chance I could still get paid for Mrs. Clover's window cleaning?"

You cheap bastard, I said to myself. *So that's why you're here.*

"Look," I said, "you'll just have to ring her solicitor or call the police station. Maybe even the detective could help you out. What was his name?"

"Grimshaw," replied Stan, sounding disappointed.

"Ok well thanks again," I said, not meaning a word of it and watched as he turned, lit a cigarette, and walked back toward the parking lot.

I stood alone under the red and yellow "Free Breakfast" banner. It flopped lazily in the breeze, and I couldn't help but think death was such a pile of shit. *Even when you're dead, someone still wants a piece of you.* My only hope was that Flossy got to heaven before the devil found out.

"God, I hate the taste of licorice," I said, slamming down my first shot of Sambuca.

"Don't worry," replied my cousin. "You'll get used to it—here's another."

She handed me the glass and without waiting, I downed the second shot in one.

From across the room, I saw a man approaching. "Who's that guy?" I asked as my cousin turned to look.

"What a wanker!" she yelled for half the pub to hear.

The man was wearing an American-style trench coat and an odd-looking fedora. He swaggered across the pub floor with such exaggeration I thought he must be somehow physically impaired.

"I'm detective Grimshaw," announced the man, removing his hat. "Been looking for you. I hear you've been out of town since the murder."

I nodded and replied, "Yeah, up to London for a bit."

"Well, I've been doing a bit of research into bricks," he continued. "Seems your family's bricks are quite the collector's item. "

"That they are," I agreed.

"And I say this in strict confidence, but it seems like the murder weapon used on your great aunt was definitely a brick."

"No kidding?" I responded with fake surprise.

He was about to continue when my cousin leaned in and plonked another shot in front of me.

"You're falling behind, cuz!" she yelled, and I held up a finger to pause the detective and quickly downed the contents.

"Do you own a Clover brick?" Grimshaw asked, sensing he was losing my interest.

· "Nope," I said. "Why? Do you think it was a Clover brick that killed Flossy?"

"Just exploring the possibilities." He got up and handed me his card. "Call me if you think of anything."

I promised I would, though I suspected he didn't think I would even remember our conversation. He adjusted his hat and swaggered away in the same direction he had come.

"What was that all about?" asked my cousin.

"Not sure," I had to admit. "But he's either got a horse tied up outside or a pickle up his ass."

It was past three o'clock when I left the pub with my cousin. She was far too hammered to drive, so abandoning her car, we headed for the train station. We were halfway down Crown Hill Road when I remembered my backpack.

"Fucking hell, cuz," said Anita. "I really gotta pee."

"You can do it round the back of the church," I said, "just don't get caught this time."

Luckily, the door to the lobby was unlocked. My footsteps echoed across the tiled floor and reaching the alcove, I found my pack exactly where I had left it.

Pulling it on, I was about to head for the exit when I glanced through the double glass doors into the church. Inside, I could see movement, and I stopped for a second to see what was happening. From where I stood, I could just make out a pair of legs awkwardly balanced on top of a step ladder. It looked like someone was trying to yank off a small object positioned above the pulpit. Curious, I watched until the job was done, and by the time the person had descended the ladder, I recognized who it was and exactly what they had been up to.

"What took you so long?" asked Cousin Drunk.

"I was just watching that John Wayne detective up a ladder," I replied.

"Oh yeah?" said Anita. "What'cha think he was doing?"

"Taking down a video camera."

"What?" said Anita.

"I know, I know, what a sneaky little bastard," I agreed. "Not sure what he's going to do with the footage. Maybe analyze people's body language or something. I hear you can tell a lot from the way someone picks their nose in public."

My dinner consisted of canned baked beans, canned steak and kidney pie, canned potatoes, and a can of Holsten Pils lager. My cousin was in no condition to cook, even sober, so a run to Tesco seemed the easiest and quickest solution.

After we cleaned up, which really only amounted to chucking everything into the recycling bin, we slumped down on Anita's couch and compared notes on the day's events. Cousin Anita confessed she got the phone number of a pallbearer she fancied. I knew the one she meant.

"A bit old, don't you think?" I said laughing.

"Maybe," she replied, "but I bet he's good at dealing with stiffys."

"Hey, I meant to ask you," I said, changing the subject. "Was there anything you wanted of Flossy's?"

"Na, I already got something," she said. "You know, I use to go round there once in a while and make tea for Rob and Floss. She always was a bit of a cow, but Great Uncle Rob, well you could listen to him all day."

"What, old Googly Eyes?" I asked.

"Oh yeah," my cousin continued. "You should have heard all his stories about the women he was banging on the side. Now he was a dirty old bugger."

My mouth hung open as I tried hard to comprehend.

"I know," agreed Anita. "I know. Anyway, one day he hands me one of his paintings. It was larger than his usual stuff. This one was all rolled up, and he tells me to keep it out of Flossy's sight. So, I take it and sneak it home. It was nice enough, probably one of his better ones, but every time I went back after that, he always gave me a wink and said someday that painting was going to be worth something."

"Do you still have it?" I asked.

"Somewhere around. Give me a push and I'll try and find it."

My cousin left the room and came back a minute or so later holding a large cookbook.

"I haven't looked at this book in years," she said. She opened it and leafed through the pages. "Here it is," she said, handing me the painting.

It was a typical Rob Clover. A bit crude and amateurish, but the painting did have a certain charm. Googly Eyes must have climbed high up on an embankment to paint the scene which looked down on a steam train rocketing out of a brick tunnel. The train was a regal black and gold, and old Rob had gone a little crazy with the steam bellowing out of its funnel.

Surprisingly, the perspective and detail were better than any of his other works. You couldn't help but feel there was something important about the painting, and I scanned the detailed brick work with a newfound respect. Flipping it over, I was surprised it hadn't been painted on a section of map. It was just plain cardboard with one handwritten caption in the top left corner.

"The 3:12 from Maldon, near Cold Norton," I read. "Any idea where Cold Norton is?"

"Not a clue," replied Anita.

I should have known better. As much as I loved the girl, she couldn't pour water out of a boot unless the instructions were printed on the heel.

"Not to worry," I said, noticing something else. In pencil, faintly scattered on the back of the painting, were a series of rough calculations. "That's really weird," I said, flipping the painting over several times. "It looks like Googly Eyes painted this from a specific triangulation."

"What?" said Anita. "Like he was trying to show us something?"

I burped and tasted steak and kidney pie.

"Yeah, exactly," I agreed. "What we need is a library. Any idea where we can find one?"

"Yep, there's one in town," Anita replied. "I went in there once to use the toilet."

"Ok great. When we pick up your car tomorrow, let's take a drive and make a day out of it. I think also it would be wise to talk to someone that knows Cold Norton or at least old steam trains."

The thought lingered for only a second before we both looked at each other.

The answer was completely obvious, and in unison we both said, "Tommy Nine Fingers."

Chapter 27

Nevel waited pensively in his red Ford Escort. He had parked on Rayleigh High Street, just down from Holy Trinity church. It was nearly eleven o'clock, and as he waited, Nevel palmed Flossy's Clover brick from hand to hand. There was a part of him that desperately wanted to attend Flossy's funeral. He could imagine how satisfying it would feel to witness the collective suffering of the Clover family, but with too much at stake, he knew he should stay away.

God, you've aged a bit, Maury, thought Nevel, seeing her for the first time in twenty years.

"A cane and everything," he said, watching her slowly pass under the "Free Breakfast" sign. "Just you wait, my dear. It'll be your time soon enough."

He wasn't sure where he was going to leave the murder weapon. His plan up to that moment was to try and leave the blood-stained brick in a family member's car, then anonymously call the police tip line. He was going to wait another ten minutes before heading to the parking lot when he spotted Flossy's backpacking relative running toward the church. *This is too good,* thought Nevel. He dropped the brick into a shopping bag and opened the car door.

"How perfect," he said, following at a distance. "I'll just slip the brick into his pack and stick him right in it. It'll take him a month of Sundays to explain where he got that brick."

He saw the backpacker enter the church and stopped. *Ok,* thought Nevel, *count to sixty, then sneak in as quickly as possible.* When finally Nevel opened the doors to the church, the service had already began. The organ was playing and against his better judgment, he sneaked a quick peak through the main glass chapel doors. *That's a pretty crap turn out,* he thought, feeling his excitement fade. *I'll just have to do better next time.*

It wasn't hard recognizing the Canadian. He stood with another woman and he could clearly see there was no backpack on any of the pews. Nevel turned and looked around the lobby. *If that was me carrying a backpack,* he thought, *where would I hide it?* Instinctively, he started walking toward the choir stairs. The only logical place would be right about . . . and then he stopped.

"Bingo," he said, reaching under the stairs and pulling out the well used pack.

Without hesitation, he started to unpack the contents. It didn't take long, and just as the organ gasped its last breath, a pile of clothes, wet socks, and a book with a hole through it, laid next to him on the tiled floor. He was about to put the brick inside the pack when he recognized one last remaining item. He knew all too well the box that Flossy had kept her husband's paintings in. He had stared at it for years, and lifting off the lid, his excitement turned quickly to anger.

"Empty, fucking empty," he cursed under his breath.

For the life of him, Nevel couldn't comprehend why Flossy's relative would have it. *It just makes no sense,* he thought. *What had Flossy been up to?*

He thought about the day they had been interviewed by the police. The Canadian hadn't mentioned anything about finding any paintings. *But he did say,* remembered Nevel, *he was going to tell Maury the bad news in person. I bet that's where the paintings are,* he concluded. *Maybe Canada was just the delivery guy?*

In the end, thought Nevel, *it really doesn't matter.* All he knew for sure was that once Maury got her hands on Rob's paintings, she would never let them go.

He heard a change in the muffled voices coming from the funeral service and guessed things were wrapping up. He flinched as the organ suddenly boomed back into life, and he hurried to return everything to the pack—including the brick. Just as three funeral home employees entered the lobby, Nevel stood up. He gave them a sombre half smile and walked past them and out of the building.

Checking his watch, Nevel saw it was just shy of eleven twenty. *Funny,* he thought, nearing his car. *It took less than twenty minutes to sum up an entire life and yet over two hours to kill her.* He unlocked the driver's door and got in. He sat for a moment before starting the engine.

"Maury, Maury, Maury," he said, lost in thought.

He tapped his fingers on the steering wheel and considered his options. *Easy, Nev,* he reminded himself, *let's not do anything stupid.* He had just taken a big risk walking into the church, and he knew he couldn't allow himself to be exposed like that again.

He fired up the car's engine and U-turned in the opposite direction. Turning on the radio, he settled into his seat and tried to relax. He had prepared for the long drive. A pack of Jelly Babies and a can of Tango rested on the seat next to him. Nevel turned west onto the A127 and fumbled with the bright coloured bag.

"Here we go," he said, aiming for a telephone box somewhere in the northeastern part of Essex.

Even if the police do trace the call, thought Nevel, *I will be home free by the time they figure it out.* Smiling, he turned up the music and grinned. It was The Doors, and Nevel, thinking he had a rather good voice, started to sing.

"The time to hesitate is through . . . Come on baby light my fire. Try to set the world on "F-I-R-E.""

Don Clover

Clover Children: Rob, Will,
Ivy, Don (missing John)

William Clover (with dog) Hambro Hill Brick Fields

Original Clover brick

"Sammy" The Budgie (1977)

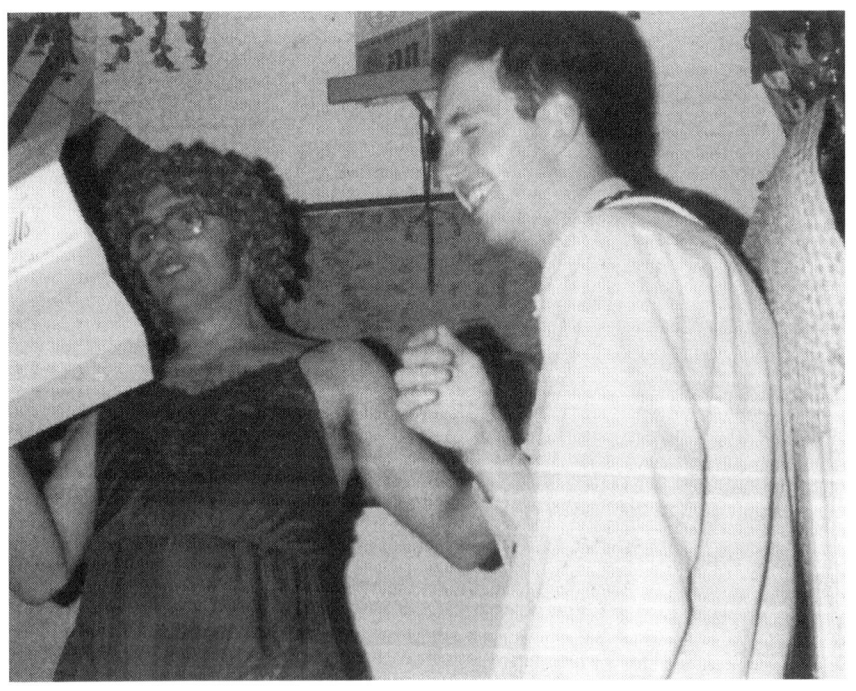

Dave's Stag

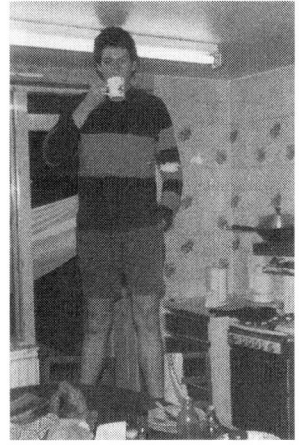

Petie Pie-Bottom

Russell

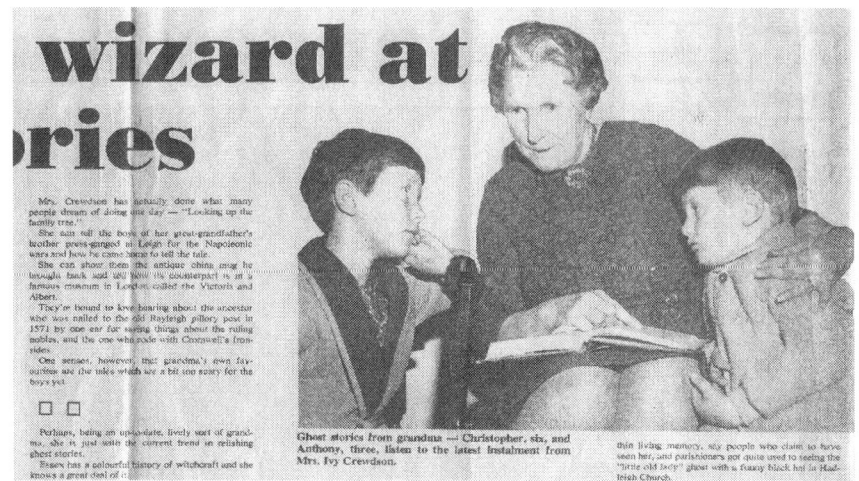

"Clover Brick Treasure" newspaper article with Grandma (1973)

Skeleton Army Logo

Cousin Anita "Cousin Drunk"

Wedding Day

Maury Clover

Flossy Clover

Rob "Googlie Eyes"
Clover

Painting by Rob Clover: "View from parlour window"

Shoreham Memorial Cross, Kent, England

Maunsell (Red Sand) Forts, Kent, England

McDuff's Castle, Fife, Scotland

Painting by Rob Clover: "Smack, Windmill, and Water"

Princess Mary Box (1914)

Mystery metal inside
Clover brick

Painting by Rob Clover: "Far-Away-Cottage"

Chapter 28

"I've got a bone to pick with you!" yelled the Time Keeper.

He stood in front of Johnathan's cave and stared into the dark cavernous space. There was no mistaking the Axe Man. He sat next to an open fire, and the man slowly looked up, annoyed at having been interrupted.

"My bones are long gone," replied the Axe Man. "Move along now before I split what's left of you in two."

Ignoring the warning, the Time Keeper stepped down into the mouth of the cave.

"I thought you said I had to 'give away what I needed' to get out of this place?"

It took a moment, but then the Axe Man recognized the Time Keeper.

"Oh, it's you," he said. "Tell me you don't need saving again?"

"No, no I don't," replied Time Keeper, slightly pissed off.

"Well then, state your business, friend."

The Time Keeper cleared his throat and tried not to be intimidated by the man's overbearing presence.

"Well . . . you're wrong, you know. I did what you told me about 'giving away what I need' but I'm still here."

"You are, are ya?" replied the Axe Man. "Well," he continued chuckling, "you must have done something wrong."

"But that's impossible," the Time Keeper snapped.

"Ah, you're just like all the rest," said the Axe Man. "You run around like a chicken with its head cut off, desperately trying to find a direction that you will never see."

"What does that mean?" replied the Time Keeper.

"It means that everything you are doing is self-serving. Stop making this all about *you*, brother. There are forces keeping you here for a reason, and my advice, if you genuinely want to leave, is to stop looking for directions to the exit."

"How's that been working for you?" asked the Time Keeper.

The Axe Man stared into the fire. The Time Keeper sensed he had pushed back too hard and instantly regretted his accusation.

"Nay," spoke the Axe Man. "I have simply chosen to remain."

"So you are hiding?" said the Time Keeper.

"You still don't get it, do you?" the Axe Man replied, shaking his head. "The Narrows isn't a wasteland for refugees, it might look that way, but it's not. This place is where you come to face your fears. It will tear you apart, or if you're lucky, will give you the strength to fight what holds you down. I died with my son many many years ago. The village, not far from here, was attacked in the middle of the night. No one was spared, and I held my son as we both bled out like stuck pigs. You ever held a dying child?"

"No," replied the Time Keeper.

"I didn't think so. Well, I'll tell ya, it's the worst, most gut-wrenching feeling of helplessness you can ever have. That shit, my friend, never leaves. I see my son walk the beaches every day. I stay here out of guilt and love, but there is nothing I can do. One day, I will watch him fade into nothing, and then, so will I. Helplessness is a terrible burden to carry."

"And this is why you helped me?" asked the Time Keeper.

"No one needs to carry that burden alone. There is too much pain here already."

His words hung in the air like a brick in midflight. They were heavy and the Time Keeper knew better than to open his big mouth again. Instead, he sat by the fire and watched as the flames illuminated the walls of the cave. He could clearly see several of the cave etchings, and in between the shadows, they seemed to dance and move to a rhythm only they could hear.

From above, the Time Keeper felt something wet touch his cheek. It was only the tiniest of specks but enough to make him look up.

"Snow?" he asked in disbelief. "What do you make of that?"

He waited for the Axe Man's reply, but there was only silence.

"Hey!" called out the Time Keeper for a second time. "Do you often get snow in here?"

He looked across the fire pit and realized he was alone. The snow came down hard. It filled the cave with thick, angry, white chunks and brushing a layer from his clothes, the Time Keeper stood up.

"Time to leave," he said, groping his way forwards, then stumbled blindly into the wall of the cave. "Ow," he said, steadying himself against the rock.

He was expecting the rough texture of sandstone but instead, he felt the smooth rectangular surface of brick and mortar. *What the hell?* thought the Time Keeper very confused. *Somehow, I don't think we're in Kansas.*

The wall was endless, and it slowly dawned on him that he was being shown the outer limits of the Narrows. It stretched to infinity in every direction, and the Time Keeper bowed his head in resignation.

"Maybe the Axe Man was right," he relinquished. "Maybe it's my own fears, not someone else's, I need to look at." He thumped the wall and turned into the storm. "I guess," said the Time Keeper, "it was my time after all."

Chapter 29

On the surface, trainspotting seems to be a futile exercise in documenting something that isn't really necessary. Typically, enthusiasts write down as many individual train engine numbers as possible, and they can be found in deep scholarly notation at most railway stations and train yards around the country.

But underneath the facade of anoraks and packed lunches, there is more than meets the eye. This clan of "loco enthusiasts" are, at the heart of it, truth seekers. Not only are they out appreciating man's ingenuity, but in some small way, they are trying to understand how a network, too large to fathom, can operate with such precision and intrinsic faith.

Uncle Tom was a die hard trainspotter. We found him fast asleep in his back garden, his "Kiss My Bass" baseball hat slumped half over his face.

I had always thought he had lost his finger getting too close to the trains, but as it turned out, his notorious nose-picking impression was the result of a motorcycle accident years ago.

"Oh, hear comes trouble," he said, opening his eyes.

"Hello uncle," said Anita, giving him a kiss. "We brought beer."

"Shit, that's how it always starts," he replied.

It was a hot afternoon and Tommy Nine Fingers readjusted himself in his deck chair. He took a swig of beer, repositioned his hat and sighed.

"Ok, what?" he asked.

Anita and I looked at each other.

"Do you know anything about a train tunnel in Cold Norton?" I asked.

"Who wants to know?" he replied.

"It's just that we have one of Rob Clover's old paintings and that's what is written on the back," I clarified.

I handed him the painting, and we waited as our uncle found his glasses and inspected the work. He had finished most of his second beer when he finally looked up.

"Well," he said, pausing to yawn, "there's several train bridges out that way if I remember, but I don't know of any tunnels. You know everything closed down years ago? The tracks were all lifted up, and most of the engines were scraped. A complete national disgrace as far as I'm concerned. When you get to my age, there's not much left of anything," he said, looking down toward his lap.

He took one last draw from his beer and dropped the empty bottle to the grass.

"I tell ya what," he said. "There's a map of Essex in the back room, let me go get it and I'll show you what I mean."

He was a little wobbly as he headed off to the house, but he returned a few minutes later, spreading out the map on his well manicured grass.

"There," he said, locating Cold Norton without any trouble.

He pulled out a pencil and was just about to draw the old track line when a gentle breeze lifted a corner and folded the map back onto itself.

"Hold the bloody thing down, Anita," snapped Tom, and possibly a little buzzed herself, my cousin flopped down spread-eagle over the paper.

"Good thinking, Anita," said my uncle, "but I think we'll get something to hold it down from the shed."

I followed my uncle up the garden path and waited till he finally produced a key from his pocket.

"Why all the security?" I asked.

"You'll see," he replied, unlocking the door.

Inside, the shed smelt like something had died. All I could see was a couple of lawnmowers in various stages of disrepair, and in the corner, what looked like a pile of ordinary bricks.

"Do you know what those are?" said Uncle Tom, pointing to the pile of bricks. "That is my brick collection."

He knelt and lifted a brick from the top of the pile.

"See, this one says The Queen's Silver Jubilee 1977. Got that on a job site up in London."

I picked up another brick and read Royal Wedding Charles and Diana 1981.

"Pretty cool," I said. "But the big question is whether or not you have a Clover brick?"

"Yes indeed, in fact, that was one of my first," Uncle Tom confessed. "Found it when they were auctioning off the Shirley House estate."

He scanned the stack of bricks and pointed to a reddish coloured brick.

"That would be the one," he said. "It's the one with the big crack in it."

I looked closer and saw a fine jagged line running down the entire side of the brick.

"What's that all about?" I asked.

"Used to see shit quality bricks quite a bit in my working days. Either it was from a poor mix, or there was some kind of debris inside the clay when it was fired. Ya know," my uncle said, shaking his head, "for all the hype over Clover bricks, you'd never know it from this sad looking specimen."

Once the map had been secured, my uncle roughed in the nonexistent train line. His pencil kept poking through the map, but eventually he sat back and surveyed his cartography. It was easy to see that the original tracks had come down from Maldon in the north. They then curved left, passing Cold Norton to the east, and from there they ran west and off the map toward Uncle Tom's hydrangeas.

"So where do you think we should start looking for the tunnel?" I asked, realizing it was a huge area to cover by foot.

"Well," said Uncle Tom, "I'm going to have to make a few phone calls first. I have a couple of trainspotter friends that would be really interested in this. You wouldn't mind if I invited a few of them along?"

"Not at all," I said, "could be a good laugh."

I looked up at my uncle, but he wasn't smiling. Things, I realized, had just gotten serious for the veteran spotter. He looked back at me with a half-crazed expression.

"I'll have an answer for you tomorrow," he said. "I got a feeling I'm going to have to call the Body Snatcher for this one."

"What the fuck does that wanker want?" said Anita back at her flat.

She had been listening to her answering machine messages, and I had presumed it must have been one of several poor bastards trying to get a leg over with my cousin. She came through from the kitchen and sat down across from me.

"That was Detective Grim on the machine. Apparently, he wants to see us both ASAP," she mocked, holding up fingers to imitate quotations marks.

"I think you're fingers are supposed to go the other way," I laughed.

"Well, whatever it is," said my cousin, "it can wait till morning, I'm knackered."

I had another couch bed for the night, and I shoved my pack off the far end and unfolded a clean sheet.

"That's weird," I said. "My pack never clunked like that before."

"What's it suppose to clunk like?" asked Anita.

"Not like that," I replied.

I went over and pulled my pack upright. I undid the pull strings and emptied everything I owned onto the floor.

"What the hell is that?" I said in disbelief.

"A brick with red stuff on it," replied my cousin, stating the obvious.

I set the brick down on a nearby coffee table, and we both stepped back as if it was some kind of bomb.

"How the fuck did it get in there?" asked Anita.

"Absolutely no clue," I said, "but whoever put it there probably found my pack yesterday at the church."

"Do you think that was the murder weapon used on Floss?" asked Anita.

"I have a bad feeling it was, cuz," I said. "That's definitely a Clover brick, look, there's even a crack down the side of it. I bet the killer was trying to set me up."

Continuing my line of thinking, I was pretty sure detective Grimshaw had been tipped off. I was half-surprised he hadn't camped out on my cousin's front doorstep, and I knew it wouldn't be long before he'd be banging on the door with a warrant.

"We've got to hide it," I said panicking. "If he finds it, we'll all be in a ton of shit."

"But we didn't do anything," argued Anita.

"Doesn't matter. I had Rob's paintings, and not much of an alibi the night Floss died. Think, cuz, where can we hide it?"

I waited with strained patience as Anita tried to think. It was a struggle, but eventually she came up with an idea.

"Mandy next door. She's away on holidays this week. What about burying it in her back garden?"

Ok that might work, I thought.

"Let's give it an hour, then climb over her fence. Do you have a black sweater or something I could wear?"

"For what?" asked Anita, looking confused. "Are you cold?"

"God, love you, cousin," I replied. "How you got his far, I'll never know."

By the time we stood at the bottom of Mandy's garden, it was one thirty in the morning. I held the brick in a plastic Tesco bag and whispered to my cousin.

"Ok, where's the shovel?"

"Why should I know?" replied my cousin.

"Because Mandy is your friend," I said calmly, "and you would know where she kept it."

"No idea," she replied.

In desperation, I looked back at the one light above Mandy's back door. It shone downwards, illuminating a single patio chair and some kind of grey plastic box.

"What's in the box?" I asked.

"Oh, it's her cat's kitty litter," said Anita.

"Ok, that will have to do."

"What? With all that cat poo?" asked my cousin.

"Trust me, cuz," I said. "A brick in cat shit is always safer than a blind dog with diarrhea."

Chapter 30

Bright and early the next morning, Tommy Nine Fingers called to say everything had been arranged. We hurried from the house, my cousin deciding a full safari outfit was required. After complaining about her hat more times than I cared to count, we pulled onto my uncle's road and into parking mayhem. Every available space had been filled. We navigated to the top of the road, and Anita turned the car around in a tight eleven-point turn.

As we passed back down the road, I noticed a large group of twenty to thirty men gathered on the front lawn of number 23. I could see Tom's wife, Dot Spot, handing out mugs of tea and it didn't surprise me to see Great Auntie Maury trying to flog her usual brick souvenirs.

"Hey, Maury," I said after walking from the church parking lot at the bottom of the hill. "Have you seen Uncle Tom?"

Her latest t-shirt read "Sometimes life hits you in the head with a brick—Don't lose faith." It seemed in poor taste in light of recent events, but I suspected even Flossy would have approved, recognizing the financial opportunity.

"Ello, my luv," she replied with a smile. "He was here a minute ago. He's not hard to miss. Oie, you still coming round tomorrow? I have those paintings you can have back."

"Sure," I replied. "I'll see you after breakfast."

"Look, there he is."

She pointed in the direction of a man dressed in a very dated orange windbreaker. His back was toward us, but as we approached, he turned and I had to look twice to make sure it really was my uncle. Gone was the decrepit old man from yesterday. Instead, my uncle bore the persona of a man in full gusto, giving orders and commands as if he was a respected army general.

"There you are," he said, putting down his megaphone. "It's about time."

"Well, we had a bit of trouble with the parking," I replied. "I thought it was just a couple of friends you were inviting?"

Grabbing a mug of tea from a passing tray, he motioned us away from the chaos and down toward the side of his garage.

"Look, I'm sorry about all this," my uncle began. "Unfortunately, there wasn't anything I could really do. You see, the tunnel we're looking for doesn't officially exist. Well, it does, but not on paper. It ended up taking me half the night to get a bloody answer and when I did, it ended up coming from Bo Snatch."

"Bo Snatch?" I asked.

"Yes, the Body Snatcher. He's like the guru of the trainspotters. Without getting too into it, let's just say he's the only man alive that's claimed all five rail networks. Brilliant bloke, knows Essex like the back of his hand."

"The Body Snatcher?" I said again, still a little concerned.

"Well, some of the loco enthusiasts take on nicknames, sort of a Superman alter-ego. A 'body snatcher' for instance is an operation where one type of train gets another style of engine put in her. Bo had a kidney transplant a few years back, so it was all kind of fitting."

"What's your spotter name?" asked Anita.

"I'm the Blue Flash," replied our uncle, standing a little taller as he spoke.

There was an awkward silence for a few seconds. I glanced over at my cousin and I think we were both relived that our uncle didn't rip his windbreaker open and reveal a skin-tight t-shirt with a lightning bolt.

"Anyway," said Uncle Tom, "the tunnel isn't on the old GNR main track where we were looking on the map. It's actually on a siding that tracks to the east a few miles."

"So what's the big mystery?" I asked. "Why doesn't it 'really exist?'"

"It wasn't built by the railway company, the tunnel we're looking for was built by the British army. And it turns out," said Tom, "it was more than just a tunnel. Best anyone can figure, there was some kind of bunker underneath the structure. We've got it dated to somewhere just before the First World War, but whatever it was used for, no one wanted it found.

So, last night I went round to Bo's. He's the only person that claims to have actually seen the tunnel. He looked like shit to be honest; his recycled kidney isn't working out so well. Not sure how long he's got left, so we started in on the Johnny Walker, and I finally got him to tell me the location."

My Uncle looked back to the front of the house, and I could see he was itching to get things under way.

"You have to understand, this is unprecedented in the trainspotter's world. Having a secret location is gold around here. When it comes to trading information, this is truly comparable to the Berlin Wall collapsing. So yeah, I got a bit excited and maybe told a few people I shouldn't have. I'm sorry, but all in good fun, right?"

"More the merrier," I said reassuringly.

"Ok then," said my uncle turning, "let's get this show on the road."

Chapter 31

Nevel's back ached. He also needed to piss but getting out of his car and relieving himself had simply been out of the question.

He had been keeping watch on Maury's Brick Shop for the last two days and a small mountain of food wrappers and cups littered the floor of his usually immaculate interior.

It was late, close to midnight, and Nevel checked his watch one last time. The street was empty, and he had clocked the last passing car almost an hour before. *It's time,* he thought, and opened the car door.

Emerging from the shadows, he walked briskly across the street. Under his coat he held a tie iron to his chest, and being careful not to leave fingerprints, wore the same black leather gloves he had used with Flossy.

Maury had locked the Brick Shop and turned off the neon sign just after seven. She had walked next door just like the night before, and through a small kitchen window, Nevel had seen her eating dinner and then watching television with her neighbouring boyfriend.

The lights to the downstairs had gone out around ten, and Nevel was sure Maury was now fast asleep, or at the least preoccupied.

He removed a small cloth from his pocket and folded it twice. Holding it up to the glass, he tapped the tire iron lightly on the cloth, then gradually increased the force until the glass gave way. It cracked in a spiderweb of shards and Nevel stopped, just to make sure he hadn't been heard.

With only the sound of a distant dog barking, he began to pry the glass out of the window. Luckily, there were only a few pieces he needed to remove, and carefully he reached into the opening and unlocked the door from the inside.

Even in the dark, Nevel saw nothing had really changed. The same shelves and cardboard displays still stood in their original positions, and he manoeuvred easily through the brick paraphernalia until he stopped at the cash register counter.

Below the register there were three drawers, and pulling out a pen-sized flashlight, Nevel tried all three. The bottom drawer was locked. He rattled the handle, then giving up, reached into his pocket and pulled out a small multi-tooled knife. Nevel crouched and tried to wiggle the knife blade between the locking mechanism and the front panel.

"Come on, you piece of shit," he said, but the drawer didn't budge.

In frustration, he stabbed at the wood. He stabbed again, and then again, and by the time he stopped, he had made a small pile of wood chips on the floor. *There must be a better way,* thought Nevel, breathing deeply. *If I was a haggard old lazy bitch,* he asked himself, *where would I hide the key?*

He started with the most obvious of places and lifted the cash register. To his surprise, in front of him lay a small brass key. He picked it up and inserted it into the lock. *Could it be that simple?* Then, with one smooth click to the right, Nevel had his answer.

He pulled the drawer open and smiled. Inside was a brown manila envelope exactly the size and shape he had imagined.

"I woo wit," said Nevel with the flashlight between his teeth, then reached down and opened the packet.

It only took an instant to confirm his suspicions. The oil finish from the paint reflected the beam of his flashlight, and Nevel quickly slid Rob Clover's paintings back into the envelope.

"Now," said Nevel. "Part two of the night's activities."

In the boot of his Ford Escort was a small container of petrol. Along with some rags and a couple of empty milk bottles, Nevel started to prepare his own version of a Molotov Cocktail.

"This'll fuck 'em," he mumbled. "Start with the shop, then make sure Maury and the neighbour's house goes up as well. Gotta love a good two for one."

He did not see the man with the dog. Only when a voice from behind asked if things were alright, did Nevel turn in surprise.

"Jesus," said Nevel, "you scared the hell out of me."

"Sorry about that," the dog walker replied, "just wanted to make sure everything was ok."

Nevel weighed his options. On him he had a pen knife, a tire iron, and a can of petrol. *What would be easier?* thought Nevel. *Hit the old man with the tire iron or blind him with petrol?* Either way, Nevel decided, he was going to finish the job by cutting the man's throat.

Nevel stood and looked at the dog walker. He had decided on the tire iron and fingered the piece of steel nervously.

"I see you have a petrol can there," said the man. "Did you run out then?"

"Well, a funny thing today," replied Nevel, biding his time. "I thought I could squeak out enough petrol to get to work but came up short, you see. Had to abandon her till this evening and then couldn't find where I parked the bloody thing."

"Yes, it's a bit confusing around here if you don't know your way around. Look, you get in the car and try to turn it over. Hand me the can and I'll pour it in."

The man stepped closer, and Nevel realized he had lost the element of surprise. In desperation, he reached for the petrol can, but it was too late. The dog walker had beat him to it and gave Nevel a gentle shove toward the driver's door.

"Ok!" yelled the man after emptying the entire contents into the car's tank.

He gave a thumbs-up and Nevel turned the key. It started as expected, and with no other choice, Nevel drove off, forcing a grateful wave.

"Keep it cool," Nevel told himself, turning out of Brick Field Estates.

He had Rob's paintings, and that, regardless of the night's interruption, was the most important thing. *As far as revenge goes,* thought Nevel, recalling a quote he once read, *"Beware the fury of a patient man."*

Chapter 32

Finally, after an hour, the convoy pulled into a farmer's field northeast of Cold Norton.

Almost everyone put on their rubber boots and headlamps but looking down at my cousin's knee-high clubbing boots, I sensed we were in for a bit of a rough go.

"Alright, people!" shouted Uncle Tom through his megaphone. "Let's stay safe out there. Find your buddy, stay in sight, and Nigel, for God sake, only blow your whistle if it's really an emergency."

Uncle Tom waved his hand to follow, checked his compass bearing, lowered his head, then proceeded to cut a path directly into the surrounding woods.

Unfortunately, the undergrowth did not help. Within twenty minutes of starting, progress had slowed to a crawl. Both trainspotters and disco clubbers wrestled with ferns and small trees until my cousin had finally had enough.

"Oh for fuck's sake," she bitched. "I thought there would be a path or something? This is like totally mental."

I stopped and turned. "What's in your hand?" I asked.

"My bloody heel," she replied. Throwing it at me, she sat down and started to sulk.

"Come on, cuz," I said, trying hard to keep it positive. "Let me have a look."

I sat on the log next to her and inspected her heelless boot. *It certainly looks far more practical,* I thought, and without a word, I pulled off her good boot and walked over to a near by tree.

With one heavy stomp, I snapped the heel clean off and threw her now matching boot back into her lap.

"That should do it," I said. "Honestly, cuz—" but then I stopped.

Sitting next to my cousin, as carefree as a naked carpenter, was none other than the Time Keeper. As casually as I could, I strolled back to the log. The Time Keeper looked amused as I tried to confront him without my cousin noticing.

"What are you doing here?" I whispered through the side of my mouth.

"Oh, just hanging out," he answered. "Came to see what all the fuss was about."

"Well, at the moment, I think we're lost," I replied, forgetting to whisper.

"It's ok," said my cousin. "You don't have to whisper. I can see him, you know. Who do you think told me to throw the heel at you?"

"What?" I asked in disbelief. "You can see the Time Keeper?"

"Who's the Time Keeper? This is Party Boy Pat," replied my cousin.

"Party Boy who?" I asked confused.

"He's been around the pub for years," explained Anita. "Don't know why no one talks to him, but we seem to have a good laugh."

My cousin looked at the Time Keeper and they both grinned at some inside joke.

In all honestly, I felt a bit put off. I hadn't considered the possibility of having to share what I thought was my own personal spirit guide.

"How long have you known him?" I asked Anita.

"I don't know really, he sort of comes and goes."

"Sorry to break it to you," the Time Keeper explained, "but there's a few others I hang out with. I've seemed to become a lot of things to a lot of different people. For your cousin, I'm a twenty-three-year-old underwear model."

"Are you telling me you hooked up with my cousin?" I asked.

Before the Time Keeper could answer, I heard a whistle blow.

"Looks like Nigel has an emergency," I said, trying to pinpoint the direction. "Let's leave that conversation for another day," I said to the Time Keeper. "Hey, Anita, which way did the whistle come from?"

"That way," pointed my cousin, and knowing her too well, I started walking in the opposite direction.

We caught up to the main group and found them standing around a large oak tree. At first, I couldn't understand what all the fuss was about. To me, it just looked like a rusted mess of twisted metal until someone shouted out that it was a motorcycle.

It took a moment but then I saw it. The bike lay on its side and had lost its front wheel and most of the engine. I hadn't a clue on motorbike history, but a couple of old boys in our party had no trouble identifying it to be an Enfield 425cc V-twin dating to around the early 1900s.

What made the motorbike so hard to recognize was the fact that the frame was suspended around the trunk of the tree. Somehow it had grown through the empty engine compartment, and over the years had lifted the entire frame several feet into the air. It was a bewildering site, and to be honest, a little creepy. The motorcycle frame sagged like a dead impaled animal, and I felt as if it had been placed there as some kind of warning.

On top of the motorcycle sat the Time Keeper AKA Party Boy Pat, smoking a cigarette. He watched as the rest of the party finally moved on, and I stepped a little closer, intrigued by the Time Keeper's nervous expression.

"You know," said the Time Keeper. "You shouldn't go any further. There's some real heavy shit around these parts."

He looked genuinely afraid, and though I had to admit I felt it too, there was no way I was turning back now.

"Why?" I asked.

He looked away for a moment, then flicked his cigarette to the ground.

"There are parts of the Narrows you don't want to see. Parts so thick with anger and pain that it suffocates everything around it. They are the places of true evil and there's no chance in fuck I'm going any further."

From our new position, the lay of the land started to make sense. We were standing on some kind of man-made embankment, and looking across forty, fifty feet, a similar mound formed a grassy "V" shape hillside. Between the two slopes, a path of flat ground curved in contour with the terrain. Like a dried riverbed, you could almost see where the train tracks had once laid, and we followed Uncle Tom down the slope to walk the final leg on the original track surface.

"There!" shouted Tom as a section of the path began to straighten.

It was thick with weeds and overgrowth, but there was no mistaking the enormity of the brick tunnel entrance.

"Holy shit," said my cousin. "You found it, uncle."

He sat down and unwrapped a sandwich. I suspected he was savouring the moment, and with a mouth full of bread, he said, "Wov course. Wot wid you wink?"

I reached into my pack and pulled out the rolled-up painting of Uncle Googly Eyes. There was no question we had found the tunnel, and scanning the embankments, I arrived at a spot I thought Googs had sat. It was roughly about three quarters the way up the south incline, and I thought I saw a rock or some kind of debris that could have served as a natural seat.

"Come on, slow poke!" shouted Cousin Anita. She grabbed my arm and pulled me toward the tunnel entrance.

The facade of the tunnel was a typical horseshoe design. It was built completely of Clover bricks, the colour and quality still holding true. The curved brick ceiling loomed like an entrance to a great Cathedral, and in places, you could still see the caked on locomotive soot, reminding me the past still hung on in many ways. Edging forwards, an array of headlamps, flashlights, and propane lanterns lit our way like fireflies in the night.

"Helllooooh!" my cousin yelled out. "This is awesome. I'm telling you, cuz, we could open our own night club down here. Imagine lights all over the dance floor, and we could have Go-Go dancers in all of those rectangular box things in the wall."

"I think they're called cut-ins," I said. "They were places to hide when a big honking train came along. Got a feeling not getting hit was the main objective if you had to work down here."

"Well, they do look a bit small. Hey, what was that band Paul McCartney was in before Wings? Didn't they use to play in something like this?"

I ignored the question and carried on until we were roughly halfway through the tunnel.

"And right there," pointed Anita, "that's where you should have the main bar."

She walked over to the space and pretended to pour a pint.

"No, you purvey bastard," she said to an imaginary customer, "you can't see my tits."

I laughed as a few fellow train enthusiasts passed by on their way back to the opening.

"Hey, you with the whistle!" called my cousin, singling out the scrawny teenager named Nigel. "Come here and flash your light on me."

Anita climbed into a near by "cut-in" and tried a few dance moves.

"That's right sexy. I'll give you something to blow your whistle about."

"Come on, Anita," I said, "stop traumatizing the poor boy and get down."

She managed one more not-so-elegant spin, then jumped, hitting her head on the roof of the brick alcove.

"Ow," she said laughing. "Thank God for my safari hat."

I was about to suggest trying it again without the helmet when from behind her, I heard a distinct mechanical clunk followed by the sound of brick grinding on brick.

Oh shit, I thought, thinking part of the tunnel was about to collapse.

"Get down!" I yelled, and grabbing my cousin's arm, we hit the ground for cover.

I wasn't sure how long we waited in the dark. I heard a few sniffles from Nigel, then running out of imaginary life-ending scenarios, I realized nothing was going to happen.

"I think we're ok," I said, removing my hands from above my head. "Nigel, point your light over to where Anita was dancing."

I waited, then finally heard him move and switch on his headlamp.

"Holy crap, cousin, what is that?" asked Anita as we stared at a door-sized opening in the back wall of the tunnel.

"I have no idea," I replied.

I took a few steps forwards and pushed as a fake section of the wall swung all the way open.

"It looks like some kind of hidden entrance," I said. "Look, you can see a bunch of stairs going down."

I was about to suggest we find our uncle when Nigel blew his whistle.

"Oh for fuck's sake," my cousin and I both said together.

He paused for a moment, then drew in another breath.

"Oh no you don't," said Anita, and in one swoop of her arm, she pulled the whistle from Nigel's mouth and threw it straight into the passage.

Chapter 33

Several theories were offered for why such a passage existed. They ranged from a bunker for storing explosives to a type of gutter system that prevented the tracks from flooding. Whatever the case, it was clear nothing was going to be proven until someone went down to investigate. Ten minutes into a discussion on insurance policies and emergency service access, my cousin Anita decided she'd had enough.

"What a complete bunch of pansies," she said. "Here, give me that," she motioned to Nigel, taking his flashlight, then crouched down and disappeared into the darkness.

"Do you think she's alright?" someone asked after several minutes. I was getting a little concerned myself, when from the bottom of the stairs, I heard Cousin Drunk singing.

"Who's afraid of the big bad wolf? All yoouuu wankers."

As calmly as my cousin had vanished, she reappeared into the flood of battery-powered headlamps and flashlights.

"Well?" asked Uncle Tom. "What's down there?"

Anita took a drink from her canteen and wiped her mouth.

"Hard to say, but there's a bunch of rooms. Creepy as shit and probably all about ready to collapse."

"Any idea what it is?" asked Tom.

"Kind of reminded me of a hospital for some reason. But I don't know, maybe a mental ward, or a jail. Who knows?"

It was decided that six of us would follow Anita back down the stairs. Uncle Tom and I would lead the way, followed by the man that had identified the motorcycle, and Nigel who wanted to look for his whistle. Bringing up the rear would be a couple in matching coveralls who had offered to bring their supplemental oxygen tank just in case.

At the bottom of the stairs, we found a room maybe half a tennis court in size. Paint flaked off the brick walls, and much of the ceiling plaster had collapsed to the floor. Around us, the sound of dripping water echoed in the dark, and as we manoeuvred over fallen planks and debris, our actions slowed to deliberate, calculated steps.

"Be careful, everyone," reminded Uncle Tom. "Some of those broken beams are load bearing. I'm not sure what's still holding up the ceiling, and to be honest, I don't want to find out."

Leading away from the central chamber, we discovered several hallways that branched off in different directions.

"Which one?" I asked, not thinking it was going to make much difference.

"That's the one I took," said Anita, shining her flashlight. "There's a couple of metal doors at the end I think we should try and open."

With no objections, we followed my cousin into the passage. To the left, I counted eight identical rooms that connected to the hall. Each contained a sink and a rusted metal bed frame, but it was clear that any remnants of human occupation had been stripped away years ago.

"We all here?" asked Uncle Tom, reaching the end of the hall.

He did a quick head count, then turned and pulled hard on one of the metal door handles. The door creaked with rust, but surprisingly, it swung open easier than expected. At first, I wasn't sure what I was looking at. A column of light shone down from a large vaulted ceiling maybe forty feet above. It looked almost alien-like, piercing the darkness with a yellowish-green glow.

"Didn't think we were that far down," I heard my uncle say, and only then did I realize the source of light was from an old skylight buried somewhere in the woods above.

The room itself was a large, cavernous space. At one end, tables and chairs were clumsily stacked, and it looked like the space had been used as some type of common area.

"Hey, check out the old cafeteria," said my cousin, pointing her flashlight at a long serving counter. "Look, there's even a Bangers and Mash special."

Surprisingly, there was still a pile of trays at the far end of the counter. Whatever plates had been left were now broken on the floor, and they crunched under our feet as we stepped closer to inspect the remains.

"Come on, cuz," said Anita. "Let's see what's in the kitchen."

I hadn't really wanted to go any further. Nothing felt right about the place. *Too many ghosts,* I thought, and I was glad to hear my uncle felt the same.

"We better get back," he announced to our group. "Obviously, this place is far bigger than anything we had imagined. Frankly, getting lost down here doesn't seem like fun."

I was about to turn around when my flashlight lit up a collapsed section of the ceiling. A large hole, presumably above what looked like the kitchen grill, revealed an assortment of wires and pipes that travelled in several different directions.

Two of the largest pipes caught my attention, and carefully I climbed on top of the grill to take a closer look.

"What do you see?" asked Anita.

"I'm not sure," I replied. "You see those two large pipes," I said, pointing the beam of my flashlight. "Well, I'm trying to figure out what they were for."

I tore at a piece of hanging ceiling tile and it instantly disintegrated in my hand. I coughed, inhaling some of the dust. It tasted foul in my mouth, and I spat out what I could and wiped the rest with my arm.

"Watch it!" cried Anita "I want the news not the bloody weather, come on, let's go."

"No, hang on, I think I see something," I said.

"Look, there's a capital letter 'C' and small 'l' on one of the pipes and a letter 'S' on the other."

"That's easy," said Anita. "'Cl' is for clean water and the 'S' is for shit. I think you found the toilet pipes."

"Not a bad guess," I said encouragingly, "but I think they're actual element symbols. 'Cl' . . . what did that stand for on the Periodic table?"

I thought for a moment and then had it. "Chlorine," I said with certainty. "But what was a pipe of Chlorine doing down here?"

"Maybe they had a swimming pool?" suggested my cousin.

"Well, that is a better guess," I said, "but I'm thinking the 'S' is for Sulphur, so I don't think they wanted pool water that smelled like rotten eggs."

"Unless maybe they were French?" said Anita.

Our laughter echoed through the great hall and again it felt wrong. It was like laughing at a funeral, but then I remembered I had done just that at Flossy's a couple days earlier.

Eventually, we reconvened at the base of the stairs. Uncle Tom stood on the bottom step and motioned his arms for silence.

"I need your word that you won't say anything about this." I had never seen my uncle so serious and to exaggerate his point, he waved his half finger at all of us. "Let me talk to Bo Snatch before we decide on anything. I have a feeling this place was never meant to be found, so the less said, the better."

"Loose lips sink ships," added Nigel, clutching his newly found whistle.

"Yes, very good," replied Tom, a little irritated at being interrupted. "As far as anyone up top goes, all we found was a big storm drain. We all clear, Secret Seven? Ok good, then let's go."

Outside, I was confident I had found the spot. The boulder I sat on seemed to line-up exactly with Great Uncle Googly's painting. The sun felt warm after the abandoned bunker, and I was grateful just to sit and soak away the chill. I still wondered what my Great Grandfather William Clover knew about the tunnel. *Maybe nothing, maybe something? Strange,* I thought, *that the tunnel was dated around the time Clover and Sons stopped production, and yet the brick job would have paid a crap load of money.*

Standing, I opened my fly. I really needed to piss, and having no real target in mind, I aimed at the long grass in front of me.

"Whatch got there, cuz!?" shouted Anita as she climbed up the embankment.

"Something so large and dangerous you're not allowed to see it," I answered.

Waving my pee around, I noticed a small rock. It was flattish and sort of round and since practice was practice, I directed my wiz dead on centre. It took a while to finish, and if nothing else, I impressed my cousin by sheer volume.

"Bloody hell, that was like ten pints," she remarked.

The wet rock glistened in the sunlight, but something on its smooth surface looked out of place.

"Hey, take a look at that," I said.

"No thanks, I don't have my magnifying glass."

"On the rock, I mean. Look, there's something scratched on it."

She came over and crouched down. "R.C.," she replied.

"Exactly," I agreed. "Rob Clover. Do you think that's what he meant when he told you his painting could be worth something one day?"

"He was a crafty one, that's for sure," she said. "Hand me his painting, will ya? I wanna look at it again."

I passed her the rolled-up painting and waited.

"Considering he was a shit painter," she said after a minute, "I reckon you're on to something. Do you think there's treasure under it, you know, like 'X' marks the spot?"

There was only one way to find out, and picking up a small dead branch, I pried the stone out of its pocket of earth.

"Are you helping?" I asked my cousin.

"I don't think so, it smells like piss," she replied.

It was tough work, considering I had no tools. My stick broke after only a few jabs and resigning myself to scooping and clawing at the soil, it wasn't long before my fingers started to hurt.

"What you laughing at?" I said, looking up.

"Nothing," she replied. "It just looks like you're taking a shit."

"Thanks a lot," I said unimpressed. "I'll have you know last week I took a poo in a vacuum cleaner and . . ."

"And what?" asked Anita.

"Hang on, I found something."

Below, I could see what looked like edges to a small metal box. Possibly brass or tin, I wasn't sure, but whatever it was, it wasn't in very good shape.

Carefully, I removed enough soil to dislodge the rectangle and pulled it from the hole. It wasn't very big, maybe three by five inches and an inch or so deep. I could just make out a head stamped in the centre of the lid and a few letters with the date 1914.

"What do you think?" I said showing the box to Anita.

"Cool, it's a Princess Mary box," she replied.

"A what?" I asked a little confused.

"Granddad had one. They're from the First World War. Apparently, some princess thought it would be a good idea to send a box of fags and tobacco to the troops on the front line for Christmas."

I looked down again at the date and saw enough letters to see that it was in fact the word "Christmas" embossed on the tin.

"Maybe the day wasn't a total waste," said Anita "Open it. You never know, there could still be some stale ciggies in there."

I set it down on the large boulder and tried to work the lid. The original hinge was long gone, but after a few persuasive pulls, the cover popped off with a jolt.

"Sorry, cuz," I said, looking inside. "No ciggies today, but there is something here."

It was an odd-looking thing and I lifted it out of the tin and held it up to the light.

"What is it?" she asked as we both stared at a small blob of yellowish metal.

"I think it's gold," I said, blowing off some dust and turning it in my hand.

It felt rough on my fingers like grit in a skinned knee, and looking closer, I could see tiny particles of red clay infused with the metal.

"That's odd," I said. "There's bits of brick mixed in with it. How did that happen?"

I palmed the metal glob and gripped it tightly. *Is this the Clover Treasure?* I thought. *One shitty nugget?* I looked down the embankment and stared at the tunnel entrance.

"Come on, Uncle Googly," I said. "What are you trying to show me?"

I looked again at the perfect Clover bricks. It was the first time I had seen a major structure with the quality of brick I had heard so much about. *Why then,* I thought, *are all the bricks my relatives have such crappy examples?* I let the question hang for a moment, then stared down at the metal glob one more time.

"Holy shit," I said out loud, realizing I had it all wrong.

It wasn't what Googs was trying to show me that mattered, it was what he wasn't showing me—no cracks, even after all those years.

"Hey, cuz," I called to Anita halfway down the hill. "I think I just figured it out."

I took a clay pottery course once. Among the shitty things I made was a bust of my head. It looked shrunken and not very lifelike, but I did learn the hard way that if there were pockets of trapped air or impurities, clay would crack or even explode in the kiln. The memory of me patching my clay head back together ran through my brain as I stared at the blood-stained Clover brick. It lay before me on my cousin's kitchen table, emitting a strong, acrid odour of cat pee.

Fuck it, I said to myself, finishing the last of Anita's tequila. *It's time to see if my theory is correct.* I picked up her pink hammer and whacked the obvious fault line along the side of the brick. Instantly, the brick broke in two, one half clunked to the table, the other remained in my hand.

"Well, what's in it?" asked Anita as I turned the brick on its end.

"Nothing," I said. "I thought for sure I was on to something."

"Well, don't feel bad, cuz. I'm sure you're not the first to be duped by the Clover treasure." She opened her kitchen cabinet and produced another bottle of alcohol. "Here, drink this," she said, pouring a clear liquid into my dirty glass.

I took a long pull, then lifted the other half of the brick just to make sure.

"Well piss on me and tell me it's raining," I said feeling the alcohol burn. "That's it."

I reached for the hammer again, and this time there was no holding back. I smashed at the clay until all that was left was a mess of broken chips on my cousin's white tablecloth.

Between the bits of brick, there was an unmistakable familiar blob. It looked exactly like the metal we had found earlier, and I reached into my pocket and placed it on the table. They were identical, there was no deny it. Whatever Googly had found all those years ago, our brick, without a doubt, had come from the same exact place.

Chapter 34

As much as he tried, the Time Keeper's attempt at self-analysis was getting him nowhere. In his opinion, there were two types of people in the Narrows. Those that had no idea where they were and those that chose to stay. Neither, he concluded, fit his present state, and for the life or death of him, the Time Keeper had no answers as to why he still remained.

If he had to be honest, he still had a bad taste in his mouth from his meeting at the Maunsell sea fort. Everyone had seemed so tethered to their previous life; he hadn't expected their unwillingness to even consider moving on. Afterwards, as he gathered the empty mugs, he still couldn't believe he was the one accused of upsetting the German. He had only mentioned the war once, but it hadn't mattered. The past was their present, and sadly, he believed, they felt it was a better place to be than trusting the unknown.

The one man that still confused the Time Keeper was his friend the Axe Man. He certainly wasn't too tired to fight, nor was he the slightest bit scared of leaving the Narrows. *No*, thought the Time Keeper, *he has chosen to stay by his own free will*. The Time Keeper already knew the reason, but still it made no sense. He had stayed because he wasn't going to leave his son. Whether from guilt, love, or obligation, it didn't matter, it wasn't his business.

"So what was the point?" he asked himself again. "What was greater than self-preservation?"

His initial answer was "nothing" but he wasn't convinced anymore. The Axe Man certainly didn't believe it. He believed his connection with his son meant more than existence itself.

"Of course," said the Time Keeper, "that's it. That's what I'm missing. It's having the faith to believe in something that I need."

He thought he had some once, but that was long ago. Faith, the Time Keeper had to admit, was a beautiful thing. In ways, he was jealous of those that found something to believe in. It didn't even matter what in the end. As far as the Time Keeper was concerned, they were the lucky ones. They were the ones that felt genuine meaning in places that had none.

"Well, fuck it," he announced. "If faith and belief won't come to me, then I'll try and find some myself."

He thought about where he would start. *A church maybe? A funeral? Now I'm getting somewhere. Hospitals,* he thought, *yes definitely hospitals, lots of praying and believing going on there.*

"Why hadn't I thought about this sooner?" he asked. "This is going to be a snap. All I need to do is figure out how to believe in something and I'll have my way out."

My mother spent a lifetime believing in something she couldn't see. Beyond her spells of insanity and desire to own a chicken, her main occupation in life was a professional hypochondriac. Her faith was strong, and by far, her crowning achievement was the lobbying and eventual amputation of her second largest toe. It was sad to think of how much pain she inflicted on herself through the years. Even when the nerve of her toe had been removed, her agony was still as real as a knife to the back.

I did manage to visit her the night before her operation. For reasons unknown, even to myself, she allowed me to cast a mould of her foot which later I bronzed. I think my mother was always proud of her metal foot. She kept pencils in it on her desk and I often wondered if she saw it as some type of memorial to her unwavering faith.

But sadly, the operation did little to rid her of the pain. The next day, my mother discovered the toe on her other foot had started to hurt, and so the process continued, destined to repeat forever.

There was always a sense of pride walking through Brick Field estates. Wiggins, the land developer who eventually bought the final Shirley House acreage, decided it would be a grand gesture to name all the roads after the Clover family tree. I walked to the end of Clover Road and stopped.

"Oh shit," I said, seeing a police car parked halfway up William's Crescent.

It was right outside Maury's shop, and thinking the worst, I broke into a run. Reaching her main door, I saw the glass had been completely smashed. My mind raced with images of a second bloody murder, and I opened the door hoping not to be a witness, once again, to another bashed in head. To my relief, the first person I saw was Maury. She was crouching down with a dustpan, and I had nearly whacked her in the head with the door as she swept up the remaining broken glass.

"What the hell happened?" I gasped, out of breath.

"Someone broke in last night," she explained. "Don't know what they wanted, but it doesn't look like anything was taken. Probably a couple of shithead kids from around the corner."

"Nothing?" I asked, a bit puzzled.

"Nope, nothing as far as I can tell."

Standing behind her was none other than Detective Grimshaw. He had on a pair of latex gloves, and holding a small fine brush, I presumed he was dusting for fingerprints.

"I've been looking for you," he said, stopping and removing his gloves. "You're a hard one to track down."

"Well, I'm here now, what's up?" I said innocently.

"What's up is that I need to ask you a few questions," he said with a tone of annoyance. "Is that yours?" he said, pointing to my backpack sitting on a chair.

"Yes," I said. "What do you want with it?"

"We got a tip that possibly you were in possession of a suspicious Clover brick. You wouldn't by chance be carrying one, would you?"

I held my arms out as if I was ready to be patted down and shook my head. "I don't know anything about suspicious bricks," I replied, "but I have some suspicious underwear if you want to go ahead and search."

Grim blew into his gloves and put them back onto his hands. He said nothing as he placed the items of my pack on the counter.

"What's this?" he said, pulling out a small plastic bag from a side pocket. Holding up the bag, Grim looked at the two yellowish globs and waited for an answer.

"I don't know. I found them in the garden," I replied. "What do you think they are?"

Grim only opened the bag for a second before resealing it closed.

"God, what is that smell?" he demanded.

"Cat piss, I think," I replied.

He placed the plastic bag on top of the heap of my clothes and sighed. "Alright, you're clean, pack it up."

"You're not going to help?" I asked, slightly indignant.

"I've got more pressing issues to deal with at the moment," he snorted. "By the way," Grim continued, "that Reggie chap from Meals on Wheels seems to be missing in action. Turns out the home address he gave us was a vacant building lot, and no one at the Meals on Wheels' office has any idea who he is."

"That is strange," I said. "He gave me a ride. Seemed like a decent enough bloke."

"You never know these days who you can trust," said the detective. "Count yourself lucky he didn't bash your head in as well."

I stopped my repacking and looked up. "Are you telling me you think he was the killer?"

"Not yet," said Grim, putting his hands on his hips, "but let's just say I have a couple men tracking down every red Ford Escort in Essex."

Once Grimshaw had left, Maury and I waited for Burt to return with a new piece of glass for the door.

"Hey, Maury," I said with a mouth full of biscuit, "any idea where the Clover and Sons ledger books ended up?"

"Don't talk with your mouth full, dear," she said, pouring herself another mug of tea.

I waited while she sipped, and then instead of another reprimand, she answered my question.

"Gave all that kind of stuff to the man who wrote the very first article on the Hambro Hill brick fields. What was his name now? Such a nice man, Nevel, yes that was it. Anyway, I imagine if they're still around, they're on some dusty old shelf at the Brick Society in London. Maybe give them a ring if you're that interested."

I was just about to ask if she ever heard of the Clover Company supplying bricks to the military when Burt walked in.

"Give us a hand, would ya?" he asked. "Just a bit awkward for one person."

I got up and carefully helped Burt bring in the new glass from his car. We positioned it in the door and I held the loose glass while Burt went and found the window putty.

"Don't you think we should tack it in place?" I asked when he came back.

"No, no, as long as we're careful, the putty should hold it until it's dry."

I watched as he patted and smoothed the putty to an almost perfect bevel edge then stepped back and stretched, satisfied at a job well done.

"Pretty good job if I do say so myself," he said. "No need to hold it now."

I stepped back and let Burt shut the door gently. Everything looked good until the door connected with the frame, and as all three of us watched, the new glass promptly fell out and smashed on the freshly swept floor.

"Feels like I just bloody did this," said Maury, tipping her dustpan of broken glass into the bin.

I laughed and thought back to Burt's complete meltdown twenty minutes earlier. He wasn't happy, but in the end, he had no choice. He put his pride back in his pocket and trudged down to the local DIY centre one more time.

"Oh, I nearly forgot," said Maury, tucking her broom away behind a display case. "In all the excitement, I forgot to give you back Rob's paintings."

She walked over to the cash register and pulled at a drawer somewhere underneath. "They're gone," she said, her face pale with shock. "What the hell?"

"I don't know, Maury, but something tells me you have your motive for the break-in."

"They were just shitty little paintings," said Maury.

"Maybe, maybe not," I replied, "but I think it's time I told you what I've been up to."

With Maury seated, I explained how I had come to find Rob's buried Princess Mary box. I also reasoned how the triangulation formula on the back of Rob's painting had led me to believe Great Uncle Rob was way smarter than everyone had thought. She looked at me bemused. It wasn't the reaction I was expecting, but I waited until she spoke.

"He was a sly old dodger, that was for sure. Come to think of it, he would say some bloody strange things. Half the time I thought he was off his rocker. The box you found was his father's, William Clover. Rob had it on his mantle after his father died. I remember now, yes that's right, it went missing one day. I'm sure that cow Flossy thought I'd pinched it. So, what are you thinking, young man? Are there more buried clues in Rob's stolen paintings?"

I looked up at her and nodded. Suddenly things had become serious.

"You know there had to be a reason why Floss never wanted you to have those paintings. I'm sure it was more than just trying to piss you off." I opened the plastic bag and handed her the two encrusted globs. "One," I explained, "came from the buried box, the other, from a Clover brick I broke open yesterday."

"Well, they look the same to me," admitted Maury.

"If my hunch is correct, and these blobs turn out to be gold, then I think we have definite proof that not only does the Clover treasure exist, but also where it was hidden."

Maury closed her eyes, and I could tell she was holding back tears. "I knew it," she confessed. "Goddamn Flossy, after all those years. I wonder if she knew all along?"

"I don't think so," I replied. "I have a feeling Great Uncle Rob made sure she was the last person to know anything."

"Hang on a minute," said Maury. "I've got something you need to see."

I followed her up the stairs to the second floor. She led me along a hallway and stopped at a closed door.

"This use to be Don's room before he died," she explained. "I have to confess I haven't bothered doing much with the room since. Nowadays, it's more of a junk room and a place to store extra stock."

We entered and manoeuvred around a stack of boxes. I followed her to a bookcase on the far side of the room, and she bent down to search the bottom shelf. Looking around, I felt I was standing in the room of a child. A photograph of a biplane hung above a well-made bed, and I couldn't help notice the sheets and pillow cases were all printed with Action Man characters. A model of a boat sat on the windowsill, and I recognized the Golden Eagle, a long-gone passenger boat that use to ferry people around the Thames estuary.

By Maury's triumphant grunt, I figured she had found what she was looking for. She straitened up and held out an overstuffed green scrapbook.

"Here," she announced handing it to me. "It's Don's," she said. "Anything brick related, that boy kept it all."

I sat on the bed and opened the book. It was crammed with loose newspaper clippings, old photographs, maps, magazine articles, and even a few handmade drawings.

"What's this?" I asked Maury, holding up a faded pamphlet.

"Oh, that was one of our brochures when we first opened. That was when old Donny was still making bricks in the back garden," she said smiling. "You'll probably want the phone number on that blue thing," she added, pointing to an old issue of the British Brick Society magazine.

I turned it over and read the back. "Mr. Oliver—Honourary Secretary." And noting his official contact number, I put the book off to one side.

A few pages later, I came across two old Polaroid photographs. One was of an over-exposed picture of a dog, but the other was of my Great Uncle Don sporting his charismatic goofy grin.

"You found it," said Maury "That's what I wanted to show you."

From what I could make out, the photo was taken in Maury's back garden. Don had his arm around another man who smiled, almost mimicking Don's expression. Behind them, in the background, was a row of freshly moulded clay bricks which appeared to have a small stone placed on the top of each one.

"What the hell?" I said, "That's incredible."

Maury was smiling. "I told you you were going to want to see it. Put a shilling in the pood, just like old dear father would. That's what he used to sing, every bloody day."

"Who's the guy with Don?" I asked.

"That's Nevel, the man who first wrote about the Hambro Hill brick fields."

I looked again, sensing something familiar about the man. He wore a short sleeve shirt and tie, his hair full and parted down the middle. It took another moment, but then it came to me with all the force of a head on collision. Without a doubt, the figure standing next to Don was a much younger version of Meals on Wheels' Reggie.

Chapter 35

Switching on a desk lamp and removing his jacket, Nevel sat and opened the packet of stolen paintings. He tipped the contents onto the desk, and still smelling a faint whiff of petrol, covered his mouth and yawned.

He counted the cardboard canvases—there were twenty in all. He placed them randomly in four rows of five, and methodically scrutinized each one as he held them up to the light.

"Think, Nev," he said to himself. "What's so important about these damn paintings?"

He yawned again and looked at the wall clock. It was nearly 4 a.m. Despite his body's urge to go to bed, Nevel went to the kitchen and switched on the kettle. He opened the fridge, hoping to find something to fill his rumbling stomach, and ten minutes later, he was sipping tea and eating the remains of a two-day old curry.

The sun wasn't due to rise for another hour, but he looked out of his kitchen window anyway. There was the familiar orange glow of the lamp posts standing guard, and above his neighbour's house, he thought he could make out the Big Dipper. Nothing moved, no cars, no people. In many ways, this was his favourite time of the day, and he savoured the moment by closing his eyes and feeling the calm he rarely was able to find.

He woke suddenly with a jolt, spilling the remainder of his tea. He wiped the floor with his sock and after brushing down his sweater, Nevel walked back to his study. It had started to become light outside. Nevel glanced at that the wall clock and was surprised it now read five thirty-six. *How quickly time passes,* he thought, *literally in the blink of an eye.*

He sat and decided to give the paintings one final look. He scanned the cards one last time and sighed. Any clue would do, it didn't matter what.

All he needed was just one small thread that would lead him to finally unravelling the Clover Treasure mystery.

There was no question the treasure existed. His dealings with Don and Maury over the years had left little doubt in his mind. The gold was there, pushed into wet Clover bricks like Don had demonstrated with small garden stones. *The only problem,* thought Nevel, *is simply finding out where the bricks went.*

Growing frustrated, he turned over each painting. Once again, he inspected the sections of the world map that made up Rob Clover's homemade canvases. Some of the cards were blank. Others had captions describing their corresponding scenes, and a few had full length folk tales scrawled in tiny, faded print. He read one called "The Shrieking Boy" and another about the Devil seeking shelter in a storm. *What a load of rubbish,* he thought, taking off his glasses and rubbing his eyes.

It was time for bed, he decided, and leaned over to turn off the desk lamp. As he reached for the switch, he absently moved one of the map pieces with his arm. It was a subtle, insignificant event, but somewhere in the recesses of Nevel's memory, an image came to mind that stopped him dead.

The image was of a puzzle he had played with as a boy. A small, cheap plastic tablet where you could slide tiles around until eventually you formed a picture. Looking now at the map pieces, Nevel couldn't believe he had missed such an obvious clue. It took only seconds to rearrange the pieces, and when he was finished, he found he had not one, but the majority of two complete pages of the world map atlas.

Nevel turned over the top left rectangle of the first page.

"Shirley House," he said, reading the title at the bottom of the painting. "That seems like a good start."

If his assumption was correct, and Rob Clover had used the map pieces in order, then the next painting should logically connect to the first.

"Well, I'll be damned," he said, reading the caption scrawled on the back of painting two. "Looking east from the parlour window."

"Ok," continued Nevel. "Let's try for three." Flipping over Rob Clover's third painting, Nevel grinned. "Bingo," he said, staring at a close-up rendition of Rayleigh Church.

The trail was there, it was plain as day. Each scene connected to the next with one common detail. Painting one was the family house. If you looked out of the parlour window of Shirley House, you had a scene of several fields with Rayleigh church in the distance. Painting three was Rayleigh church in full frame with the village of Rayleigh in the background. Nevel flipped the next card, and the next. It all held true. They were all a series of painted snapshots that showed a path directly through the Essex countryside. *Incredible,* thought Nevel, *the old bastard knew all along.*

Unfortunately, the second page of the atlas was not as complete. Nevel had managed to skip several missing pieces without losing the trail, but when he came to a painting of a river, windmill, and an old sailboat, he had to stop.

The problem was that there were three pieces missing between the river scene and the final painting. Nevel could think of at least three rivers that Rob Clover could have painted, but without some other identifying detail, he was well and truly stuck.

Nevel turned over the last scene. He hoped he could somehow recognize the location, but there was nothing unique about a commoner's thatched cottage. A woman and her dog could be seen walking up the front garden path, and Nevel was certain that this was where Rob Clover's hunt had ended.

Whether the bricks were laid on purpose or by accident, Nevel didn't care. All he knew was that somewhere, near a river, by an Essex windmill, a treasure awaited that he believed was rightfully his.

Chapter 36

The flat was empty when I arrived at London Bridge. I turned on the kitchen light, then glanced through the living room window, marvelling at how different the city looked at night. I had a lot to think about since my visit with Maury. The image of Don with Reggie, or Nevel, had really thrown me for a loop, and it was now clear that his appearance on the day I found Flossy's body had not been a coincidence.

The previous day, I had managed to get hold of Mr. Oliver from the British Brick Society. He seemed a nice enough bloke, but when I asked about a member named Nevel Fink, I sensed a hesitation at the other end of the line.

"You see, we had a little trouble with that member," he began. "A bit overzealous might be a good way to put it. Unfortunately, we had some complaints regarding his conduct. A little too aggressive was the general consensus, and sadly a few weeks ago, he assaulted one of our guest speakers. We had no choice but to revoke his membership. As a lifetime member myself," continued Mr. Oliver, "I understand how us brick lovers can get pretty wound up over things, but that sort of behaviour was just inexcusable."

Before I rang off, Mr. Oliver had suggested contacting the Brick Development Association in London about Clover memorabilia. He explained they often stored items for the society, but without any official list, as far as he knew, there could be pieces of Stonehenge still sitting there.

To take my mind off things, I turned on the television and watched a cooking show with two rather large women wearing motorcycle helmets. They were just about to extract a blancmange from a Victorian pineapple mould when I heard footsteps climbing the final set of stairs.

Peter appeared in the doorway, followed closely by my old friend, Russell. Russell had dispersed with his cardboard arm and was now carrying a rather large shoulder bag.

"Hey, Potato Man," I said. "How's it going?"

"Not so good," Russell replied. "Had a bit of a disagreement with my new flatmates," he admitted.

He swore to me he didn't know anyone was home when he had mixed stolen pool chlorine with acid he had smuggled out of school.

"All I was trying to do was fumigate the place," he said with genuine sincerity. "I hate rats. Ok, the cat, I admit, I should have thought about, but what a bunch of pussy roommates. Just because we all lost a bit of consciousness, I didn't think they needed to call an ambulance."

I could tell he was still really annoyed, so to take his mind off the pending lawsuit, I tried to put a positive spin on things.

"How did you ever figure out how to combine acid with chlorine?" I asked with mild interest.

"Easy," replied Russell. "I've been reading a lot about toxic gases lately. My main source was this old turn of the century chemistry book I found in the Science library. Turns out, mustard gas was pretty nasty stuff back in the First World War, and though it was banned by some sort of convention, both the Germans and the British had some up their sleeves."

My gut had started to twist before I asked the next question. "Tell me again, what kind of acid do you mix with chlorine to make mustard gas?"

"Sulphuric," replied Russell.

I closed my eyes and knew exactly what had been going on at the secret tunnel bunker at Cold Norton. It all made sense. A brick job paid in cash, trains arriving in the middle of the night, even wet clay bricks to hide secret money. No wonder, it was a complete hush job. Cold Norton was a secret lab experimenting in chemical warfare. The last piece of proof I needed was to find the Clover Brick account ledgers. If there were no entries recording purchases or deliveries to the British military, then it would confirm a top-secret government agenda right under everyone's noses.

"I got something for you, Russell," I said, keeping my thoughts to myself. "Here, I want you to take a look at these."

I handed him a plastic bag containing the two yellow encrusted globs.

"Any idea what it could be?"

Russell held up the baggie and looked. "Well, it's defiantly some kind of metal," he said.

"Do you think it's gold?" I asked with an inflection of hope.

"Not sure about that," replied Russell. "Could be lead, could be a lot of things. Any idea of a date?"

"Somewhere around 1909, 1910," I answered.

He looked at me for a second and I could see his interest peak. "What's with all the crusty shit?" he asked.

"Brick dust," I replied. "Both of the blobs were found in the middle of fired clay bricks."

"Why would anyone put metal into a brick around the First World War? Maybe some sort of military purpose?" he thought out loud.

"What do you mean?" I asked.

"That science book I read had a chapter on the early development of radiation and nuclear applications. I'm wondering if what you've got here is some prototype for gamma ray protection."

Russell could see I looked a bit disappointed. My entire theory hinged on the blobs being made of gold.

"I'll tell ya what. Leave them with me and I'll take them to school tomorrow," offered Russell. "There's a couple of mates that owe me some favours at the lab. We'll run some tests and then we'll know for sure."

I found the Brick Development Association just off Bloomsbury Road. It wasn't hard to miss. The building dominated the quaint surrounding area, and I pushed the revolving doors and stepped into the lobby.

"Who are you looking for?" asked a security guard, putting down his newspaper

He seemed a little accusing, and I sighed, sensing it was going to be one of those days where everything took twice as long.

"No one gets upstairs without a pass," said the guard, looking smug.

"Ok," I replied. "How do I get one?"

He turned and handed me a green piece of paper. "You fill this out and then mail it in, shouldn't take more than a couple of weeks."

"Yeah, no, that's not gonna work, I'm afraid. Can you just make a call and let someone know I'm here?"

The security guard, obviously put out by my inconvenient request, got up, walked to the other end of his desk, then lifted the telephone receiver. I waited, and then waited some more until finally a well-dressed man in a grey business suit stepped out of the elevator and approached.

"You must be the young man wanting to see some historical brick records?" he asked with a cheery tone.

"Yes," I said, shaking his hand, "but why all the hassle?"

"Hassle?" the man asked, looking puzzled.

"Oh, just your security guard," I said, motioning to the man reading his newspaper again. "He's a bit of a dick."

The man from the Development Association, surprisingly, didn't miss a beat.

"Ah, yes well we're all a bit on edge at the moment since the fire. We had a photocopier catch alight yesterday, and we were all a bit put off having to leave the building. Nothing damaged, but I imagine it could have been a lot worse."

He led me back to the elevator and we descended two floors to the sub-basement level. At the first door we came to, my well-dressed chaperone pulled out a pass card and swiped it over a locking mechanism. The door hissed open automatically, and lights began turning on above us. We walked down the hallway, passing several more doors, then stopped at one marked "Records Room." I waited again while a multi-digit code was punched into a security pad, and I heard the click of the door lock confirming our authorization.

"This is the one you want," my escort said, tapping a clear plastic box the size of a large microwave. "Gets requested all the time. Just let me know when you're done, and I'll take you back upstairs. Oh and just remember," he added, starting to walk away, "big brother is watching." And he pointed to a small black camera mounted on the ceiling.

Well, I thought, giving him the thumbs-up, *if building security depends on buddy at the front desk, then they are all in serious trouble.*

I heaved the box off the shelf and placed it on the floor. Removing the lid, the first and most obvious object I saw was a brick. I couldn't help but feel somewhat of an authority on Clover brick quality, and lifting it up, I came to the conclusion it was a rather shit example. Flipping it over, I read the words on the brick's frog.

"D. Clover," I said with a smile.

Somehow, one of Don's demonstration bricks from Maury's back garden had found its way to the B.B.S. I remembered the photo from his scrapbook, and I bet dollars to doughnuts a small stone was hidden within the clay.

Putting Don's brick to the side, I next lifted out a plastic bag with the 1972 May issue of the British Brick Society newsletter. I unzipped the baggie and leafed through the publication.

"Hambro Hill brick field and the Clover's Buried Treasure," I read.

In my hands was the story that had started it all. One three-page article that unbelievably had stirred so much public interest, and most alarmingly, caused the brutal murder of my great aunt. It was credited to Nevel Fink. *If that is truly Reggie's real name,* I thought, *then it is probably time to pass this information on to Detective Grim.*

Next, I pulled out a very worn wooden brick mould. It was simple with no more than a few pieces of wood fitted together. There was no question it was original, and I wondered how many thousands of bricks it had produced.

Then finally, with the florescent lighting buzzing above me, I pulled out the last identical items—two black, well-worn, leather binders. At a quick glance, the first book I opened was clearly the Clover Accounts Payable ledger. The earliest entry dated to 1905, and flicking through the pages, I found multiple entries for tools, horses, fuel, and most importantly, wages.

"One pound, sixteen shillings, and ten pence," I said not, knowing if that was a good or bad weekly wage.

I flicked to the last entry on October 25th, 1910. There were only a handful of general expenses listed but surprisingly about the same number of employees. *So what the hell happened?* I thought, picking up the second binder.

"Ok, now we're getting somewhere," I said, realizing I was holding the Clover Accounts Receivables.

As far as I could see, things had been going well. Clover Bricks had a steady list of clients, and it was only getting better with the addition of a railway siding that connected onto the main London line.

Not until the middle of 1909 did I notice a downward trend. Nothing in any side ledger indicted a reason, but it was obvious that something had plummeted sales to only a few local house builders. Cross-checking, I looked back at the accounts payable and compared the outgoing expenses to the decrease in revenue. Everything seemed normal. The number of employees stayed the same, and I realized it wasn't until the last year of the Clover Brick Company that funds started to hemorrhage left, right and centre.

So why wait to lay-off workers and cut down expenses? It all seemed like bad business unless, I suspected, William Clover was bankrolling his company with cash. Gold coins, to be precise. Out of curiosity, I skimmed the last few delivery entries of Clover Brick's final days.

One delivery was for Rayleigh Church, apparently for an addition to the rectory. Another was for the post office in Rayleigh High Street, and still another was for the rebuilding of the public toilets at Rayleigh Mount.

It was only when I read one of the last deliveries was for a cracked windmill foundation, that I realized I knew all of those places. Not because I had driven by them or actually visited the sites, but because they were the locations of Uncle Googly Eyes' paintings. They all matched. Every single one of them.

"Holy crap," I said out loud. "Old Rob's paintings were trying to tell me something after all."

I cursed, knowing that it did little good now. The paintings were gone, and though I had company names and delivery addresses, without the corresponding paintings, I had little chance of deciphering what the exact connection was. Turning to the last page, my disappointment sank even lower. The final delivery entry began on the last line.

"Delivery to builder, Tom Shelly. Ten standard pallets of brick to the site location of—"

And then, nothing. The rest of the entry on the following page was missing. I could see the tear marks where the final entry had been removed, and I stared dumbly in disbelief. Someone had beaten me to it. *Fuck,* I thought, *and fuck the security guy, and even his dog if he has one.* I was screwed. Without that final address, any hopes of discovering a message from beyond Googly's grave, was gone.

I wasn't in a particularly talkative mood as I walked back to the elevator. I was pissed, and my escort, sensing my mood, was wise to say nothing. As we waited for the elevator, the silence was broken by a rumble of wheels. Turning, I watched a maintenance man push a charbroiled photocopier toward us. He was yelling to hold the elevator, but it still hadn't arrived by the time he rolled up.

"Not every day a photocopier spontaneously combusts," said my escort, grateful for the interruption.

The man looked at me and I saw he was a little unsure of what to say. "Well, no harm done in the end," he said. "Besides, this building used to be some sort of bunker in the Second World War. Don't suppose there was much chance of the fire spreading."

Whether that was true or not, it didn't matter. What I did sense though was the maintenance guy was not telling the whole truth. He kept looking at the man in the grey suit, and when I said my goodbyes on the main level, I slowed my exit just enough to hear their conversation mention the words "tampered" and "no accident."

It was a stretch, but I couldn't help wondering if possibly the fire was set to destroy something in the storage facilities, maybe even the Clover Brick ledgers. It was a bit far-fetched, but if someone could bash an old lady with a brick, I wouldn't have put it past them to try and set a building on fire.

As I left, the security clerk was diligently working his way through a ham and tomato sandwich. Behind him, several monitor screens went unattended, and if I had really thought about it, I could have mooned the cameras, and no one would have been the wiser.

Personally, I've only been naked twice in public. The first, I had no control over at Dave's stag night, but the other, I was fully aware of my intentions.

The occasion was my ass-faxing party on the last day of my warehouse job. It was time to move on anyway, *but what better way,* I thought, *to close the door on another chapter of my life, than to sit on a photocopier and fax the image to my least favourite manager.* If I had only written the words "kiss my ass" across the two white cheek impressions, all would have been well. Instead, I decided to do the honourable thing and signed my name to it.

It was, in all sincerity, a purposeful act of intent. I had come to the conclusion that in life, some bridges were meant to be burned, and for the first time in my life, I took control of my future. Never again would I be hired by that company, and I saw it as more of an insurance policy against forgetting how miserable the job actually was.

As always, my buttocks served me well. They had even reached legendary status by the time I called to get my old job back a year later. I could have really used the money, but an ass fax was an ass fax, and there was no chance of a rehire.

I never regretted my goodbye party. I know my younger cocky self always had my best interest at heart. Not only did I learn how to quit a job in style, but I taught my elder future self that I was worth much more.

Chapter 37

I almost didn't recognize the Time Keeper. He stood leaning against the wall of Southwark Cathedral, and if not for his robe, I would have dismissed him as another homeless street vagrant.

"What are you doing here?" I asked, exhausted from my walk.

"Just came out of a funeral," he replied.

"And how was that?"

I waited as the Time Keeper pulled his robes over his head.

"That's better," he said, finally pulling his costume free. "Yeah, the funeral was very interesting. All a bit of a laugh."

"How's that?" I said, thinking death usually took the "fun" out of "funeral."

"Well," said the Time Keeper, "I mainly sat with the dead guy and watched how badly everyone overacted."

"Did you know him?" I asked.

"Nope," he replied. "I also went to a wedding there yesterday," he said, changing the subject, "and last night crashed a birth at Guy's Hospital across the street."

"Why would you do that?" I asked.

"To find out what people believe of course. Thought maybe I could believe it too."

I stared at him for a moment not knowing how to respond.

"Hum," I finally grunted. "I'm not sure belief is something you can really sign-up for. I think it usually goes the other way around."

"Maybe you're right," agreed the Time Keeper, somewhat deflated. "To be honest, I don't think I felt it anywhere. First off, funerals are for the living. Can't say it does the dead any good, except for the entertainment

208

value. It's more like a question of hope than belief. I mean, no one knows for sure what comes next, so just in case living isn't a total waste of time, people show up at funerals, to at least pretend the dead are going somewhere. The wedding was just as bad. If there's anything close to 'belief' at a wedding, I would rephrase it as 'thin cautionary optimism.' You should have heard it. One couple was wagering if the marriage would last more than eighteen months, and others were guessing if it would be the bride or groom who would cheat first."

"What about Guy's Hospital?" I asked, looking for some positivity.

"Now that was something. A birth is a true fucking miracle. One of the purest things I have ever witnessed. Wouldn't say the room was full of belief, but you couldn't help but feel some kind of reset with a newborn."

I had to agree, but looking at the Time Keeper, I could tell something still troubled him. "So what's wrong?" I asked. "You look like shit."

It took a moment, but I had guessed correctly.

"You know, there's a reason why I didn't go with you to the tunnel?"

"Did that have something to do with the bunker?" I replied.

"You found it," said the Time Keeper. "Wasn't sure you would."

"Well, you can thank Cousin Drunk for that," I said.

"Any idea what it was used for?" asked the Time Keeper.

"Best guess," I said, "some kind of chemical warfare experiment, mustard or chlorine gas, I think."

"Spot on, Charlie Brown," he replied. "But what you don't know, and why the place had to be abandoned, was that there was an accident in the underground labs. You'll never hear about it, but a lovely cloud of that mustard shit escaped out of the facility. It lingered for a while, killing a few farm animals, but then it drifted east, and finally settled on the grounds of a local primary school. Any idea what mustard gas does?" he asked, turning toward me. "Well, I'll tell you. It burns away the soft skin first. You know, behind the knees, under the pits, the tissue of your eyes. Then it goes for the lining of your lungs and closes up your throat. Beyond the blistering, you end up drowning to death from fluid build-up in the chest. What a nasty way to go," said the Time Keeper, shaking his head. "Seventeen children died that day, and you know what else? None of them knew they were dead."

"So they're trapped in the Narrows?" I asked, beginning to understand the horror.

"It's fucking terrible," said the Time Keeper. "I can't go there anymore. Even for me, their cries and screams still curdle my stomach. So don't judge me when I say I need something to believe in because that shit gives me no hope. As far as I can tell, there are no rules in this universe. Good things happen to bad people and bad things happen to the good ones. It's as fucked and random as any of us are going to get."

"What do you want then?" I asked, having reached the end of my patience. "How can I help you?"

"I want you to get me the fuck out of the Narrows. I don't know how, but I am asking you, begging you even, to find a way."

He stared directly at me. His face had a desperate pained expression, and I understood the Time Keeper was just as helpless as each of the dead children.

"It's gold, motherfucker!" shouted Russell as I walked into Peter's kitchen.

By the amount of empty beer cans on the coffee table, I guessed he had been waiting for me most of the afternoon.

"7.2 grams, give or take, to be precise," he announced.

"No shit," I replied smiling.

Russell belched and stood up. "Take a look at the report," he said, pointing at an envelope on the counter. "Should give you a bit more information."

He left to take a piss, and I sat down and turned to the first page. Reading carefully, I realized the report was an analysis of my yellow blobs of metal. From what I could tell, there had been several tests carried out, all leading to the same conclusion.

"What the hell is gravimetry and a flame atomic absorption spectrometer!?" I yelled as Russell turned off the bathroom traffic light.

"It's brilliant stuff," he said, entering the kitchen and cracking open another beer. "You see, you gotta convert metal ions into an atomic state, then heat the fuck out of it. It's based on the principle that ground state metals absorb light at specific wavelengths."

"And you did all of that today?" I asked, completely lost.

"Well, just on my lunch break but . . . yeah. Flip it over," he said excitedly. "The crazy shit is on page three."

I flipped over the stapled pages and tried hard to understand what I was seeing. "DNA results?" I mumbled. "I thought that was for living things?"

"It is," replied Russell. "Just for shits and giggles, we did a standard analysis on both of your blobs. If you can believe it, there's a couple types of DNA mixed in with your gold."

"How the hell is that even possible?" I asked.

"No idea, but you can't argue the facts. Look at the chart," said Russell, pointing. "Both of your globs contained matching human and porcine DNA."

"Human and pig?" I replied, genuinely surprised.

Logically, I thought, *since both sets of human and pig DNA matched, it was probably a decent assumption that contamination occurred at the time of firing. Ok, a pig,* I thought, *was plausible. Animal fat was a good fire starter, but a human body? That was dodgy shit even with the best of explanations.*

"I made a couple calls this morning," said Russell, "and it looks like each of those little golden nuggets are worth somewhere in the region of one hundred and fifty pounds. So the only question I have left is where can you get some more?"

"That's just the problem," I replied. "I don't know."

Russell looked disappointed to say the least. I figured he had already worked out the logistics of gold extraction on a grand scale, but there was simply nothing I could do.

Screw it, I decided. "I'll go cash the nuggets and you round up your mates. See you at the George around seven. Let's shit face through the money and finish this thing off in style."

The precious metal exchange was sandwiched between a McDonald's and a betting shop. I found it after a ten-minute walk from Liverpool

Street station, and stepping inside the small front room, I entered a world of chintzy fake marble and plastic Romanesque columns.

An old man in his late sixties shuffled into view behind thick bulletproof glass. He wore a white shirt, black trousers, and a sparkling gold tag with the name Frederick printed on it. My first impression was that the man didn't quite belong in such a faux establishment. I would have pegged him as the owner of an old dusty antique shop, wearing a ratty cardigan with the elbows worn-out. Regardless, I stepped up to the window and waited for my man Fred to size me up.

"Can I help you?" he said, barely audible from the other side of the glass.

There was a small metal tray built into the countertop, and I lifted the lid and placed my baggie of gold inside.

"Good morning," I said. "Just wondering how much you'd give me for my gold?" I asked.

I closed the metal lid and Fred slid the inner tray over to his side. He stared at my two blobs for a second, then told me to wait as he disappeared out of view. I hummed along to a few bars of an instrumental version of "Eleanor Rigby" and waited. It didn't take long for Fred to return, and this time he was carrying some small bottles, a flat palm-sized stone, and a jeweller's examination pad.

"If this is gold," explained Fred, "then I'm going to find out what karat it is by placing different strengths of acid on the gold scratch. If the acid doesn't dissolve the gold, then that tells me it's at least that karat indicated on the acid bottle. Understand?"

I nodded and watched as he took out both of my gold chunks and scraped them against his flat stone. He lifted it up so I could see through the glass and confirmed with another nod that there were indeed two well-defined golden skid marks on its surface. He repeated the process of dripping different strength acids onto the gold skids until he announced a winner.

"They're both twenty-two karat," he said without any emotion, then reached into a drawer and pulled out a small digital scale.

He placed each of my blobs on the scale and read out the numbers. The first weighed a total of 7.48858 grams. Fred placed it on his examination pad and weighed the second.

"Humm," grunted Fred. "7.50106 grams."

I waited as Fred said nothing and rolled around my second lump of gold in his hand. He was thinking about something, and all I could do was stand and tap my fingers to another watered downed rock classic.

All of a sudden, he looked up at me as if seeing me for the first time. "Where'd you get these?" he asked as if a personality switch had been turned on.

"My back garden?" I replied.

I didn't think telling him they came from bricks would help matters, but I did add that I thought it possible they could have been coins at one time.

"Funny you should say that," he replied. "That gold content is bloody close to 7.32240 grams."

"And what's the significance of that?" I asked.

"Well, given both nuggets are 91.67% pure, and allow for whatever those stone fragments weigh, I reckon what you got are the melted down remnants of two gold sovereigns."

"A sovereign, wow, that's old-school *Treasure Island* talk," I joked.

"No," corrected Fred. "That would be pieces of eight and they would have been Spanish silver dollars. Sovereigns were circulated up until the early 1920s. An Edward the Eighth sovereign is arguably the rarest one of them all, but I guess that's a moot point in your case."

The date fit perfectly into the Clover brick field operations, and I was convinced, or at least 91.67% convinced, that gold coins were the reason Clover bricks cracked. I had heard Great Uncle Don had taken the leftover bricks from the last ever kiln firing and given them out as Christmas presents to his relatives. I suspected my gold blobs had come directly from two of those bricks.

"How'd you know all this anyway?" I asked.

"I used to have a shop selling coins, stamps, and cigarette cards. That's of course till these wankers came along and undercut me out of a job. Now I have no choice but to work for them."

Shaking his head, Fred tapped a few numbers on a calculator and said he could offer two hundred pounds in total for the gold. I had checked the Times newspaper earlier and knew the going rate was roughly one-fifty a piece. I did the math and came to the conclusion that a thirty-three percent finder's fee was complete bullshit, but I needed the money, so I agreed.

I pulled the ten twenty-pound notes from the tray and recounted just to make sure. Tucked in-between two of the notes was a small piece of paper, and reading it, I recognized it was a phone number.

"If you find any more," said Fred as hushed as a glass partition would allow, "call me. I've still got some contacts. Get you a better deal than these tossers."

There was one more place I wanted to try before heading back to London Bridge. It was a bit of a hike up Curtain Road, but I owed it to the Time Keeper as it seemed he was in need of a pick-me-up.

I felt the money in my pocket. There was something suddenly real about holding cold hard cash. I thought about Flossy and the strange appearance of multiple DNA, and it began to sink in just how deadly this journey had become. Instinctively, I turned my head and looked behind me. I hadn't thought I was being followed, but I realized from that point on, I would never be completely sure.

As luck would have it, the market by Peter's old house was in full swing. It was a struggle, but eventually I fought my way through the crowds and reached the stall I had visited several weeks earlier.

Nothing had really changed. The book stall was still as disorganized as before, and the several stacked boxes of random books gave little clue as to what their contents held.

Reaching for the nearest pile, I picked up a dozen or so books and grinned. Each had a hole drilled through the centre, and I wondered what drunken idiot had ruined another pub's swanky decor.

After about a half an hour, I came across two possibilities. One was a hardcover titled *Ghosts, Spirits and the Afterworld,* and the other, though a bit harsh, was a ratty paperback called *Demon Exorcisms.*

Somewhere in those pages, I hoped, was the answer to the Time Keeper's problem. *Hell, who knows? Maybe there is an answer or two in there for me. Anything seems possible with the way things have been going,* I thought, and I paid my four pounds with all the optimism of a one-armed man in a second-hand shop.

Chapter 38

What kind of an address is Faraway Cottage, thought Nevel. He held up the ripped ledger page and read the handwritten scroll one more time.

"Faraway Cottage, B-on-Ch? Where the hell is that?"

He hadn't been having much luck lately, and in his opinion, the Clover brick delivery page was the last straw in a string of unfortunate events.

Most regrettable was his outburst at the last B.B.S. meeting. The speaker, without question, had deserved everything he had gotten. Brickmaking, he believed, was a sacred hands-on tradition, and anyone promoting mechanized brick production deserved to be taught a serious lesson.

To add insult to injury, he had received a letter shortly after the incident stating that any attempt to attend a future B.B.S. meeting would result in the involvement of the police.

What a bunch of hypocritical twats, thought Nevel, still indignant about the entire incident. As far as he was concerned, the B.B.S. would go on his revenge list right after the bloody Clovers.

He was also disappointed to hear the Brick Development Association hadn't burned like he had hoped. His rewiring of the photocopier should have done the trick. He had positioned the machine strategically to ignite the surrounding papers, but like everything lately, his plans had gone to shit.

Nevel let out a sigh and tried to calm himself. He knew he was close to finding the Clover treasure. All he needed was one lucky break and considering even his plans to burn down the souvenir shop had failed, he didn't think it was too much of an ask.

Come on, he said to himself, *what does B-on-Ch stand for?*

Getting up, he walked over to his record player and lifted the plastic lid. It took a couple of attempts, but after a few moments, he set the needle down at the start of his favourite track and closed his eyes. It was a haunting slow melody that filled the room. Beethoven was one of Nevel's favourite composers, and he sank to the sofa and stilled his mind. For whatever reason, it was "Moonlight Sonata" that always did it. Something he couldn't explain silenced the voices in his head, and as the sombre piano continued to swell and dip in sadness, his thoughts became to clear.

Nevel stepped off the boat feeling sick. He had parked on the opposite side of the river and had realized too late that the Burnham ferry and his sausage roll lunch were not a good mix.

He probably would never have visited Burnham-on-Crouch if it wasn't for his library research. In a moment of pure genius, Nevel had realized it was the windmill in Rob Clover's earlier painting that would be the key to the location of the cottage. All he had to do was identify the correct windmill and "Faraway Cottage" might not be so "faraway."

He had tried his best to hide his frustration with the volunteer pensioner. She shuffled around the book stacks like a sedated sloth, but finally she produced an 1896 area map of Essex that proved to be his long-awaited lucky break.

After locating all the possible mills, he had narrowed his search down to four. Battlesbridge was ruled out immediately as it only had functioned as a watermill, and the windmill at South Ockendon he dismissed for its location next to a landlocked moat.

It was only when Nevel saw the map icon for a windmill on the River Crouch that he believed he had found what he was looking for.

"B-on-Ch" could only have meant Burnham-on-Crouch, Nevel decided. It didn't even matter to him that the windmill had been dismantled. All it would take, presumed Nevel, was a local to point him in the direction of the windmill, and with a bit more luck, Faraway Cottage.

Nevel made his way up to the High Street. To his right was an odd clock tower built over a pedestrian walkway. There didn't seem to be much else of interest, so he turned left and headed west toward a row of shops.

The first shop he tried was an estate agency. Nevel figured someone selling houses in the area would have to know a little of the local history. He showed the girl behind the computer both the windmill and the cottage paintings but received only a blank stare for his time.

He had better luck at an antique store a bit further on up the High Street.

"That's right," said the shopkeeper. "I used to play on the ruins years ago. Of course, it's all changed now, always does," he added.

"Nowadays, the ruins are part of a posh hotel and spa. My missus had her nails done there just before Christmas."

"What about this picture?" said Nevel, handing the painting of Faraway Cottage to the man.

"Could be one of a hundred houses back in the day," he replied, shaking his head. "Never heard of a cottage called that. You know," the man continued, "back in the day, all the houses around here used to be thatched. Reminds me of a story when—"

"Yes, yes," interrupted Nevel, feeling the man would talk all day. "Got to go, I'm afraid. Have to make the ferry."

Backtracking slightly, Nevel found an outdoor patio and sat down at an empty table and chair. The air was thick with the stench of rotting seaweed, and as he waited for his tea, Nevel watched as several sailing boats traversed the murky river.

At the next table, he noticed an elderly couple sporting matching tracksuits and running shoes. He guessed they were local, and casually Nevel slid his chair over and introduced himself. It didn't take long to disperse with the pleasantries, but once again, all he could confirm was that the local windmill wasn't standing.

"Couldn't help but overhearing you were talking about the Faraway Cottage," said the waiter with his tea.

Surprised, Nevel turned. "Yes," he replied a little taken aback.

"Well, I passed it this morning down by the marina. All you do is go down that there street and when you get to the river, turn right. Can't be more than a ten-minute walk."

"Are you sure?" asked Nevel.

"Aye, been there as long as I can remember."

Nevel didn't wait to drink his tea. He threw a couple of pound coins onto the saucer and immediately took off.

Running was possibly a little ambitious for Nevel, having never exercised in his life, and when he nearly knocked over a small boy with a bucket and spade, he slowed to catch his breath. The sun was hot and sweat had already soaked the back of his shirt. He held out the cottage painting in front of him, and as his breathing returned to normal, he began comparing each building he passed.

He knew the cottage had probably changed through the years. A different roof maybe, or even a full addition added on. He wanted to be sure he didn't miss anything, and he methodically analyzed every brick structure until he arrived at the Yacht Marina.

Something isn't right, he thought. There were no more brick buildings anywhere. All he saw were fields surrounding the inlet, and for a moment, he wasn't sure what to do. *Was the waiter wrong?* thought Nevel. *Is this some kind of bloody joke?*

He was about to turn around when he noticed several boats dry docked on large wooden blocks. *Maybe this is something,* thought Nevel. Admittedly, he had faint hopes, but having come this far, Nevel had nothing left to lose.

"Vitamin Sea," he read, wandering through the boats in various stages of repair. "Very funny."

"Seas the Day" brought a small smile, and Nevel could only shake his head at a boat called "Nauti Boy."

He came to the end of the row and stopped.

"Shit!" said Nevel.

In front of him was one last boat. It had obviously been there for many years, and by the looks of the fishing boat's rotten hull, there was no chance it was ever going to sail again.

"Bloody hell," said Nevel, reading what was left of the boat's namesake. "Furl Away Cuttage," said Nevel in disgust. "You stupid, stupid boy. What a complete waste of time."

He stood, trembling with anger. With one swift kick, he split a hanging plank in two, then turned and walked back to town.

The rest of the afternoon only left Nevel more frustrated. His attempt to engage the local librarian was met with an indignant "shhh" and his inquiries at a charity shop and Baptist church only left him with a pair of used socks and a book of church fundraiser raffle tickets.

Eventually, Nevel made his way to number 107 Station Road. It was hard to tell if the building they called the Granary Hotel and Spa was actually the building next to the windmill in his painting. So much had changed in the makeover that without comparing it to an original photograph, Nevel couldn't be sure.

He felt a little underdressed walking into the hotel reception. The antique furniture, high ceilings and wrought iron chandelier gave the impression it wasn't a place for millers and farmers anymore.

He closed the door behind him and found that the front desk was unattended. *Well, that helps,* he thought, relieved at not having to explain himself. *Maybe I can pull this off without talking to anybody.*

Feeling a bit like an intruder, Nevel slowly made his way around the main lobby. He was hoping for a possible photograph or painting of the original mill, but it seemed the interior designer of the rebuild had run with a theme of the 1800s working class.

To the right of a grandfather clock, Nevel found a framed map. *This could be interesting,* he thought, and was leaning in to get a closer look when a door opened at the other end of the room.

An oversized lady wearing a terry cloth robe and flip-flops came into the lobby. Their eyes locked for the briefest second, but choosing to ignore Nevel, she waddled through a side door and left in the direction of the pool.

From the outside, he could hear children splashing and screaming, and deciding to follow in the same direction, Nevel entered the adjacent room.

It was furnished in a similar décor. *The only difference,* thought Nevel, *is the strong smell of chlorine.*

High above an ornamental birdcage, Nevel found what he was looking for. It was a lithograph print with the caption Burnham-on-Crouch Windmill and Granary 1889.

"Perfect," he said with satisfaction and lifted Rob Clover's painting to compare the details.

At first, the granary in the print looked suspiciously like Rob Clover's rendition, but then Nevel's heart sunk, realizing they were two different types of windmills.

The windmill in Rob Clover's painting was definitely a smock type of structure, there was no question. The standard sloping, horizontal weatherboards and rotating roof cap could not be mistaken. Even the overall shape was a dead giveaway which resembled an old-time farmer's smock.

Unfortunately, this was not the type of windmill Nevel saw in the lithograph. It was blatantly obvious the structure turning its sails was nothing more than a simple post windmill. *It isn't even close,* thought Nevel. He checked again, but in his heart of hearts, he knew the entire day had been a complete waste of time.

He flopped down on to a plush maroon couch and closed his eyes. He could still hear the shrieks of the kids playing in the pool, and he clenched his teeth to try and suppress his anger. He had come to the end of what he thought would have been ultimate payback, and now, as painful as it felt, he had to admit defeat.

As if on queue, the long case clock from the lobby chimed four long drawn out gongs.

"For whom the bell tolls?" said Nevel, regaining his composure.

It was a quote he knew well. From what he could recall, the bells were rung to symbolize the death of humanity, and suddenly he had his own answer to Hemingway's question.

"It tolls for the Clovers."

Chapter 39

I had to admit I was not thinking clearly as I opened the door to Maury's shop. The small London pub party the night before had gotten quickly out of hand.

To start, one of Russell's friends had pulled their trousers down and showed the entire pub their impression of a "brown-eyed Susan." That had led to a series of fights, Russel getting his hand stuck in an empty pint glass, and Petie Pie Bottom wearing a tea cozy on his head proclaiming he was king of the Hobnobs.

I had woken the next morning in a bathtub somewhere in Hammersmith. Except for a slight limp, I thought I had survived the night relatively unscathed. I checked for freshly penned tattoos, of which there were none, and then limped across West London, eventually finding a train to Rayleigh, and on to the relative safety of Maury's shop.

I was pleased to see Burt's door glass had remained intact, and stepping inside, I saw the familiar face of my great aunt bagging a couple of rubber bricks for a customer.

Beside her, a new display had been set up, and I stared for a moment, trying to make sense at what I was seeing. Two life-sized cardboard cut-outs stood before me. One was of a man looking suspiciously like Burt, dressed up like a chimney sweep from *Mary Poppins*. The other was Maury in some late Victorian garb, holding a tray of scone-looking cakes.

I dropped my pack and walked over to the display. In complete amazement, I reached for a book on the display shelf and turned each page of Googly Eyes' paintings, accompanied by historical recipes from the nineteenth century.

"But I thought the paintings were all gone?" I answered, still in shock.

"Well, yes," said Maury. "The originals are, but wasn't that what you were so upset about?"

"Eel Pie, mash, and sheep trotters?" I asked.

"What do you think? All we needed to do was match a pile of Victorian recipes with Rob's old paintings and flog the lot for a tenner."

"Bloody hell, that was a quick turn-over," I said. "You don't miss a trick?"

Maury smiled. "Not when there's money to be made, dear," she replied. "The printers did a good job, don't you think?"

As I took a closer look at the pages, I started to recognize many of the scenes. Still fresh in my mind were the addresses from the Clover ledger delivery pages, and in my head, I automatically began to match up locations with recipe pages.

"Oh, by the way," she said, "that detective's been calling for you again."

"Any news on Flossy?" I asked.

"No idea, but he's pissing me off. Calls twice a day now. Could you please do us all a favour and shut him up?"

Ten minutes later, I was on the phone to Detective Grim.

"Have you heard from that Reggie chap?" asked Grim. "We're still wanting him for questioning."

"Well, I've got a bit of news for you," I replied. "Not that I'm telling you how to do your job, but it turns out Reggie's real name is Nevel Fink."

It took a few minutes to explain, but when I had finished, the detective mumbled a half-hearted acknowledgement and promised his team would entertain a line of inquiry.

Happy to move on to another topic, Detective Grim asked me if I knew anything about an unsolved missing person report dating back to 1910.

"It just came across my desk the other day," he continued. "A brown envelope, no return address, just photocopies of a dated constable's notebook and some basic fact gathering. Bit of a long shot, but the last known whereabouts for this man was a witness stating a man of similar description was seen entering the premises of the Hambro Hill brick fields in Rayleigh. Ever heard of anything like that in your family history?"

"No, not a clue," I replied, instantly thinking of the DNA samples found in my gold blobs.

"Right then, call me if you do."

Grim rang off before I could answer, so I placed the phone back on its receiver and went to see what Maury was doing in the kitchen.

"Eel pie," she said with an unconvincing grin.

I wouldn't have put it past her, but as she handed me a large, steaming slice, I could tell it was nothing more than some sort of meat and veggie concoction. Filling the remainder of my plate with boiled potatoes and lifeless veggies, I sat down and explained how I had confirmed my yellow globs were indeed twenty-two karat gold.

"Can I ask you something, Maury?" I said, stuffing the last remaining potato in my mouth. "The detective mentioned an old missing person report connected to Hambro Hill. Any idea what he was talking about?"

There was a moment's hesitation before she answered. "You be minding your own business. The past is the past and what's done is done. No, there's nothing to the story."

Abruptly, she got up from the table, took my empty plate and walked to the sink. She stood for some time staring out of the window, ignoring the dish water that threatened to overflow.

"What's been going on with you and Burt?" I asked, bringing Maury back.

"Oh, well you might as well know I've moved in with him. Just can't shake the feeling someone's still watching."

"Hey, that's great," I said, genuinely happy for the old girl.

"So take my room if you want," she said, wiping her hands on a tea towel. "Save you the stairs if you need to go pee in the night."

"Oh fuck off, will you?" I said, waking to see the Time Keeper standing at the end of my bed. I looked over at the cheap digital alarm clock and groaned. "It's one thirty in the morning. What do you want?"

"Sorry," he said, somewhat apologetic, "but I was wondering if you had given any more thought to our last conversation?"

"If you are referring to how you wanted to disappear, then yes, I am thinking about it right now."

I rolled on my side and pulled the bed sheets with me. For good measure, I held a pillow over my head and tried to fall back to sleep.

"You still here?" I asked after a long silence.

"Yep," replied the Time Keeper alarmingly close to my ear, and I sat up to find him sitting next to me on my bed.

"Ok, ok, let's get this over with," I said, turning on a small bedside lamp.

I swung my legs out of bed and groggily made my way over to my pack. The books I wanted were zipped in a side pocket, and I fumbled with the flap till eventually they came free.

"Right," I said, beginning to focus. "There's a bunch of different ways to try if you really want to do this. I don't quite understand spiritual suicide, but I guess that's your own choice."

"I'm just done, mate," said the Time Keeper, trying to explain. "Whatever is supposed to come next, I'm ready for. If you can find a way, then you'll be doing us both a favour. At the very least, I'll stop harassing you in the middle of the night and you can get some decent sleep."

"Can't argue there," I said, and opened the first book to one of many dog-eared pages. "Well, firstly it says if I ignore you then that might make you leave. There's little chance of that, so let's just move on. Here it is," I said, opening the book to a chapter on spells. "I'm going to read out a banishing spell. Not sure what's going to happen, but it sounds pretty serious. If you're not here at the end of it," I looked up at the Time Keeper, "it's been nice knowing you. You ready?" I asked.

The Time Keeper nodded solemnly and I began to read.

"Ecce Crucis signum, fugiant phantosmata cunta." I said it again louder, and then repeated it a third time almost yelling.

The room was silent as I looked up to where the Time Keeper had stood. He was gone. *Fuck,* I thought, *it really worked.*

"That's the worst Latin I have ever heard. Your pronunciation was terrible."

"Christ," I blurted, turning to see the Time Keeper standing behind me. "You know, you're a real tosser," I said, trying to hold back a smile.

"That's quite possible," said the Time Keeper. "What else you got there?"

I turned to a page near the end of the second book.

"I was leaving this for the finale, but I guess now is as good a time as any."

I got up and walked down the hallway to Maury's kitchen. It didn't take long, and when I returned, I had a breakfast bowl, some packets of herbs, a box of matches, and a few lose cigarette rolling papers.

"You're rolling a joint at a time like this?" asked the Time Keeper indignantly.

"No, no, don't get all bent out of shape. This is what the book calls a 'smudging.' All you do is burn dried sage leaves and it's supposed to drive shit heads like you away."

I had no idea how to use rolling papers. It seemed simple enough. I had watched Burt roll perfect cigarettes enough times, but it took several attempts and some coaching from the Time Keeper to produce three fat misshapen spliffs.

"So now what?" asked the Time Keeper, staring at the breakfast bowl.

"Well, I'm going back to bed," I said. "I've got a feeling this will take a while. Why don't you take a seat and after I lite the smudge, see if you have an uncontrollable urge to run from the room?"

In bed, I got the first whiff of the burning herbs.

"Is that how sage is supposed to smell?" asked the Time Keeper through the darkness.

"I couldn't tell you," I mumbled half-asleep. "Maury didn't have any."

"Then what the hell is that stink?" he asked.

"Dill, thyme, and a pinch of oregano. But don't worry, cooking is all about the substitution, or is that soccer? Anyway, I'm sure it will all be fine. Breathe it in and let's see who's here in the morning."

I woke again around 4:30 a.m. to piss. The Time Keeper was gone, and shuffling through the darkness, I managed to kick over the bowl of smudge. It clanged as it overturned and feeling a sore throat, I coughed, wondering just how much smoke I had actually inhaled. I found the small closet toilet across from the kitchen, and in a semiconscious fog, I impressed myself by landing the majority of my pee into the bowl.

What's with this cough? I thought, hacking again. Possibly a bit heavy on the oregano. Making a detour, I fumbled into the kitchen and found a dirty glass in the sink. I turned on the tap and tasted a slight hint of whisky as I chugged. It felt good on my throat, and I was ready to head back to bed when I heard a thump, like a piece of furniture falling over.

"Oh shit," I said, realizing the sound had come from the shop across the hall. *Is this another break-in?*

I made my way over to the door that separated Maury's kitchen from the retail store. There were more random sounds coming from the other side, and I coughed again, unable to suppress my hack.

There was no time to think. I yanked on the door handle and jammed open the sliding bolt. With one powerful kick, the door flung open, and instantly I was hit by a wall of heat and bellowing smoke.

Instinctively, I stepped back and covered my face. *Christ, that's hot,* I thought, seeing the shop fully engulfed in flames. There was no stopping it and no hope of salvaging anything. Rubber bricks and t-shirts burned. Display counters crashed, and Maury and Burt's cardboard cut-outs blazed like two Roman candles on Guy Fawkes night.

Chapter 40

The joke shop was always the centre of my childhood social anarchy. Not even an hour-long bike ride would dampen my hopes of disrupting a world of oppression.

Hot sweets, tiny rolled explosives, stink bombs, fart powder, plastic poo, it was all there for the taking. All selling the idea of embarrassment and empowerment to an eight-year-old.

I'm not sure if I was aware of any of that at the time. What I do remember, however, was bringing home two smoke bombs on April Fool's Day genuinely believing that yelling "fire" would be a great practical joke.

I waited downstairs to make sure the smoke had a chance to fill the bathroom. Next, I was ready with my swimming goggles and a plastic cup. When the moment was right, I would yell "fire" and put on the goggles, suck the cup over my mouth, and make it look like I was wearing a WWII gas mask.

Unfortunately, I did not know what linoleum flooring was made of. Its main ingredient was solidified linseed oil, and combined with ground cork, and calcium carbonate, my plan took an unforeseen turn.

Without a doubt, I got the impact I was looking for. My father raced up the stairs and was engulfed in a cloud of smoke as soon as he opened the door. Probably, my makeshift gas mask tipped my father off. He did not instantly run to call the fire brigade.

Instead, he looked at me, and letting my plastic cup drop, I said more in the form of a question, "April Fools?"

The confusion that followed did little to assert my dominance over my perceived oppression. My mother ran up the stairs with a saucepan of water, and after many minutes of shouting and arguing, a large burn hole in the bathroom floor appeared through the dissipating smoke.

I should have known something was wrong. Nothing had worked quite so well in the past, and it was only with the addition of actual flames that made me think the bombs were a pretty good deal for fifty pence each.

I'm not sure what happened to me, I can only think it probably wasn't pleasant. Nevertheless, the hole remained. It lurked under the bathmat like a dirty secret for years. I guess it was much like sticking ripped wallpaper back on with strawberry jam. The aesthetics of life were easily covered, but the messy truth was never far under the surface.

We sat on deck chairs as dawn crept into the sky. From the other side of the road, Maury, Burt, and myself watched as the souvenir shop burnt into a charred non-descriptive heap.

There was nothing anyone could have done. The fire brigade had arrived quickly and though they fought valiantly, their best outcome had been containing the fire to only one house on the road.

The neighbours had also come out to see the blaze. People stood in their night gowns and pyjamas. They shook their heads and like good tax-paying citizens, gave their uneducated opinions on what the firefighters were doing wrong.

One old boy was in the midst of recalling the London Blitz when a side wall, ceiling, and the entire second storey suddenly came crashing down. There was no question it was the end of an era, and I wondered if that meant the Time Keeper was also gone too.

We were silent as we took in the spectacle of flashing lights and sirens. Only when the cast iron bathtub torpedoed down into what was once Maury's cellar, did Burt finally speak.

"How's your insurance policy, Mar?"

"Maxed out," she replied smiling. "Start packing your bags dear, retirement just landed on our doorstep."

"It's a shame," she continued after a pause. "I would have liked to have saved a photo album or two."

I felt bad. In front of us was the total destruction of her life, and the reality of finding anything of value seemed almost impossible.

Certainly, my backpack was toast. That went up in flames along with my clothes and what was left of my two hundred pounds. Gone also, I realized, were the recipe books that I believed were the key to solving the whole Clover Brick mystery.

"Fucking hell," I said, summing up what everyone was thinking. "It was all right in front of us, what a bloody waste."

Again, silence fell until Maury abruptly stood up. I looked at her and sensed something had changed. At first, I thought it was defiance, but when she spoke, it was clearly something else.

"No use staring at the past," she said, wiping a tear. "A dead cow is a dead cow." She turned to Burt who was trying to free himself from his own deck chair. "You know what, luv?" said Maury. "The best thing about the past is that it shows you what not to bring into the future."

He smiled and took her hand. "Well, we best get on with it then," he replied and without a second look, they walked to Burt's house and toward a future I guessed they both were ready for.

It was pointless for Burt to shut his front door. His kitchen had been deemed the official command centre, and all morning there had been a constant barrage of police, fire, and investigators, mainly wanting to use his toilet.

I had been trying on some of Burt's spare clothes and was surprised that most of them fit. I stared in a full-length mirror and laughed. 1966 was apparently a great year for fashion, and though I appreciated Burt's dated apparel, my next stop would have to be my favourite Rayleigh charity shop.

Downstairs, Detective Grimshaw had made an appearance. He had taken it upon himself to give us an update, and we listened as he read out the facts, trying on a very bad New York accent.

The fire was apparently out. The fire crews were in the process of hosing down the last of the hot spots, and Maury's house had been officially deemed unsafe for habitation. Considering the second floor was now in her basement, I was relieved the police had figured that out all on their own.

Grim finished by dramatically folding shut his notebook. He seemed a little lost at what to do next, so I asked a question.

"Have you heard of any probable causes yet?"

Grim adjusted his trousers, then with a flare of the dramatic, he looked both ways down the hall to make sure no one else was listening.

"I can't say anything official," he finally replied, "you understand, but just between you, me, and the lamp post, I heard the arson investigator mention something about 'classic burn patterns.'"

He left giving us a U.S. army salute, and I stared at Maury who looked away, fidgeting with a small locket around her neck.

"Arson?" I said. "Are you kidding me? Not to address the burnt elephant in the room, but what aren't you telling me, Maury? Did you set the fire for fuck's sake?"

"No, you stupid boy," she replied, still looking out the open front door.

I followed her gaze, and for a fleeting moment, I thought I saw a red Ford Escort drive by.

"It was my late husband Johnny that told me," Maury began. "It was so long ago now, I never thought he would ever find out."

"Who?" I demanded.

"Bloody Nevel," she said with annoyance.

"You think he started the fire?" I asked.

Maury didn't answer, but I could tell I was right.

"There was a body," she said, continuing her story. "From what I was told, it was the body of a man that was clearly distraught. Apparently, he wandered into the brick fields and got into some altercation with your Great Granddad William. I think he shot himself in the end and it was my poor Johnny that had to help get rid of the body."

I thought about it for a moment and remembered my gold blob DNA test results.

"He was chucked in with the kiln bricks that were getting fired," I said, almost not wanting to believe my own words.

Maury nodded.

"Holy shit," I said. "But why not just tell the police?"

"If my facts are right," she said, "the local constable was a devout Christian that was tightly in cahoots with the Hadleigh Salvation Army. I reckon the last thing Clover Bricks wanted was to give 'the powers that be' a reason to shut them down for good."

"But I'm confused," I said, trying to connect the past to the present.

"I think if my suspicions are correct," said Maury, "the body of the dead man was Nevel's father."

"What???" I said, even more confused. "How the hell did you come up with that?"

"It's what he said years ago," replied Maury. "You have to remember, he became really close with old Donny. One night, we were in the kitchen having a cuppa when I asked Nev why he was so passionate about bricks. He looked straight at me with a crazy deadpan expression and said, 'You can't get blood from a stone, but you can get blood from a brick.' I wasn't quite sure what to think, so I asked him what the Dickens he was on about. It turned out Nevel was completely loony. I've never heard such rot. He told me this long-winded story about his mother being killed by a brick in the Skeleton Riots and his father never returning from Essex after searching for the murderer. It wasn't until I quizzed him about dates that I realized his father could have been the body in the kiln."

"I presume you never mentioned it to him?"

"God no," replied Maury. "He was obsessed to the point of madness. Somehow he had taken it upon himself to revenge his family on the company that made the fatal brick. His whole life was devoted to trying to find out which Essex brick company it was."

"And what was he going to do when he found it?"

"He never actually said," replied Maury, "but I don't think burning down a building or bashing someone's head in was out of the realm of possibility."

At a loss of words, I turned again and watched the traffic drive past the open front door. Cars slowed as they rubbernecked the devastation, and for the first time in my life, I felt concerned for my safety.

"If it was him," I said eventually, "do you think he'll be back?"

"I wouldn't put it past him," Maury replied. "We're all still alive."

As if on cue, our conversation was interrupted by a car pulling up outside the house. I recognized my Uncle Tom A.K.A "the Blue Flash," and he walked up the garden path shaking his head. He carried a garbage bag in one hand, and when he got to the kitchen, he handed it to me.

"Thought you might like some clothes," he said.

I sifted through the pile and settled on a Sex Pistol's t-shirt with the words "Never Mind the Bollocks." Somehow, I found it fitted the moment.

There wasn't much left for me in England. I had drunk and shit myself through the last several months and I found myself broke, badly dressed, with no mystery to solve, and in fear of my life. *Not a bad way to leave a country,* I thought smiling.

It was decided I would stay with Tommy Nine Fingers till I could figure out a way home. We were just walking out the door when Burt spoke.

"There's a rainstorm coming, I can feel it," he said. "Let me get my spare rain jacket from the car boot."

I really didn't think he was right, but as we walked down the driveway, the sky turned a dark and ominous grey as predicted. Burt opened the rear of his car and leaned into the space. He grunted as he moved a large cardboard box that was blocking his emergency stash.

"What's in the box?" I asked, helping him lift it out of the way.

"Oh that," said Burt, his upper body still hidden in the boot's interior, "that's the other half of those recipe books we ordered. They were too heavy to move, so I just left them here."

In disbelief, I ripped the sealing tape off the top of the cardboard. Sure enough, inside were forty-eight freshly printed recipe books, all clad with identical prints of Uncle Goog's original paintings. I picked up a small manila envelope that lay on top of the pile. Opening it, three small oil paintings slid out.

"And these?" I asked Burt as he finally emerged.

He squinted at them for a second, then remembered. "Those were the extra paintings that never got used. I guess we still have a few that weren't stolen."

"You still got that old map of Essex!?" I yelled to Tom over a sudden gust of wind.

He nodded and I smiled.

I put the box minus one copy back into the car, and left Burt confused as I spontaneously blurted out, "Game on, bitch."

Chapter 41

"Move along!" shouted the police officer, trying to speed up traffic.

All morning, there had been a steady stream of slow-moving cars. *It's typical,* thought constable Plod, *how a bit of smoke can attract half the bloody population of Essex.* A red Ford Escort slowed, and the driver rolled down his car window.

"I'm so sorry to stop," said Nevel, "but please tell me there were no fatalities."

The police constable was not impressed. To hurry things along, he once again warned the driver to carry on but added that the only fatality was a one-eyed pet goldfish. Nevel kept up the facade of relief as he drove away, but underneath the cool exterior was a seething acidic fury.

"What in God's name does it take to kill a fucking Clover!?" he yelled as spit peppered his steering wheel.

He drove to the end of the road and turned into an unusually busy petrol station. There was a lineup for the pumps, but Nevel bypassed the idling cars and found an open parking space at the side of the station's convenience store.

Inside, his mood did not improve. Customers stood oblivious of their surroundings, and Nevel had to restrain himself from picking up a can of Tango orange drink and crushing it over the nearest person's head.

Eventually, he found what he wanted. He couldn't wait to pay, so he ripped open the packet and jammed five soft Jelly Babies into his mouth. The change was instant as he bit down on the chewy treats. He closed his eyes, savouring the flavour, and drifted back to the last memory of his parents.

He saw his parents dressed in shiny army-like uniforms. He heard his father say they would be late if they didn't hurry, and he felt a soft kiss on the top of his head as his mother passed him in the hall. He fuelled his memory by adding three more jellies into his mouth, and saw his father turn to him at the last second. Crouching, his father pulled a small, crumpled bag from his pocket.

"Don't let your mother know I gave you these," he said with a wink. "Be a good boy for your grandma, and we'll be home soon."

He smiled and got to his feet. His father put on his peaked Salvation Army hat and walked through the front door and out of Nevel's life forever.

The confectionery "Jelly Babies" had been around a very long time. They were a soft bite-sized gelatin, shaped like plump babies in a variety of colours. They were not called "Jelly Babies" back then. The modern-day version had gone through several different relaunch campaigns, and as Nevel waited for his parents' return, the irony of chewing "Unclaimed Babies" would haunt him for the rest of his life.

As an adult, Nevel did not believe in coincidences. He believed there was absolute purpose in everything. He believed his father had given him the bag of sweets for a reason, and after many years of interpretation, Nevel was convinced each Jelly Baby had a personal message to aid in his revenge.

Looking down, Nevel was happy to see he had picked a red Jelly Baby out of the packet. It was his favourite, and licking the starch powder off its belly, he clearly saw the embossed letter B. For Nevel, the red B had always stood for "Blood." He believed it stood for violence as a means to an end, and as he bit down hard on the sugar baby's head, an image of Flossy suddenly came to mind.

Orange was about his journey, and the green crying baby was a symbol of dark human suffering. Yellow, believed Nevel, represented the riches of redemption, and the black, the evil the Clover's had inflicted onto his family. The last Jelly Baby was pink. It reminded Nevel of his own innocence. The innocence that was taken from him, the memories he was deprived of. As he chewed, there was no question it fuelled his anger. He had been savagely torn from a life that had awaited him, and it was clear, to gain a new life, he would have to destroy the past and anyone that was connected to it.

Nevel threw the empty plastic bag into an outside bin. With a finger, he picked out a small clump of jelly stuck between his teeth and stared at what seemed like an unending line of cars waiting to use the pumps.

For some reason, a man pumping petrol into a white Vauxhall Astra looked familiar. Unconsciously, Nevel stepped back, and leaning slightly to the left, tried to get a better look.

Inside the car, he recognized the passenger. It was the Canadian from Flossy's back garden, and instantly Nevel knew this was no coincidence. He grinned in affirmation and without hesitation, turned and walked back to his car.

He reversed out of his parking space and manoeuvred into position. At just the right moment, he forced his way in front of an exiting Jag and turned onto the road, three cars behind the driver of the small white compact.

Chapter 42

The Essex map Uncle Tom rolled out onto his dining room table was dated 1912. It was probably original, but even in my limited knowledge of shady Essex history, I knew it was still considered a modern survey. Holding down the curled map were two halves of Tom's Clover brick. He had wasted no time after we pulled into his driveway, and picking up a hammer from his garage, Uncle Tom had walked directly to his back garden shed. It took only one solid hit to make "Doubting Uncle Thomas" a believer. The Clover brick snapped in two, and after brushing off the dust, a gold encrusted nugget revealed itself, identical to my last two finds.

"Right," said Tom. "What are we looking for exactly?"

I put the recipe book down on the table and opened it to the table of contents.

"We're looking for the delivery locations of the last batch of fired Clover brick. I'm not saying all, but some for sure are going to be filled with gold coins. All we have to do is follow Uncle Goog's path."

"Where do we start?" asked Tom.

"Easy," I replied, opening to page eight of the recipe book. "Shirley House—Boiled Calf Head."

Tom reached for a small plastic box of drawing pins and jammed a blue headed point into the map. It stuck firmly into Daws Heath Road, and without Tom caring, into his dining room table beneath.

"Next?" he said.

I flicked through the book and found what must have been the next corresponding scene.

"Looking east through the parlour window—Mutton Curry," I read out loud.

In the background of the print, I could see a small church beyond the plowed field, and I told Tom to hold on while I made a connection to the next painting.

"It's Rayleigh Church—Spotted Dick," I confirmed, looking at a close-up painting on page thirteen.

"Got it," replied Tom, and I heard him thrust a second pin deep into his map.

After the best part of an hour and two beers later, we had successfully identified Flour Soup, Broxy, Coburg Loaf, Mince Pies, Water-souchy, Brown Bread Ice Cream, Gruel, Marrow Toast, Kedgeree, Heron Pudding, and an enticing boozy kind of dessert called Syllabub.

"What's next?" I asked, staring at a painting of a large grassy hill.

"That's Rayleigh Mount," Tom replied. "Used to be an old Norman Castle."

Far in the background, in very minute detail, I could see a river painted into the horizon.

"What's the river north of Rayleigh?" I asked.

"Has to be the Roach," my uncle replied, cross-referencing the map for confirmation.

There was only one logical painting left to connect Rayleigh Mount. It depicted a small boat sailing past a mill house and windmill.

"Ah," said Tom, turning to take a look. "That's called an Essex-smack. They were used for fishing and hauling stuff around the turn of the century."

"Is that like a Glasgow Kiss?" I asked, but my uncle didn't reply.

He had tied a string in one continuous line around each of the coloured pins, and he held it, poised to connect it to the next location. After a minute, he looked up, shaking his head.

"There's no windmill marked on the map," he said. "I know Canewdon had one once, but that burnt down along with all the witches. Hang on a minute," he said, leaving the room "I have a book somewhere."

He returned with two more beers and a small paperback. He tossed me the beer and I pulled up a chair.

"Knew there was a reason I kept this," said Tom.

Conveniently, the book was titled *Essex Windmills* and since there didn't seem to be any particular order, we started at the beginning and tried to match our windmill painting to the book's sketches and old photographs.

"Here, I think that's it," I said about two-thirds the way through.

Tom picked up the recipe book and compared it to a grainy black and white image.

"I think you're right, old boy," he said with a smile. "Even the mill house next door lines-up perfectly. According to the book, the last owner of the windmill, Mr. Herbert Manning, was actually born in it. Let's see, what else does it say? Blah blah eldest son Fred . . . mill settled to one side, three pairs of stone, a bolter, declared unsafe, dismantled first half of the 20th century. Well, there you have it," he said, grabbing his anorak. "Finish your beer, we're off to find Windy Miller."

From what I remembered, Windy Miller was a character from an old children's television show called *Camberwick Green*. In one episode, poor old Windy Miller drank too much homemade cider, and if I recalled correctly, he had to have a snooze behind the mill. I knew how he felt. After a sleepless night, no breakfast and three beers, my eyes were heavy.

"Hey, wasn't that where you got stripped naked?" blurted out Uncle Tom laughing.

I peered out the window just in time to see the sign for Battlesbridge flash before me.

"Yep," I said, groggily swearing I saw my underwear hanging from a fence post.

"So, what's in Barling?" I asked Tom, pulling myself upright.

"Not a hell of a lot," he replied. "Went there once for the Christmas lights. The whole main strip on Church Road gets lit up every year. Not bad for a small town of a thousand people. The best bit of history though is beyond River Roach at a place called Foulness Island. Apparently, back in the eighteenth century, the local men had somewhere between six and fourteen wives."

"How'd they swing that?" I asked.

"Turned out there was a marshy type of malaria going around. All you had to do was bring in a girl from the outside and she rarely lasted a year. Not a bad turn over, wouldn't you say?"

We both laughed and Tom mumbled he should take his wife there for a day trip at some point.

"There's always a hope," he added with a wink.

Pulling on to Wakering Road, I reached down for Burt and Maury's cookbook. I flipped it to the back and pulled out the three loose paintings that were not used by the printer.

One was a close-up of the windmill's granary. The second, a field of horses and stables, and the last, a detailed close-up of an old shipwrecked hull.

"So what's our plan?" I asked.

"Hang on," said Tom about to overtake a tractor.

With his foot to the floor, we careened over to the oncoming lane, and I prayed nothing was coming around the bend. After signalling back to the left side of the road, he spoke.

"Reckon we'll try and find the old granary if it's still standing. It looks like you have a detail of it, right?"

I nodded.

"Then," he continued, "we figure out the sequence of the last pictures and see what we come up with. If nothing else, there's a local air strip I've always wanted to check out."

It didn't take long before we came to a stop just past the cemetery wall of All Saints Church. We parked in a clearing at the top of Church Road and looking east, I could just make out Barlinghall Creek above a line of trees.

"Which way?" I asked as we got out and stretched.

From his jacket pocket, my uncle pulled out his book on Essex windmills. He flicked to the chapter on Barling, and I watched as he studied the accompanying photo.

The Norman Church of All Saints could clearly be seen in the background of the windmill image, and after a series of turns and cross-checks, Uncle Tom pointed his half finger and proclaimed north was our best bet.

Across from us, on the other side of the main road, was a series of nondescript council houses. One half of a house had been painted yellow, and above the door, I noticed a hand-painted sign.

"Millfields' Cottages!" I called out to my uncle.

"Looks like we're on the right track," he answered back, already several steps ahead.

"Can I ask you something?" I said, catching up. "Do you believe in ghosts?"

"Do you mean have I seen Harry lately?" replied my uncle.

"Who's Harry?"

"You know, the man in the monk's costume," he replied.

I stopped. "What?"

Tom turned and looked at me. "I thought everyone in our family knew about him?"

"News to me," I replied.

"Funny, never actually saw him," continued Tom. "When your cousin was young, he kept going on about a man in a robe. Had a few words with the neighbour, let me tell you, but after a while, he would tell me what chair he was sitting in or where he was standing. Gotta say it freaked the shit out of me, but after talking to a few of your aunts, it turned out he was pretty much a regular with all the kids."

"Wow, he really got around," I said.

"Yeah, I suppose so. Not sure who he was. Maybe a long dead relative, but after a few years, Bloggs stopped talking about him and none of the nephews or nieces remember him now."

We stepped on to a strip of well manicured grass and waited for an approaching car to pass. When it was safe, I followed Tom in single file until he stopped, kneeing to inspect something I hadn't noticed.

"Ha!" he cried out in triumph. "Any idea what those are?"

Leaning against a fence post were two stone circles. They were maybe twenty-four inches across and five or six inches thick. Cut into the surface were a series of diagonal lines, and at first glance, they looked like stone bicycle wheels. Trying not to look completely clueless, I stepped a little closer and read a small plaque fixed to the outer stone.

"Mill House," I read, and in true scholarly form, I announced it had something to do with a mill.

"They're mill stones, clever clogs," he said sarcastically. "It's what ground the corn and wheat into flour. It was the whole reason you built a windmill."

We got up and walked past the stones onto a driveway of interlocking blocks. A Mercedes was parked further back toward the house, but it did little to obscure our view.

"It's the mill house," I said. "One hundred percent."

I held Great Uncle Goog's painting up, and without a doubt, the house standing before us was as close to the rendering as we were going to get.

"See any cracked bricks?" I asked.

"I bet there's a few, but we'll never see them. Too much plaster and paint covering them," replied Tom.

We both stared, amazed that we had actually found what we had been looking for. In front of us was genuine proof that we were truly onto something big.

Chapter 43

Summer was definitely drawing to a close as we stood in the Mill House driveway. A cold wind had picked up, and I held on tight to the paintings as they flapped in the autumn breeze.

From our vantage point, we could see a farmer's field across the road. Beyond, there were horses grazing in a fenced paddock, and I watched for a moment before recognizing the scene from one of Uncle Goog's paintings.

"That's it," I said, pointing to the road leading to the stables. "It has to be."

My suspicions were confirmed as my uncle and I retraced our steps. We made our way past his car and down a narrow road that led toward the stables. There were no questions needed, the riding stable sign said it all.

"Welcome to Barlinghall Stables," it read. "Established 1910."

"Look," I said, pointing to an old brick out-building. "See near the top, two rows of cracked bricks. One or two poorly made bricks, maybe, but several whole rows? That's no coincidence."

My uncle did a quick count. "Thirty-eight bricks," he announced. "How much again was one of those blobs worth?"

"About one hundred and fifty pounds," I replied.

My uncle gave a whistle and shook his head. "Fifty-seven hundred quid just staring down at us," he said. "Bloody hell. What pictures do we have left again?" he asked, a little more motivated.

"Ok, we have a painting of a shipwrecked hull, then the two paintings in the cookbook. Salmagundy is a plowed field with cows, then Tripe and Onions is the final brick cottage with a toddler, dog, and a MILF walking up the garden path."

"Well, let's see what's down at the river," said Tom. "Seems like a good place for a shipwreck."

It didn't take long to find the water. The sound of motorboats and seagulls led us around the bend till suddenly, where the land met the river, we came across a large, abandoned ship that was permanently wedged into the shore.

"Well, that was easy," I said.

If that wasn't enough, just upstream, maybe fifty or so feet away, I could see a second decaying boat rotting in the mud. Unfortunately, it was clear neither boat was the subject of Uncle Rob's painting. One was made of steel and the other, though of wood construction, was too long and narrow to be in the running.

A car horn startled us both as we stood wondering what to do. From behind, a car reversed toward us, towing a small aluminum boat. The driver seemed in a hurry, so we stepped out of his way, realizing we had been standing in the middle of a boat launch. We watched as the car backed its trailer half into the water and then stopped with a loud crank of the hand brake. The man got out and looked at us.

"Well, don't just stand there," he said. "Give me a hand."

I looked at my uncle and shrugged.

"Come on, come on," said the man impatiently, and I rolled up my hand-me-down jeans and took off my shoes and socks.

It didn't take long. All that was needed was a quick unwind of the boat winch, and after a few decent pushes, our new friend's boat was in the water. My uncle, wanting nothing to do with the murky cold sludge, decided to hold the boat's rope. He waited till the man had parked his car, then on his return, found his opportunity to ask.

"Just wondering where else we could find some more wrecks around here?" he said.

The boat owner thought for a second. "Just go on up that foot path there," he said, pointing to a worn-out trail behind us. "There's a good one caught up in the salt marsh just at the end of it. I'd take you there in my boat, but there's nowhere to land. It's all just one big mud pit."

He took the rope from my uncle, and in one leap, jumped onto his outboard and drifted free of the shore. It took him a couple of tries, but the motor finally spluttered to life, and he chugged off downstream without giving us a second look.

The walk was pleasant enough along the water's edge. The tide was going out, and a slew of different sized watercrafts had aligned themselves in the middle of the river as if on some kind of flotilla parade.

It was Tom that brought up the topic of Harry again. He had always been curious why the monk had only been seen by kids.

"What makes you so special?" he asked, sounding a touch jealous.

"I don't know," I said. "Maybe we're connected somehow, like having a best friend you don't really want."

We walked for a few minutes in silence until my uncle spoke again.

"But he must want something? All ghosts have some message to give or a wrong to put right?"

"I think he's trapped to be honest," I said. "Maybe he's just looking for some peace."

My words hung in the air as we came to the edge of the salt marsh. It was just as our boat friend had described—one big muddy shit hole. In places, the river had carved snake-like paths, and we found the wrecked boat in between mud piles, rotting like the carcass of an animal. The whole area even smelt like death. I couldn't quite put my finger on it, but if I had to guess, the smelly tang reminded me of cleaning out a fish tank.

"Let's see the picture," said Tom, putting on his glasses.

I handed it to him and waited. There were a few grunts, but finally my uncle announced we had the right ship.

"It's definitely a smack," he explained. "And look, it's still got blue paint on it like in the painting."

"Why a boat?" I asked, wondering why my great uncle had taken the time to paint a wreck.

"I wouldn't be surprised if this was some kind of loading pier at one time," said Uncle Tom. "You have to remember those boats were like our modern-day lorries. They delivered all kinds of stuff to the coastal farmer—paper, candles, shingles, bricks, even farmyard shit."

"Do you think there's bricks on it still?" I asked.

"Are you going to check?" my uncle answered with another question.

"Fuck no," I replied. "The only mud wrestling fantasy I have includes a couple of naked women and a midget for a referee."

I pulled out the cookbook and flipped open the scene of the grassy clearing.

"Two clues left," I said, suddenly looking up.

Above us, we both heard the sound of an aeroplane. It had been getting increasingly louder, and it was my uncle who first spotted the contraption breaking free from the clouds.

"Cor blimey, would you look at that," he said transfixed. "I think it's coming in for a landing."

Without realizing it, we had found ourselves on the flight path for Barling Airstrip and we watched as the single engine plane dipped and levelled in preparation for contact. We couldn't have had a better vantage point. The plane roared over our heads, and instinctively we ducked even though it was a good hundred feet above us.

"My God, it's a Morane-Saulnier!" Tom yelled above the noise.

"What!?" I yelled back.

"It's only one of the rarest planes from the First World War. See, look, you can tell by its parasol wings."

"Like an old Victorian umbrella?" I replied.

"Well, yeah . . . no," said Tom. "It's just that the wings were mounted above the fuselage and aren't attached to anything. In the end, the air force threw a machine gun on the front and fucked a whole whack of Germans."

I could see by my uncle's reaction his trainspotter senses had kicked in. He was half running back down the path, and I kept up with him until we reached the stables. A little out of breath, I stopped and waved him on.

"Go, see your plane, I'll catch up later."

"Won't be long!" he called back, jingling his car keys. "Looks like rain anyway."

Chapter 44

It felt strange being alone. Maybe it was the rumble of an impending storm, but suddenly everything felt slightly sinister. I had lost sight of the plane. It had disappeared below the tree line, and I figured I would take my time and walk through the paddock and woods that presumably led to the end of the runway. I was about halfway across the field when I felt the first drops of rain.

"Perfect," I said mockingly.

I knew better than to think I was in for just a light shower, and by the time I had legged it into the woods, the sky had opened with a loud and violent downpour. There was nothing to do but wait. I sat under a large old oak and watched the rain come down. At my feet, a few leaves had already given up on fall. They lay dead among a scattering of acorns, and from somewhere high above, I heard a small bird sing a few notes of weak protest.

"Ouch," I said, catching my hand on something sharp beneath me.

I had presumed I was sitting on a fallen tree limb but taking a closer look, I saw several rusty nails sticking out of what looked like an old rotten fence post. Not far off, I noticed another post standing semi-upright. I counted ten steps to reach it, then counted ten more in what I thought was a straight line. Sure enough, under a thin layer of wet leaves, I found the remains of a third post hole. The curious thing was that the fence didn't make sense. It led deeper into the woods, finally disappearing into a tangle of thick bush.

"Hang on a second," I said, pulling out Maury's cookbook.

I flipped it to the final cottage painting and stared. A fence ran the entire length of the picture.

"Oh come on," I said, "that couldn't be the same fence?"

In truth, I wasn't sure what to think. My mind's eye had imagined the cottage still perfectly intact, but the reality was something I hadn't really prepared for. *I need to find my uncle,* I thought. The rain had almost stopped, and as luck would have it, beyond the last of the trees, I spotted the runway.

If I had been paying attention, I probably would have stepped over the mound of mossy grass. But, as it turned out, I flailed through the air and landed hard on my ankle in a rather unnatural way. The pain was intense, and I cried out in dumb frustration.

"Fuck, fuck, and fucking fuck!" I yelled, holding my leg.

I curled into a fetal position and waited for the pain to wash over me. It took a few minutes, but getting my breathing under control, I pulled myself up and limped back to the offending mound.

In anger, I yanked at the solid mass and managed to pull it free from its resting place. I wasn't sure what I was going to do with it. I wasn't going to kick it, so instead I found a stick and thrashed at it in hopes of at least teaching it a lesson.

I had just finished getting my point across when I saw the letters. In my futile lashing, I had somehow dislodged several sections of moss and what I thought had been some type of rock revealed itself to be something quite different. The first letter I saw was an O and then the letter V came into view. After a bit of scraping, I had the word "OVER" and then, seconds later—everything made sense.

I let my fingers trace over the word. I wasn't sure what to feel, but to further validate my find, I rolled the chunk of masonry onto its side and discovered that all ten bricks of the cement cluster were cracked. If archaeologists were right to claim that three bricks made a wall, I thought, then ten cracked Clover bricks cemented together could only mean one serious building.

"Holy shit," I said. "I think I found it."

As if on queue, a new sound filled the sky. A helicopter had taken-off from the airport, and in the aftermath of the storm, I figured it was on some type of air-sea rescue mission. It passed low over head, but since there was no chance it was stopping to help some idiot who couldn't walk straight, I got up and worked out a hoppy-limpy dance, similar to being tied naked.

I found the cottage door first. It lay flat and sunken in the ground, its green paint still holding on to its rotted wooden planks. Next, I came across an old, crumpled pail, and then not long after, a rusted bed frame. I passed several dodgy looking farm implements, and trying not to get impaled, I limped slowly around each one, narrowly missing a half-buried tiller.

I was wondering when my last tetanus shot had been when I suddenly found myself standing in a large rectangular opening. The remains of a fire and broken glass littered the far end of the area. A few logs had been positioned around the charred remains, and apart from some empty crisp packets and a condom wrapper, there was very little evidence of any other human activity. I looked once more at Goog's painting and limped a little closer to the ashes. From the painting, I could clearly see two chimneys, and pulling back some singed ferns, I discovered the ashes were actually in the remains of an already existing brick hearth.

"Holy crap," I said as I yanked and tore more of the thick undergrowth. "It's a goddamn wall."

Before me, well hidden and almost reclaimed by nature, stood a wall of Clover bricks. It was only partially intact, but there were enough bricks to suggest a two-storey cottage exactly like the one in my great uncle's painting. In all, I counted thirty-eight layers of bricks, all cracked and presumably all hiding Clover gold. Thirty-eight high, twenty-six bricks long, I calculated, call it a bit under a thousand, times one-fifty, that's one hundred and fifty thousand pounds.

To prove I wasn't mad, I picked up a loose brick and smashed it against another that lay by its side. It separated cleanly, and without any doubt, I examined the exposed broken ends and found the same familiar golden blob. The back wall of the cottage was just as hidden as the side. It was at least three times the length, and I pulled at a few random sections of overgrowth, each time finding another area of cracked bricks. *That's something like half a million pounds,* I thought.

"Would you like a Jelly Baby?" a voice from behind suddenly whispered.

I knew that voice and instantly I froze. *Christ, what is Nevel doing here?* I asked just as a sharp blow snapped my head to one side. It was a powerful, merciless strike, and staggering, my sprained ankle gave way, and I toppled to the ground.

"Nevel?" I managed to mumble before a second blow connected with my outstretched arm. "Fuck!" I yelled. "What the hell are you doing?"

Above me, Nevel stood chewing a red Jelly Baby. I could see small droplets of blood dripping from the brick he was holding, and it suddenly occurred to me the fucker was trying to kill me. *This is bad,* I thought, desperately trying to drag myself out of harm's way. He looked possessed with rage and he lunged again, this time narrowly missing my head.

In shear panic, I felt around for anything I could use as a weapon. Something sharp poked my hand, and in desperation, I held up the neck of a broken beer bottle.

"Suck on this, mother fucker!" I screamed, jamming the broken glass into Nevel's leg.

With a satisfying thud, it sunk deep into the muscle. He looked down briefly, as if slightly amused, and then all hope vanished as he raised the brick high above his head and grinned.

Chapter 45

"Bugger," said Nevel, thinking he had been spotted.

He had passed the uncle and boy not five feet from the road but looking back in his rear-view mirror, he realized neither had paid any attention.

He had been following them since the petrol station, and things seemed to be heating up. After a two-hour stakeout at the uncle's house, he had tailed the white Astra until a slow tractor had forced him to lose sight of the car. Somehow, he had missed their parked car as he sped through the village. He had gotten as far as the Mucking Hall crossroads when a gut feeling made him turn around.

Except for that one slight hiccup, thought Nevel, *I'm getting pretty good at this detective thing.* He parked at the far side of the church and waited. *What are they up to?* he thought, tearing open a fresh pack of Jelly Babies. He pondered his own question and sucked silently on a decapitated head. As far as he knew, there were no standing windmills in Barling. *Even if there are,* he thought, *without the three missing paintings, no one will be finding anything.*

It wasn't long before the boy and the uncle reappeared. For a panicked moment, Nevel thought the two were walking directly toward his car, but with relief, they turned on the other side of the churchyard and disappeared out of sight. Nevel got out and popped the boot. He reached for a small hand shovel and raincoat, then walked into the churchyard.

Turning east, Nevel looked for a grave close to the road. He found several that would do and choosing one as far away from the church as possible, he began clearing debris while nonchalantly peering over the church wall and down the narrow road.

In the distance, he saw them. From what he could make out, they were pointing at something high up on a building. *What's that in the boy's hand?* thought Nevel, watching papers flap in the wind. *Papers,* he thought, *that look suspiciously like paintings.*

"Blast and double blast," he said with a pang of anger. "How the hell did they get those?"

It didn't take long to find them. The boy and uncle had made it down to the water's edge, and he watched from behind an overturned rowboat as they helped a boat owner launch his aluminum runner into the frigid channel.

They were close, very close, decided Nevel, clearly recognizing one of the three missing paintings. He had to concede they had done their homework, and he felt annoyed remembering his wasted day in Burnham-on-Crouch. *Why did I go there instead of Barling?* he pondered. The delivery notation was perfectly clear.

"B-on-Ch," he recalled.

Burnham-on-Crouch, what else can it mean? Barling-on-Crouch doesn't make sense, that is completely the wrong river. Barlinghall-on-Creek is a possibility, but I don't think so. Barling-on what then? he asked himself. *Barling-on-Ch, Ch, Cheif, Chum, Cheese, Chalk. Chimp, Churp,* and then he had it. *How dumb am I?* he thought, reprimanding himself. *Barling-on-Church,* he concluded. The damn cottage was in Barling and on Church Street.

From the conversation he was hearing, Nevel calculated he had a good hour head start. He smiled, picturing the boy and his uncle knee deep in the tidal mud, and wasting no time, he turned and started up Church Street with a renewed sense of purpose.

So where would someone build a house around here? thought Nevel, looking around. He had spent several nights painstakingly studying every detail of the cottage painting, but nothing, in any direction, seemed remotely familiar.

Just then, two horse riders approached from the rear. Nevel stepped aside to let them pass, and as they drew parallel, he gave them a casual wave.

"Looks like rain," said the rider closest to Nevel.

"It certainly does," he replied. "Hey, tell me something," asked Nevel, hurrying to keep up. "Do you know of any old cottages around here or abandoned buildings? I belong to a forgotten history club, and I was told there were a few places around here."

The woman closest to Nevel pulled lightly on her reins, and her horse stopped without protest. Nevel guessed she was in her sixties, and by the way she handled her horse, he figured she had probably ridden most of her life.

"I really don't know, luv," she said, looking down at Nevel. "Nothing really comes to mind. What about you?" the woman asked, directing the question to her riding partner.

Nevel could see her companion was at least half the woman's age. She had similar facial features, and it wasn't a hard stretch to think the two were somehow related.

"Come on, mum," she replied with an air of disbelief. "Really? What did you always tell me not to do over here when I was a kid?"

The mother looked confused for a second and then spoke with a tinge of embarrassment. "Oh for Pete's sake, how silly of me. Yes, yes, of course, over there." She pointed with her crop to a distant clump of trees far to the right of the road. "If you follow that tree line," she said, continuing to wave her whip, "you'll find whatever is left of that old farmhouse. It got condemned years ago. Not sure why it wasn't pulled down. Anyway, it's a bit of a death trap as far as I'm concerned. After Cynthia's brother came back with a nasty gash in his leg, I forbid my two to go near it again."

"Thank you, you've been most helpful," smiled Nevel.

"Just mind how you go," said the woman, kicking her heels into the side of her horse. "Hate for anything bad to happen to you."

He watched as the riders carried on up the road. *No*, thought Nevel, *nothing bad is going to happen to me. The boy and his uncle, however? Well, they might not be so lucky.*

Nevel found the cottage remains with little trouble. He sat for a long time and considered the ruins a holy place, the final end to a pilgrimage he had endured for many long years. *Surrounding me*, he thought, *is the*

first real compensation for the horrors of my family's past. He supposed killing Flossy had got the ball rolling, but now with such a massive amount of gold, Nevel felt his life was about to change dramatically. *There will be talk shows,* he thought, *a book deal, and I will insist on a new in-depth investigation into the death of both my parents. No one will blame me, how can they? It's obvious my family were the victims here, and any incidental murder along the way will clearly be seen as justified.*

Tilting his head upwards, it occurred to Nevel it was raining. He spread his arms open wide, and then, in what he believed to be a moment of true redemption, heard the applause of a thousand souls rejoicing his victory.

Nevel felt his arm muscles strain as he fought through the underbrush. The weight of eight Clover bricks was obviously too much and he made a mental note to buy a wheelbarrow before his next visit. He was on the verge of dropping the stack when he heard an agonizing scream.

What was that? thought Nevel, a little unnerved. *That sounds like the boy,* and as if on queue, a second more groan-like cry came from the direction of the airstrip. *Whoever it is,* he concluded, *they aren't sounding good,* and for no other reason than his fascination with human suffering, he dropped the bricks and went to investigate the source.

I was right, thought Nevel as he watched the boy from behind a tree. He felt no urge to help, in fact to the contrary, the more the boy writhed in agony, the greater joy he felt.

Nevel reached down into his raincoat pocket and touched the handle of his small trowel. He felt the sharp serrated edge, and though it would be messy, he was confident he could cut the boy's throat with little effort. *No,* thought Nevel, feeling that wouldn't do. *There has to be a more fitting end to honour my family.* Leaving the boy, he retraced his steps back to the bricks he had unceremoniously dumped. Bending down, Nevel picked up the closest Clover brick and felt the weight in his hand.

"This will do nicely," he said, and with no great rush, turned once more, back to the helpless boy.

It didn't take long. A pair of odd-looking footprints led straight into the cottage ruins. Nevel tightened his grip on the brick and slowly crept toward the unsuspecting boy. He had already drawn his arm back, poised to unleash a damaging blow, when Nevel suddenly stopped himself again. *No, no, no,* he said to himself, *this isn't the way. I want to see his face. I want to see his reaction when my brick crushes the side of his skull.*

Noiselessly, Nevel reached into his left pocket and pulled out a half-eaten bag of Jelly Babies. He was reminded of how Doctor Who from the television series had a habit of offering Jelly Babies to intergalactic monsters, and Nevel couldn't think of a better blind side.

"Would you like a Jelly Baby?" he said, ready to strike.

The boy turned at the offer, and Nevel smashed the Clover brick as hard as he could into his head. The result was instantaneous. The boy's mangy leg buckled, and his body dropped to the ground with a satisfying thud. To Nevel's surprise, he did not lose consciousness. He had hoped his first blow would have been enough, but instead, Nevel received a volley of insults from a very alive and angry victim. *He just doesn't get it,* thought Nevel, raising the brick for a second time. *What a complete insensitive piece of shit.*

Once again, he aimed for the boy's head and launched a blow even more vicious than the first. This time, there was no doubt in Nevel's conviction. *That's a guaranteed "home run" as the Americans say,* he thought, and flinched slightly, anticipating the spray back of blood. But it did not come. At the last possible second, the boy rolled to one side, and Nevel, carried by his momentum, could do little but feel the impact of the brick as it hit the hard packed earth.

Damn it, thought Nevel, *this isn't the way it was supposed to be.* He had always prided himself on killing smart. Even for entertainment purposes, he had always, always, planned and controlled every move. Getting up, he felt the hatred boil. With almost blind rage, Nevel swung the Clover brick around in a circle, ready to pounce. There was no mercy now, all he wanted was blood and justice.

Suddenly, Nevel looked down. *What the hell is that?* he thought, seeing a piece of broken glass sticking from his leg. He stared at it for a moment, feeling nothing. *That's it?* Nevel thought, *that's the best you've got?* He smiled at the pathetic attempt and knew it was over. Nevel raised the Clover brick one more time. It was the moment he had waited for his entire life. With both hands gripped tightly, he launched a final blow that even the boy could not escape.

Chapter 46

"You made it," said the Time Keeper, stoking the fire of an old Victorian cooking range.

"I did?" I said, opening my eyes.

"Of course you did, welcome to the Narrows."

"What?" I replied, very confused. "That makes no sense."

"Well, yes, it does. Not sure if you recall, but right about now you're in the process of getting your head bashed in with a brick."

I touched the side of my head and tried to remember.

"Oh yeah," I conceded. "How's that working out for me?"

"Not so good, I'm afraid, but never fear, there are infinite possibilities to your outcome."

"I'm glad you think so," I replied, trying to stand.

"Easy," warned the Time Keeper. "Don't move so quick. Hate to have you puking again."

In front of me was a worn-out table and chairs, and I pulled a chair out and slowly sat down.

"Why are you wearing the monk robes again?" I asked, taking a better stock of my surroundings.

"Oh, I don't know," replied the Time Keeper, turning, "just thought I would look official."

"Does that mean I'm dead and you're the welcoming committee?"

"No, no," he replied. "We just need to figure a few things out first."

Behind the Time Keeper, on the stove mantel, I recognized two small porcelain statues. They had been handed down in my family, to the first girl of each new generation.

"Hey, I know those dogs," I said. "Where am I again?"

"Shirley House," replied the Time Keeper. "Thought I'd bring you back somewhere kinda familiar. Have to say, it wasn't cheap getting a hold of the memory."

"I appreciate the effort," I replied, "but this was all way before my time."

The room was bigger than I had imagined. A bookcase leaned against the far end wall and an armchair, presumably Great William Clover's, nestled at an angle close to the hearth. There was only one window to the room. From outside, I could hear the wind scream as it rattled the panes and snow blew thick, obscuring any true sense of time.

"What's with the upside-down flowers?" I said, noticing several bunches hanging by the front door.

"Lavender," replied the Time Keeper. "It's always been a popular herb. Even the Romans were big on its healing powers."

"Talking about that, what happened to you? The last time I checked, we were making homemade smudge to commit a bit of spiritual hari-kari?"

I must have touched a sore spot because the Time Keeper didn't respond. Instead, he walked over to the table and sat down.

"I was wrong," he said matter-of-factly.

"About . . . ?" I asked.

"Trying to escape a place I thought I was trapped in."

"So you weren't?" I said, trying to keep up.

"Only in my thinking," he replied. "The problem was I looked at the Narrows as a place that wouldn't let me go. But the reality was quite the opposite. I didn't know how to leave. You see, all along I was thinking like every other In-Betweener."

"And how was that?" I asked.

"That I wasn't 'me' anymore. That I was broken, you know? All used up. But then I figured it out. Dying doesn't change anything. It wasn't being human that defined me, it was everything else I was made of that counted."

"Makes a lot of sense," I said, "but why do you think you were broken?"

"You don't know?" asked the Time Keeper, a little surprised.

"No, why should I?" I answered. I stared at the Time Keeper until he realized his mistake.

"Oh, of course," he said, slapping the side of his head. "That's right, your present hasn't caught up to my past yet."

"Well, when will that happen?" I asked, a little frustrated.

"I wouldn't worry about it," he replied. "You'll never see it coming, even if you tried. Just remember it isn't what happens to you, it's how you 'deal with it' that counts. Remember my axe-wielding Viking friend?"

"Sure," I replied, "great guy."

"Well, I couldn't figure him out. All along he had the choice to leave the Narrows, but he never did."

"Why?" I asked.

"Exactly," replied the Time Keeper. "Exactly, exactly, exactly."

"What?" I said, confused.

"No, not *what* but *why*," corrected the Time Keeper. "Why do we do anything? Isn't that the ultimate question? And before you say it, the answer isn't 42."

I shut my mouth; it was exactly what I was about to say. "It's hard to say," I finally said. "*Why* just sort of happens. I can't really explain why we do anything other than it comes from a place on some instinctive, deep, unconscious level."

"Sounds a bit like the definition of love?" suggested the Time Keeper.

"Yeah, a bit," I agreed.

"Then it's the *why*, above everything, that eventually will set you free."

"It's time," announced the Time Keeper, quickly standing up from his chair. "You have to go. Now."

"Where?" I asked.

"Back," he said with no other explanation.

"But my head," I protested. "What about my head?"

"Don't you worry," replied the Time Keeper. "I've got it covered."

He pulled at his leather necklace, and I heard a snap as it broke. In his hand he held his gold medallion, and with an urgency I hadn't seen before, the Time Keeper thrust it into my palm and closed my fingers around it.

"Hurry, there's no time left."

As if to emphasize the point, a violent tremor suddenly shook the room. I grabbed at the table edge and watched as the oil lamps flickered then died, plunging the cottage into absolute darkness.

"Go!" shouted the Time Keeper. "Unlock the door and run!"

Before I had time to move, a second quake, and more jolting than the first, knocked me to the ground. I pressed my hands to the floor, then recoiled in panic as I felt something sticky and viscous.

"What the hell is happening!?" I yelled, lunging through the darkness.

I had no clue where I was. The darkness felt infinite, and it was only blind luck that my hand fell to the latch.

"Come on, come on!" I screamed, finally connecting the Time Keeper's key with the lock. With every remaining ounce of energy, I wrenched open the door. "Christ!" I yelled, trying to shield my eyes from the light.

It felt like I had just been punched, and turning, I caught a glimpse of the Time Keeper for perhaps the last time. I watched, transfixed, as he reached out in front of him. Only the whites of his eyes showed as he swung at something only he could see. I knew he was leaving the Narrows, I could feel it. But surprisingly, I wasn't sad, just happy he had found a way.

I broke my stare, realizing the memory of Shirley House was dying. Blood oozed from the walls as floorboards twisted and picture frames smashed. Just as the roof collapsed, I made my escape. I braced myself against the onslaught of the storm, and as a wave of crimson debris crashed toward me, I leapt across the threshold, telling myself there was no other choice.

Chapter 47

I have only seen into the future once in my life. The entire experience lasted a total of five seconds. But that was plenty of time to doubt the scene that popped into my head and then plenty of time to become a believer. It didn't scare me. I felt empowered, even special, having witnessed the universe with its trousers' down.

The premonition I saw was the flagpole of my back garden tree fort crashing down on the boy from next door. He was rather annoying if I recall, and if I had cared, I would have tried to warn him, but I didn't. In my defence, I didn't believe it would happen. That flagpole and its Union Jack had stood for years, and yet right before my eyes, the scene unfolded exactly how I had envisioned it five seconds earlier. I don't think "Stiffy Stephen" was hurt too badly. I presume he limped back over the fence, but sadly I had little concern for his well-being. Instead, my attention lay on trying to make sense of what I had just witnessed.

My best explanation came from when I was even younger. I had thought that all you needed to do to get into a movie on television was put hinges on the screen. Just step in through the open space and jump into the action. I saw my experience was not that far removed. It showed me just how thin the curtain of reality really was and that the illusion of time was only one of multiple options on the television channel selector.

I felt nothing. Not even a single hair on my head moved. It was strange, like I had become numb to the world, and I wandered, lost, until I climbed a large snow-covered hill.

By the time I had reached the top, the storm had settled. I stood, knee deep in snow, and looked out over a valley that seemed to stretch for miles.

What the hell is that? I asked, looking at an object in the distance. *A cage, maybe a box?* I wasn't sure, but whatever it turned out to be, I knew it was waiting for me. When I finally approached, I realized it was much larger than I first thought. It was a room made of glass, and I stood, watching, trying to make sense of the unfolding drama.

Inside, nurses wearing brightly coloured scrubs frantically moved with deliberate intent. Important machines beeped and flashed, and a jigsaw puzzle of multi-coloured wires ran like out of control spaghetti toward the centre of the room. *Crap,* I thought. *Maybe that's me in there? Death by brick to the head.* With both hands, I started to bang on the glass.

"Hey!" I yelled. "Let me in, I can help, let me in, please!"

But no one heard. *Why does it matter?* I thought. *If I'm dead, then my body is no good to anyone.*

"I'm so sorry," I finally heard myself say. I had no idea why I was apologizing, but it felt like it needed to be said.

I was still watching when the room went black. It was if the power had suddenly been yanked, and like an old television set, all that remained was a small white sphere in the centre of the room. I took a deep breath and turned.

"So what now?"

I had no plan, no direction, no idea what to do. I breathed in again and coughed. I could taste something acidic, and clearing my throat, I spat into the snow.

"Burnt garlic?" I questioned, not understanding. *Where did that come from?*

Then, without warning, a thick greenish fog coiled around me. It became so dense my visibility reduced to almost nothing.

"Jesus," I said, feeling my eyes start to burn. "What is this shit?"

As my cough became a steady hack, I lost all sense of direction. It was as if I was floating in some out of control dimension, and if not for the sound of a whistle, I doubted I would have ever found my way out.

"Who's there?" I croaked, hearing the whistle again.

There was no reply, but I was sure I saw something move. It was hard to tell just what until a figure of a man came running toward me. He appeared out of the fog with his hands clasped around his throat, and I stepped aside, convinced he was about to run me over. He wore what I thought was an army uniform. It was caked with mud, and before I could make sense of what was happening, another soldier, just as panicked, rushed past.

"Jesus fuck," I said as a horse suddenly collapsed less than five feet in front of me.

Then, one by one, the bodies started to drop. They seethed and convulsed on the ground, and all I could do was get out of the way and hope death came quickly. Without warning, I was knocked backwards. A soldier fell motionless on top of me, and before I had a chance to pull myself clear, another body crashed down on top.

"Get off me!" I cried desperately, reaching for any type of hand hold.

Damn it, I thought. *This is not how it's going to end,* and feeling the leg of a fallen horse, I pulled myself from certain suffocation.

Stumbling out of the carnage, I came upon a series of dug out trenches. More dead bodies scattered the passageways, many having collapsed only a few feet from the top. *What a fucking mess,* I thought.

I knelt and brushed a light dusting of snow from a body a few feet away. Their eyes were blank and lifeless, and only then did I realize, to my horror, I was staring into the face of a small child.

"Oh Christ," I whispered, unprepared to accept what I was seeing.

I cradled the stone-cold body and felt nothing but helplessness. I had nothing left in me to give. My tears fell and my heart broke, and I understood that the only fault of the innocent was trusting the past.

Chapter 48

A psychic once told me the best way out of a desert was to walk a straight line. A little ironic, I had thought, to pay money for the obvious, but it has always served me well, so maybe they knew something I didn't. I picked a direction on the horizon and started to walk. The terrain was much easier than before. The fog had lifted, and only a thin crust of snow covered what appeared to be nothing but a barren, forgotten wasteland.

Occasionally, I would find an abandoned object. The first was a rusty old baby carriage half buried in the ground. One of its wheels was missing, and it looked wrong somehow, just left to rot in the middle of nowhere. Then soon after, an assortment of clothes appeared. Everything from baby outfits to worn-out jeans and t-shirts. Even old shoes lay carelessly across my path, and I made a game of kicking them out of the way. In the air, high above, papers blew in the wind. They looked orchestrated like migrating birds, and I watched as they moved and twisted in an unspoken understanding.

For some reason, everything looked familiar. An old broken toy, a faded comic book, even a flat well-used soccer ball.

"Hang on a minute," I said. "This is all my shit." No wonder I recognized it. What the hell was it doing here?

"And that's my dad's old Ford Cortina," I suddenly said, recognizing the old burnt-out car.

I hadn't thought about that in years. The car had caught fire on a family trip to London, and though it hadn't blown-up, it never did drive again. Amazed, I climbed onto its roof and scanned the horizon. Around me, wreckage from my past sprawled in every direction. I could see no end to the multitude of discarded memories.

"Jesus," I said, not knowing how to feel.

On one hand, my memories had made me who I was, but on the other, they lay helplessly dying around me. I was looking, I realized, at the sum total of my existence. Everything around me had guided me to where I stood. All of my past was here, and I suddenly understood that each and every moment of my life had both meaning and purpose.

The wind had picked up again as I tied the last of the draw strings. It hadn't taken long to put the old family cooking tent back together, and though I could hear paper and other debris slap against the outer canvas, I knew my past wouldn't hurt me.

Inside, things were very different. A fire pit smouldered in the middle of the floor, and the walls of the tent, though I thought were only dusty fabric, gave the illusion of damp cold rock. It took me a second, but then I smiled. *I remember this place. It was the one safe place in my mind I used to always go. An impenetrable cave that protected and hid me when things got bad. How could I have forgotten?* I asked. This place had saved me many times over, and I felt suddenly ashamed having betrayed myself for "grown-up" insensibility.

Kneeling, I picked up a handful of sticks and threw them on the dying fire. Instantly, the kindling crackled and spat, and I couldn't help but feel reprimanded for my long stay of absence.

"Yeah, yeah, I'm here now," I said, edging closer to the fire.

It was tempting to lie down. The tongue-like flames moved in a hypnotic rhythm, and though sleep beckoned, I knew it would be too easy to give up and stay in my cave forever. Instead, I sat motionless and listened to the sounds of my past. The muffled shouts, the breaking of glass, children screaming, even old Flossy's heckling laugh. Next to me, I swore a budgie flapped its wings, but turning, I saw only shadows flickering off the walls.

I drew my knees closer to my chest and squeezed. It didn't matter how small I tried to make myself, the voices always knew where I was. In ways, my past had served me well. It had protected me, taught me, and prepared me for the future. All that remained were simply used up stories that blew and eroded into obscurity. It was a nice place to visit, I decided, but in the end, there was nothing new to see.

The pain of my past only made me stronger, the tears of my past, only braver. Even the worst heartache I understood, in time, would only make me love deeper.

Chapter 49

To be honest, the last thing I expected was to be confronted by the appearance of a large brick wall.

"Where the fuck did that come from?" I asked as I crawled from the tent.

A brick wall wasn't something you just missed, and I gaped at its sheer magnitude, seeing no end in sight. Against the base of the wall, metal and trash had started to pile up. If I hadn't known better, it looked like the entire wall had scraped along the ground, gathering everything along its path.

So this must be the edge of the Narrows, I realized. I reached out and touched the rough clay surface of the brick.

"Hum," I grunted. "Clover brick, of course."

I looked up to the top of the wall. It towered above me like a medieval fortress. *How the hell am I going to get up there?* From somewhere high above, a single piece of paper floated down toward me. I watched as it gently circled and twisted and then finally came to rest on the frame of my old bicycle. Curious, I pulled myself onto my mother's rusted washing machine and reached for the flapping page. In the top right-hand corner, my name was scrolled in pencil.

"I remember this," I said, reading the title I had underlined twice. "Attacking a Castle in Pictures."

The first drawing was of soldiers tunnelling under the ground. There were also forty pigs in the scene, apparently waiting to be herded down the passage and set on fire. *It seems reasonable enough,* I thought. *The heat of forty burning pigs might just collapse a castle wall, but looking around, I didn't think I was going to find too many volunteers.*

The second drawing was of a catapult called a French trebuchet. It launched projectiles at a castle, although in my version, the object sailing through the air was a stand-up piano. I never did like that piano teacher.

My work contained an obsessive amount of blood splatter. From what I could see, arrows, swords and battering rams seemed to generate the most impressive carnage. It was a bit disturbing, I had to admit, but then what eight-year-old didn't like a decent Jackson Pollock massacre?

The idea of building a tower came while looking at my last drawing. It was clear I had spent a lot of time on the scene, and I was still impressed by how many ways I had detailed soldiers losing their limbs. The subject of the attack was a siege tower. Basically, it got rolled up against a castle wall, and soldiers simply climbed to the top and hopped over the battlements.

"So how about it?" I said to myself.

Bicycles, appliances, playground equipment, it all can be used, I thought. My crap was everywhere, and for once, I was glad my past was worth remembering.

I really couldn't tell how long it took. There was no real way to tell. Maybe a week, a month, time had become insignificant.

The biblical Tower of Babel, built to reach heaven, stopped after an estimated one hundred and seven years, and for all I know, it could have been the same for me. The only real difference was that I didn't want to get to heaven. I just wanted to get the fuck out of the Narrows.

Standing back, I stared at my creation with pride. It was beautiful in its own pathetic way. Through the construction, I had been forced to re-examine my past, and by deciding what I still could use, I was left with a monument I was truly proud of.

I yanked on my mother's clothesline one last time. I had set up a pulley system using the roller from dad's Suffolk lawn mower, and I watched as the final two planks lifted into the air.

My tower was about as stable as a mobile home in a tornado. It swayed dangerously from side to side, the grinding and creaking of metal only reminding me of how fragile my past held in the balance.

It was the last time, I hoped, I would have to climb the bloody thing. Only two planks separated me from freedom and damned if I was going to screw it up.

My confidence, as I climbed however, dwindled by the time I had reached the top. Along the way I had discovered a few alarmingly loose support beams. I had long since used up anything decent to lash my structure together, and I could only pray that electrical wire, duct tape, and fishing line, would hold until I had made my jump. Catching my breath, I tried not to look down. I untied the clothesline and carefully positioned the final two planks into position.

Nervously, I eased my body up onto the highest platform and swallowed hard. *It's now or never,* I thought, trying to steady my shaking knees. I blew out one final breath, then crouched, ready to launch. Just to be sure, I checked the distance to the top of the wall one more time.

"Easy-peasy," I said, trying to convince myself, and before another thought entered my head, I started my count down. "Five, four, three, two, two and a half, two and a quarter," I said, hesitating. "Two and a bit, two and a smaller bit." A momentary pause, and then, "FUCK IT . . . one!"

The pain was intense. Instantly my hands burned with sharp, seething fire, and I hung helplessly as I watched blood trickle down the inside of my arms. *That's not good,* I told myself, trying desperately to swing my leg up and over.

Below, I heard the tower groan. It didn't sound like it would be standing much longer, and it was obvious there was no turning back even if I had wanted to let go. I kicked again, and miraculously my foot caught just the edge of the top brick. With everything I had, I heaved and twisted my body until finally I cleared the wall.

"Fuuuccck!" I yelled, landing hard on some viciously sharp glass.

It had been cemented to the top edge of the wall, and my hands and leg stung as I gently tried to coax my impaled flesh from the shards.

I was just about to congratulate myself when a crash of metal screeched from below. My tower had collapsed, and I felt a twinge of sadness as my memories hurtled back to earth, transforming into junk once again.

It didn't matter. I knew where they were. I waited as the aftershock reverberated through the wall. It was only a low rumble, but instead of it fading, I felt the intensity only grow stronger.

"That's not right," I said, pulling myself up. "What the hell's going on?"

I steadied myself the best I could and peered over the edge. It took only a glimpse to understand.

"Christ," I gasped as my arm scraped against more glass shards. "The wall's fucking moving."

To my amazement, the wall began to gather speed. It seemed almost pleasant at first until we hit the first bump.

Ok, I thought, *fun time is over,* but my problems had just begun. If I had just been dealing with ups and downs that wouldn't have been so bad, but the wall slithered sideways, and I was tossed into the air like a defenceless rag doll. I tried to hang on, but it was no use. My fingers slipped from the smooth joints of mortar, and I careened high above the wall until I crash landed, impaling my shoulder in the process.

I felt everything now. Whatever the Narrows had taken away, my summit push had brought it all back. The wind chilled me, my wounds burned and ached, and even the rising nausea in my stomach crept back like an old annoying friend. Instinctively, I tried to reach out to hold my wound, but there was no time. Once more, I was thrust skywards, and again I crashed down onto the wall, this time raking my arm across its glass teeth.

It's useless, I thought, feeling more pain than I had ever imagined. The phrase "death by a thousand cuts" came to mind, and I braced myself for the next jolt, thinking I would be dead in half that number. I could see blood now, starting to seep from my wounds. However I tried to hold on, it didn't matter. I was being torn apart, thrown and diced like carrots, and there was nothing I could do but wait for the end.

"Please!" I cried out. "Please someone help me, someone, anybody!"

But no one came. I was alone, abandoned, and incredibly pissed-off.

I was too weak to care why the wall eventually stopped. My blood-soaked clothes stuck to my skin like wet toilet paper, and I gulped small shallow breaths in hopes of minimizing the pain. I lay motionless, exhausted and crushed on the unforgiving brick.

"What did I do to deserve that?" I asked, spitting up a glob of bloody phlegm. "I thought I had done everything right?"

I didn't expect an answer, but from somewhere behind me came a voice.

"You don't learn by doing everything right."

"Time Keeper, it's you. Help me," I groaned.

I was still unable to see him as he raised my head and shoulders. He cradled me in his robes, and I felt a warmth pacify my broken body.

"You did it," I heard him say. "You made it out of the Narrows."

"Barely," I replied. "It didn't want to let me go."

"I know," agreed the Time Keeper. "The wall doesn't give up the dying easily. It knows you too well. It knows your fears, your weaknesses, even your doubts. It does everything in its power to keep you surrounded until you lose all hope."

"I was pretty close," I confessed.

"No way," replied the Time Keeper. "You made your decision to be free a long time ago. Now get up," he said, lifting me into a standing position. "The trick is you have to heal yourself, even when it hurts. Remember, where there is pain, there is also great love."

I stared at him, not sure of how to respond, but the Time Keeper's eyes answered for me. They were old, wise, gentle eyes, that looked at me with such compassion. I knew, I felt, he was right.

"This is where our journey ends," he said, still looking at me. "It is the only way for you to truly understand who I am."

"But why?" I asked, then stopped. I had answered my own question.

"Thank you," said the Time Keeper. "Because of you, I have lived my *why*. There is no better gift to take with me."

He paused for a final moment and then turned away. I watched for a time until he disappeared over a crest in the brick path, and I knew he was gone.

Once again, I was alone and unsure of what to do. Looking down, I was surprised to see my hands had started to heal. Scars of white ridges bound my palms, and checking my other wounds, I found similar bands holding together in tight defiance.

"Fuck you, wall!" I shouted with newfound conviction. "I'm still here, you mother fucker!"

My cries echoed into the surrounding void, and I laughed, realizing it was my scars that were making me whole again.

On an impulse, I pulled the Time Keeper's key from my pocket. It looked simple enough, but if I had learned anything from the Time Keeper, it was that my five basic senses were rather limited beyond the art of survival.

"So," I asked my talisman, "what can you show me that I can't see?"

I lifted the key to my eye and stared through the oval-shaped opening. To the right were the Narrows, to my left, absolutely nothing. Well, maybe not nothing. Even a vacuum of nothing had some sort of matter and antimatter battling it out to become something.

Maybe that's it, I thought. *Maybe it's the unseen struggle that really matters. That makes the universe complete and keeps everything in constant motion. Sometimes you win and sometimes you lose. It's just how you put yourself back together that counts.*

I put down the key and stood facing the void. It had a bluish tinge, like a cloudless clear sky, and closing my eyes, I felt a waft of tiny pin pricks radiate through my body. It was a bit like being mildly electrocuted. It didn't hurt, but as I stood there, I felt completely embraced, knowing that somehow my entire past, present, and future were all one in the same.

"Oi," came a voice loud and clear. "You, my dear, need to bugger off."

I felt only a presence, but there was no mistaking the gruff, weathered essence of my old Great Auntie Flossy.

"Floss?" I said. "Holy shit. Where are you? Are you ok?"

"Of course I'm ok, you silly boy," she replied.

"I just thought—" I continued.

"Yes, yes," she interrupted. "Well, none of it matters now. Everything happens for a reason, doesn't it? A brick to the head, a squashed ant, it's really all the same. Now, open your eyes, poor child."

I did as I was told and found, standing next to me, a woman in her twenties, looking somewhat familiar. She wore a long satin gown, and she reminded me of a 1930s movie actress. It hugged her body in all the right places, and there was no denying a sexiness that instantly got my attention.

"Wow, who are you?" I asked, hoping to see where things might go.

"Who do you think?" she replied.

"Christ, Flossy? What the hell happened to you?" She was absolutely beautiful, and I felt instantly embarrassed for having such purvey thoughts.

"You can be any age you want in this place," she winked. "Nice to have my legs back and a pair of boobs that don't sag."

"I bet," I replied, not knowing what else to say.

"Did you get the bastard that bashed me in?" she asked.

"That's still to be determined," I said. "I'm kind of in the middle of it right now."

"Well then, you better get back and finish."

She was right, of course, and I took her last words as my queue to leave.

"I guess I don't get a choice to stay?" I asked.

"There's always a choice," she replied, "but not the choice you think. You know there's a lot of things you can't see that demand your belief," she said, looking into the great nothingness. "But I tell you, faith and fear are the two real buggers. All you really have to do is decide which one you believe in more."

Is it that simple? I thought. *Does the real meaning of life come down to just one single choice?*

Flossy turned and smiled. In her hand, she held a long antique cigarette holder, and with all the poise and grace of Audrey Hepburn, she inhaled deeply and blew out a stream of bluish grey smoke.

"Well, it's a start," she replied, answering my thought. "So what do you think? Faith or fear?"

I stepped closer to the edge of the wall and leaned over. "Nothingness" was a very long way down. I swallowed hard and took a deep breath.

"I think faith comes from my heart," I replied, "and fear from my head. You can convince yourself of anything in the end, but you can't ignore what you feel forever. All I know is that my heart never lies."

I stepped over the shards of broken glass, and with an involuntary gasp, I fell, and let go of any control I imagined I had.

Chapter 50

My arse was really wet. My legs and back were also, but it was my soaked buttocks that registered first as I opened my eyes. I could feel the soggy ground beneath me, but I did nothing to rectify the situation. Instead, I lay perfectly still and stared up into the sky. The storm clouds were gone, and I watched as small wisps of clouds swirled above me like smoke from a cigarette. In the distance, I could hear my name being called, but something about the sky's beauty made me reluctant to answer.

"Bloody hell, nephew, what the blazes happened to you?"

It was my uncle. I felt my head being lifted and something soft, presumably his raincoat, being shoved under it.

"It was Nevel," I replied, a little hoarse. "He just came at me with a brick."

"Jesus," said Tom. "Where in God's name did you get that axe?" he asked.

"Axe?"

"Yeah, the medieval looking thing sticking out of his back."

"What?" I replied, trying to sit up.

It was not a good move. My head started to spin, and all of a sudden, I felt the urge to throw up. Laying back down, I caught a brief glimpse of Nevel, maybe six feet away. He was lying face down in the mud, and just as my uncle had described, an ancient warrior's axe was lodged at a forty-five degree angle in the back of his lifeless body.

"I have no idea," I mumbled, trying not to black out.

My mind raced as I tried to remember, but nothing came. The last recollection I had was of Nevel's crazed face as he attempted to smash my head to a pulp.

"I'm so sorry, I should never have left you," said Tom. "As soon as I pulled into the airstrip hanger, I knew something was wrong. Your friend Grim was there along with a few of his cronies, one of them the guy we helped to launch his boat. Turns out the police picked up Nevel's trail back in Rayleigh, and they had been following him all day. Who knew he was following us? But apparently it all turned into a county wide surveillance effort and we, my dear nephew, were the bait."

"Is he dead then?" I asked.

"As a door nail," replied Tom. "You Clovered him good."

He leaned down and took a closer look at the side of my head. He dabbed gently at it with a clean hankie, and by his expression, I knew it wasn't pretty.

"We're going to have to get you out of here," he said, scanning the woods for help. "Those idiots couldn't organize a piss-up in a brewery," he grumbled, and having seen too many war movies, my uncle drew in a breath and yelled at the top of his lungs, "Medic!"

"I found it," I said to my uncle who was still tending to my wound.

"Found what?" he replied.

"The cottage, the gold, it's all there."

He stopped and looked at me. "Are you sure?"

"Look behind me, see the walls. They're all made of cracked bricks. That's it, we were right all along."

"Dear God in heaven," he said, breaking into a wide grin. "How the hell did you find it?"

"I just followed the clues. It wasn't hard once you had all the pieces."

"Jesus," said Tom, suddenly aware he shouldn't be laughing in front of a dead man. "Do you think that's why Nevel was here? Do you think he figured it out too?"

"By the look in his eyes, I'm sure of it, uncle."

"Then he must have been the one that stole Rob's paintings and burned down the shop," said Tom.

"Yeah and finished off Flossy," I added.

"Christ, what a bastard. At least you gave him what he deserved," said Tom.

"I guess, but honestly, I don't remember any of it."

"Well," said Tom, "let them figure that part out. Here comes Detective Grim now."

From a thicket close to one of the cottage's walls, Detective Grimshaw appeared, trying to free himself from a grappling weed. With a final grunt, he pulled himself clear and stared, a little worse for wear, at the scene in front of him.

"This is a fine mess," he announced at an attempt of sarcasm. "Kinda looks like a scene from Buffalo Bill. All we need is a few Red Indians and I'd call it a rodeo."

"I have no idea what you're talking about," said my uncle, "but this young man here needs some first aid."

Detective Grim stepped toward the body of Nevel and squatted. The skin of the dead man was a pale ashen, and Tom hoped even the detective could figure out the cause of death.

"Well, that's a shame," Grim said nonchalantly. "Would have made things a heck load easier if he had just got off his horse nicely."

He stepped over the body just in time to see two ambulance attendants appear.

"Ah, the cavalry," Grim announced.

The paramedic team ignored the comment, but I heard a faint "twat" come from one of them as they separated to assess the casualties.

It didn't take long for the other attendant to pronounce Nevel dead. Hearing it, I wasn't sure how I felt. I wasn't particularly proud to have actually killed someone, but if that was the case, my head injuries, I hoped, certainly justified a bit of self-defence.

"Ok," said the medic. "Looks like we've got a fractured ankle, head trauma, a possible concussion, and more than likely, a skull fracture."

"Well, at least I'm doing better than the other guy," I said, trying to lighten the mood.

"We'll be back with a stretcher," said the attendant. "Just stay put and don't move."

From my vantage point, I could see Detective Grimshaw unravelling a roll of police scene crime tape. He had tied the beginning end to a tree but had somehow managed to get his legs wrapped around the rest of the roll. I watched as he attempted to unravel himself, but in the end, he lost his patience and ripped the tape into several unusable pieces.

"You know," said Grim, turning toward me, "you have a lot to answer for. Something's just a tad bit fishy here."

"What do you mean?" I asked.

"How was it that he attacked you with a simple brick, but somehow, with a busted foot, you were able to get behind him, find an old rusty axe, and land it clean between his shoulder blades?"

"Beginner's luck?" I guessed.

"Yeah, pull the other one," he replied.

"The truth is, Detective," I said, "I don't remember doing it."

"Well, that's very convenient," he said. "But let me play along. If it wasn't you, then who was it?"

"I don't know, maybe he did it himself, you know, fell back on it or something?"

"Well, you can bet we'll be getting fingerprints and a full autopsy to say the least."

I was getting tired of trying to defend myself. The damp ground had started to chill my body, and I slid my numb hands into my front pockets and tried to ignore Grim's verbal diarrhea.

What's that? I thought, feeling something metallic. For the life of me I had no idea, and slowly I pulled the object out and brought it up to my face.

"What cha got there?" asked my uncle.

I recognized it instantly. "It's the Time Keeper's necklace," I replied.

"Do you mean Harry, the family ghost?" he asked.

"Yes," I said, understanding what he meant.

"He's not coming back," I said with a pit in my stomach. "It had to be the Time Keeper that finished off Nevel."

"Impossible," said Tom. "There's rules about those things with ghosts."

"You're right," I agreed, "but he must have broken them to save me. I guess he thought I was worth it."

"Why?" asked Tom.

"Exactly," I replied.

It was hard not to hear the medics returning. They sounded like they were having trouble manoeuvring the stretcher, and I suddenly had a vision of being dropped like an injured soccer player being carried off the pitch.

"Here they come," said Tom, "Tweedledee and Tweedledum."

"Fuck," I said with genuine concern.

"Oh, don't worry, it'll all be fine," he said. "My only concern is what are we going to do about the gold?"

"Well, it's sat undisturbed for the last eighty years. I think it will be ok for a bit longer."

"And what about our story with the detective?" he asked.

"Just tell him the truth," I said. "We were looking for a historical Clover brick building and we found it. Nevel was some kind of brick nutcase, and presumably he lost his shit trying to be the first to discover it."

Before I could say more, the medical attendants arrived. What I thought was going to be a makeshift stretcher was in fact a full-on metal gurney on wheels. *Christ,* I thought, as they transferred me onto its mattress. What were they thinking?

I could see the cottage as they slowly off-roaded me back to the air strip. It stood proud in its state of erosion, still holding a secret that had very nearly remained forgotten.

I didn't care about the gold anymore. The Time Keeper had shown me the real value of living, and I was determined to do just that. I would honour him and everyone in my past who had counted on me to continue. We were all connected. It seemed so obvious. There truly was no beginning or end. The universe was not still.

Thankfully, my ride got smoother once we hit the short grass of the runway. In total, three runways cut through the large hay field, and my ambulance was waiting, its blue lights flashing, next to a tower of straw bales.

A second ambulance, presumably to take Nevel, slowly made its way down an adjoining runway, and I closed my eyes as the adrenaline-filled day slowly took its toll.

I was just about to be lifted into the back of the ambulance when I heard his voice. *Of course,* I thought. *Who else can it be but Detective Grim?*

He strode over to me with all the usual swagger of an old-time cowboy and tipped his hat to one of the attendants. I stared at him for a moment and tried hard to look past the facade. *Somewhere in there,* I thought, *is a real person with real feelings.*

"Yo'll have anything to add?" he said, pulling out a notebook and licking the tip of his pencil.

"Nothing comes to mind," I answered.

"Nothing?" he asked again.

"I don't think so," I replied.

"Well, what's that?" he asked, pointing at the Time Keeper's necklace in my hand.

"Oh that. That's just an old keepsake I carry," I said.

"Looks more like one of those lollipops kids suck on," said Grim. "You know, the ones with the little white stick."

"Not sure what it's supposed to be," I replied.

Grim put away his notepad and sighed. "Well, for what it's worth," he said, "I liked the green and yellow ones the best."

"Was that the same kind the detective from that 70s show use to suck on?" I asked. "You know, the bald one?"

"Kojack," Grim replied without missing a beat.

"Yeah, that's right," I said, remembering. "But what was his famous catch phrase?"

"Who loves ya baby?" he replied, giving a half-decent impression.

"Who loves ya baby?" I said again to myself.

It was a question I had never really thought about, but for the first time in my entire life, I honestly felt I knew.

Chapter 51

Rob Clover pulled his bicycle out of the garden shed and smiled. He enjoyed his Sunday rides through the Essex countryside. Best of all, it was a day's relief from his nagging wife, Flossy, and that, he thought, was worth the miles of leg-aching hills he planned to ride.

He checked he had all the supplies he would need. Paints, brushes, a sandwich and thermos, a puncher repair kit, and a rolled-up piece of thin cardboard that stuck out the top of his pack. He knew it was going to be a long ride, but he felt that this was the day he would finally finish the painting of the tunnel.

Since the death of both his father, and most recently, his mother, life had drastically changed for the son of a debunked brickmaker. Shirley House and all its land had sold, and thinking back, if he hadn't visited Daws Heath Road the day the bulldozers leveled his father's office, he would never have found the box.

It appeared in the rubble quite by chance, and rescuing it from certain destruction, Rob sat under the last remaining apple tree and pried open the lid. Inside, he found a small brown envelope with the words "in case of my premature death" scrolled in his father's handwriting on the outside sleeve.

Intrigued, he tore open the seal and discovered three folded sheets of paper. The first, an account ledger listing dates and amounts of several payments made to the Clover Brick company. Each amount had been entered as "cash sovereigns," and as far as Rob could tell, they were all related to the same job.

He whistled as he came up with the final tally in his head. *That is some serious money,* thought Rob, *but why the paranoia?* He unfolded the second paper and read the heading: "Top Secret British Army Tunnel Project."

"What the hell?" said Rob in disbelief. "This is what spy novels are made of. How could father have been wrapped up in any of this?"

To Rob, it made no sense. He would have remembered seeing something back in the day. The only army soldiers he ever saw . . . and then he stopped.

"The night trains," he said. "Of course, how stupid of me. It was a secret government job."

As he read, Rob understood exactly what he was holding. It was an insurance policy his father had hastily made in case he was deemed an "expendable liability." It listed dates of meetings, the names of his handlers, and every army personal service number William Clover could recall. *Christ,* thought Rob refolding the paper, *this is heavy shit.*

On the last page, Rob found a large red X marking the secret tunnel location on a hand drawn map. He recognized several of the landmarks around Cold Norton, and noticing the Purleigh Bell pub, he figured he would take a day to investigate, then end with a few pints of stout.

There is only one remaining question, thought Rob. *What the hell happened to all my father's money?* He hadn't remembered the family ever living the high life.

He put on his bicycle clips and wheeled his push bike to the front of the house. Rob turned and looked through the front living room window. *Good,* he thought. *The old bat isn't there to see me leave.*

He tapped his pocket just to make sure the small brass box was still there.

"No way you're getting your greedy hands on this," he mumbled.

He swung his leg over the cross bar, and without looking back, Rob Clover pushed off toward the north bank of the River Crouch.

Oftentimes in life, thought Rob, *answers and information come from the most unlikely of sources.* Such was the case when he finally learned the whereabouts of his father's gold.

It was Don that gave him the answer. He lived with their brother, John, and John's wife, Maury, and on a visit one Sunday to their newly built house, Rob had grumbled that a milkman's wages would never pay for a place like theirs.

"But you have lots of money," said Don.

"What do you mean?" asked Rob.

"I mean, we're all rich. I gave everyone a brick for Christmas when Hambro Hill shut down."

"I remember," said Rob, "but that wasn't much of a gift. You didn't even wrap it," he said jokingly.

Don wasn't smiling. "The brick was the wrapper," he explained. "The gift was inside."

"What? Inside the clay?"

"Yes," replied Don. "Father's money. That's where we put it every time the army trains left. In the wet bricks."

It took a minute for Rob's brain to connect the dots, but when it did, he suddenly realized why his father had been so angry to find out that the last ever batch of Clover bricks had been delivered.

"Dear God," said Rob, having no other words to describe the pit in his stomach. "No wonder father looked like he was going to murder me that day."

"Wait here," said Don. "I'll show you."

Rob waited as he watched his brother run to his bedroom. When he reappeared, he was holding a familiar Clover brick, and Rob followed his brother out the kitchen door and into the back garden.

"See," said Don, suddenly throwing the brick down hard onto the concrete patio.

Rob looked down just as the brick broke and feeling rather pleased with himself, Don pointed at an obvious clump of something dusty yellow and grey.

"Told you," he said, finally picking up the chunk and handing it to Rob. "No more money worries, brother."

Rob Clover knew there wouldn't be many chances left to see the Cold Norton tunnel in operation. Steam trains were becoming a thing of the past, and he waited, brush poised, ready to add the final touches to his painting.

He could hear the locomotive coming. Its whistle reminded him of a screaming child, and when the train eventually burst out of the tunnel entrance, Rob flinched from the shear violence of the machine.

"There!" he yelled, adding a large amount of white paint to his canvas. "You can never have too much steam."

He worked the paint till the sound of the train faded into silence, then stepping back, he stood and admired his work.

"Bloody good job," he said, agreeing with himself. "I think that'll do it."

Rob wiped his brush on a rag and was about to reach for his thermos when he remembered the brass box in his pocket.

"Right, let's find a place to hide you," he said, pulling it out.

He opened the lid and took out the yellowish glob one more time. It had been several months since Don had revealed their father's secret, and though the melted clump had sat on top of Rob's mantel in plain sight, he sensed Flossy was beginning to get a little too curious.

Next to a small boulder that he had been using as a seat, a smooth flat stone caught his eye. He picked it up and held it in his hand.

"This will do," he said, holding the stone and the glob together. Then, with a series of grinding strokes, Rob scratched several gold lines onto the flat surface. "R.C." he said, looking at his handy work. "Don't think I'll forget that in a hurry."

After burying the box, he sat for a long time. Rob sipped his tea and watched as the steam from his thermos swirled and floated away. He wasn't sure why he had wanted to paint the tunnel. He knew there were no gold coins hidden in its bricks. *Maybe,* thought Rob, *it is my testament to the last great engineering feat that Clover bricks ever built.*

He had found the rest of his father's gold. That was the least he could do. For many Sundays, he had biked around the Essex countryside, retracing the last batch of Clover brick deliveries. In some weird, twisted way, he felt closer to his dead father, but knew, at least in his lifetime, there was no chance of ever getting any of it back. The gold was gone, sealed up in the walls of churches, windmills, stables, and a cottage that if he wasn't mistaken, old Tom Shelly had built.

There is only one slim chance for recovering the gold, concluded Rob Clover. *It's a long shot, but at some point, far in the future, the bricks will eventually crack. They always do. Impurities or large bits of aggregate invariably cause nature to try and reject the imperfections. Maybe someone will figure it out,* he thought. *Maybe someone who cares enough to learn the family history. All it will take is to understand the clues.* The only problem was that the clues, at the present, were still very much hidden.

As he began to roll up the dried canvas, Rob had to admit he was getting better. He had only started painting as a way of documenting the final delivery sites, but as his interest grew, so did his attention to detail and perspective.

When, at last he had visited every site, Rob laid the paintings out on the dining room table. There were over twenty he counted, but not all were the actual delivery locations. Many were what he called "connectors," simple landscape paintings that geographically joined one delivery site to the next.

His idea was to create one unbroken path from Shirley House to Tom Shelly's cottage. A few scenes he had to recall from memory, but keeping the route historically correct made Rob feel he was stopping—or at least preserving—time, for a future generation.

Rob climbed to the top of the embankment and turned one last time. He never did find out what the army had used the tunnel for, and in the end, he didn't want to know.

If anything, he was just grateful to have witnessed the steam train one more time. He knew many people would never have the chance, and lately he had recognized that it was those small everyday moments of wonder he now lived for. Even the simplest of things, like the way wind rippled across a field of wheat, made him pause, and in those briefest of moments, he believed he was happy.

This, he said to himself, *is my time, my moment, my now. The future will come when it is good and ready,* and he honestly didn't think anyone would give a shit what his life had meant anyway.

But he knew, and that was all that mattered. Even the gold really meant nothing in the end. The only value, he believed, was in a life well-lived, and it was up to himself, and no one else, to take his ordinary life and make it extraordinary.

Epilogue

I had no idea why the hospital cast my dead daughter's hands in plaster. As I held her lifeless body for the last time, I knew she was far from this world. Whatever peace her tiny hands were supposed to give, only made it worse.

I am a fixer, I see potential in everything. My instinct is to breathe new life into old, yet I have had to accept that not all things can be fixed. Some are simply broken before they were ever first put together.

I hide my loss well. The tears are gone, but the memory of the pain remains. The death of the "potential" is one of the cruellest of all. There are no words left to answer the everlasting question of "What could have been?"

But I hold no grudge; there is no war to wage. Nature always wins, that's just simply the deal. Regardless of my daughter's thirteen days of life or one hundred years, I have learned we all have two lives to live. The second begins when you realize you only have one.

I see her among the tombstones. She visits me in my sleep. Occasionally, I will catch a glimpse of Alison from the corner of my eye.

She is the Time Keeper. I understand now. My present finally caught up to her past.

She flickers between the seconds, just out of reach, but forever, by my side.

Acknowledgements

I have no idea how this book came to be. It certainly didn't start out as one, but like most creative endeavors, I have found the "Art" is all in the process.

Without the help of so many people, whether they knew it or not, I wouldn't have been able to drag myself across the finish line. Admittedly, it was a hard slog, but I am so grateful for every second of the journey.

My biggest thank you would have to be to my grandmother and her brother Rob (Googs). They had the fortitude of typing out their childhood memories and leaving me with eighteen pages of stories and characters that became the basis for my inspiration. Of course, they are all long gone now but the stories remain, and in some way, they live on in their words and the hearts of the reader.

My deepest thanks to my parents. Though they both passed somewhere between the beginning and the end of writing this book their encouragement and insight to my family history has brought me closer to better understanding where I came from and who I am.

Thank you, Colin Crewdson, for answering my random questions, and thank you Victoria Williams for all the great pictures and investigative work. A special thanks also to Peter King from All Saint Church in Barling.

To the musicians I have played with through the years. Thank you for the moments that only we could have created. Ed Roman for offering me an opportunity when I needed it the most, Chris Taggart for simply believing in me, Tom Gerencser for the Freeedoommm, Pauline for speaking your heart, Tammera for your compassion, Rob Holiday for never giving up the faith, Steve and Lucy for always seeing Red, James Heidebrecht for being so gracious, Mitch Girio for never being a sucker, Greg Howley for GLH 9, Lynn Scott for not holding grudges, Chris Murray for staying true to his calling, Barry Harris for your vision, Kimberley Pritchard for your unrelenting support, and Tim Ronan for inspiring me to be a better human being.

Also, my respect and gratitude for everyone at Tellwell Publishing especially Scott Lunn, Lyndon Trinidad, and my awesome editor Katie Beaton.

For technical support I can't thank Kirk Schuller, Seri Gee, Michael Jack and Steve Wood enough. And for the reassurance that I'm semi-sane, thank you Rob Arnoth, Todd Hayen, and Ted Edwards, for confirming which way is up.

Lastly, and most importantly, I wish to thank my family. Through all this time you have given me your faith, trust, and support and you have allowed me the greatest opportunity to live the best life I could imagine.

Thank you. coco

About the Author

Originally a native of Essex, England, Antony has considered Canada his home for the past forty years. Having spent time at the University of North Texas and the University of Toronto, he received a Bachelor of Fine Arts from York University in 1998.

Among his artistic endeavours, Antony owns and operates a custom stained-glass studio, drums professionally, and has discovered a passion for writing that has led to this book, his first novel.

He lives with his family in the rural community of Pefferlaw, north of Toronto.

To listen or download the official soundtrack to *Strawberry Jam on Tuesdays*, please go to www.jamontuesdays.com

Printed in Great Britain
by Amazon